THE BLUE TAXI

THE BLUE TAXI

a novel

N. S. KÖENINGS

Little, Brown and Company

NEW YORK   BOSTON   LONDON

Little, Brown and Company
Hachette Book Group USA
1271 Avenue of the Americas, New York, NY 10020
Visit our Web site at HachetteBookGroupUSA.com

First Edition: October 2006

The characters and events in this book are fictitious. Any similarity to real persons, living or dead, is coincidental and not intended by the author.

Library of Congress Cataloging-in-Publication Data

Köenings, N. S.
    The blue taxi : a novel / N. S. Köenings. — 1st ed.
    p. cm.
    HC ISBN-10: 0-316-01061-8; ISBN-13: 978-0-316-01061-0
    Int'l. ed. ISBN-10: 0-316-01846-5; ISBN-13: 978-0-316-01846-3
    1. Traffic accidents — Fiction. 2. Married women — Fiction.
3. Widowers — Fiction. 4. East Indians — Africa, East — Fiction. 5. Africa,
East — Fiction. 6. Man-woman relationships — Fiction. I. Title.

PR9130.9.K64B58 2006
823'.92 — dc22   2005031609

10 9 8 7 6 5 4 3 2 1

Q-MART

Book design by Fearn Cutler de Vicq

Printed in the United States of America

For house crows everywhere

Vunjamguu, East Africa, 1970s

I

❧One

The plus in Sarie Turner: a minus for the widower's youngest boy. An accident, it was, in the bright Kikanga neighborhood of seaside Vunjamguu. For the unseen, sudden child? A *gongo* drinking driver, big blue Tata run amok. Great low rumble and a thrash, metal bending with a wail. A fall—a slip and tender snap—and cries and shrieks and shudders from those close enough to see. Next, the tremors of a riven street, belated shatterings of glass. A squeal, an interrupted skip. What else? Among others and perhaps the very least, but, still, one thing: at some distance from the fray, unexpected and intent, a simmer and a bubbling in a tall, ungainly woman who had not bubbled before.

Sarie Turner did, like others in that nest of high-housed, sooty streets, hear the rich commotion as it happened. But because she didn't see the Tata shedding its old brakes, taking its hard teeter, didn't see the stumbling boy's quick pitch, was still coming round the corner, she couldn't fathom what it was. In fact, she thought, *C'est quoi?* The bright perfume of burnt and bleeding things came flooding up her nose. Aware of Agatha's small hand tightening at her own, Sarie felt that she should hurry. But she'd gone very still, her eyes and mind a blank.

Her daughter's fingers fell away and Sarie next experienced in her knees a looseness that, traveling up her hips and thighs, nearly caused her to collapse against the stationer's window—where, behind the oily glass (shocked, too), a steno pad threw off its dust and several ink pens rolled slightly to the side. Sarie felt the window hot and smooth against her shoulder and wondered why she couldn't see. She brought herself upright again and noted then that her own eyes were closed. She opened them.

Sarie squinted in the light but could not see her child (Agatha, while her mother's eyes were shut, had run on to find things out). As the street came into view, Sarie's stomach tilted in its house. She swallowed, turned the corner, too. She identified a crowd but, slow to see the obvious as she was, still didn't understand. She wasn't used to being dizzy, that squeezing in her chest, a blurring at her temples that took some time to clear. *What is it that's happened?* Was that Agatha, just there? When Sarie had caught on that the scarlet-stippled log her only child sat holding on the banks of India Street was no log but a leg that had been unhooked from its owner, it was too late for her to scream. Somewhere between her collarbone and chin, a scream-shape came careening to a stop — she gasped.

She was not alone. The others had screamed punctually, just after the bus hit, and now they only stood, unnerved, making tender sounds like *mm* and *oh* and *haaa*. A newsboy, head-cocked, knee-bent like an egret in a pool of fallen print, stood frozen in the sun. A small round woman the color of a cashew, gray hair middle-parted like a book, eyes as deep as bowls, clutched her racing chest with two immobile hands. Hovering like a specter from white smoke and toppled coals, a coffee salesman, tongue an arrow, held fast to his curls. In the plump and muted hush — breath-breath, gasp-gasp, and everything so *slow* — everyone was still. Everyone, that is, except the boy to whom that log — no, leg — belonged.

But the newly fractured boy, whose accident this was, wasn't screaming either. Rather, there slipped from other parts of him, as from mysterious insects, a range of thrums and squeaks. There was:

from a shaggy head with opaque hair, a wincing; a creaking from the thin-boy trunk-and-thigh; and a steady, anxious droning from the one leg he still wore, which he clutched as if to keep it safe with two surprisingly big hands. The sounds his body made, delicate and soft, would have—somehow Sarie and the gaspers sensed that this was so—put further screams to shame.

Sarie, one brown knuckle tucked into the hollow at the base of her tight throat, wobbled on the curb, aware without quite knowing why that she was being called upon to *think*. To Sarie's left, squatting, showing flowered panties, Agatha was quiet, too. Brave child, she had not considered screaming. With care, with eerily professional aplomb, with love, perhaps, she had neatly folded down the cuff of the blue sock at the end of that lost limb as if preparing the loosed thing for a party or for school. Fingers lightly resting on that wounded, dappled skin as at the keys of a piano, Sarie Turner's daughter calmly oversaw the stranger's separated flesh in a square of city shade. Behind her, the split doorway of an alley lolled open like a blouse.

Despite everything else, perhaps because at times like this the mind moves rather strangely, Sarie thought, *She looks nearly like a picture,* and she was briefly proud. In all of her nine years, Agatha had never been a worry, *pas une fois,* and why should she be now? Seeing Agatha so serious and unruffled—sensing something of herself there and by this sense reassured—Sarie ceased her gasping and took stock. She pressed her lips together and turned towards her right. There, not on the sidewalk as she was, but in the middle of the road: the now one-legged boy, squeak and drone gone soft.

The hardy, sticky pool of red that seeped around his little hips and what had earlier that morning been a round and boyish knee made Sarie, of all things, think wistfully of sauces she did not know how to make. This culinary wish, its ordinariness, its very saucy plainness, coincided with a jarring and extremely strong desire to ensure that that boy's hair and chest and thigh kept making hopeful tunes. That the urge was visceral was curious, for Sarie—as she well knew herself, as her husband Gilbert often thought, and others had asserted in frustration—was not given to communion. But, oddly, there it was. Already. Accidents transforming.

Dutifully, she turned once more towards Agatha, to make sure she was all right. She was. Perfectly at ease, having understood, perhaps, that there would be no parties and no lessons any longer for the leg, Agatha had begun unlacing the brown shoe so the thighless foot might stretch its toes a final, dear time. The shoe? Not new, but still; Sarie noted, *Bata,* by the way. She briefly had the thought that she herself would like a pair of dark brown Bata pumps, someday, but she knew she oughtn't linger: *To think about the shoes! A wounded boy, just there. A boy missing his leg!* So be it. *She* would help him, yes. *C'est moi,* she thought. *C'est moi qui vais l'aider.* Agatha would soothe the shin, and she herself would take firm charge of that other, altered body. With an able, manly finger, Sarie tucked a strip of yellow hair behind one of her ears, and, deliberate now, like a hefty praying mantis, she lifted up one foot and prepared. She set the raised foot down, lifted up the other, and took into the street seven crucial steps that would, before she understood it, change the things she knew.

She was not alone in moving at that moment towards the injured child. As she set off, a neat, close huddle formed, hiding him from view. Oh, concealment of the target, so fresh and speedy on the heels of Sarie's taking aim! That urge inside her trebled. She felt needed by the world, as she never had before, and she went forward quickly. The swollen hush, its muted *mm*s and *oh*s, died down as she moved, and a babble rose instead. Ears and heart arush, Sarie made out this and that: some in the assembly, whispering at first, wished to ascertain the cause of what they saw. Buses were no longer what they had been, sure, but was that up-country driver drunk? And did this sorry boy not have a mum or dad or uncles? What had he been doing, foolish, in the road? Here, the coffee salesman ventured that the boy (so it seemed to him) had been hunting house crows with a slingshot. The middle-parted woman, with an authoritative look, declared that boys these days— coffee-man included—had no common sense. She smoothed down her brown sari and commandeered a slightly wandering green eye towards the wounded child.

Sarie hurried forth. Enormous in her orange flip-flops, not unsteadied by her speed, she cleared a heap of rotted mango peels, eight pointed lady-fingers fallen from the gray-haired woman's basket, and also the rough slingshot, which Agatha would later learn indeed belonged to that felled boy who whimpered in the road. As Sarie came upon them, those around him parted like a sea. The driver's tout (a thick boy from whose lips protruded a thin twig), an able litter-woman (palm-frond basket heavy on her head), the coffee salesman, a watchman in a military cap, the woman in the sari, and the newsboy (papers now aswirl in a ragged play of wind) all stepped back to make way for the madam. Some among them, skeptical, prepared to be amused. They wondered what, exactly, the racing woman thought she might achieve. And—this Sarie did not hear—some of them imagined that she would have sound knowledge to apply that they themselves did not.

In this last, granting foreigners all kinds of super-expertise, people are frequently mistaken. For example, Sarie did most definitely not possess a bright Mercedes-Benz with which she could convey the patient to a luxurious private clinic; nor was she a doctor; and she was not related as far as she'd been told to any European football stars, actresses, or presidents. She was not even, as most who had not heard her speak assumed, English. But she had, as humans do, lived through a great deal, and she could be effective: as it happens, orphaned by a War, shuttled to the Colonies at a very early age, Sarie Turner (née Genoux) had been after all brought up by dexterous Nursing Sisters, and she'd taken some things in. It was thus neither fame nor power, but a vague and rusted habit coupled with a *feeling,* that pushed her towards the boy.

The members of the huddle watched. Sarie was: long, big-boned and ample, topped with desert-colored hair as unkempt as her housedress (dingy, yellowed, with faded flowery marks)—a personage, indeed. She landed from a leap over a pot-hole near the little crowd, and, hands on hips, hiked up that yellow shift—revealing as she did so two bright pomelo-sized knees—and squatted, wild-haired, in the center of the road beside the wincing boy.

She lost a flip-flop on the way. The litter-woman, moving with a grace that kept the basket on her head absolutely still, slid the bright thong over with a push of her big toe (her own flip-flops were blue). The night-watchman offered up the cardboard sheet on which, at lazy times, he napped. Sarie took it, sat, stretched her own legs out, and, oddly dainty, crossed them. She leaned over slowly.

As her big head cast a shadow on the boy, she began to whisper. Sarie did not say, "Your absent leg will cast a spell on my green daughter." Nor did she utter anything exceptionally prophetic, like, "Your father, *nom de Dieu,* will knock my apple cart." In fact, Sarie, who was Belgian in some way, though she had left that place too long ago to recall with any freshness its damp and gloomy clime, found English rather tricky and would not have spoken daringly like that, for fun. Sarie made mistakes. She twisted sentences around. She didn't always know the meaning or the import of the words she put together. She sometimes did not think as clearly as she could. But she had seen sick and wounded people in her life, and she had seen them tended. So she offered him distractions, small and tender things that in her long-gone youth she had been apprenticed to dispense. "My Agatha likes very much the candy, will you like some in a while?" And, "You want to stay alive to grow so tall and be resembling your papa." And, "Nevermind, now. Nevermind." And, "Please."

She wished the others were not watching her so closely. She did not like so many eyes on her—did not like even her own husband to look too long at her legs or her elbows or her face—and the heat from all the bodies and the sun felt a bit like melted wax. *Vous me dérangez,* she thought but did not say, aware that someone else's comfort, at this moment, mattered more than hers. She closed her eyes and shook herself and made herself forget them. *I am needed, après tout.* Indeed, she felt that she was acting well, that she was at that moment exactly where she should be.

The boy's eyes shut and opened, too. As Sarie touched his poor, slick brow, it did occur to her that he was not much older than her child. She gave the boy a smile. Glad that wounds had never fazed her, she felt strong. To one or two mean hoots and overall approval, which Sarie did not hear, she tore a length of cotton from her dress and fashioned him a tourniquet.

While there is little charm in losing a good leg, there was that day in the thronging bubble of Kikanga—well apart from the appearance on the scene of a sometime European nurse—a sort of luck at work. A timely-spacely wrinkle. First, in the jam-packed busy streets between this corner (India meets Mahaba), the Theosophical Society's hunkered yellow palace, the clock tower with the four round faces that look every way at once (each with its own mind), and the eggplant-radish-onion stands of old Kikanga market, there were several charitable clinics founded, as it happened, by the Aga Khan himself. On that day, two were sorely understaffed—one by a long-awaited wedding, the other by a funeral. A third was sadly understocked—thanks to the ill will of an official who would not let in the medicines from Delhi for the fee to which he had long ago agreed, and who was causing in a smoky room beside the harbor a bitter little scene. A fourth, however, was full of stuff and staff. This one—square, clean, pink Kikanga Clinic—was just two blocks away. The boy was, from the moment of the crash, therefore, not too far from help.

Another lucky object by that sticky place? On the second floor of egg-blue Mansour House, which overlooked the sharp joint of India and Mahaba, and was occupied by Bibi Kulthum, her fine son Issa and his clever wife Nisreen, there lived a brand-new telephone that was eager to be used. Black, still smooth, not yet gummy from the air's thick oil and grime, the thing sat brashly on a table near the balcony; it was cushioned in high style by a yellow doily Bibi's son had asked his wife to purchase, to make certain Bibi understood the phone was there to stay. A forward-looking man, Issa had gone to great lengths to acquire it, and had in doing so, he said, brought the future home. Nisreen, admiring of her very busy husband, and a worrier, felt it might be useful. But while Issa had struggled to convince his mother that amenities like this one were milestones to success, Bibi was suspicious: entreated and cajoled, she had not used it yet, and had said she never would.

As she often was, Bibi had been seated on the woven mat that softened the hard floor of her Kikanga-facing balcony, thread and needle ticking in her lap. Because her ears were not what they had been, she neither heard the boom nor caught the rush of birds escaping like applause from the drama in the road. She didn't hear the shouts. No, wrapped up in her work—a square embroidered hanging she intended for Nisreen—she hadn't heard a thing. But, because Bibi had another, special sense, a skill she'd had since childhood, she did look up from her embroidery at the very moment that the brakeless Tata bus veered around the corner and next knocked the slingshot-aiming boy right on his little back and tore one leg clean off.

The skill? As a child, like many other children, Bibi had been open to the world, sensitive and curious. She wondered about words she overheard, dampness on a face, paper bits that didn't burn, twigs in patterns on the ground. Such wondering's not special. So? What was Bibi's talent? One: when it suited her, she knew how to be still. Two: she had, since a crucial period in her youth, almost without fail focused her bright eyes and set her mind to work at *exactly the right time,* looking up from chores and meals and stitching just as a new development that would busy tongues for weeks, a truth that had only been suspected, or an event that none could have imagined spilled onto a scene. So she'd learned that Mrs. Dillip's husband had abandoned her at last, that the creditors were coming, and that a certain cousin whom she loved had exposed her secret parts while climbing up a clove tree. Bibi, people later came to say, was more perceptive than a house crow, knew things before they happened—even if the happening was soundless, sneakier than snakes.

She was less prone now to hiding under shelves to see what she could see than she had been as a girl. She couldn't hear as well. But the sharpness had stayed with her. Urged on by the feeling that she should, she looked up and out into the street just before the bus collided with the widower's little boy. That was as expected, looking up at the right time. Not new. But on this special day, there was, it seemed, something else at work. Something that had snuck up inside Bibi without her knowing that it had. It was as if Bibi, who had never in the past required an assistant, who one could trust to know the goings-on well before they went, had on this day been accorded an extra sort of push. Insurance.

What would really stay with Bibi? Above the Tata's foremost window, in curly painted letters, turquoise blue and white in shades that matched the thread in her own hands, were the very words she had been stitching. *Al-Fadhil,* the Utmost, Kindest One. *Al-Fadhil!* God's name on bus and cloth! Was this not much more than a lucky-look-up at collision? Was this not a super perk, to make doubly-triply sure that Bibi Kulthum was informed? She and he—the boy, whom she could see between the concrete moldings of the balcony, framed by a neatly crafted opening shaped precisely like a heart—were, or were they not, *stitched* together in a cosmic bus-to-balcony alert? The undeniable conjunction, the fact that between herself and the scene there was a heart drawn in the air, and that the bus that hit the boy proclaimed God's Almighty Kindness just as she was doing in her lap, prompted Bibi to deploy a courage that surprised her only later.

She had not touched the thing before. Insisting that she had never needed one, and why should she start now? and, hadn't she grown up and borne four children without a hitch or flaw? she had frankly refused to; but Issa, stopping wisely short of saying that three of those four kids (himself the one exception) had fallen ill and died almost right away and think what might have been if they had rung a doctor, had subjected her, as youth these days were wont to do, to lectures. Issa had talked on and on and on, and Bibi, because she loved him very much, had heard some of what he said. And so, well drilled despite herself by her modern son "in case anything should happen" (and what a thing had happened!), Bibi lifted the receiver—which was heavy, which she did not know how to hold—and used the only number (also lucky) that she had learned by heart.

One eye on her own *Al-Fadhil,* the other on the phone, she tapped and tapped as she'd been shown and waited for the click. The operator spoke. Bibi gave the number of nearby, cool Kikanga Clinic, where bright and promising Nisreen was none other than the woman at reception. *Click-click. Click.* And *click.* An unseen switchboard ticked, then gave over to a clatter. A voluminous quiet rose. Bibi held her breath. At long, impatient last, there came a rolling ring. Nisreen, accustomed to emergencies, picked up at the first shiver of her very own black box and, after expressing her surprise at hearing Bibi's voice, listened to her mother-in-law relate the news that a holy Tata bus had smashed into an ordinary boy just outside their building. The bus, said Bibi, had sent that boy's four limbs aflying (arm, arm, leg and leg) in each cardinal direction. "Do something!" she said. "*You* work in a clinic!" It was Nisreen's job to "do something," of course, and she would have, quite regardless. But hearing Bibi so excited made her do it faster. As she dropped the telephone, leapt up from her seat, and raced into the ward, she did not ask herself if her limp made her seem lame. It escaped her mind completely to wonder how she looked. Driven, brave, she found the orderlies and doctor and told them what she knew.

Therefore, with Bibi's timely vision and Nisreen at reception, Sarie's actions were perhaps not as weighty as they felt. She'd made the boy more comfortable, and may have stemmed his blood at a semicrucial juncture, but no more. After she'd secured the yellow cloth, whispered some more things, and was about to press a testing hand to the small boy's pounding wrist, a troop of medical assistants descended on the scene. Their leader gave the order for the members of his little group to take the boy away, which, without a gasp or shout, or—to their credit—so much as a blink, they did.

Two of the assistants, scolding her for touching what they argued was now theirs, took the leg from Agatha. At the ominous pinching in the recess of her chest, she did the only thing she could, causing the two white-coated men to falter, stamp, and sigh: as the leg was taken up, she stood to tie the shoelace back again. It was a skill that she was eager to display (recently acquired with her father's single pair of dress-ups), and (bright girl) she also feared that that shoe might be lost: she would not be rushed. Medical assistants frowning all the while, poor leg in midair, the shoe was tied up snug.

Once the dislodged limb, the boy, the clinic-folk, were gone, the compact huddle loosened. The street, with all the things upon it, came slowly right again. The stationer's index cards fell back in relief and waited for new dust; the pens rolled into place. The pavement settled down. Bystanders who had screamed and then gone absolutely still now shrieked in retrospect. Some hooted. Others, hands on heads, reminded themselves and their neighbors patiently that God-must-not-be-cursed-no-matter-what-no-matter-what, and tried to give Him thanks for His mysterious work. The coffee-man announced to no one in particular that the bus had burst as though from smoke into the day. The woman with the wandering eye recovered from the shock and noted with dismay that some produce had been lost. The litter-woman saw a heap of coco husks and thought that she might pluck them. The paperboy, who had thrilled to being on the scene when new news came about, gathered up his now outdated sheets.

Hisham's Food and Drink was open by this time. The owner, named not Hisham but Iqbal, brought out a bucket full of passion juice and a set of metal cups for the watchers who remained. This

he did because all humans are involved in this big life and sometimes need refreshment that should not be bought. For Agatha,
however, because white children can for good or ill inspire certain
things, he made a show of proffering a straw. The litter-woman
drank without tilting her head back. The coffee salesman, prefer-
ring his own beverage to theirs, did not accept the offer. The newsboy, whose days out in the sun were thirstier than most, came back
for a refill, which he felt he deserved.

Upstairs on the balcony of Mansour House, Bibi happily took
up her stitching once again, stopping now and then to shake her
head in awe. *Won't Issa be surprised, how I've mastered his appliance?*
She was happy with herself. She tucked her chin down towards her
chest and smiled into her lap. *At how modern his ma is?* Nisreen
would tell him, too. She'd heard that phone ring all the way around
the corner, after all, and picked it up herself. And, more than this!
Had not Bibi's scandal-seeking sense been accompanied by por-
tent? Had she known all along, without knowing that she did, that
an *Al-Fadhil*-bearing bus would surge into the day? Had she, in deciding for *Al-Fadhil* on that hanging instead of something else
(*Kids are wealth, A marriage is a tomb, Business is a blessing*), been fingered by the cosmos? Not simply to catch things as they fell, but to
forecast with her work? While Bibi stitched and mused, below on
India Street the driver's tout, fearing that the next professionals to
swoop might hold handcuffs and batons, snapped his fingers and
then vanished. The driver was long gone.

At home again that day and for the following five, Sarie mentioned to her husband several times that she wanted to discover where the hurt boy lived. But Gilbert Turner was suspicious of, and did not like: *involvement*. Much better, he thought, to let the world unfold around oneself and, as a rule, *not make any stink*. He therefore did not believe that Sarie should involve herself expressly in the life-business of strangers. For five days like a husband and a father, he did manage to dissuade her. But Agatha, who could not stop thinking of the limb she'd cared for in the sun, wished to find out for herself if the shin and calf and foot had been sewn back onto their owner. She seethed with anger at her father, pouted at her mother, and stamped her little feet. "Leave well enough alone!" said Gilbert, and, "Forget it, won't you, now?" when Sarie asked again. He added something about sleeping dogs, which Sarie did not understand, and sent Agatha outside.

Sarie's husband did not like involvement because it made him feel unsafe. As many people do, Gilbert masked his shyness with elaborate shows of expertise that were sometimes impressive. He kept up a fair library that experts might have thought an amateur's good show. In leather, paperback, and cloth, the writers of his books purported to lay bare the logic beneath peculiar local lore, exhaustively detail the mores and the habits of this land's many tribes, and explain *how natives are;* others, less imaginative, discussed the (so they said) obscure ins and outs of agricultural procedures under tropical conditions, described how boats and homes were built; still others tried their hand at generating history. From his volumes, thumbed and eyed and loved, Gilbert had acquired, in some measure, the tenor of authority.

Drawing on the things he'd read, and also on his days in the Colonial Service (when more able men had drilled him), Gilbert said—among other things—to Sarie: "Muslims won't consort with any likes of us, my dear." He was reading at the time a pamphlet that seemed relevant, and he had gleaned from Sarie's talk (about Hisham's Food and Drink, a mention of the Aga Khan) that Muslims the boy's family must be. He found some pleasure in the word "consort." He tried it out again, this time for himself. "We can't *consort* with Muslims, dear. Just think!" Sarie turned to face him and did not, for once, speak, which pleased him. Thusly, he thought, gaining ground, he added, in a tone he meant to be consoling, "My dear, what will you ever do? What will you ever do if they should want you first of all to be *unshod of your shoes,* and leave them in the hallway?"

Gilbert liked to view himself as a strong man and as an able husband. And so he often told himself that Sarie, no matter what she said or did, was a fragile thing, unsure of what she wanted, and that she needed him to tell her what to do. Sarie was aware of this and sometimes played along, but there were limits to what she could accept. Her days, aside from making small, plain meals, keeping track (if absently) of Agatha, and wishing without making any plans that life was rather different, were not exactly full. And Agatha had reached a restless age. With her "when-can-we-where's-his-leg's" she had become a nuisance. From what was but did not seem to be a notably long distance, Sarie looked at Gilbert. She weighed her knowledge of him with her eyes. *J'complete,* she thought. Indeed: although he wore a singlet and a shirt, she knew precisely where, below two ashen nipples, the flesh sagged from his chest. She could have pointed out exactly where the soft mass of his belly was dimpled and was not. She knew without having to look how many ribs he had. And she was tired of his talk.

She breathed out through her nose. "If that is what the Muslims want," she said, "then I will take them off." Demonstrating—in one motion, without losing her balance—Sarie slipped her two big feet from her orange rubber thongs. Gaining some momentum, feeling contrary and sure, she went on: "It is not as if I had the sandals to unstrap. *Regarde!* One, two." She put the shoes back on, then slipped them off again. She did a peppy dance step on the rust-red, tattered rug. "It is not"—and here she sighed—"as if I had some stockings. Or fancy Bata pumps." For the moment she had given up on giving in to Gilbert. Daring, really, almost happy, she placed one of her large feet square onto her husband's lap. "See? It takes no time at all."

Sarie's toes distracted him. She did not often touch him. Gilbert moved his pamphlet to the side, adjusted his small hips, and smiled indulgently at her. "Oh, Sarie." He wrapped a round pink hand around her weighty ankle and looked up at his wife. Sometimes Sarie's looks and height slipped Gilbert's mind completely. Was that the little nose he'd liked, with the hint of lioness about it? The soft shoulders that were strong? Was that the ceiling fan, just beyond her hair? On their wedding day, he thought, the flush of love had made her seem so small! He looked back at his hand, her ankle, at her toes, which flared and curled towards him. Oh, he knew she wanted shoes. He wished she would forget. "You just won't understand," he said.

Sarie, aware still on that day that husbands need attention and timely, kindly acts, softened her approach. She leaned down from afar and kissed him on the brow, which, despite the argument at hand, thrilled Gilbert's thin hair. She crooned: "I understand much more than you can know." Gilbert, not quite catching what she said—hearing, in fact, *I understand,* and nothing of the rest—was touched by Sarie's gesture and the sweet smell of her face. Perhaps, he thought, she didn't really mind his lack of permanent employment, his staying in during the day, skimming his old books, his wandering in the afternoons and evenings. She loved him, after all. Is that not what wives were for? Sensing that her husband had gone mild, was dreaming, Sarie put an end to the debate. "I am taking Agatha today," she said, "and we will see that little boy."

Gilbert, bested by her touch, relinquished his objections. She had leaned down from the distance of her body and come close. Had pressed her toes against his thighs and had not pulled away, when, beneath her arching foot, his loins gave out a shiver. She had kissed him, after all. He could still, he imagined, feel her mouth on his bare brow. *Let her do just as she pleases,* Gilbert thought at last. *What harm is there in it?*

Completely unaware that Sarie would soon access some freedom of her own, he crossed his feet, which were doughy, damp, and he smiled up at his wife. Decided to be generous. *Fair is fair, old man. Why shouldn't she go out?* "All right," Gilbert shrugged. "Do just as you like." Sarie put her foot back on the floor. Gilbert sighed and turned back to the pamphlet: *His Holiness in Africa: An Account of Dr. Saheb's Tour of Light and Love Among the Vunjamguu Adherents.* He himself was planning, reading done, to take an early evening stroll to the Victorian Palm Hotel, where he hoped, as always and as idly, to find a fellow ex-colonial on the lookout for a partner in a business. Someone who would notice all he had to offer and who would take him on in a reassuring, easy venture that would unfold for him at last the future, which he vaguely dreamed of now and then but did not know how to find.

In the bedroom, freed, Sarie called to Agatha. She put on her best dress, a light gray thing with small white dots, short sleeves, and a scooped neck. With a finger and saliva, she nudged accumulated grime from a yellow vinyl purse. Into it she slipped a pen and five pineapple sweets wrapped in glossy paper. "We are going," Sarie said. "Are you now content?" Agatha did not answer, but she nodded, satisfied. She sat down on the bed and, watching in the mirror, aped her mother's moves. She did not have a purse, but she rolled her shoulders and her neck like a woman making an assessment of her looks, and, once Sarie was done, asked to be assisted with the zipper of her own best thing (a long purple-buttoned smock with a radish-print design), and smoothed down her dark hair. Sarie zipped her up and clipped her daughter's mop with a cracked, worn plastic pin that had, in its first days, resembled a chameleon. Engrossed in the next room, Gilbert put his lightly smelly feet on Sarie's favorite table and set about imagining himself desired and aglow among the dignitaries who were pictured milling pleasantly about a bird-filled Chancellor's garden. *Peacocks,* Gilbert thought. *Surely there were peacocks.*

On the streets, the light was fierce, but Kikanga Clinic's world was dim and still and cool. Sarie stood still for a moment on the threshold, relishing the air. Agatha, waiting for the flashes in her eyes to quit, blinked six times in quick succession, then raised her eyebrows high before blinking again. Everything looked green. Directed by her mother, Agatha moved spryly towards the heavy wooden chairs that waited by the wall. Feet adangle, she sat looking up with one eye closed at two framed pictures of the famous Aga Khan—each of which, healthy and avuncular, almost but not quite like the other self, flashed a winning smile. The ceiling fan wheezed idly.

Sarie smoothed the dotted dress down over her thighs and moved up to inquire. The receptionist, a narrow girl with fine, long hands and a sturdy pair of glasses over two perfectly round eyes (Bibi's own Nisreen), looked patiently at Sarie. Nearly dropping but retrieving one pineapple sweet that had got caught on the cap, Sarie fished her pen out. She zipped the purse back up, leaned forward towards the girl, introduced herself, and explained why she had come. "It was me, you see," she said. "It was me who tried to help."

Nisreen had heard about her from the medical assistants, who had, as it turned out, described Sarie very well. But they hadn't said she'd helped. Nisreen cocked her head and said, "I see." She didn't say it meanly. She looked past Sarie, towards Agatha (the girl, she'd heard, who'd prevented them from going till she'd laced up the one shoe). "My daughter," Sarie said. She looked down a moment at her dress, then swayed a bit from hip to hip. "I, too. We want to see him. How he is." She was not sure how to proceed. Sarie did not go out much, not to visit people, and not to speak to strangers. She also did not know what happened, ordinarily, to boys who'd lost their legs so suddenly. She had seen abrasions, stab wounds, ulcers, too, sometimes broken arms and toes, small things plucked, removed, and once an amputation, but nothing quite like this. Was he still at the clinic? Sarie clenched her jaw. Had he, perhaps, died? She didn't ask these things out loud, but Nisreen understood.

Because she was obedient and responsive above all, before thinking to be careful, Nisreen answered Sarie's question. "He's at home," she said. The boy had been released. "He's going to be all right." Resting one long finger on a page of the reception book, where coordinates were noted, she read Sarie the address, and Sarie, on a weathered scrap of paper she had slipped from Gilbert's special drawer, wrote the following down: *Tahir. Majid. Ghulam. Jeevanjee. 10 yrs. Fthr. M. G. Jvnjee. Kudra House. Flr. 2.*

Feeling pleasantly accomplished, Nisreen closed the book and slid it gently back onto its shelf. But, watching Sarie fold her piece of paper, it occurred to her, a little late as usual, that she now felt some doubt. Should she have done what she just had? Should she not have asked more questions? Gotten *her* address? Nisreen stood silently and wavered. Biting at the inside of her cheek, she looked across the tiles to the bright doorway, thinking. Sarie had zipped up her yellow purse and was about to go, but, seeing the receptionist so quiet, she felt suddenly uncertain that the interview had ended. In Nisreen's heavy glasses, a pane of street appeared: a small transparent man pulled a cart behind him; a gleaming Fiat swerved. Sarie wondered briefly how well Nisreen saw. Ought she call her daughter and go on with her mission, wave thank-you from the door?

Here's what was at work: while dutiful Nisreen most often did exactly what was asked of her without skipping a beat, she was also sometimes moved by a desire to step in, to let on what she knew. And Nisreen, on second thought, was not convinced that visiting the boy would be a good idea. But what was she to say? She gave Sarie a look designed to make her pause. Just as, in Northern lands, many Europeans do when speaking to a foreigner, Nisreen enunciated clearly: "You are sure you want to visit? You are certain you're quite sure?" Nisreen's voice was gentle; she felt torn. Visits to the sick were right, of course. Nisreen conducted many on her own. But this! A European with a child, and the Majid Ghulam Jeevanjees. Well, this was something different. Should she say? Should she not? If she did, *how* would she? Fingering the glossy desk, Nisreen hesitated, almost spoke, then gulped. Expectant, Sarie frowned.

Nisreen tapped the counter twice with her long thumbs. She thought: *An Englishwoman, after all. I shouldn't even care.* Englishwomen were well known for doing as they pleased. But Nisreen also thought: *A woman, with a child.* Nisreen cared for children. She leaned away from Sarie, put weight on her good leg, and touched her stomach briefly. What if something happened to the girl? She looked back up at Sarie. "Well." Nisreen pressed her lips together. "What if. Well." Shyness was a struggle. Nisreen took a breath. "Perhaps the boy needs rest."

Nisreen's soft suggestion, coming after such a pause, caused Sarie to stiffen. Gilbert's croons came crouching in her ear. Perhaps she shouldn't go. What if Gilbert was correct? Perhaps she would, as he had said, be *well out of her depth.* Perhaps this girl was thinking, just as Gilbert had, about the Muslim boy, the father, these very Jeevanjees, the mistakes Sarie might make. Something like *No good can come of it, my dear.* Off keel and embarrassed, Sarie stepped away. She thought of sleeping dogs, and blankets, almost said, "Yes, let the sick child rest. You're right. I will not go today." But she also thought of Agatha. They, not Gilbert, and not this narrow girl, had been witness to a thing far greater than themselves. *They,* not she, had recovered gracefully at Hisham's Food and Drink. Sarie turned around. Agatha, enthralled by the framed pictures and the cool clinic's smooth walls, as usual seemed calm. Her dangling feet were still. Agatha, Sarie told herself, would not be swayed by doubt. She was too intent on that boy's missing leg. And, thought Sarie, imperial in her way, *Who's this bony girl to intervene in our own affairs?*

No. Sarie stretched her neck and described a circle in the air with her substantial chin. She brought a finger to her ear, pried Gilbert's warnings out, and flicked them to the floor. She would not go back to the old flat to admit she had been bested, would not leave this clinic in defeat. *On y va,* she thought. *We go, no matter what there is.* Had she not felt required by the boy, the road, the world, that day on the corner? Sarie squared her rugged shoulders and looked Nisreen in the eye. "I am sure that we must visit." She turned to Agatha and said, "Or not?" And though her daughter hadn't stirred, Sarie felt confirmed. She looked back at Nisreen. "We have to go, you see."

As if in response to Sarie's declaration, the electric current dawdled and the fans failed with a thunk. In unison, Sarie and Nisreen turned their faces to the ceiling. The skin on Sarie's bare arms puckered and unpuckered. In the corner on her chair, Agatha looked up but did not cease to scratch a bug bite at her knee. In the stillness, Nisreen thought about the Jeevanjees. Oh, she was not at all concerned that this ungainly woman would not know where to store her shoes, or that she might reach out for a biscuit with an unsuitable left hand. That such things might occur, she didn't even think. Yellow hair and naked arms aside, Nisreen was definitely not protecting Jeevanjees from Sarie.

In Kikanga, the busy heart of downtown Vunjamguu (mixed and thumping: shops and homes and buses, restaurants and bedrooms, an office here and there) people know each other. It's a bustling place, for sure, and Vunjamguu keeps growing. But contrary to what some social thinkers claim, cities don't split people up so much as they mix them all together—indeed, until some of them fall sick from so much neighbors' news and dream of building for themselves a refuge in the country, to which acquaintances will travel only if they must. People here *hear* things. And Kikanga in those days was even more like a big village than now: all kinds of people in close quarters, blood relations and the rest, generous and not, eavesdroppers on every single side as well as up and down.

Nisreen, because she'd married Issa, and because they lived in Mansour House, where secret-monger Bibi hummed and surveyed all day long, had heard more things than most. Though Bibi hadn't left the house in several years, she had once done the rounds, and she had heard enough at weddings and at funerals to last ten gossips' lives. And since she now lived on the balcony, almost, waiting for that *feeling* and scouring the faces of the houses on India and Mahaba streets for happenings in windows, she was also up-to-date. Bibi noticed things, and, to top it off, had a good imagination. If there was a tale to tell (and sometimes when there wasn't), Bibi could produce it. About the slingshot-aiming boy's sad dad, the Majid Ghulam Jeevanjee whose name Sarie had set down, there was plenty to be said.

Here's what Bibi told Nisreen: Majid Jeevanjee, known once to two or three as Ghuji, had long been widely called Mad Majid Ghulam. The glum events that had earned him that sharp name were proof beyond a doubt that people do not always match up to a type. Jeevanjees, case one. Mad Majid Ghulam did not resemble in the least what anyone with ordinary feeling about Jeevanjees might think. Oh, yes, he was somehow a cousin to the famous family's coastal island branch. And was related also to the kingpins who had so stevedored, dubashed, and even, frankly, *built* great cities to the north. A Jeevanjee he was, by birth and blood and flesh. But he was nevertheless not what people in Kikanga expected Jeevanjees to be. Here's the very thing: he was not, as his older brothers were, as his parents and their parents had once been, and as so many other Jeevanjees were, too, a thundering success.

Hard jaw working fast, arms spread apart before her, palms turned slightly up, pleased that Nisreen had for once taken time to sit and appeared prepared to listen, Bibi had begun: "I know exactly what you're thinking. 'Those Jeevanjees have got it made. Money in their veins. Jubilees and Garden Parks, import-export, cloves, and newspapers, to boot.' Oh, and how can I forget? You are also thinking, to be sure, 'Railroads in the brain.' But sometimes"—Bibi leaned a little in and made her voice important—"accidents and luck, my dear, are a stronger thing than blood. Oh, yes, little Nisreen." Here Bibi had smiled especially for her, a crow-smile that had made her eyes glint. "Can change destiny . . . *Pahp! Pahp!*" Bibi snapped her lips apart, releasing puffs of air. "Right before your eyes."

Here's how. Majid Ghulam Jeevanjee had begun his grown-up-journey in the world with a well-stocked wholesale shop and a respectable inheritance from profits made in cloves. Later on, he had run a paper. So far, so good, you say. But no. The businesses, one-two, like dominoes, had failed. First: a storm with thunderous fists sent forty kapok mattresses and six new sofa sets (love seat, ottoman, and couch) floating down the streets. The wholesale shop was ruined, soaked, then washed thoroughly away. Not one wall left standing, not one wet thing returned. Majid Ghulam's older brothers, who had given him the shop because (they'd said) little can go wrong with a Jeevanjee in charge, thought twice. Ghuji had not brought the rain himself, of course, but he must have—mustn't he—done one thing or another to have *his* shop disappear while others stood up tall. Perhaps they'd understood already that he wasn't made for things like that; perhaps the shop was proof. Knowing themselves able, the brothers had with considerable daring turned to the illegal acquisition of stereos from abroad and to the smuggling of rice. They did not take Ghuji on. But, still, a brother is a brother and so on, a load that can't be shed. They gave him something else. "Stick fast to the paper," his two brothers said. Hadn't certain Jeevanjees elsewhere done well in publications? "Words can't float away."

Second: the *Kikanga Flash and Times* had seemed a better proposition. Majid Ghulam might not have luck with shops, but he had, as everybody knew, been capable in school. Had won some prizes, even, been praised by British masters (kneesocked men and hatted ladies all who, so they said themselves, "could spot artistic temperaments even in *this* dark"). Here, Bibi had reminded Nisreen and the pillows that, though some years before Majid, she *had* been to the same school as he, you see, had grown up on those islands, too, come to Vunjamguu at the same time, and her memory was sharp. *She* relied on evidence; she *didn't* make things up. And so. And so Majid Ghulam, who liked words a fair sight better than mattresses and chairs, had taken up the newspaper with a sense of, shall we say, *adventure*. Those who watched him had felt hope: he'd lost the stuff for sure, but here, if anywhere, a poet might make good. Words are better for a reader than kapok beds and fans.

But just because a newspaper is rife with little fictions doesn't mean that dreams can make it run. A paper is a business. This Majid was a poet. A verse, the man could read; a market, he could not. The *Kikanga Flash and Times,* once abrim with hot, delicious news, became the *New Kikanga Times: For Vunja's Thinking Folk.* Tripling the section kept for poems (a modest dose of which did reassure the readers that they were people of good fiber and also guardians of tradition), highlighting the student essays, he squeezed the starlets and the football players out. Driven, Majid was. The failure of the mattress shop had brought about in him a fierceness of *ideas.* As others put it: it was not just sofa sets and mattresses that softened in the rain. Even as the customers complained and the brothers looked up from their radios long enough to shake their rice-filled fists, Majid Ghulam persisted with the poetry, and essays on "What Every Man Should Read." The poems! He did not even stick to only local kinds—which rhymed! Which thrummed with meter that could hit you in the face! Or the local epics, serialized, with morals that should make a person think!—which could have, maybe, with the giving out of prizes, caught on in the end. Instead, Majid Ghulam, a man who'd read books printed in England, who now and then wore neckties, whose father and his father before him had played billiards, and bridge, too, with probity and glee, was sometimes Modern like a donkey. Majid chose free verse; the papers stayed unsold. Oh, one-two years on dwindling funds. A weekly, then a monthly, and then finally, bitterly defunct. The *Kikanga Times* were up.

Some did think this failure simply a mistake. Other Jeevanjees had failed at various things. Some businesses just didn't work; it happened. Yes, all right. But they'd always come back shining, wait and see. That's what Jeevanjees are made of, or? Resilience. A no-man-or-state-shall-bring-me-down demeanor. But with no sign of revival, with no help from the brothers, what had at first seemed a series of forgivable miscalculations here, and here, and there, became something else instead. The busy talkers and rethinkers of Kikanga identified the root of Majid's trouble, and suddenly those losses were not flukes. Pedigree aside, this Jeevanjee, this aberration, was not a man for business. Moreover: he was stuffed full of bad luck and had perhaps been made that way. Ill-starred from the first. Not just vague, eccentric, which some successful men can be, but a business-curse and poison: "Not just 'so strange I-will-wear-a-hat or learn-to-play-a-trumpet,' no, but *bad*. Bad luck," said Bibi. "A bad-luck man, indeed."

How could it have happened, to a very Jeevanjee? In Kikanga, where people make pronouncements, the new belief was this: either from a holy place, or from somewhere, *someone,* else, there had come an interference. Either God (Who cannot be second-guessed) had made it thus, or someone—this was Bibi's leaning—had slipped a sticky finger in his food when he was just a boy. "You know." She gestured to her skirts, slipped a finger in her mouth. "Like so." Nisreen laughed, then blushed. Bibi was insistent: Majid was fated to disaster. "Look now," Bibi said, replacing her wet digit with a chunk of almond burfi, "what happened to his wife."

To his own shock and pleasure, Majid Ghulam Jeevanjee, as men and women do, fell in heady love. He even managed to get married to the darling of his choice, who had, as luck (it seemed) would have it, fallen for him, too. Hayaam, a distant cousin, a round-faced, pleasant girl with great dark eyes and slow, thick hands, was smitten by the narrow man. Because she had not excelled in school, was not as light-complected as good parents might hope, and showed no sign of having either special skills or embarrassing desires, she was not unsuitable for sad Majid Ghulam, either. And he was, after all, a Jeevanjee. Quite so. A catch, if only for his name. Members of her family convinced themselves that all the talk of bad luck in Majid was nonsense, and, gladly, proudly, even, let their young girl go. Majid and his new bride fell into the happy tick and sway of married love, with eyes and hands for none but one another. They did not even mind when Majid's older brothers, who could spot a deal from very far away, sold up all their radios, accepted final payment for a ton of Thailand rice that they had not yet received, and skipped Vunjamguu for England, promising them money but abandoning them all.

Oh, magical Hayaam, reverser of ill fate! For several years, Majid and Hayaam appeared—though no one knew quite how— to prosper, and those who'd made pronouncements wondered if they had been wrong. Narrow Majid plumpened up and went about with smiles on. Hayaam glowed and glowed so brightly that in her parents' eyes her shine made up for what Majid lacked in gold. And the real shape of success? Proud, dutiful Hayaam fashioned for her dreamy poet-husband three good-sized, noisy kids, all of them strong boys. "Like you'll make for my Issa." Bibi tapped Nisreen's long leg with a hand like a warm claw. And Nisreen had giggled, said, "Go on!"

News of Majid's offspring at first seemed rather fine: from the moment each could move, the boy-children gave signs, as all Jeevanjees should, of mathematical prowess. They counted every-thing—toes and beans and stones, and parents—noted down their totals (30, 3,064, then 8, and a lovely, lovely 2), then counted up again. Plus-plus! Things looked, at last, to be turning to the good. Had everyone been a bit too quick to speak? Could Majid have some Jeevanjee in him? A slow, small kernel, but a true one nonetheless, that had simply taken its own time to pop beneath the concentrated sunshine of a brave, sweet-tempered girl?

Well, no. Alas. Bad-luck men do not turn good-luck just like that. And misfortune leaves a mark that is often hard to separate from the thing that left it there. The bad luck some thought might have gone away came back to him eightfold or even ten. Before the tide of talk had turned, before people could too thoroughly forget how they had sworn that to dumb Ghuji nothing good could ever come, Hayaam and Majid's boys were forced to learn the sad art of subtraction. When love-of-Majid's-life Hayaam set out to get her Ghuji their fourth child, well, just like that, proving now to one and all that M. G. Jeevanjee was nuksi, kisirani, failure through-and-through, darling Hayaam died. It's true the fourth boy lived, he did, he was the very one who'd had four limbs until the week before, so Hayaam's death was not a thorough minus. But what a loss, indeed. Nisreen gasped, and Bibi squeezed her hand.

People went right back to naming what was what. Majid Ghulam was not destined to prosper. See how he ruined what he touched. "Clear as water, don't you see? The man is not good news." Bibi then went on to say that Majid's weak heart had gone sour and that his mind had suffered, too. "What else could we expect?" She stretched her neck and brought her hands together. Majid Ghulam went mad. "Crazy, don't you know? Shouts. Sees things that aren't there! The man," she said, "has had a *short.*" Bibi showed Nisreen exactly what she meant: she slapped her temples with her palms, rolled her eyes back, growled, pointed in the air at something neither she nor Nisreen saw, and shook her little knees. "Short circuit!" Almond crumbs went flying. Nisreen had laughed and laughed, then all at once felt tears in her eyes. She'd looked away from Bibi.

Nisreen was not unsusceptible to bad-luck explanations; she knew that misfortunes added up can make a person like a dog, fit only to be shot. And surely little Tahir Majid's fall the week before on India Street was not good luck at all. But on some days, Nisreen turned away from neighbors' talk of destiny, mixed romance with science. She had read about psychology at school, and she had private doubts about whether Mr. M. G. Jeevanjee, or anyone, was bad-luck through and through. She wasn't sure—not knowing him herself—if he had really lost his mind. Perhaps, she thought, Majid Ghulam's reported habits (his wandering outside in the night in nothing but a singlet, his sleeping in all day, his brow-beating of passersby, the shouting out of windows, all since Hayaam's death) were not the bad luck coming back. *No,* thought generous Nisreen, *they're signs of love and grief. Majid Ghulam's depressed.* Nisreen thought that if her man died one day like that, without warning in advance (she thought of Issa and her heart hurt), she might act strangely, too. Deaths were planned by God and only God, she thought, not by stars or sticky hands, and grief could bring on madness. If Issa died, would people say that Bibi's gummy hands had lingered on the food? Nasty mother snuffs her only son? Worse yet, that poor Nisreen herself, with her froglike, failing eyes, that limp she tried to hide, and, most telling of all, her neither-round-nor-swelling stomach, had caused her husband's doom? Been a bad-luck girl herself?

Nonetheless. It was one thing to look upon M. G. Jeevanjee from safely far away and treat him kindly in her thoughts, another to agree that he should be sought out. Bad-luck man or no, Majid *was* peculiar. And peculiar men should be kept at one arm's length, at least. Especially the long and naked arms of Englishwomen who were not at all informed. For what did Europeans know about the right sort of protection? And, further, like dust fevers and syphilis, infidelity and hatred, bad-luck-grief-or-madness, or whatever the thing was—would it not be contagious?

At Kikanga Clinic, the high fan twitched, then started up again. Sarie fiddled with the long strap of her purse. Agatha slid down from her chair and came to stand beside her. While Nisreen considered Sarie and the child, Bibi's voice resounded in her ears, with headlines from the *Flash and Times of Sad Majid Ghulam*. Nisreen saw them in her mind. In longhand, teasing script: "Incorrigible!" In bold: "Unpredictable, What's More!"

Nisreen drummed her fingers on the counter. One last time, should she speak, or not? She couldn't. She decided to keep quiet. Sarie Turner, biting at her lip, waiting for a sign, clearly wished very much to go. *Maybe,* thought Nisreen, *maybe fate is hard at work. Who am I to intervene? Let the woman go.* "Well, you're right. It is very good to go." Nisreen felt an urge to make the visitors feel especially at ease, tell them something that they might not know. "He lost that piece of leg, but he will walk again," she said, nodding at the child. "We are waiting for his crutches."

Sarie shivered in the ceiling fan's new wind. She didn't like to think it, but she knew that it was true: she *had* wished for encouragement. She was relieved to get it now. She felt that she had won a battle, small, but nonetheless, with Gilbert and even with this girl. Sarie stood up straight and laughed, happy, loud. "All right, then. *Merci bien!*" Sarie waved her fingers at Nisreen. "That means 'thank you,'" she explained. "Thank you very much." Ready to go, too, Agatha gave each Aga Khan a wink. Nisreen—because what else can be done when a thing has been decided but help destiny along—said, "You will find it, then. Kudra House. It isn't very far."

As Sarie and her daughter stepped out of the cool clinic back into the glare, Nisreen remembered something else. She rose on her bare toes to see if what they'd told her—what Bibi had repeated all week long, since the crash that *she herself had seen* and her triumph at the phone, what the orderlies had said—was true. It was. Sarie Turner, though decked out in what might have passed for some people's best dress, was wearing rubber thongs: worn out at the heel, cracked around the rim, and orange, exactly as they'd said. For shame! Amazing. Nisreen, more to please her Issa's mother than from any love of telling tales herself, made certain no one saw her; then she made a call.

"You're sure?" Bibi wished to know. "You're not mistaking one white woman for another? It's the very same?" Nisreen reassured her. "She's left here just now." Nisreen could tell Bibi was grateful, this a bright spot in her day. "I'm not going to move, my dear little Nisreen," she said. Indeed, she was going to settle on the balcony so she could keep her eyes fixed on the back of Kudra House— which she could see, just there, just a sliver of an alley and a little dab of green, could see as plain as day—until the sun went down.

Even if she didn't quite believe everything she heard, Nisreen did like a story. And though she didn't do it by herself, when Bibi talked and talked, Nisreen sometimes let her mind play, too, come up with things to wonder. What was going to happen? She pressed her chin against the handset, smiled into it, and sighed. "She's going there on foot," she said. Bibi was a little disappointed that Sarie Turner did not have a car. "Walking, did you say?" But a walk would let her see the pair, and it made her think of something. Might not so much sunlight spoil a foreign woman's brain? Sunstroke was an issue, yes? Nisreen concurred that Sarie Turner should have worn a hat. What if *she* went mad as well? If Mad Majid harangued her, would she call in the police? Bibi laughed into the telephone (which was not so strange now, not such a bad thing) and asked, would Sarie Turner—because Englishwomen were often mannish, after all—slap his face and kick his groins herself?

Bibi had a little more to say before Nisreen hung up. With rapid breath: "That man. Do you know how mad he is?" There it was, the same old story, what had happened when somebody named Alibhai Mustafa died, trampled by an ox. How a person named Rahman had asked Majid for a funeral donation and had been kicked out of the house. Bibi told this one a lot. She imitated Mad Majid Ghulam. " 'Burials are a good-for-nothing waste, Rahman! Death a cruel joke!' " And how the three big sons tipped a bucket down into the courtyard when their father told them to. "Not human boys, they are! No, devils! I can see him now, can you? Rahman! And nicely dressed, he was. Wetter than the sea." Bibi purred, and Nisreen wondered if this poor Rahman—so frequently, so excitingly, wet through—was really a relation or if Bibi'd made him up. She could almost hear the creaking of excitement in Bibi's little neck. "Mad Majid Ghulam," said Bibi, "is capable of anything. Anything at all."

Energized, Bibi told Nisreen to please now let her go. She had a balcony to guard. *Let fools reap their foolishness,* she thought, *while others sit and watch.* She stood up from her seat. Before taking

Nisreen's call, Bibi, having finished the *Al-Fadhil* stitchery and moved on to something else, had been fashioning the bright tail of a peacock at the heart of an old sheet. As she replaced the telephone and straightened up the doily, Bibi took a hard, long look at that stitched bird. Yes, those feathers looked quite nice. She paused. She put a hand up to her mouth and tapped her bottom lip. *What if? Perhaps. Just think!*

Ever since the miserable boy had been hit by that big and holy bus, Bibi's pins-and-thread box had taken on a tantalizing shine. What if in her old age she *were* developing a gift? Granted a reward for having caught so many secrets on her own, unaided by foretelling? Hadn't she woken just the day before with a peacock on the brain? A feathered dream with cries that woke her in a sweat? Had she not seen the bird again on the back wall of her mind when she rolled her soft msala carpet after prayers and pulled on her old dress?

Could it be? *The peacock?* No. Not really. Could it? Bibi pressed a tooth into her lip and moved her mouth around. *Can Majid Ghulam Jeevanjee have any preening left?* Thinking of her balcony and how from it she could now and then distinguish exactly what was what, she stood. *Perhaps, perhaps!* She gave the bird a final squint, a haughty, knowing sniff. "Well," she said into the room. "Anything could happen." Anything, indeed.

Kudra House was one of many pastel-colored multistory mansions that had sprung up in Kikanga at the century's broad middle, dreams aboil, hopes high. Built by eager and determined people whose grandmothers and -fathers had finally arrived, they had been proof of joy. Ashok Building, 1931. Hormuz Villa, 1936. Premji Mansion, 1947. Honesty House, 1954. Some mansions bore the names of sons whose star charts had foretold skill in family trades, or, as with Hormuz Villa, the names of bobbing boys procured after a gaunt parade of girls. Others were a comment: Honesty House a fearless declaration, Happy House a dare. Others, like Tanga House, and Kudra House as well, were named after the places whence initial riches came, in sisal or in cloves.

In the days before bad luck grew to be, for some, another name for Independence (and the snatching-up of homes), the houses in Kikanga had been beautifully kept up. Rich in windows (in some a dozen on each floor), with finely painted shutters and impeccable facades, some reached out into turrets or bulged roundly at the sides. Many boasted high box balconies made of well-placed wooden slats, so that prosperous ladies could peep inquisitively out and never once be seen.

In Majid's father's time, the houses had been flowers for the city's thrumming heart, each a light and lovely color set off by the sun. Hormuz Villa had started out a buttery yellow, Premji Mansion a blue more tender than the sky, the Happy House a mild

rose-apple pink. Kudra House, a fine example of this earnest building style, had once been painted green—a powdery, smooth color,
like pale pistachio ice cream or a newborn's knitted socks. But by
the time Majid Ghulam's boy had lost his leg and Sarie went with
Agatha to see him, Kudra House had long been on its way down: it
looked more like a ruin.

Thirty years of heavy rains had soured that first green, and now
that Kudra House was owned no longer by the Jeevanjees but
rather by the State, no funds were left for painting. As if a gigantic
woman's eye had with its weeping bled mascara down the walls,
the outer face was streaked with sooty black. The few remaining
patches of a sweet, inviolate color battled now with water stains
and diesel grime and dust. From gouges in the house-face strange
tufted grasses grew. Here and there, the shutters had come loose
and, gone to kindling for clever passersby, could not be retrieved.
At this window dingy curtains hung, in that, a homely gloom. The
wooden balcony had lost many of its slats. If a woman were to sit
there, Bibi had once said, a bad-news boy, if he was smart, could
look up from the sidewalk and right into her skirt.

But still. As Nisreen had promised, Kudra House was not far
from the clinic. Beyond the bus stand's clang and rattle, past the
sweet smell of a table where a bearded man made cane juice at a
creaking metal press, Agatha and Sarie crossed a narrow alley lit-
tered with old things and reached their destination. Sarie coaxed
the slip of paper from her purse. At the foot of that once-glowing
house, she and Agatha looked up towards the roof and saw the
name embossed, which they both read aloud: *Kudra House, 1932.*
Squinting at her mother's note, Agatha said, "It's on the second
floor." They found the chipped black doors ajar, and, Sarie, nervous
but determined, and Agatha, exceptionally calm, stepped carefully
between them.

They found themselves in a neatly private place. The courtyard was so quiet, the air in it so fresh, that indeed it seemed to Sarie as if the busy streets outside, with Hisham's Food and Drink, with cool Kikanga Clinic and the dusty ashok trees—with Bibi at her balcony, though Sarie didn't know it—and even with their own dim flat on Mchanganyiko Street, were very far away. Another world entirely. And although Sarie was accustomed in the courtyard of their building to seeing unknown neighbors' clothing dangle in the wind, and chickens, and an ancient taxicab that never moved and maybe never had, and wire coils that vanished and appeared, this, a house meant for a single family (a dynasty, in fact, and Sarie, to her credit, vaguely knew that this was so), was something rather different. Closed.

As in most Kikanga courtyards, there was washing and the waxy, yellow smell of soap. Somewhere, water dripped. Nothing special, then. But perhaps because it served few people, these details seemed to Sarie evidence of comfort and a privacy she could only envy. On a sagging length of twine, two undershirts, bright white, surrendered to the breeze. An orange gown with ruffled sleeves swung lightly to and fro. A violet skirt, with pleats. There were also modest signs of care: flowers growing out of tins; ten o'clock roses, crimson, that had already closed; violet brinjal blooms; a slender pepper plant. In the gutter just along the wall, a breadfruit seedling toiled, twin leaves, new and languid, just starting to unfurl.

A white cat with a tufted coat and several bald spots stepped into the courtyard from the street, which Sarie had already forgotten. Attracted by its sores, Agatha bent to touch it and it fled, a wary glow in its pale eye. From up above, in the still and quiet air, a parrot hollered, "Who's there, who's there, who?" Agatha, with her sharp ears, imagined that she heard a scurrying of feet. In her mind's unformed eye, she saw girls with blue-black braids move swiftly to a kitchen where they would ably squeeze up juice. She thought she heard the soft, seductive scrape of a brand-new biscuit tin being taken from a shelf. But Agatha, unlike Bibi, was not yet on the verge of discovering a gift. She was wrong about the girls. As Nisreen could have told her, Kudra House had none.

Sarie, stepping backwards, caught her flip-flop on a stone. She stumbled, tilted her strong chin towards the roof. The parrot cried again. "It is Mrs. Turner here!" Sarie called, long neck arched, and waited. At first more swollen silence and a thickness in the air. Then came a response. A lean boy, bright-eyed and bare-shouldered, hair ashine with dressing even in that dusty light, leaned out over the windowsill and grinned. He spoke quickly, brightly. Sarie did not understand. The ground uneven at her feet, she almost fell again. She swooped both hands towards her hips and up, found her balance for a moment. "We've come to—" she began. But when Sarie had stood tall, smoothed her dress, and looked up to him again, the boy had disappeared.

There was a scuffling in the stairwell, one soft thud then another—the hot sound (Agatha imagined) of a boy pulling on a cotton shirt and buttoning it up as he moved down the steps. And then, beaming, smelling of fresh aftershave (lemons, pepper, glue), Ismail Majid Jeevanjee—the oldest of the sons whose birth had caused no grief—stood expectantly before them. Sarie thought to introduce herself again, but with a graceful sweep of a long arm, the boy showed them up the stairs as if he already knew exactly who she was. (He did. Words travel, after all. *This* must be the woman who had braved the road in her cheap shoes and whispered spells into his brother's ear while that little girl of hers sat fooling on the sidewalk with the sorry, severed limb.)

*   *   *

They did have biscuits, in the end. Majid's big boy number three—heavy, slow Habib, with great sad eyes and a soft gut—was sent out to the shops to fetch a roll of Nanjis. The downstairs neighbor (Maria, loyal, Christian, sour, owner of the vivid orange gown) was dispatched to make tea by Majid's second son: thin, sharp-tongued Ali, who called down to Maria from the balcony ("Oh! Maria, *weh!*") without so much as a please. Smooth Ismail, who as number one was wiser if not better than the rest, dutifully took charge and went to rouse his father. Next, yawning in a singlet, Majid Ghulam Jeevanjee emerged to greet his guests.

Mad Majid in the flesh. How would Bibi have reacted, presented with this body? This waker did not look emphatically unhinged. Not quite the debauched crazy. Rather, he looked tired. Majid Ghulam, or Mr. Jeevanjee, as Sarie called him for a time, was not as mad, not anymore, at least, as Bibi had made him out to be and not as helpless as Nisreen had thought. Their theories, founded principally in any case on hearsay, had not kept up with the times. Oh, he had grief and fury in him, yes, in pounds, in pishis and frasilas, many hundredweight. Majid had *not* been lucky. But, while the first few years of widowhood had certainly entailed the ravages that Bibi could recall—Rahman, the insults, the wild waving of arms, the giving-up-on-bathing, the shouting in the street, and other things, and more—long grief had also, finally, brought a quietness in him, something like a dullness, which neighbors with a taste for stories full of action did not think to bring up (quiet, after all, was not much good discussing). This Jeevanjee was tired. Widowhood and failure had snuffed the brightest of the glow he'd had as a poem-peddling youth, as the owner of a rag; and the loss of little Tahir's leg-below-the-knee had been a wild and unexpected blow, smarted every time he passed the bedroom where the recovering boy still slept, every time he woke. How could such a thing not further test a hopeless, brooding pa? Even Sarie noticed that the man seemed pretty glum.

He'd just risen from a nap, and, scratching dumbly at his chest, Mad Majid was just then neither dangerous nor mad, but a tired picture of great sorrow. He came out from his bedroom slowly, an old and rumpled dress shirt trailing in his hand. He stood bleary in the hallway for a moment, pulled one sleeve up clean, and struggled with the other. His long, bare arms were bony. He did not quite understand who the woman was, not yet, and he did not look Sarie fully in the face until he had buttoned up his shirt (not well, not ably: second button at first hole). Before raising his head, he rubbed his stubbled chin and cracked his square, hard jaw, eyeing the chipped floor with a dazed air, as if remembering a stain.

Sarie briefly felt that they should not have come. The strange man had been sleeping, after all, and deeply, so it seemed from how his eyes looked narrow and his mouth a little caked. And surely he was worried for his youngest son. Sarie swallowed lightly, dryly, and her lips twitched taut and back a moment, like a person who has privately become aware of making a mistake and hopes no one will see. Perhaps the boy was worse, not as well as the receptionist had promised.

In another room, the unseen parrot squawked. Majid Ghulam, looking up at last, could not suppress a yawn. In bed, he had been dreaming a sharp dream—a dream with a blue rainstorm, a brass coffee set with cups, a fountain pen. A doctor without arms had been hopping over puddles. In sleep he had acquired the impression of himself in a costume, in a cumbrous, feathery suit, trying something, trying. Ankle-deep in water, he'd felt tiny creatures slither round his feet. A sucking at his knees. Watching the pale woman in his hallway (a nervous presence, polka-dotted, pearly in the frowsy light), Majid Ghulam, not yet abandoned by the dream, felt confronted by a beast. Part giraffe, part camel. How single-toned this woman was, and tall! A foot taller than he was, at least. Was the woman real? He had to tilt his head. A view: Sarie's dappled skin brought him closer to the world; he was startled by her freckles. Majid Ghulam passed a wrist bone hard against his mouth, then, unexpectedly, gave Sarie a smile.

It might have been a grimace, but it made Sarie feel more confident, and hardy. She plucked once at the fabric of her dress to right the narrow skirt. She took a preparatory breath of chalky, windless air and leaned in towards the man, ardently extending her right hand, which Majid Ghulam took and then, dismayed by its heat, perhaps, by the fact that it was real, let go rather quickly. She thought: *I am intended to be here! I will make this a success!*

They spoke at the same time. Sarie's voice was earnest, loud. "We came—"

Majid Ghulam, remembering as though from another long-gone dream the gestures of respect, placed two hands flat against his breast and bowed his head politely. "Welcome—"

Sarie, unsettled by the elegance of Mr. Jeevanjee's address, lost her train of thought. She shifted all her weight from side to side and back. She said, "I am Mrs. Turner." And then, "Your son." She was glad she'd written the names down. "Tahir." She did not know what to say next.

"Mrs. Turner. Ah," Majid Ghulam said. Sarie said, "The clinic." Majid Ghulam now understood that she had come about the boy. His heart rose for a moment—had she come about the crutches? Was it still too soon for that? But Sarie said, "The accident." Behind her, she felt Agatha's cool shape atwitch. She gestured to her child. "My daughter." Agatha frowned up at him, then bit her lip and smiled. Sarie's big eyes widened. "We were there, you understand?"

Majid Ghulam squinted. He looked down at Agatha and nodded slightly, not unkind. "Ah, yes." His mind was coming clear. He'd heard about her, too. "Thank you. Yes." And, "Good," he said. Then, "Grateful."

He shuffled to the parlor. With a sense that things were moving to some second stage, Sarie followed him. Agatha came, too. Ismail and Ali hovered in the hallway. They eyed each other, shrugged, and, quiet, leaned against the wall to watch. Majid Ghulam asked Sarie to sit. He took the chair across from her, on the other side of a long, low, broken table. Sarie noted its carved feet, the nice curve of the legs. *A coffee table,* Sarie thought. *Antique.* As pictured in old magazines. As Sultans must have had. Agatha settled on the floor.

Elbows planted on his thighs, clasped hands hanging in between two bony, trousered knees, Majid Ghulam Jeevanjee looked at her and waited. Tense but almost beaming, tight, like a man unused to company but eager to behave. His scrutiny made her shy. She squirmed. Her legs were too long for the space between the blue settee and table. She twisted her big hips, now this way and then that, trying to get comfortable. Agatha looked up at her and Sarie had the feeling that her daughter thought her too big and ungraceful. She frowned and rearranged her hair.

Awkwardness. It is through just such times, of course, that certain seeds are sown: without intending to, Sarie showed Mr. Jeevanjee her upper thigh, doughy, muscular, dimpled at the flank. Did he notice it for what it was? Was he alert enough by then, awake enough to see (*A thigh!*)? Or did it simply seep into his consciousness somewhere and shift a shadow in his head, as weighty flesh can do?

His head. Above it, brassy pendulum at work, an old wall clock from America or Switzerland glinted in the light. Sarie by and by stopped twisting. She sat instead sidesaddle, her knees high and

together. She watched him. Yes, the man looked tired and unkempt. Perhaps even dirty. But there was something fine about
him, too. With the clock atick behind him, just above his head, she
thought that Mr. Jeevanjee, in slightly different light, might look
particularly important. *A man with things to do. A man who thinks of
time.* It struck her that she would not have been surprised to see
a man like him—shaved and better dressed, of course—managing
a railway station or a restaurant or working at a desk. And while
her husband had once had a rather large desk of his own, it occurred to her to ask herself, *Ces jours-ci, does Gilbert have a watch?*
Sarie didn't think so. She sucked idly at her cheek. There passed
between Majid Ghulam and his guest a solid silence, heightened by
the parrot's intermittent squawks.

Majid Ghulam leaned back a bit. His fingers loosened. Perhaps
because in this half-waking state he was not quite himself, or perhaps because he found her height, her freckles, and her forthrightness refreshing, Majid Ghulam—who *was* unkind when the right
opportunity arose—felt that he had been presented with a rare occasion to which he should rise, sensed that something different had
come. "Well. You are Mrs. Turner." Sarie answered, "Yes."

When faced with an odd happening, still moving in a funk, one
can sometimes resort to ritual and rules. Drawing on the manners
he had witnessed in his father and his wife, this Majid Ghulam did.
As though expecting waiters or the members of a staff, he looked
briefly away. He then turned back to her and said, "Maria will
bring tea." Sarie nodded, was impressed. *Ils ont une servante,* she
thought. Her voice a little like the voices of British ladies she had
known once and not liked very much, Sarie said, "Oh, tea. Yes, I
am sure that will be nice. Yes. Thank you." She plucked at her gray
hem and noticed gratefully in passing that Agatha was sitting well
and looked appropriately polite.

Next there appeared Maria, plump and sturdy, thick-ankled and dour, bringing tea in a red thermos that entirely by accident matched the color of her headscarf. Because the Jeevanjees never had real guests—or hadn't, once Hayaam was gone—and the few relations who still came knew to bring refreshments of their own, Maria, understanding that this was an Occasion, had also brought up seven rare kaimati balls she had acquired the day before and had been saving for herself; though once she'd set them down, she had a second thought. While Sarie didn't notice, Maria (who was not an ordinary Christian, who had recently been *saved*) looked her down and up, lingered on *that leg,* and made up her own mind. She set the dumplings on the table with a clatter, wished she hadn't brought them, gave Agatha a warning look as if to say, *And these are not for you,* then pounded down the stairs.

Sarie, who didn't get enough sweet things at home, though she loved them so, was agreeably surprised. "What sweets!" she thought, and said aloud. She did enjoy kaimati! Majid Ghulam blinked. He gestured towards the plate, and Sarie, who had wished to be good-mannered, had wanted to act right, forgot herself a bit. It was good to be polite, but Sarie's mouth was singing: *Sugar! Oil!* She ate four in quick succession. Majid Ghulam was not upset. He'd forgotten what guests should be. His own mouth moved a bit as Sarie chewed and chewed. He felt that he should speak.

Unused to teatime's polished back-and-forth, he felt something in himself come loose, a pain that had been sticking in his heart. He'd tell *her.* She'd listen, yes she might. It was something he'd been longing to announce, an indignation for which the aunts (who'd come to visit little Tahir out of duty and because their greatest pleasures sometimes lay in other people's grief) had chastised him. "So petty!" they had said. "Think of what's important! Don't dawdle on what's done! *Do* something instead!" He had been, without knowing it, perhaps, longing for an audience. Tasteless, possibly, too soon? But how often was he faced with someone who had come explicitly to sympathize with him? Why accept a guest at all if doing so did not bring the host relief? What Majid Ghulam told Sarie was a story that, had the *Kikanga Flash* still lived, would have taken the front page. Gesturing to the calamity that had brought her to the house without naming it directly, Majid Ghulam talked about the shoe, the very shoe that Agatha had loosened and laced up, and which had, in the end, been lost.

He leaned forward, placed one hand on the table and one on his own knee. "Do you know what? Do you know what, Mrs. Turner?" Sarie made a listening sound, a *hm?* Like this, Majid Ghulam explained: while he had gotten most of his son back from the doctor, he had not retrieved the second Bata shoe. "They kept the shoe!" he said. He paused. Sarie, eating, nodded, and Majid Ghulam went on, surprised at his own speech, the active, busy sound of it, pouring from his throat into his ears and hers and the front room. Sure, the doctor was embarrassed. But Majid felt that he was being had, was hurt. "They were lying, I believe, you see. How could a shoe be lost?" While Sarie chewed and swallowed, careful, Majid Ghulam puffed out his meager chest and gestured with his hands. Above his head the ticking clock approved. "Right in front of me, he called up all the nurses for a scene." Majid Ghulam pressed his lips together and worked his aching jaw. Sarie wiped her fingertips, leaned forward.

She could picture hospitals, of course, could muster up enthusiasm for talk about their failings, and she felt reassured. *He is telling me a story. Things are going well.* She smiled at Mr. Jeevanjee, and, bolstered by her silence and the kind look on her face, he spilled out the rest: how the nurses quaked and trembled in the hallway, bit their lips in sorrow, shook their practiced heads. And how, despite the for-show-finger-wagging and one or two quick winks, the doctor was unable to extract from them an answer. "Nobody would say, Madam!" Majid Ghulam told her. His voice suddenly grew soft then, no longer quite a storyteller's voice but rather like the voice of someone who has been telling a tall tale and all at once recalls that it is not tall, but true. He looked away from her. "None of them spoke up. Told me best I should forget." Sarie made a pleasant listener's noise. He raised his head again and fixed her in his sights, as though she alone could help him "They said, 'What is it with the shoe?' "

Sarie thought how long it was since anyone had thought of her as "Madam." It made her sweet and calm. She looked down at Agatha and wondered if she'd noticed, but Agatha, who was looking at the plate, hadn't heard a word. Sarie turned back to her host. Aware of Mr. Jeevanjee's bright eyes, she told herself, *I must be sympathetic.* She redoubled her support. "It's terrible!" she said. "So sorry!" She could see the man had suffered. She did think (ever practical), *What is a boy without a leg to need a second shoe?* But she was wise enough just then to keep that to herself. Bata shoes *were* fine. She said, "Terrible," again.

An aside. What several people at the clinic knew but had not said was this: a mild but inexperienced orderly whose own father's leg had been devoured by gangrene had slipped that Bata shoe from Tahir's dead leg in the night. The dead leg was a right leg, after all, as his father's at home was. Perhaps that little shoe could fit his barefoot dad! But he'd miscalculated things. His father's foot was small, it's true, but not that small, and the shoe now like a rotted fruit or secret sat smelly and accusing beneath the worker's bed. Absconding with a dead man's hat or coat might be one thing, but this! Stealing from the dead leg of a little boy whose other parts were very much alive! Well, that was harder to admit to; he was too ashamed to bring the item back.

But the fact of this small sin—if sin it was at all—neither Sarie nor her host could know. And it really didn't matter. What Majid Ghulam remembered most, what rankled—he was in the corners of his mind aware that showing too much feeling to a stranger can turn them speedily against you, and tried to tell this part without being too serious—was how the doctor left things, how unhelpful he had been. He'd offered Majid Jeevanjee a decorative apology, then moved quickly away from talk of search and compensation to the future, which, if Majid played his cards right, the doctor thought—of all affronts!—was really rather bright. "Two arms and one leg! I know some with less! You must be looking now to what he *does* have left, I say." He'd laid a fawning hand on Majid's heavy arm (just a little anxious, knowing very well, of course, that this was Mad Majid). "Come now, my dear sir." Then, far more intimate, too much, and steering Majid towards the door: "What's a shoe, *yakhe,* in the face of life and death?" Majid Ghulam shook his head at Sarie, sighed. " 'What's a shoe,' indeed!"

A shoe *is* nothing, in the face of life and death, it's true. Even Sarie would have said so. But she liked to feel indignant, and it pleased her that her host was so visibly upset. *He is opening himself,* she thought. Were not Mr. Jeevanjee's dark eyes undeniably aglisten? Did his voice not seem particularly warm? "Indeed," she said. The lost shoe was an insult, yes, it was. A sign of bad times in the land, if people who are meant to heal a child can't care for his possessions. And Sarie also felt superior: where *she* had been a nurse, nothing, not a thing, had ever disappeared. (Well, a *person* had, just once, but *that* story is for later, in a little while.) The lost shoe was an abomination, and she said so. The mean echo of a loss that was already too much to be borne. She shook her head and looked at Mr. Jeevanjee with both her blue eyes wide. "I can't believe it," Sarie said. "I have never heard, exactly, anything like this."

The shoe theft was thus not, in each and every sphere, an unproductive thing: it joined Sarie to her host. Majid Ghulam was unaccustomed to arousing tenderness in strangers. What a long time it had been! When Sarie Turner said, "It is truly a surprise what happens in the world," he found himself feeling rather soft, and bare. "Yes, indeed, it is," he said, repeating Sarie's words as though they had been issued in a difficult new tongue. "What happens in the world can be truly a surprise."

While her mother and the father of the boy she'd come to see sat commiserating in their very grown-up way, Agatha, who could not wait any longer, crept up to the table and took two kaimati for herself, leaving only one behind. Her movement brought the sugared balls to Majid Ghulam's attention. And, without knowing what he did—though his late wife would have stopped him—he plucked the last one up.

What else took place in Kudra House that, though she squinted on the balcony and willed her eyes to grow, Bibi didn't see? Not much. A lot. The boys stayed watching in the hallway, whispering through cupped hands. Dutiful Habib had come back from the shops with biscuits and, holding these, not wanting to interrupt his father, joined Ismail and Ali. As their daring father placed a sweet ball in his mouth, Ali, the quickest and most wicked, said a racy thing about Sarie Turner's legs, and Ismail gave out a long and knowing laugh. Habib, embarrassed, good at seeming even slower than he was, pretended he'd heard nothing. But Majid Ghulam, aware of rustles in the hall, dusted off the crumbs that had fallen to his lap, cleared the sugar from his lip with a quick pass of his knuckles, and called out for the Nanjis.

Later, he pulled out an old exemplar of the paper he'd once owned. Sarie was relieved. Despite her bravery with Gilbert, her insistence that she was more than equal to all things, that she had dealt with many kinds of people in her interesting life, she did feel out of practice. The newspaper was perfect. It was something she could read, in English. It also gave Majid Ghulam a simple space on which to focus his bright eyes. He hadn't meant to ogle Sarie Turner's legs. In fact, he had not been aware of doing so until he picked up the last sweet. He didn't think he had such looking in him—not with Hayaam dead and Tahir broken practically in two. He was therefore also glad about the paper, which (like many other things) he had not shown anyone in years. Bringing out from underneath the chair a favorite issue of the old *Kikanga Times,* he thought how proud of it he'd been. "My specialty was poetry," he said. He tapped the yellowed pages, closed one eye and pursed his nose and lips to show how seriously he took it. He wished that he owned glasses. "I increased the room for verse." Sarie nodded in encouragement, and Majid Ghulam, taken by her kindness, admitted that he had, in long-gone days, written poems of his own.

Sarie reached out for the paper. She liked a man who made things. Disheveled, this man was, she thought, but, still. *He has a clock that marches! And he writes! He has a girl to bring him up the tea!* Writing, really writing, things that no one else has said, was something to admire, wasn't it? (Nevermind that Gilbert now and then submitted ramblings to the Historical Society or threatened to write books. *This* was something else.) And *poetry!* She liked the thought of that. Her freckled face lit up. How well this outing had turned out! She'd not only been *consorting* with the Muslims (for

Gilbert had been right, she thought; *Those names!*) but meeting
with, imagine, a thinking, writing man. An intellectual, indeed.
"You write *verse!*" she said, knocking one of her big knees against
the coffee table but not feeling any pain. "Mr. Jeevanjee, you mean
you are a poet."

Majid Ghulam raised a hand up to his breast, suddenly embarrassed. "No," he said, "I am an amateur, that's all." But part of him
was pleased. "You are generous," he said. Ali elbowed Ismail and
pointed with his chin. Habib looked away. Their father the poet!
Ali laughed and Ismail shoved him, told him to be still. The
grown-ups carried on. Sarie folded up the paper and handed it to
Mr. Jeevanjee. Majid Ghulam urged Nanjis on his guest. Though
the kaimati balls had filled her, she took two to be polite. She
twitched a little on the settee, moving her cramped legs.

At last, Majid Ghulam understood. He pulled the coffee table
to the side so that Mrs. Turner could stretch her limbs and sit with
greater ease. Sarie sighed. Her big thighs disappeared beneath a
dotted hem. She felt seen, and cared for. It was all right for Mr.
Jeevanjee to have been looking at her legs, she thought, if this was
how it ended. Perhaps he had been noticing her thighs so frequently in order to determine how to give her room. What a grand
outing, indeed! Sarie, who could pick a side and stick with it
awhile when it occurred to her to do so, decided then and there
that not only was her visit so far a success, but that she *liked* this Mr.
Jeevanjee and was having a good time. She felt she should repay
him, that it was her turn now to find something to say. An offering.
"I grew up in Jilima," Sarie said. "The mountains."

Majid Ghulam was genuinely surprised. "Here?" he said. He
cocked his head and looked sideways at her. "Mrs. Turner, you are
local!" Sarie did not smile. "I lived with nurses there," she said.
"The Sisters." Majid Ghulam did not know what to make of that.

"Your mother and your father?" Sarie shook her head and pressed her knees together. She looked up at the clock and told her host she'd lost them very early. Majid Ghulam expressed sympathy, shook his tilted head. Sarie said—a little loudly, as though his sorrow were misplaced—"But I do not remember them!" She sat up in her seat. She hadn't come to talk about herself. "I'm used to it," she said. And, as if in explanation, as if husbands could eclipse the value of one's past, she tugged lightly at her earlobe, cleared her throat, and said: "My husband was attached to the Vunjamguu High Court. He was in the Service."

Majid Ghulam did not wish to pry. He did not press her further. Sarie had the fleeting thought that this was a relief. Taking charge again, she asked about his wife. A poet with three sons must have somewhere a Mrs. Perhaps she had gone out and would come back at any moment with shopping bags or news. But, no. Majid Ghulam looked behind him for a moment as though making certain that he would not be overheard. "Oh, Madam," Majid Ghulam said. "My only wife is dead."

It was thus for Majid Jeevanjee an afternoon of firsts. Everyone he knew already knew about Hayaam. And because they thought of him as mad, they rarely came to see him; and if they did come close and speak, they didn't dare say anything that might provoke his madness. But there it was. He'd said it, and saying it was strange. "What can anybody do? She died many years ago, may she be in peace." At the fresh announcement of something so familiar and so old, Majid was disconcerted by a feeling: a little pang rose up just below his ribs and something in him flinched. Yes, he was still sad, for wasn't he just that? Sad and Mad Majid? But when he unfurled himself again, he became aware of an even stranger thing: the pang had given way to a conviction that, despite the sweet kaimati, he might now have a biscuit.

Hunger? Hunger and not grief? He was alert enough by now to be taken quite firmly aback. Was it Tahir's missing leg that made him hungry, suddenly, for filling empty space? Did his hunger stand for wishing old things to come back? Or for—this he could not think too clearly then, not with Mrs. Turner polka-dotted and life-sized on his very own blue settee—new things to replace the older ones that kept being subtracted, shoring up the gloom?

Sarie Turner said, "I'm sorry," pushed the dish towards her host, crossed her easy legs, and elaborately adjusted the collar of her dress. Majid Ghulam said, "Thank you." Looking for a moment all the world like a person plucking a soft flower, he took another Nanji.

At their father's nod, the boys took Sarie Turner's daughter, who had been patient all this time, who had been waiting just for this, to see their little brother. One and one-half legs covered by a patterned cotton sheet in the room he shared with Ismail, Ali, and Habib, Tahir Majid Jeevanjee was sleeping. Ali, like a dart, poked at the boy's pillow, shook him by the shoulder. "Here," he said, "is the last living person in the world to have seen your missing leg." Clever and impious, Ali had turned it all into a game, pretending from the day Tahir came home that the missing limb would be returned to him as soon as it was found. Ismail and Habib were grateful. "Dad's a paper man, remember. They'll put ads out every day. Full page. *Wanted: Leg! Last seen on India Street.*" Ismail rolled his eyes. There was only one newspaper in those days, and on its rather military board no Jeevanjee had allies. Tahir knew full well it wouldn't happen, but he let Ali have his way. Tolerant, he blinked.

Agatha, though she'd had visions of the leg sewn back on herself, could tell Ali was lying. The older boys did not impress her. She thought his brother's teasing might make Tahir cry—a prospect that neither pleased nor troubled her but of which she took note. What did happen surprised her. Tahir Majid, undeterred by the guest's newness, reached out for her arm and pulled her in towards him. Agatha allowed it. Like her mother, in a way, Agatha was curious and could also be impassive. Tahir took up the border of the sheet with his left hand and whispered, "Do you want to see?" He gestured with his pointed chin towards the odd place on the bed where the soft sheet simply sank, just below his knee. Tahir was a wounded boy, for sure, but he also had good sense. Displaying his own stump with pride was better, after all, than moping or pretending he was whole.

Agatha did not need to be asked twice. She wanted very much to see. She clambered up beside him, and Tahir raised the heavy sheet, invited her to peer into the cotton-flowered gloom. The brothers' silence was complete, and Agatha forgot them. In each room of the house, it seemed—down the hallway in the parlor, and here in their own bedroom—female shapes were ushering new times. Agatha, more brazen in some ways even than her mother, having seen what she had come for, pulled her head out from the tunnel Tahir Majid had devised, and tugged a pillow from behind him. "I need this," she said. She sat beside him firmly. Tahir, wincing but hospitable, gave his guest more room.

She'd surprised him, too. Propped up on one elbow, she asked him if it hurt. His brothers didn't like to ask, even soft Habib; they already knew the answer, didn't like to hear it. With Agatha so close to him and stark, Tahir almost said that yes, it did, it did, and not a little, either. That he felt the absent calf and foot as keenly as if they were still there. He might have added that having lost a leg had brought him new embarrassments, that the clever brothers had to bear him to the toilet if he needed to expel a poop (though this they did with a solemnity and tenderness that they had never shown him in his fully four-limbed days). He might have told her that when the distant aunts came (bringing their own juice, and nuts, and sweet, dry, yellow cake), he knew they came because they had to, because what had befallen Majid's little boy was too-too-terrible, they said. That he could tell from how they passed the cashews, chomping, busy lips asmack, that they did not hold out much hope. "Two cripples in the house! Mad Majid whose mind should have a walking stick, and this! Now *this!* What else should we now fear?"

They spoke their thoughts out loud when they believed he was asleep, more softly when they thought he was awake. Suddenly the crafty brothers—clever, yes, but unreliable, indeed—appeared more viable to the big aunts than he did. Even his Aunt Sugra, who people said was good, whispering to Tahir (was it just a month ago?) that he was the only hope, the only boy whose head for numbers might not put him in jail—Sugra had turned to leggy Ismail and Ali, and even stout Habib, the slowest of them all, and, holding out her hands, told them they were all their poor baba had left. That it was up to them now. Sugra! The only one who gave them money, came to visit; who could manage Tahir's father when nobody else would. Sugra, who still loved them! A sore betrayal, it had been. But Tahir didn't say these things to Mrs. Turner's daughter. He waited for her lead.

Pushing at her bottom lip with a sharp but creamy tooth, Agatha considered him. She asked again: "Really, does it hurt?" Tahir felt exposed. The skin around his eyes went tight; he sniffed, and looked away. But he remembered what the aunts had said (they had gotten it from Iqbal, at Hisham's Food and Drink). *This* was the girl who had unlaced and laced his shoe, done something to his limb while the firmer parts of him lay well across the road.

Aunt Yasmina had told Sugra that this girl had not flinched. That she had sat there on the sidewalk (panties showing, nevermind!) and watched over Tahir's fallen leg as though it were a baby goat or doll. Had spoken to it, even. Agatha was perhaps not, thought Tahir, a guest into whose shoulder he could cry.

With a valiant shove of lashes, he swept his tears back. "It doesn't hurt. It itches." He pushed his thin chest out and pressed his lips together. "It doesn't hurt at all." If Agatha could push, insist, then he could do it, too. She closed one eye; he could see the wet pink point of the girl's tongue. He exhaled, and said, again, "It itches. Didn't you hear right?" He pulled the sheet above their heads and motioned down beyond the bandaged absence to make sure she could see. If Tahir's leg could be put back, thought Agatha, the foot would reach just there, to a swirl of printed leaves. Tahir loosed his fingers from the sheet and let it flap down very gently over Agatha's bent head. She pulled it back to show him she was frowning. "The bad thing," Tahir said—Agatha felt here that she ought to pay attention—"is that now I've lost my slingshot."

Sarie came to call her. Agatha slid gently off the bed and faced him. She noticed how his eyebrows slanted towards each other, pointing to his nose. She returned the pillow to him, then reached out and pinched his face. "I don't think it's true," she said. Her words were like a hiss. Tahir felt the tautness at his eyes return. He blinked. She whispered: "I think it hurts a lot." Then, as grown men dismiss matches, she flicked the soft part of his cheek with a rapid parting of her forefinger and thumb, and skipped towards her mother. Leg and cheek both smarting, Tahir took his pillow back and held it, not sure what had happened, or if he should be glad.

Sarie hesitated before stepping towards the bed. They'd come for his sake, after all. And yet now that she was in his room, she faltered. Out on India Street, she had stroked this child as intimately as she (sometimes) stroked her own. As we touch, strangers though they be, those whose pain is great enough to warrant unabashed care: one dispenses with formality. Yet now she felt that he was owned, by that nice Mr. Jeevanjee, even by the house, by the long-dead mother whose name she had not learned, and by the empty chairs between the beds, meant for visitors whose vigils were expected. She felt that touching Tahir Jeevanjee might require a permission from his father that she had not obtained. *He never knew his mother.* It occurred to her that in this way she and Tahir Jeevanjee were very nearly linked, but she was not one to stop for long on sad and tender things. She focused on the boy.

Other women come to sit themselves down here. They touch him. She saw an army of them, heavy, scented ladies dressed in pinks and blues—colors the Kikanga mansions had once been—women meant to be there, petting the sick boy and speaking very softly. Comfortable and right. She knit her light eyebrows together. Thinking—of the once-bright wife and visitors (whose absences had weight), the height and girth of Kudra House, the parrot squawking in the gloom—made a heavy knot in her. She wanted to behave in such a way that if Mr. Jeevanjee had been a witness (he was not; subject to an unknown lightness in the other room, he was eating biscuits, still) he would find her actions irreproachable and right. So she leaned in above the boy and tugged softly at the covers. "I am sure that everything," she said, "will soon be going well."

Tahir could not make out the features of her face. He noted only that Mrs. Turner's hands were freckled and that she smelled faintly of talcum—not the kind Aunt Sugra wore, which smelled of wood and roses, but like what mothers patted on their babies' chests and rumps after they'd been oiled. Agatha, also tugging on cool cloth, pulled her mother's dress. Sarie, used to Agatha's imperium, sighed, and gave her the five pineapple sweets. Agatha eyed the brothers for a moment; then she made her choice. Firm, she took smart-mouthed Ali's bony hand and opened it with hers. She liked a challenge, too, and she could see that he was sly. Too surprised to pull away, he trembled nonetheless. She slipped the sweets into his palm then closed her fingers tightly over his, pressing to make certain they would stick. She had made him nervous. "No telling what girls like that will do!" he later told his friends, who, though they'd seen the smuggled magazines in the corners of the paan shops, had never spoken to a white child, let alone had one pull open their hands. Agatha released his shivering fist and pointed at the patient in the bed. "They're for him," she said. She was looking at Habib, sensing even then that Habib was the softest, could be counted on to make sure that kindnesses were done. "All five of them. For him."

As the Turners left, Majid Ghulam walked down the stairs behind them. He was barefoot, still, and Sarie was aware of the light shuffling sound his flesh made on the steps, something like a whisper. She thought she felt his eyes fixed on the middle of her back. At the bottom, in the doorway, Majid Ghulam behaved like a good host, as a decent person should. He even said to Mrs. Turner that he hoped she would return. That she and her small girl could visit any time. Agatha—he smiled at her so that the corners of his eyes curved down like two arrows—Agatha, he added, hadn't seen the parrot.

Outside it was cool, still light, but promising a heavy evening blue. On the balcony at Mansour House, Bibi craned her neck and thought she saw a heavy figure in a dress stumble in the alley. "Orange, yes, I think," she would later say. "A trampy little rag, too short to be believed."

{❀}Four

At the Turners' own Kikanga building (Mchanganyiko Street, number 698, concrete, pale, and gray), Gilbert was ready to go out. He considered waiting until Sarie had come home. He liked to say good-bye to her from the doorway while she sat in the kitchen. If Agatha was in, he also liked, sometimes, to pat her on the head and feel for a quick moment the gloss of her dark hair, though it was always, he thought, cold, not quite as heads should be. He wondered what had kept them. But waiting—that was silly. Approximating a *harrumph* of the sort Colonial types had often given out, Gilbert sniffed. Narrowing his eyes, he looked once more into the kitchen, shrugged, stretched the muscles in his neck, and stepped out of the flat.

As was Gilbert's custom, he wandered by the seafront at the ragged edge of town. Ahead of him, thick, high jacarandas and flame trees in full bloom made the avenue a tunnel. Between their arching trunks, the water, a hard metallic blue inlaid with seaweed black, extended flat and low towards a yellowing sky; farther out, unpeopled islands shimmered, mangroves silver-green and creamy in the tricky ocean light.

Up the road, the city's forced activity was ending. Families from nicer places like Uzuri and Matumbo would arrive in pickup trucks (old and rusted, sure, but given what those days were like, impressive, the best that could be had). In chatty well-dressed groups, they'd head out for a treat: the Old Empire Cinema, or the

Frosty for a cone. Tired paperboys would make a final round before climbing into buses; custodians and the tea-ladies would be packing up their things; the High Court's final case would close, and the wide brass-studded doors would part to spill the witnesses and others gently down the steps. Gilbert, at his best when things were slow, enjoyed this time of day. And, while not, as others were, seeking easy times to cap a taxing day at work, he was also hoping to relax. He was headed for the Palm.

The Victorian Palm Hotel, in the sense of beds and baths and rooms for strangers' sleep, was not really a hotel. Though some gentlemen did spend days and nights there doing various things, it was for throats and stomachs only. Gilbert went in the afternoons and on some evenings to *this* waterfront establishment because, following Independence, the Yacht Club had been moved to the far side of Scallop Bay and, with all the new-found freedom, he could not afford a taxi. The old Yacht Club had sat just above the harbor and, affording its fine patrons a wide view of the sea and of the hulking ships that ferried wood, cement, and cashews up and down the coast, had once been painted white with lyme, so white it hurt the eyes. Oh, it had been frequented by awesome men who did things: men who went into the interior and emerged with tales about the natives and their ways; Service men who smelled of wind, faintly of tobacco, and of an enviable, complicated sweat. Men who — Gilbert often thought, with a tingling in his chest — men who'd smelled of History.

That old clubhouse was now crumbling, and no human had reclaimed it. Gilbert once — and it had made his neck hurt, his hands go soft and slack — had even seen a cow there, grazing at the tufted grass that had come up in the doorway, and, blade by shiny blade, was cutting up the floor. *People who made History,* thought Gilbert,

*have now been replaced by. Would you look at that. Nothing more than.
Livestock.* Considering the old clubhouse too much could bring a
twitching to his eyes.

Having receded from the city center just as the real colonials
had (ousted from imperial bomas and barred holdouts on the sea),
the current club was now simply out of reach. The moneyed ones
who chose to stay and who, destined for abundance, had had better
jobs and pedigrees than Gilbert, Empire-or-no, armed with fat
bankrolls and blueprints, Embassies behind them, resided now, as
the relocated Yacht Club did, in the resplendent northern suburbs'
luxuriant repose. Slowly but encroaching surely on the bush, villas
lolled out there—gracious, boxy things, floored with speckled tiles
and also rich in windows, surrounded by walled lots where hardy
seedlings grew: hibiscus, jasmine on the breeze, drapes of bougainvillea; somberly patrolled by braided watchmen, sharp spears in their
hands.

Gilbert's feelings about Independence and the Empire it appeared to have outdone were not particularly straightforward. Like
many small-time men, he desired and did not desire wealth. He
thought equality was good, in right measure for himself and, osten-
sibly, for others; but, ambivalent, he also felt that there was something indiscriminate about the rattling new times. His loyalties were
scattered. He was given to emotive declarations and to surges of re-
sentment, now aimed here, or there. When the remaining ex-colonials
had picked up and settled out of town, and the local powers with
them, Gilbert felt at once superior and defeated. Bright enough to
see he'd never make a mark, he did not try to catch up. So he gathered what he'd saved, and moved not out but in.

He took Sarie and Agatha to the small streets of Kikanga,
where they would be, he'd said, "in the thick of things." That he
did not wish to be, exactly, in the thick of anything was well beside

the point. Gilbert, reader that he was, could talk. It was a Gesture for the People, he had told his family. Not for rich ones or for white ones. At the time inspired by the banners that promoted national love, he had felt that in committing to Kikanga and its throbbing streets and shops, he might stake a small claim of his own on how things would develop. He would turn his back on those who'd moved to Scallop Bay, on the hierarchies of Empire, and would, he said, declare himself a local. As the new government advised, he would be self-reliant; he would make himself *belong.* One result of this move inward (which was also, though he didn't like to say it, all he could afford) was that when the Yacht Club snuck away from the main harbor, it also snuck from him. And so he justified the Victorian Palm Hotel, where lesser men would gather. And though it was not what he'd been used to, and not really first-class, Gilbert had, in time, come to love the place.

There by the seafront, those who lived in town, those who still had aspirations but didn't have a car (or did but could not find or pay for petrol or for parts), came to consume beer, a variety of spirits, pallid chicken stews, and, now and then, kebabs. Office men from Vunjamguu came, fountain pens like flowers at their pockets, brassy watches on their wrists; others, stiff in new Kaunda suits, flanked by women in bright gowns like those of Jackie O. and the soon-to-be Queen Noor. City men whose lives unfolded in the heart of Vunjamguu, who ran shops or managed buses, came now and then in pressed white shirts and achingly creased pants. Russians came, with sad light eyes and purple faces; clusters of gray-suited men from China, shiny pins on their lapels.

Because Gilbert knew most of them by sight, he was convinced that they must know him, too. Indeed, at the Victorian Palm Hotel, Gilbert felt, almost, that if he could only *cut a figure,* he might someday fit in. Someone there—he smiled shyly at himself, smoothed his hair and checked the buckle of his belt—someone there, one day, might see him for what he really was and offer him a drink.

Sometimes he would find another man who, like him, had not gone after the end came, a man whose fortunes, modest all in all but better than his own, might be a source of hope: Rathke, for example, who with a little capital would any day now fund a passion for rapid photo printing, or Göethe Bienheureux, who dreamed of raising pigs along the seashore and of producing delicate spiced sausages he would call Bienheureux Coast Joy. But Gilbert's favorite, the only one he would have called a friend, was Mr. Kazansthakis. Kazansthakis, known also as the Frosty King, ran the Frosty-Kreem, which his father and *his* father had made and run before him. It was Vunjamguu's oldest and most famous ice-cream shop, where developments were sweet and romance filled the air.

The truth: Kazansthakis had met his final darling in that very place. A clever, well-built Polish girl (youngest child of prisoners of war who had, after another, earlier end, likewise found themselves still there while others raced back home), she had come in with her sister and ordered up a tricolored helping of cold stuff which she then asked him please to cover in a coat of chocolate syrup— this with such great charm that young Kazansthakis winked. The smiling girl winked back, and he fell steamingly in love. They wed. At the party, a towering ice-cream cake that *did not melt* was served. The lovely business bloomed. Oh, how locals flocked to them for sundaes and for cones! People of all ages, colors, and persuasions. A bustling, bristling business that brought people together!

Gilbert, despite the need ajitter in his stomach, his fear of dissipation, could not help but admire their success; he was not jealous of the Frostys. The ones who'd been born rich, who now had homes in Scallop Bay, he could easily resent: the Greenleafs and the

Thorntons, who sent roses and carnations all over the world; ruddy Mr. Remington, with his throaty, booming voice, who ran a hunting outfit from the bar of the Ambassador Hotel and spent his days procuring kills (and the trinkets that announce them: lion skins and heads, stools on zebra feet, the choicest rhino parts) for princesses and magnates; nervous, dull Jim Towson, with the exclusive beachfront lot, whose big wife Hazel, redoubtable, effective, ran Committees as though the British had not left (the woman also had, to Gilbert's horror, a soft spot for his Sarie). But Gilbert couldn't, even at his smallest, bring himself to think unkindly of the Frostys. His approval of the pair was made possible in no small part by their goodwill (they both treated him quite genuinely, he thought). But more important was the fact that they weren't real colonials in the first place, not as *he,* he liked to think, had been. History had not so much put them on the top of things or nursed their dreams of grandeur as it had thrust them to the side and shoved them through the cracks. And, thriving, they'd popped through.

If Gilbert envied Kazansthakis and his wife, it was for what he saw as the uniqueness, the freshness, of their suffering, and for all their work and vigor: she had been a prisoner, after all, born behind barbed wire, and the Frosty King had come from quick, smart people who had once run for their lives. The Frostys, Gilbert felt, were in a completely separate league, distinct from him and all his kind: he found that he could love them.

Kazansthakis was, in fact, well-disposed towards Gilbert. The Frosty King liked knowing things, and, though he didn't care for books, he admired those who did. He frequently stood Gilbert Turner drinks while Gilbert told him what he'd read. After he had spoken, the Frosty King would never fail to say, "Mr. Turner, you were meant for greater things than this. Tell me something else."

And Gilbert would produce another anecdote, another, and another, until the Frosty King's green eyes grew soft and it was time for him to go.

That evening, the Frosty King was at his usual patio table. "Ho! Gilbert! Mr. Gilbert Turner!" Gilbert sat down gratefully. Kazansthakis motioned to the waiter for a thick bottle of beer. "What's cooking?" he asked Gilbert, with a wink. The Frosty-Kreem was just beside the Cinema, of course, and, despite the hard work needed at the parlor, Kazansthakis often left things to his sweetheart so he could daydream in the dark. He liked foreign expressions and was given when intoxicated to mimicking the moves of kung-fu stars, cartoon men, and cowboys. "What's up, Doc?" he said.

Today, thought Gilbert, pleased, he might tell Kazansthakis about the Dawoodis in the pamphlet, whose Holiness had met with ministers and shopkeepers at several fashionable places and who, Gilbert had been interested to see, encouraged all his followers to contribute to whatever nation pressed its laws upon them (those Dawoodis, Gilbert thought, *knew* how to fit in). He smacked his narrow lips, rubbed his hands together, and began. He told the Frosty King about the fete for Dr. Saheb at the great Jubilee Hall. "A quiet man," he gravely said, while Kazansthakis drank. He would have liked to say a little more—how fine the beard was on the fellow, how pleasant the walled gardens—but Kazansthakis had not yet had enough to drink. "No beards and little diplomats for me, my friend. No stories of the State. Or God." The Frosty King was rather spiritual, in truth, but he did not like Religion. "What else? Give me something better."

Gilbert's drink arrived, and, while a quick boy popped the cap, he thought about the accident. "Well, here's an odd thing." He told the Frosty King that Agatha and Sarie had come upon an accident the week before—an Indian boy hit by a bus, relieved of half a leg. And that instead of leaving well enough alone, today they'd gone on an adventure. "Wouldn't give it up. Said she had to go." Gilbert looked down at his wrist the way a person with a watch might. Then he sighed, and looked out at the sea. "She's still there!" he said. "She hasn't come back yet!" It was more a show than a display of real feeling. His impatience had passed and, once settled at the Palm, he wasn't really curious. But he felt a little snubbed, had expected Kazansthakis to support him in his disapproval, even his disdain. But the Frosty King, Gilbert was unsettled to discover, was not on his side.

"Of course, of course," he said. "She found him in the street! She should not let him go." The Frosty King went on to say he thought that people linked in accidents were joined by holy forces quite regardless of the distances between them. Hadn't Gilbert seen the films? Did he not believe in Providence, or Fate? Gilbert did not care for whimsy. He had not considered such a possibility before and, sipping his thick beer, decided that he didn't think much of it. That was very well for all the groups described in Gilbert's books, with all of their *beliefs,* and perhaps for kung-fu fighters, too, whose codes of honor were apparently remarkable, but he himself could not subscribe to such a view, interesting as it might be. Sarie was not joined, in his opinion, to any legless boy. He said so.

The Frosty King insisted. His ruddy face lit up. "No, no, no. It's very beautiful," he said. "A drama, man! I'm telling you, you're wrong." He liked very much to hear the story of the bus, the missing limb, the visit—which was going on exactly then (Mad Majid pulling out the paper), while they were sitting at the Palm. "Just wait, why not, and see? I'm telling you that something will come of it. As it must. Your venerable Sarie must at no price let go." But

Gilbert hadn't ventured out in the ebbing afternoon to discuss in any detail Sarie and the boy, or the wounded father, who was, he thought in passing, probably from Gujerat and certainly a salesman. Why was the Frosty King so keen? He even asked his friend why *he* hadn't gone along. "Maybe," Kazansthakis said, aware that he was teasing, "that father's a Dawoodi. At last, my friend, you'd meet a person from the pages of your books!" Gilbert didn't laugh, and Kazansthakis, who knew that Gilbert could only take so much, sighed, and turned back to the pamphlet. "All right, then, my Tonto. I'll be good. To the holy man, on-ho!" He waved a big hand in the air to bring another round. "To the Jubilee." Gilbert, grateful for the second beer, found some things to say.

The Frosty King drank, too. And eventually his face took on the dreamy look that Gilbert waited for. He listened. He was so lulled by Gilbert's talk he ordered ten kebabs on slender sticks to keep him at his side. Behind them the sea turned and the sky became a lucent velvet blue. When the Frosty King at last told Gilbert it was time for him to go, he put his palm on Gilbert's back and said, with yet another wink, "I'll be here tomorrow. Be sure to come prepared." In fact, the Frosty King would be in place at the Victorian Palm every afternoon for five more days, while the Frosty-Kreem's old freezer underwent repairs. The business would be closed. Gilbert, pleased, promised he would come. Why not? Kazansthakis smiled. As he often did, he said, "I like you, Gilbert Turner." As Kazansthakis raised his eyebrows, Gilbert knew the Frosty King was trying something out that had been witnessed in a film. "I've told you once, I've told you twice, and I will tell it you again. There's more to you than one might think, I say." Gilbert shook Kazansthakis's hand with a good feeling in his chest. Five days of a closed parlor meant five days of little tales.

*   *   *

"Why not come tomorrow? Come tomorrow if you like," daring, flailing, uncertain Majid had said to Sarie's little girl, and, yes, they did, they did. And so. For five afternoons that followed one another, each of which brought Mrs. Gilbert Turner and Majid Ghulam Jeevanjee to the brink of interesting things and the Frosty freezer back into top shape, Gilbert sat at the Victorian Palm Hotel and told Kazansthakis stories he had plucked out from his books. At Kudra House that week another schedule was also ratified. Something there, though no one wished to name it, was, holy force or no, eagerly astir.

A tale of transformation for a widower and wife, delicately told. Let's put it like this. Day one: On the patio of the Palm, at a graying three o'clock, Gilbert started with a mystery, a strange, alluring fact. "The places where Sikhs died along the railway to the north have now become famed shrines. Sites of tragic accidents are now piled with gadgets, photographs, plastic blooms, and beads. Pilgrims go to visit." Kazansthakis was intrigued. In Kudra House, Ismail and Ali, who sometimes did odd jobs, were out. Tahir was asleep. Habib showed Agatha the parrot. It spoke out in the kitchen: *"Allahu akbar,"* it said. Habib pointed out the window at the mosque to show Agatha the source, nodded in approval when he saw she understood. She sat beneath the swaying cage in awe, saying *"Allahu akbar"* now and then, until the bird said "Tahir" and she remembered why she'd come. With soft Habib beside her, she went to watch him sleep.

Day two: The Frosty King ordered an entire roasted chicken and several kebabs, then watched Gilbert eat his fill. "What is it today?" he asked, once Gilbert had leaned back from the table, wiped his mouth, and belched despite himself. And Gilbert, who had found a biographic book about a Cardinal from France, announced, "The White Father Missionaries wore those long white dresses in the hopes of being taken for a troop of Mohammedans. This peculiar outfit has now become their costume." Kazansthakis liked this one so much that he bought another round. At Kudra House, Majid Ghulam located several more issues of his long-dead, much-loved paper and read from them to Sarie. There was a poem called "The Pomegranate," which left a pink scent in the room. To clear the air, Majid read another, "Cat, the Thief of Meals." Sarie felt greatly, kindly entertained. She thought, although perhaps it wasn't true: *I have always liked the rhymes.* Agatha showed Tahir how to make a Jacob's Ladder with a knotted piece of string.

Day three: The Victorian Palm was sorry, but there was no beer left from the Congo. Would they accept a reddish local brew? Kazansthakis ordered chicken stew and gin. Gilbert, who had looked very hard the night before, recited what might have been the most astounding tale of all: "When Nkama Ndume, local king on Kudra, the green island, became angry with his staff, he made women sweep the kitchens with the pillows of their breasts." "He *what?*" asked Kazansthakis, though he'd heard every word. Gilbert played along, repeated himself proudly, like a student showing off. Kazansthakis hid his eyes and laughed, until a ferry boat gave out a throaty toot and the Frosty King turned red.

At Kudra House, the coffee table with the animal-like feet had not snuck back to its ordinary place. Sarie sat with ease. She had the odd, delightful feeling that the furniture would remain just as it was for a nice, long time to come. Over milkless tea (brought up by Maria, who scowled at Sarie all the while), Majid Ghulam revealed that as a child in the green islands (where Bibi, too, had grown) he had played football on the beach. Sarie sheepishly admitted that she did not know the game's rules, although, she added, no doubt other Belgians did. Habib went down to shoot marbles, leaving

Agatha and Tahir in the bedroom all alone, where each child took a nap.

Sarie, having found her purse beneath the settee, and about to fetch her child, turned to Mr. Jeevanjee and said, suddenly surprised by the truthfulness of it, and how deeply she was feeling, and by saying it out loud: "It is nice to have a friend! Someone I can visit." Majid Ghulam's face fell open, and Sarie closed her eyes a moment, suspecting she was not equipped quite yet to see what might be there. "Come again tomorrow," Majid Ghulam said, lightly holding to his stomach but not looking away.

On day four, Gilbert did not get the reaction he expected. "When Livingstone finally, really died at last, they left his heart in Zambia and hid his lungs in Zanzibar, beneath the tiles of a cathedral. The stitched-up, empty body was brought next back to England, where they built for it a chapel." Kazansthakis, like many other people, had little patience for the famous Dr. L. He had heard this story one too many times and did not believe it anymore. In fact, he was annoyed. "Where've you been, my mister? You think no one has told me? That I'm just off a plane? Next the head will be in Egypt and his liver in Kasai. Stomach with the Swazis, God knows what in France. No, no, no, my friend. Another story, please."

In Kudra House, Sarie found herself nodding on the settee, wondering why she was so tired, and amazed that she could feel so free in someone else's house as to yawn luxuriously without minding her mouth. Majid, forgetting not only himself but also who she was, advised that she lie down and take a nap, which was what Hayaam would have suggested in a long-gone, happy time. And he remembered with a gulp what he had not forgotten once in years: that Hayaam was not there. He was drowsy, too. Sarie, not so far gone she could not sense what might be a mistake, said, "No, thank you!" and did her best to stay awake. In the other room, Agatha taught Tahir a song about creatures speeding on the shore to join a turtle dance. "The Lobster Quadrille," she said to Tahir, round mouth like a fish. "Too far, too far," she sang. "That's what the snails feel like while everyone jumps right in. That's how *you* would be." She laughed. This time, when they left, Majid Ghulam took Sarie's hand in his and held it for a little longer than might have been expected. He said, "Tomorrow, Madam Turner? Tomorrow, you'll come back?" Sarie, sharp ache in her throat, thought Mr. Jeevanjee looked sad, and beautiful, indeed.

Day five: Gilbert, on his second drink, confessed to Kazansthakis that, despite what people might surmise about old Mr. Turner, he was more a thinker than a doer. He would be very glad, he said, to while his life away. But wouldn't it be sweet if someone hired him to dream? If he were officially involved in something that could feed him? Kazansthakis, who liked to help his friends but also felt that there were limits to what successful men could do without risk to themselves, was not sure what Gilbert meant. He wished to change the subject. He coughed, and motioned to the sea, where fishermen in spidery boats were preparing to go out. He said, "And what a life we have, old man." Distracted, Gilbert let the words sink in, and, smiling, he agreed.

In Kudra House, Tahir's wounds were healing. Though there were still odd pains down there, where nothing really was, he lied a little less when he announced it did not hurt. Nevermind, he'd think, he'd moan when she was gone. Agatha at his request pulled out a science primer from underneath the bed. Tahir talked about the planets. Agatha wondered: were there not still other unnamed orbs up there for new people to find? Tahir didn't think so. "They've learned everything already." He left the book in Agatha's damp hands and slowly fell asleep.

On the other side of Tahir's door, Sarie and Majid Ghulam found themselves alone in a brand-new, necessary way. They had just come from the very balcony through which Bibi said some underclothing might be seen (Sarie's on that day were white). Majid Ghulam had pointed out the seedlings he was hoping to transplant one day to the courtyard—pomegranate, coconut, a kisukari stump, and a little henna bush in reclaimed metal tins. Gardening had been his wife's affair, he said. But he couldn't let it go.

Sarie didn't mind the mention of a wife who was, she thought, long gone. She was glad he had been married and that he no longer was. It made her host mysterious, in command of secret pains she felt she should respect. And, while she was not the sort of person who cared much for potted things, the plants made her feel young. She thought the trees were lovely, and although it is the kind of thing one says wholeheartedly and later does not mean, she confessed to her new friend that she often wished she had a garden, too. Majid Ghulam could feel his toes already perched at the slippery edge of an abyss. Eyes moist, offering another woman pleasure from what dead Hayaam had taught him, he said, "Oh, come to enjoy this one, anytime, oh, anytime at all—"

Sarie, caught between the doorway and the city, which she could make out vaguely through the slats, felt something gentle and demanding in the air. Majid Ghulam wrung his hands. Sarie raised her light eyebrows and blinked. She lost her balance, steadied herself with his arm. His elbow bone was sharp, but just above it, beneath the cuff of his pale shirt, there was a plumpness Sarie found surprising. No longer startled by her height, he looked up at her, barreled bravely on. "You can come here to my home and we will bring a chair for you to sit, on this old balcony. You have no garden where you live."

Sarie followed Majid Ghulam inside. Ismail and Ali were at work, and Habib (how lucky!) had gone to watch the heaving buses take off for the north. The door to Tahir's room was closed. The hallway's heavy air was smooth and soft and blue. Sucking at the inner flesh of both her cheeks at once, Sarie found herself examining the back of her host's head. Considering: *How blue the light is here. How nicely Mr. Jeevanjee is swaying now as he moves forward in the hall. My host is like a reed on the edge of a brown pond.* A fierce, barbed tingle came tripping through her limbs.

When Majid Ghulam turned around to look at her, meaning then to say, "And now we will have tea. I will call down for Maria," he caught Sarie Turner looking at the space where his own head had been, and right before his eyes, she turned the rich plum color of Ribena Concentrated Syrup. Next—suddenly—Mad Majid Ghulam pressed himself against her. His hands met briefly at the back of Sarie's neck, slipped along her spine, then, riffling as though through a drawer to find the urgent thing, moved across her back and then all over her front to part the curtains of her dress and feel her freckled flesh come loose and tepid in his palms. Sarie touched him, too.

Later, Sarie wished it had been slower than it was, so that she could make a calendar of small and sweet events: *First he . . . and then I and then he, oh yes. And then I, yes, and then we and then I and then he again and I knew and he touched and I and I and I*—Sarie would have liked to savor it. But Majid, from the moment that it started, wished he could forget how it began. He wanted to remember not the first betrayal of an ancient, dear love but a not-too-loved familiar clutching, an act he had committed many times before that did not mean so much. He wished, that is, to feel himself already in the midst, already at sea and too far from the shore. The shore: the fact of his now-mangled little boy, the growing needs of three two-legged sons, Sugra, with her endless energy and the kindness which so helped him but which he could not hope to repay, the Kikanga set who called him Mad and Sad, the hungry, talky aunts, Maria with her Bible looks, the ruins of the paper, even old Rahman, and everything, everything, that he had ever been and ever wanted to forget.

At sea they surely were. Sarie had had scant experience with romance. And so she mimed the movie actresses she had seen in one or two hot films at the Old Empire Cinema. She released and squeezed her lips in patterns in the air. Expecting that she might eventually feel Majid's tongue against her mouth, she bent down to match him, pressed her brow against his neck and sighed, keeping her eyes closed. But Majid on that day was not interested in kissing. For one thing, Sarie's mouth was far. He remained intent on that long chest and stomach, which he rubbed, she thought, like the lamps she read to Agatha about, from which amazing spirits come. To Mad and Sad Majid, the space between her shoulders and her jutting hips was dangerous, unchartable and vast.

While the embrace — sudden, hectic, endless — wound on and up and round the parents in the hall, Agatha watched Tahir. Perhaps connected much more tightly to her mother than either of them would have cared to know, she felt a thick confusion, a warm coal in her chest. While Sarie shivered in the hall, Agatha thought for an endless, awful moment that perhaps Tahir had died. As Majid Ghulam Jeevanjee, failed widower, businessman, and poet, pulled Sarie Turner across the way a bit so as to prop her up against the peeling wall, Agatha was pulled closer to the boy. She let the book drop to the floor and leaned in towards him, where, chest tight and steaming still, at last she heard little Tahir snore. While Sarie bent her knees on the other side of that room's door so Majid Ghulam would not be hindered by her stature, Agatha kept careful track of Tahir Majid's slight, but yes, still, breathing. Eventually she was so lulled by it that she, too, closed her eyes and slept.

When Sarie came to wake her, Agatha felt fresh. Sarie was no longer flushed. Her yellow hair was dark now, that peculiar shade of green that wetness can bring on. She had just poured water on her face. Majid, who had brought the battered bowl, had watched her, bent over by the window, tip the water out over her high cheeks with a beaten metal cup; he had wished that she were standing naked there instead of in that horrible old dress, that he could watch the water trickle over that long body, of which he was—too late to turn back now—already enamored.

"We have stayed enough," Sarie said to Agatha, hurrying her up. "When we get to our home—" She paused, stroked her daughter's brown-shoe-polish hair. "When we get to our home, your father will no longer be there." She meant that Gilbert would have headed for the watering hole, would be telling stories at the Palm. But she was also right, of course, in quite another way.

Though she could not have said, exactly, with what eyes she was concerned, Sarie cast a furtive look behind her as she and Agatha arrived at their own building on Mchanganyiko Street. She wondered if they had been noticed coming in, her with her hair wet, heart drumming so loud, but thought, *Who can be there, looking? Who would care, or know?* Nonetheless, she shivered.

This should be said, and clearly: despite Gilbert's now-and-then democratic dreams, the Turners were not rooted in Kikanga. Apart from one or two acquaintances of Gilbert's and the formidable

Hazel Towson—who thought Sarie should be serving on Committees and whose sporadic visits always soured the air (and were they not overdue for one, any day now, any day at all?)—the Turners did not socialize, not of their own will. They did not lounge on any stoops; nor did they have a balcony on which they might have become fixtures. But for awkward waving from the stairwell or the courtyard on their way to somewhere else, they did not know their neighbors.

To her credit, Sarie was aware of one or two. The one she saw most often was an Arab from the islands, a Mr. Suleiman, old but not infirm, who listened on occasion to the radio in his parlor, pale blue door ajar; he sometimes stood beside the broken taxi—also blue, but brighter, like the sky—where he peered into the windows or fingered the sad chrome. There was also, now and then, a Comorian lady who sold thumb-sized vials of scent from an old cane chair beneath the meager shade of a gray thorn tree, where she muttered to herself and fanned her potent wares, and sometimes an assortment of small children, whose brave Churchgoing parents, hardworking and pious, were rarely seen outside. If they saw her, these children sometimes ran towards her and then away. (Here, Agatha was better. She traveled now and then in a very different world from the one her parents knew. She kept mostly to herself, but she could sing those children's names. Sarie, for her part, did not even know if they knew who she was.) A wise person might ask: in the heart of Vunjamguu, in mixed and mad Kikanga, can such a state of things not be the fruit of arduous labor, of an insistent and unnatural closing-of-the-eyes? For sure, for sure. Indeed. Bibi would have howled and slapped her wobbly thighs. Nonetheless, on her return from Kudra House, Sarie had the feeling that something, someone, saw. Perhaps, although Sarie didn't know it, the watcher from the balcony only four blocks down had left an imprint on the air, an eyeball-shake-and-shiver that had lingered in the breeze. Sarie felt observed, and the feeling made her cold.

She urged Agatha to silence and led her slowly up the stairs. In the landing's patchy gloom, she closed her eyes and conjured up a look she'd caught on Mr. Jeevanjee's thin face. The tremor—the thought *I have been seen*—dissipated in the half-light, and she shook herself a bit, felt alone and clear. Her final steps were brighter. She pulled Agatha along, and in a moment she was laughing; yes, she was excited about what she and he had done. Or, *après tout,* what Mr. Jeevanjee had done. Hadn't the sweet man ("Majid Ghulam," she whispered) without any preamble at all pressed himself upon her, and she, willingly, succumbed? She thought, *He conquered me,* sent Agatha to wash, and lay down on the bed.

When Gilbert came back home from drinks at the Victorian Palm, Sarie, who had stepped out of the bedroom at the *whoosh-whoosh* of his tread, saw him as though through a colored haze. She felt rather kind, protective. Her pink Gilbert, *Mon petit mari rose,* damp with beads of dew. How sweet an unsuspecting husband, protected from a shock by a thoughtful, able mate, could look!

That evening, everything in Sarie's tilting world looked clean and good to her: her dear, silly legal man, Agatha's soiled hands, the cracked and dirty tiles.

At the sticky table, Sarie fed Gilbert plain rice boiled in water, and when he as usual suggested that she might have spiced it up or tried to be inventive, she only smiled at him and did not even sigh. In the hanging bulb's dim light, Gilbert appeared fragile, delicate, and rare. She noticed, noncommittally, the purplish age spots on his pate. *The skin spots make my husband's head resemble eggs found in the nests of little forest birds. C'est précieux, après tout.* He was, she thought, the only man to whom she'd ever been and would ever be deceitful; as such, as the husband of the woman who had not long ago embraced Majid Ghulam Jeevanjee so daringly and hotly in Kudra House's hall, wasn't Gilbert Turner finally, if modestly, historic? Sarie felt important, too. *Yes,* she thought. She beamed.

Though often unperceptive, Gilbert was susceptible to gentleness. And it *was* gentleness he sensed, though it confused him, seeping like a halo from the contours of his wife. Belatedly inspired by the sayings of His Holiness (who felt, or at least maintained in public, that all peoples in one place were best conjoined in mutual assistance), he thought to repay Sarie for that unexpected smile by washing up the dishes. Sarie, not surprised to see that things were moving in her favor, said, "Oh, yes. Please. Of course."

Later, in Agatha's small bedroom—no more than a closet— Sarie read aloud from a book that they had borrowed at the British Council Library. It was *The Adventures of Aziz,* in which Taj al Maluk, Prince of the Green City, falls heels over head for charitable Dunya, a comely, charming girl with an aptitude for making things from silk. While Agatha curled fists into her only pillow, tricky, energetic Dunya swore she'd kill off any husband foisted on her with the strength in her own hands. Agatha sleepily approved, and Sarie, satisfied, put her child to bed.

Gilbert, who had been reading by himself in the next room, came in once Agatha had dimmed. He could, it's true, only kiss his daughter when she could not respond. With Sarie looking on, Gilbert pecked the sleeper chastely, then turned lightly on his heel. He fell asleep soon after, with (having taken a brief rest from the *Tour*) a book about the merchant sailors of the littoral on the table near the bed.

Sarie felt her limbs and skin still mightily aglow. Too awake to make a show of lying down, she stood before the mirror. With a plastic yellow comb once designed to look like marble, she smoothed down her wild hair and thought that she looked fine, perhaps not as far into her middle age as she now was, perhaps closer to forty. She gave her own reflection a subtle plotter's moue. When she finally joined Gilbert in their hard and narrow bed, he was snoring just as Agatha in the next room was (*ruffle-ruffle-hoo*). The bedsheet trembled gently at his mouth. He was as good as absent now; she was almost by herself. In the quiet-but-unquiet stillness of her family's soft sleep, the very air around her shimmied in delight.

In the darkness, wet winds rose up from the shallows of the city; a haphazard rain swept in. More stains appeared on the face of Kudra House, and in the courtyard of the Turners' building, a shed that held the neighbor's chickens lost a good part of its thatching to a well-placed gust of wind. Infected by his second book, Gilbert dreamed of Indian Ocean kingpins and their mutinous retainers skulking in the mangroves, while Sarie, smiling, dreamed of warmth and love.

Five

Sarie woke the following day thickened with good sleep. All night while the rain fell, she had been curled against the narrow, dear form of Majid Ghulam Jeevanjee. The Mr. Jeevanjee she'd dreamed was not the Mr Jeevanjee with whom she'd tussled in the hall just the day before. This dream-man was Majid Ghulam after weeks of care and comfort, a known lover: a brave man whose bliss she knew and who had seen (and wordlessly, graciously agreed never to throw back at her) how weeping spoiled her face. The dream-Majid-Ghulam was slack and comfortable beside her. Throughout the night he'd raised his hand up to his chin to rub a beard that grew there, then set his palm to rest again on his familiar lover's flank. Oh, marvelous and sweet! But when Sarie awoke, the nocturnal man was gone. She found not only that the Mr. Jeevanjee she'd dreamed was different from the one she could recall with her eyes open (in her dream his fingernails were clean, his arms a little stronger), but that she was, sleep-creased and stiff in places she had not noted for some years, in bed beside her husband.

Gilbert, who was used to waking by himself and often stayed beneath the covers until Sarie called for breakfast, was touched to find her there. Remembering the previous evening's kindness, made daring by it all, he even thought he might, curling up to Sarie from behind, persuade her to collude with him. How long it had been! But Sarie groaned and pulled away. Not reconciled to being where she was, skin wrinkled from the pillow and her arms, she gave her real-life man a disapproving look. Gilbert, fixed by her blue gaze, stilled the hand that he had been about to slip between her arm and ribs, dropped his fingers to his chest, and blushed.

Gilbert was the kind of man who kept a blush, sometimes for as long as half an hour, an outrage, a berry-colored shame that sometimes made Sarie despise him. She had no patience for his skin just then, no wish to be accused. She moved her tongue across her wide front teeth. She frowned. As though Gilbert had been privy to her dreams, as though he sensed that he was not, perhaps, the easy master of his home, she said, "What will you *do* about it?" Lip pushed out like a fist.

Gilbert disliked squabbling and was not skilled at repartee. He didn't answer, said, instead, "Make us breakfast, won't you, love?" He stood up then, and, bent over at the middle, bloodless shoulders sagging, plucked his brown robe from its hook and went down the hall to bathe.

Sarie lay back in their bed and pulled the sheet over her face. All the charm she'd felt the day before and for all of that wet night had been wiped conclusively away by Gilbert's roaming hands. She thought: what could the world be like if there were not a husband of whom she had long been disillusioned? The cloying, serious gloom that had replaced the lovely night distressed her. How humid the air was.

She had heard a phrase once and she had kept it for herself: *I do not dwell on things.* Dwell. She had liked the double meaning, once it was explained: the living, and the pouting that was also like a swoon. *I do not dwell on things,* she sometimes said in her own mind while other people talked. But here she was, adwell. What promises Gilbert had made, with the Sisters (*Oh, les soeurs coupables!*) assisting. The Sisters! Amélie and Brigitte, Clothilde, and all the others, too, had told her he'd been meant: *"C'est ton destin, petite!"* they'd said, over washing, steaming bedpans, crusted cups—her destiny, God's plan. They had made it sound as if nothing could be done, as if she had no choice but to welcome the man in. That man, the pink young man with traveling dust in his brown hair and emotion in his eyes, had seen her and had wanted her and had asked if he could have her. And the Sisters had said yes excitedly, and shining, as if they'd been awaiting him for years. As though Sarie must have been waiting for him, too. "This is a sign from God," they'd said. "You're his." And Sarie had believed them. They insisted she'd be cared for, that she would have a future. One or two of them had even, humbled by the bliss of married lives that they had never known, cried and held her tight.

But, Sarie thought for the first time, perhaps they'd wanted to be rid of her. Hadn't heavy, satisfied Clothilde said, "If you don't go with him, what can *we* do with you?" Hadn't they all said, "You can't live your life here"? But, no, it wasn't all their fault. She *had* thought, hadn't she, that she was supposed to go with him, let him take her from the clinic and escort her, like a prince, closer to the sea, to a kingdom of delight. It all seemed a sad tale. She knew now it hadn't been a plan, no divinity at all. In fact, she thought, it was car trouble that had sent Mr. Turner and his Magistrate down to the Jilima Mission, to ask if they could stay. There had been an accident, something with a donkey Sarie didn't know, exactly. A broken strap or fan, perhaps, a dislodged, leaky valve, a puncture in hard skin. But whatever belt or metal piece had failed, Sarie had got married because of trouble with a car.

What stories he had told! There would be a house and garden by the harbor. She would be admired. He would be promoted. But of course Independence came, and with it, all that went. *What if I had not accepted him?* Sarie rubbed her mouth with a long hand. *If*

I'd met Mr. Jeevanjee instead? The very question hurt her, and she turned to rise from bed. But thoughts of Mr. Jeevanjee, it seemed, kept on popping up, no matter how she tried.

Aware of Agatha gabbling to herself in the next room—Taj and Dunya, threats of murdered men—she wondered for a moment what Majid Ghulam Jeevanjee liked to have for breakfast. How *did* people like him, widowers, poets, men from those green islands, *Jeevanjees,* get moving with the day? Samosas, was it? Gruel made from some grain? A sweet, light-scented pastry? Confronted with the item, would Sarie know its name? And would she ever in her lifetime learn how it should be cooked? She drew the sheet away, ran her fingers hard across her face, sat up, set her feet on the cold floor, and strode into the kitchen.

After breakfast, Gilbert, unfaithful in his way, put down the book on coastal merchants and replaced it with a favorite, a slender teal-gray volume called *The Mohammedan Peoples of East Africa's Coast Lands.* Oh, how he was glad about his books! How they calmed him, how they promoted in his heart a sense of order in the world! But let us tell the truth: he was not a conscientious reader. While Gilbert loved the varied books with a constancy and ardor that were probably unmatched, and took great pleasure from his ownership, he gave them less than all of his attention. He did not read them through and through, not as they had been written. Gilbert loved their shapes, what they hinted about *him,* far more than their intricate, sometimes difficult insides. He loved to hold the volumes open in his lap, to gauge their width and heft, to feel the paper with his palms. Holding books like that, with care, made Gilbert feel like—yes. A professor. Like a man who *understood. Like,* he sometimes thought, *the man I really am.* When he did cast his eyes down among the pages (which he *did* do, yes, he did, sometimes), he was often more intrigued by the appearances of things, their outlines, than by their inner cogs.

In the cherished books, Gilbert sought out vivid anecdotes and clear-cut section headings. Statements in bold print. Single sentences, or pairs of them, not often more than three, that jumped from off the page. In the book on merchant sailors, he had liked to learn that slaves came to the coast from Yemen and also from Circassia. Oh, Circassia! In *Mohammedans,* Gilbert found expressions he was curious to try out on fellow drinkers at the Palm: "prestation," "affine," "rights in rem," and more. Gilbert practiced his pronunciation softly, just under his breath, while Sarie clattered in the kitchen. Then he looked at his high bookshelf, reassured and proud.

As her father read, Agatha wandered out into the courtyard to find pebbles and to watch the neighbor's chickens recover from the storm. As Sarie did each day, though she knew that Agatha never strayed into the road and that the only car to speak of was the broken Morris taxi, which could neither run a person over nor even give a growl, she said, "Look out for the cars!" and Agatha ignored her.

Later, in the bedroom, Sarie watched another Sarie in the dresser mirror. The yellow light from the three windows, tinted with the residue that gums all city glass, showed up Sarie's wrinkles. A veritable bunch of them around each of her eyes, and a slight but undeniable new give at the skin of her long throat. Dissatisfied, she frowned. She peered a little closer. The mirror showed a shadow at her lips—coffee? A mustache? She licked a finger, wiped.

The blouse she wore, with wooden buttons she'd stitched on herself, displeased her. Like all of Sarie's things, it had been purchased secondhand from a man who sold old clothes. Acquired from a vast array of church groups, hospitals, old-age homes, and, thought Sarie, grim, *Even from the morgue,* the cast-off clothes of men and women from the U.S.A. who'd moved on to other things were sent past the Equator to the wretched, wretched South. Indeed, thought Sarie: A reminder to the people of exactly how things stand between themselves and the Great North, of how mighty powers churned. *We wear past decades on our skin,* she thought, *because we're stuck in time. The world goes on sans nous.* The blouse, 100 percent U.S. cotton, now as thin as paper, suddenly seemed twice as old, twice as shabby as it was.

Sarie laid a hand across her belly, which, between two thick and sturdy bones, was neither flat nor round. She measured that soft space with her palms, not only for herself, but also on Mr. Jeevanjee's behalf: for her (*Perhaps!* she thought) new lover. She felt less worn, less aged. *A lover. A man other than mine.* The very thought refreshed her; she almost laughed out loud. But he was not quite a lover, was he? A *lover* was a man one had allowed to go as far as men can go, and she had not quite done that. Or was a man whom one permitted to explore most of one's upper skin and squeeze what was still covered also like a lover? Sarie wasn't sure. *Would* she let him, if he tried? Did she want him? *Yes,* she thought. She did. She puffed her chest and lips out, flexed her calves and thighs. But next, the thought of Majid frightened her. She held a hand out to the air. As though Gilbert were not reading in the parlor and Agatha not squatting (shameless) in the sand just beyond the lowest stair, she felt thoroughly alone.

Sarie, like all women, had a past. Hers, as all pasts are, was particular, and not. There'd been, in brief, parents dead too young (run over by a car while Sarie played elsewhere), an avid aunt who had just taken vows and who, when she set out for the Colonies to spread the Light of Might, took little Sarie with her and soon after died herself, feverish and crazed, as many like her do. Accidents aplenty, unexpected change. One death to another. But there'd been steadiness as well. Sarie's past, the part of it a person could explain, the one she could remember clearly, what she thought of as *the real past,* had begun in earnest at the Jilima Mission Clinic, one hundred rutted, hilly miles from seaside Vunjamguu. The clinic: pain and sickness, health. Blood and spit and bruises, sporadic wails and cries, and the pungent, complicated smells of potions of repair. A heady mix, indeed. Things that make strange tales.

She'd been, when Gilbert met her, "our assistant, Sarie," lacking formal training but certainly a help, a not-bad girl with heft, a girl who could be taught. When he had seen her in that hallway picking up a tray, when she had turned to him and said, "Hello!" he had had a momentary vision, truth be told, of what beauty might be like. In that dim, cool light and the bright air, so palely blond, she was! What dearly freckled skin! *What girlish muscles,* he had thought, *in those able arms.* He'd fallen then and there, that Gilbert who so rarely saw young women and to whom those he did see said: "Hello!" But he had, from the first, enamored somehow of himself and made uncomfortable by pain, understood the clinic as a place she should escape.

He was delighted when she left with him; and though he'd found her past romantic, once settled in the city (tiny garden, tiny house, and no view of the sea), he found that he did not delight in Sarie's reminiscing. When she started, if he could, he'd squeeze her hand and say, "Not now, sweet," or turn his eyes from her. His stomach, among other things, was weak, and he did not encourage her, though now and then he did regard her life with awe: before Independence, most of all, Sarie's past—the mission clinic part of

it, though he did not like to think of it too clearly—had sometimes made him proud.

In those days, not long after their marriage, in the breezy hallways of the courthouse or at a gathering where serious drinks
were served, if Gilbert was confronted by a District Officer (lips
asmacking, chest plumped up) who presumed to "set poor Turner
straight" about the natives and their ways, he sometimes took a
deep breath of his own and, to take them down a peg, would say,
"Indeed? *My* Sarie worked inland, you know." And so, oh, yes, she
had. And not too badly, either.

Methodical and unimpressed, she'd had, despite herself, perhaps,
an aptitude for care. In little ways, she helped the sick grow well,
the damaged find some comfort, and the dying void themselves.
She'd wiped teary cheeks and bottoms with the same unfocused
ease and had been particularly good—though Gilbert found this
odd—with those among the pregnant ladies who thought to brave
the clinic, hoping it would offer up a magick that a home midwife
could not. What arrays of peoples she had seen! Gilbert liked the
names. He'd think, awed again by Sarie's height: *my wife assisted at
the birth of Chagga infants, Gogo babies, Haya kids, and Sumbawanga
triplets!* Gilbert, who read rather faithlessly but with an eye to customs and beliefs, imagined all the varied babies wearing colored
beads and goodluck stuff to match their tribe and place. And Sarie,
just beyond them, officiating, gowned in white, and wise.

When Gilbert felt the smallness, the pettiness, of his own clerk-
ship at the courthouse, or when too many colonials had passed
through town with their interior tales, it cheered him up to think
that he was married to a woman, in a way, who was really an ad-
venturess. How capable she must have (*must have, really*) been. But
if—as she rather often did—Sarie spoke out on her own, she

made him feel ashamed, of her and of himself, and Gilbert's pride dried up.

"A Maasai girl," he'd once heard his new bride saying at the Gymkhana, where on a sunny, cloudless afternoon there'd been a garden party. Just beyond the patio, a polo match on the soft grounds (hollow thuds and gallops carried on the breeze) gave the gathering and its linen-covered tables (cloth clamped down by pewter weights) a fine, Imperial feeling. Closer in, rooted in red pots, miniature palms swayed. Across the garden path, but loud enough for all the men to hear, Sarie had continued brightly. "The spear, it passed completely, *tout à fait,* through her awful foot! Stuck in there for days!" Sarie held her nose. "The smell!" Her cup rattled on its plate. A little much for pleasant company. Rather. *Too vivid,* Gilbert thought, though old Jim Towson from the farms and Majors Daltry, Copeland, could tell far harder tales to men in other rooms with whiskeys in their hands. *Oh, dear.* Didn't several ladies near Sarie step just a bit away to supplement their tea or reach for walls or men? Here and there, a gasp. *Too vivid, for a woman.*

Sarie, unschooled (*Not quite all she seemed, my man,* Gilbert told himself again, again, again), mistook the gasps for interest. "Oh! Oh! *Écoutez!* And then!" She could not be stopped. She told them next about that region's rice and flour magnate ("A *Bohora* man, you see," as though the word determined the affair), who came bleeding to the clinic with two fingers hanging off, a stab wound in his thigh. "A fight with his own son, imagine, for a dark girl from Dodoma! And he already, *s'il vous plaît,* had a pleasant wife at home. A fine lady with the jewels." Sarie (*Was she drunk?*), with the devious look a salesman might put on to tantalize a customer who is almost out the door, added, "And yet"—a head tilt to the men just across the way—"do they not say that the races are not permitted to and must not be making love?" How the small word "races" rang out through the party like a bell. Did the polo players pause, out there on the field, the palm fronds give a shake?

Triumphant, laughing, feeling she'd done well, Sarie gestured at the ladies with her flowered saucer. Oh, the shudders that politeness could not quite conceal or perhaps in fact depended on: Major Daltry's latest conquest raised a girlish hand; Jim Towson's sturdy Hazel, licking her front teeth, brushed nonexistent smudges from her shirtfront and wondered whom Gilbert had married ("Lost her parents, did she?" as though it were Sarie's fault), while the men, attention drawn, fell silent. Several of them were unnerved, crossed over to the gathering of women and sought their spouses' hands ("As if," Sarie later said, "to say it wasn't true!").

How on that afternoon Gilbert wished that he had picked another wife, a girl, instead, come straight to him from England, docile, eager for a match. Or some honorable Nairobi horseman's leggy, stable child, not *this* peculiar one, whose memories were unspeakable, who had, it sometimes seemed to him, no real History at all. Whose past was an affront. He begged Sarie in the future to exercise restraint. "A wife, you know," he said, "can make or break a Service man."

In the backseat of someone's car (Brickman? Masterson, perhaps?), Sarie had scowled deeply at her husband, then looked out at the waves as they spread from Seafront Road. This was not what she'd agreed to. In fact, in her whole life, she asked herself, to what *had* she agreed? Blown by winds, instead! A sorry, tattered flag with not even a pole! To calm herself, she thought, *The water of the ocean is bluer than my eyes.* Then she thought about Jilima and wished she had not left. Years later, now, wondering whether with Mr. Majid Ghulam Jeevanjee she had taken a misstep far greater than at any garden tea, Sarie thought again about the mission clinic and the hills, and (for the first time rather urgently) about Sister Angélique, whose story—luckily for Gilbert—she had never raised at any public function.

The journeys of some people gesture with their motion to the hidden heart of things and leave deep marks on others. For Sarie, the first day after her moment in the hall with Mr. Jeevanjee, Sister Angélique loomed large. Born Angélique Magisse, efficient and hardworking, Angélique had been much older than Sarie, twenty years perhaps, a very grown-up woman. *Not much younger,* Sarie thought, *than I myself am now.* Sarie had admired her, as the other Sisters did, but from a distance made of awe: a girl child's adoration. Angélique, she'd thought, was perfect. Suited more than anyone to Jilima and its trials.

Pinafores and fingernails as clean as clean could be, Angélique never cried or shouted. Faster and more forceful at her work than any other Sister, she could disinfect and wrap a wound in the time it took poor Amélie to uncork an aspirin jar, could pluck a splinter from a toe, dab-dab, and wish its wearer well while slow Clothilde had only located the tweezers and coughed three times for show. And Sister Angélique was handsome. Small and strong, well-shaped. With stiff red hair and small sharp teeth. A beauty, in her way, brash and quick and vivid. The old men who cycled up with fish always hoped that *she* would come to the back gate, not Sister Brigitte. The boys who tried to sell them chickens liked her best of all. Indeed, the Fathers who drove down once a week from the town of Uchuipo often winked at her, inviting her to whiskey and tobacco in the frothing purple dusk. And Angélique was game. She praised them, shared their bawdy jokes, and, blowing smoke out of her nose, laughed into the night.

If she was occasionally unseemly, her straighter mates forgave her, because she was generous and skilled. They found excuses for her manner. She could not be, the Sisters said, Belgian through and through. She was too fearless and too vivid. "There is some Ireland in her," Sister Brigitte (who was bald) would say, enamored of that hair. Or, thrilled and also horrified, "A Frenchman in that family, at least. Perhaps she was adopted."

The most regular of patients, too, had ideas of their own. In the very center of Angélique's broad forehead, slightly raised, smaller than a circle of confetti but larger than a speck, was a perfectly round mole that matched the rusty tint of dry Jilima earth. The patients said, "She was meant to be a Hindu, a Banyan from the north. All that white-white skin is but a trick and a mistake." The patients (themselves certainly not Hindu but feeling well within their rights) proposed that Angélique's poor mother had been visited one night by a Brahmin spirit-man whom Angélique's poor father had been too busy doing other things to ward off from his bed. "And spirit-lust is strong, or not?" Perhaps Angélique's cuckolded pa had been herding humpless cattle or minding a big shop. They imagined the girl's mother very pale and mole-less, smooth as glass or water. Angélique, for reasons of her own, perhaps, never set them straight. She laughed with patients, too.

When Angélique, the pillar, the pistol, the one with too much spark, with more agility than anyone they knew, fell in with an indigene, Sarie, tender, was still young, making herself useful in the kitchen and the grounds, learning to wash bandages and identify a fever. One Sunday, as a buttered sky grew scarlet at the rim, a Kuria cattle-thief came into the clinic with an ulcer on his leg. Sarie saw him coming and ran into the ward to say a person had arrived. But he was not exactly welcome. Because Sister Brigitte thought he smelled bad, like cows and heat and dust (if she passed close to him she sneezed), they put him in the bed nearest to the window. This he didn't mind; that bed afforded him a fine view of the mountain and, by implication, of far-off Kuria-land, which, with a little give-or-take, does lie just beyond.

Brigitte, though very good with ulcers, didn't want to treat him, and he was passed to Angélique, who (wise girl!) did not think he smelled. The cattle-thief was quiet. He had, in general, a surly look, which Brigitte would in later stories say should have been a warning: it presaged all of his perversions, as had—if only they had measured it!—the sharp slope of his skull. For Angélique, however, who turned out to be as skilled as anyone with treatments of the leg, he now and then displayed a rare and lovely smile. She tended him. He gestured to the mountain, and Angélique, able with her hands, made clever gestures back.

The cattle-thief stayed with them for two weeks before walking into town, hobbling but not weaving, aided by a slender walking stick he'd fashioned expertly himself. Sarie had been warned away, and she had not approached. But she saw him make the cane from the kitchen window. He spent hours sitting on a rock, whittling away. She had thought him picturesque and serious. He said he would be back. He had business in the area before heading home to Kuria-land and would return before the journey for a final checkup and a cleaning of his leg. Sister Clothilde later swore that just before he left, she saw him speak with Sister Angélique on the far edge of the grounds, beneath the biggest tree.

"She grew bright in the face," Clothilde would tell them with a shiver, "red as the leaves on that big croton, and redder than her hair." Hands twisting in her lap, eyes closed, Clothilde—who later swore she'd loved her the best!—would moan, as if she and only she could have prevented the disaster. "I told myself right then that that one—*that one!*—he is coming back. We have not yet seen the end." Nevermind the cattle-thief himself had told them he'd be back, making signs that even Brigitte, elaborately wheezing, could not fail to understand.

He returned one month after his discharge with two milk-cows in tow, elegant humped beasts with patient eyes and strong, fine legs and rumps. This russet pair he tethered to a post behind the clinic, not far from the trees. He came into the kitchen, asked for Angélique, and then requested tea (*demanded,* rather, this they later saw). This time, though, he left the cattle at the mission; he slept and ate in town. There, Clothilde would say, rubbing her soft gut, she observed him more than twice behaving oddly at the Mukhtar Drink Emporium: eating chocolate biscuits, which he washed down with a Fanta, skin-bag at his feet.

Sister Brigitte was as unhappy with the cows as she had been with his scent. When he came out in the mornings to visit Angélique so she could help him with his leg, Brigitte told him they could stay until he left. But she also made it clear, eyes tearing all the while, that it should not become a habit. "What if everybody did it? Eh?" she'd tell him, finger wagging at the sky as if a herd of cloudy cattle lived there, dying, simply dying, to taste the clinic's grass. Sarie had made fun of her, poking with her finger at the air, and plump Amélie had slapped her. Three days later, Angélique was gone. The two milk-cows remained.

Amélie insisted that she had seen her go. At night, afraid of the dark toilets, she had stepped outside to pee. "I watched her slip over the wall," she said, "with nothing but a penknife and a ten-inch stick of sugarcane held in her two hands." The penknife glinted in the moonlight, and the foamy smell of fresh-cut cane came swirling through the grounds.

At the news that Angélique had vanished, Sister Brigitte— aware of Amélie's propensity for self-important fictions—thought perhaps that Angélique had simply gone to see a patient in the hills and been detained there overnight. Then, as though it made any sense at all, as if Angélique were the sort of Sister who would do so—as if such a thing were *simple*—she thought, "She's simply wandered off." She sent the gardeners out, and asked the cook to look. To a Jiji man who repaired shoes in the next town (and who had come in with his nose broken very much in two), Brigitte gave an antique pair of German boots in exchange for any news. The shoe-man sent Brigitte a thank-you: the boots had sold for a high price, and his nose was very fine, but he'd sniffed nothing of the Sister. No one else came forward.

The Fathers were called in. Maudlin, they polished off two bottles of good scotch. Not completely without pleasure, they came up with scenarios. For certain, a misfortune had befallen her. She had been dragged from bed by force. Subjected, even, in some still-unknown locale, to complicated tortures at the hands of pagan men. From the very start, they suspected the involvement of a man, or men, dark men with terrible intentions. Failed converts—possessed, as natives were, by devils, maybe—performing nasty but delicious tortures on a Sister! They did not voice their fears out loud to the Sisters, but Sisters, too, have rich imaginations. They feared the very worst.

On the quiet clinic grounds, the russet cows consumed the grass, and everything went brown. Sister Amélie, the first to give up hope of a fantastical return—she'd seen Angélique heave off herself, she knew it was for real—assigned a local boy to graze them. With Brigitte's grudging approval, she ordered the milk sold. Clothilde, who had enjoyed access to cream, came around soon after, and she and Amélie put their heads (and two and three) together. Double chin aquiver, Clothilde announced, "He's taken her just like a cow!" A tear snuck into the crook beside her reddened

nose. Clothilde had turned to Sarie and had held her, had damp-
ened Sarie's smock. Amélie, counting up the change from that
morning's sale of milk, nodded and agreed: "A cow!"

They did not consider this: perhaps, perhaps, that Kuria man
had made a fair exchange. What if he'd taken her just like a
woman, had been fairer than was due? Who expects two head of
cattle for someone taken as a *lover?* But the Sisters didn't see things
in this way. *They* understood the natives, didn't they? And the
Fathers, who wrote books in their spare time, confirmed the local
lore: Kuria men, it is widely known, employ a special paste, which,
when rubbed into the forehead of a cow, will give that beast false
memories and a fitful, homesick sense. Thus cursed, to Kuria-land
that cow will walk, unaided, undeterred by lack of food or water
or even fear of death. All over the highlands, it was known, beasts
had gone unswervingly away, lost to their real homes until firmly
in the keeping of the thief whose paste had marked them. Kuria-
cows they never were, but such they helplessly became. Hadn't
people in Mangombe lost three thousand dizzy head to such a pilgrimage trumped-up?

And so he'd treated Angélique, the saddened Sisters said.
Perhaps just beneath the croton tree, so familiar to them all, he had
daubed that charming mole with potent Kuria paste. Oh, there
could be no doubt! Possessed, she had scaled the mission wall and
gone to do his bidding. Kuria-woman now, erstwhile Nursing
Sister doctored by a patient. She was lost to them already, on a
strange, amazing journey the Sisters could not bring themselves to
fathom. She was a warning to them all.

Two months after Angélique had gone, and hope been given
up, an American nurse named Betty, from the nearby Baptist
Center—a healthy woman in her fifties, large, white-haired, and
pink—brought the Sisters eggs. While Betty rested in the garden

(partly green again, recovered from the cows), Sarie, young, efficient in her way, fastened newly laundered bedsheets to the
clothesline with curved pale wooden pins. Betty said, offhand-
but-not-offhand, stretched out in the sun, "This Angélique of
yours." Sarie, young, was still willing to be led. She looked up
with a clothespin clamped between her lips. Sheet in hand, she
waited. "It's really just too bad." Sarie didn't think old Betty
sounded sorry.

Betty looked back at her evenly and spoke as though imparting
a deep secret: "That's what happens here," she said, "when you take
this place to heart." Betty didn't move her eyes, though she rolled
her shoulders greatly and righted her thick neck as if preparing for
a leap. Her dark eyes narrowed, almost disappeared. Something in
the air went cold, a bifurcated breeze that touched only Sarie's
throat and the plump part of her calf. "Those men. Don't even
think about it, honey. Don't you let that happen."

Sarie hadn't thought about it, or anything to do with men, ever
happening to her. But she missed Angélique, and she did wish, like
the others, that she hadn't disappeared. Betty was intent, and what
she did next shook Sarie. Her eyelids taut and wide, mouth stiff,
Betty raised a plump pink finger to her forehead and ran it horizontally across the furrow in her brow. "That's what happened,"
Betty said, spreading unseen paste above her eyes, miming the era-
sure of everything but love for nasty Kuria-men, long-horned
cows, and scrub. "That's what happened, now." She rose, and she
poked Sarie in the chest. "Look out." In the dull gray morning
light, Betty's soft, short hair was whiter than the sheets. Clouds
shifted. A thick and gummy stillness replaced the little breeze. Betty
wiped her forehead with a handkerchief, which she then tucked
into her bosom. The thing between them passed. Betty took possession of the basket she had set beside her. She made a show of

wistfulness, shook her head with a tight smile. "That Angélique of yours, my girl. She's gone and done it now." This time, as though to someone else that neither of them saw, Betty said again, "Oh, yes. She's gone and done it now."

For a while there were sporadic sightings, each as dreamed-up as the last: a mad white woman dressed in rags, hunting on the plains, bare-breasted, astride a hot Ankole cow. Or Angélique, sunken, battered, red hair shorn, spotted at the harbor of busy Vunjamguu, making for Odessa with her passport and the pocket-knife, both nicked, a glazed look in her eyes. Or, milder, but even more disturbing: Angélique, happily done up in dusty local gear, golden baby or perhaps a red-haired black boy nestling on her back, purchasing tomatoes at a market north of town—then gone, as local women were.

Eventually, however, the Sisters left off gasping, and, one by one, gave up on the whispers. Brigitte once again denounced all smells that came from patients as if no one with a dreaded stink had ever passed her way. Clothilde undertook a diet. Amélie thrilled to selling milk as if she'd brought the cows herself. Thus the Kuria-man was excised from their anguished hearts, forgotten, and Angélique grew stiff and distant in their minds. She had surely got what she deserved. If they spoke of her sometimes, they said her name aloud, and even with distaste, but with no hint of sorrow. The Sisters had been healed. They couldn't know what had really happened, nor would they ever learn. And, besides, far more serious than perversion, scandal, or abduction, even pure desire or unsurpassed affection discovered where one least hopes to find it, there also was a War on: Europe, battles bulging, camps and bloated trains. Other things to think of.

*   *   *

In her bedroom, hands now on her head as she bent over, thinking, Sarie pictured Betty's finger sliding on her brow, how pale her hair had been. She smelled the fresh sheets in the air. What had the Kuria-man told Angélique beneath the croton tree, or from his mountain-looking bed? Was any of it true? When she thought about her own surprising man, she reassured herself. She was not at all like Sister Angélique. Oh, no. No, she wasn't. She was not. She had not *done the thing. La chose,* she thought. Not yet. She looked into the mirror, steeled herself: "Mr. Jeevanjee has never stolen cows. He is no bad-smelling Kuria-man with an ulcer on his leg. He knows how to read. And I" — she touched her brow and neck — "I have yellow hair."

After an hour in the courtyard, Agatha came into the bedroom. "Look," she said. She opened her closed palms and let her new-found stones spill across the folds of her parents' unmade bed. Intent on her pebbles, she didn't see how very still her mother was, or how she stood, sideways to the mirror, fingering her hair as though uncertain it was hers. "Kudra House," said Agatha. "Nineteen thirty-two. When should I get dressed?" And, "We're going to have juice."

"We are not," her mother said. Upon a second, unmoored vision of Betty's moving finger, and a third and fourth, Sarie had decided that she surely wouldn't go. She'd been foolish to think of going back so soon, to think of it at all. She had herself in hand: she would make a lunch for Gilbert; she would take Agatha to market, seek laundry soap and beans.

Agatha was dogged. "When we go today," she said, "I'll wear my purple dress." "You will not," said Sarie. Agatha kicked the air, tossed a pebble at the wall. But Sarie's resolve held. She needed, she decided, a little time to think. Indeed, what if going back to Mr. Jeevanjee spelled a great disaster, as great as Angélique's? *What if,* she thought, *he makes me disappear?* Agatha complained. She cried, she stamped her feet, she pounded at her mother's legs with vigorous fists, but Sarie, once she'd made her mind up, could not easily be moved. "The Jeevanjees need time," she said. "We have visited enough."

They did not go back to Majid Ghulam's house for four long, dreamy days. During those four days—because at the start of an affair one feels a great variety of things—Sarie sometimes thought the thoughts she felt a newly chosen woman should: *I will take my time, I shall like to savor this, to think*; alternately, she felt she had been mad to go at all—that by her dismissal of the girl with glasses at the clinic, who had been (hadn't she?) somehow issuing a warning, she had sealed her fate. She wished for an alternative: she wished to do it all again, to say instead to the receptionist, "You're right. We will let him rest. Give him our regards," and go right home, straight from that pink room. And there were happy moments, too; when Sarie danced before the mirror, hugged her own self tight and stroked her great, long hips. If thrilled like this, she wondered what Agatha would look like if she did not belong to Gilbert. If Majid were her child's real father, Sarie asked herself, would Agatha's pale skin have come out nutty brown? Would those high brows be dark? Would the willful girl have had poetic leanings (which, in her current incarnation as the daughter of a man who couldn't, Sarie thought, put two words old or new together in a bright or interesting way, Agatha, it seemed, most certainly did not)?

What if her own hair were *not* as yellow as gelled ghee? She wondered what sort of clothing Majid's long-dead wife had worn, and *would they look well on me?* She took her wonderings with her as she moved in the drab flat. She scrubbed the kitchen tiles, imagining the floor in Kudra House, its furred, brown, bare cement gone black and damp beneath the flakings in the scarlet paint. She peered out of the windows thinking she saw not Mchanganyiko Street but Libya, another world, indeed. What if *she,* and not the nameless love, had been married by the poet in her youth?

But a simple cough from Gilbert, a shuffle in the other room, or a look from Agatha, who *did,* no matter what, look very like her father—that round, round face, those light brown eyes like clear glass beads beneath such opaquely brown hair—and who resented both the interruption of their visits and her mother's recent habit of *staring* at her so, could make Sarie lose her happiness and think, *I'll forget it ever happened.* At such moments, considering the back of Gilbert's head or a dimple in her daughter's arm with enormous concentration, *I will,* Sarie would think, *forget this man completely.*

❈ *Six*

M ajid also wavered, side to side, and down, and down, and up. He paced the hall and balcony of Kudra House; he walked the stairs from top to bottom and to the top again, then back. At the bottom, in the doorway, Majid stood as Sarie had, looking up the pitted steps into the bluish gloom. From this position, he made forays into the courtyard, which made Maria think that there was something wrong: at the far end Majid looked at the old tap as if he'd never known that it was there, rusting and sporadically aspurt; he eyed the upper rim of the old wall and noted, frowning, like a visitor from other realms, the passion vine that, having snuck across from an unseen neighbor's root, now clutched the coral bricks; he walked down the narrow alley to the metal door, felt the street arush behind and almost pressed the panel out, almost crossed the threshold; then he turned around and moved back towards the stairwell, as if he'd come in from the street. As he walked below, he wondered what the big woman had seen, in their crumbling place, and him.

That she'd looked at him at all caused Majid some amazement. That she had kept on doing so, that she had returned so many times, that she had pressed his body to her and might do so again—it seemed beyond belief. He had never, never, thought that such a thing could happen. Yet it had. There was a stirring in him, familiar and yet not. It made his skin feel strange. As if he were aswell. *It must be,* Majid thought. *I am.* How odd! He felt himself grow ample, filling his old clothes! Indeed, in the days after the embrace, it seemed almost to him as though, despite himself, a younger version of Majid Ghulam, a healthy one whose arms could lift a mattress without effort, whose fingers might undo a door-bolt without pause, a young man who could laugh, were threatening to push old bereft-and-angry Mad Majid to the side.

He thought about his body, about his own and Sarie's: the electric rattling between. Recalling Sarie's limbs, how greedily, how quickly, she had wrapped them all around him, Majid Ghulam felt restless, nauseous and excited. *How wild she was with me!* He recalled her as ferocious, nearly in a rage. He even thought she'd clawed him, growled a little in her throat. That ardor! It cannot have come from the pale woman alone. Had it been called up in Sarie Turner by something within him, a force he had not known? This thought pleased and jarred him. Yes, at some moments in his unraveling's early wake, Majid felt like a new and different man. His body changed, his mind shook. Was it the biscuits that they ate? The clutching in the hall? The showing of the paper, after so many yellowed years? Majid didn't know. And though he did not quite yet put any pen to paper, he remembered, almost, too, what it had been like to face an empty page and will himself to fill it. To make a mark, out there, outside of himself. He thought of this: *Were you not once a poet?* Had he not once been so very full of clever words that they spilled out of him unsponged? Had he not once or twice been *really* listened to? Had he not had certain special, urgent things to say? Been praised for his fine wit? And in those days, he thought, had he not understood why a girl or woman might look to him and smile?

The braver feelings were of course countered, too, by rather opposite emotions—emotions that in fact were not new, and had priority, had squatters' rights, over any thoughts of happiness, which were arrivistes, indeed. Inertia: the sort described in Tahir's science primer, the inertia of a body that has too long been at rest. He was widowed, after all, a man who'd lost his wife. Or was he? Though Majid would not have seen it, it is also possible to say that widower Mad Majid was not. For widowers can recover, can emerge from forty days of managed grief with the unpleasant, perhaps, but inevitable impression that life itself continues. Successful ones go on to take up other wives, to father other kids. Triumphant widowers take strolls to ease their sadness; they linger in the world and find their wounds grown dull. Mad Majid, instead, had languished, had never taken strolls, and had never felt before that life, skipping on without Hayaam, might show him a new thing. Perhaps he was no widower at all. Not yet.

For years—and it had made him crazy, wild, unkind—Majid Ghulam Jeevanjee had refused to countenance the passing of Hayaam, the dear, bright-eyed, heavy-breasted, fine-ankled, laughing sweet first love. When in the cruelest of tricks she had exchanged her living self (which he'd been firmly promised!) for a whimpering baby boy, Majid had (here Bibi was right) as good as lost his mind. He had, almost—had it not been for Cousin Sugra, who was strong and never failed to say exactly what she thought— not gone to the funeral. He had almost failed to hold a maulid later on, after forty days had passed, when grief, it is assumed, will have softened its mean grip and made room for a smile. *He* hadn't held it, really; Sugra had, taking over, smacking him to make Ghuji behave, though he had, uncontrollable, anyway announced to everyone (the cousins, the few still loyal brothers who'd wired from Toronto and from London, to the neighbors, who first eyed him softly, then with fear, to passersby, who hadn't asked) that there was nothing now to live for. That he wished everyone would die. (That wet event with old Rahman, which Bibi liked to tell and tell and tell, was not made up at all.)

Unspeakable, such things! Too much! What was *not* all right to say, what *no one ever said*. One said, instead, "The blade of life does sting, my dear, but we will not flinch, indeed." One said, "Get hold of yourself. Withstand this. It's all part of the plan." One said, "We've all got an appointment, a promised time, with God. There's nothing to be done." And even, "Buck up, love, this was meant to be." How could it, though? How could such things be meant? Hayaam, after his failures, after the lost shop, the paper, after the embarrassment of not being a success, had been the sweetest, truest thing, the venture that had bloomed. He'd found himself unequal to it and upset, despite the grievers' wisdom, the wisdom of it all. What good was life if all ended in death? What good was love, indeed?

Majid Ghulam forgot to eat, grew frail, and also ceased to bathe. While the abandoned sons grew large because Sugra was determined that they should, his once-good teeth went bad. He cried, he swore, he shriveled. He did what no good Jeevanjee, what no good man, had ever done in the whole swath of human history; he did what faithful humans mustn't: he stopped attending funerals and weddings. And what's more, stopped making contributions to family events. Majid would not—do listen close—would not give a shilling for incense or a shroud, or even for the sugar to make funereal sweets. He said: *I would rather die.* Rebuffed at first, then wounded, by Majid's transformation, people stopped asking him for help. They knew what he'd become. They called him Mad Majid, and they did not come to call.

He spent weeks in his own room. He dreamed of furious things, and woke to even worse. He saw things in the shadows, moving in the walls. He felt visited by shapes. He was afraid to cross his room at night alone. He hated knocking sounds, and sounds of married life that came to him over the walls, from other houses, from the city's air itself: the toothy scrub of graters, the clack and shift of pans in basins of cold water, the flap of carpets in the air; these things made him shout. Indeed, Majid had lived (or not lived) nine solid empty years—of rage, then sleep, and finally of worn and gummy grief. He had not killed himself, not with acid, knife, or pill. But he'd done as good as.

And yet, see how Sarie Turner, with her thick, long legs and those—he thought—*kind* eyes, had made things suddenly seem light! How at the first appearance of her small but chubby and not inconsiderable breasts beneath his gaze and then his own excited hands he'd felt a kind of sway, a circus in his mind! How easy it had been! The import of what had taken place in his own hallway— the simplicity of it—stunned him. In just one moment he had felt the floor shift, the air throw off its coat, the evening light a balm. He'd felt joy, and joy. A manliness, a cheer. He hoped she would return!

But, prey to sorrow and to fear, he also asked himself the following, and the question made him sick: if it could be replaced so deftly by a hunger for round biscuits, for the flat and endless heft of a foreign woman's back, and for the awful, hot excitement of his hands between his tired legs in that old and sagging bed, what *had* the madness, all that long, long grief, been *for*? And had he really meant it?

In Majid's version of the thing, Sarie Turner had thrown herself quite shamelessly at him, and he, long loyal, so he'd thought, to life-lessness and Hayaam's death, had caught the woman squarely in his arms and felt a shivering at his core which he had heretofore re-served for sleepy fumblings with his, yes, nine-years-dead, once lively, comforting Hayaam. Illicit grapples with his loins were bad enough, wasting bright seed on a sheet. And with a woman who was dead, much worse—a sin of the first order! How could he?

But thinking now of a live shape, the possibility of Sarie Turner, who still breathed—a much greater transgression, Majid thought. Dreaming of Hayaam and thrilling sadly to her in the night . . . wasn't it a version of fidelity somehow, talk of sin be damned? *This,* with Sarie Turner, was a special kind of treachery. Still, had the embracing been his fault? No, he thought. She *took* me. He had not desired it. Sarie Turner was a fleshy accident, Majid told himself, for which he had not asked. He cursed her and himself. And in the rippling of his skin, the thoughts he could not help but have—of limbs, and mouths and loins—he discovered a new fear, a strange one: had it always been Hayaam behind his eyes at night? Because, to tell the truth, it hadn't been so difficult, clutching Sarie Turner, not as difficult as he thought it should have been. But if he could so easily take hold of her, had he already practiced touching other women in his sleep? Had he been disloyal to Hayaam well before Mrs. Sarie Turner showed up on the steps? Majid began to wonder if his memories of that first and only wife—*Hayaam! Hayaam!*—were true. Did he know, precisely, with any certainty at all, into whose place Sarie Turner had (with his permission, this he knew) made such a decisive and significant advance?

In a yellow envelope that Majid kept beneath a metal mathematics box that he had won at school (compass, ruler, pencil, chart—for planning things just so), he'd saved three photos of Hayaam, which he had never shown the boys. In the early days of grief, he'd studied them, had held them to his heart, had on several nights kept them by his pillow to see her face on waking, had thought to make a shrine. But in later years, he had rarely pulled them out. For he had memorized them, hadn't he? Had he not carved, in tears, an image of Hayaam in the tender darkness of his chest? In his mind's eye, he could still—could he not?—call her up exactly as she'd been. Before stepping towards the drawer and clasping the brass handle, he pictured the three photos in his mind. *There* would be Hayaam, draped in lavender, as he well knew, seated on the sand of Scallop Bay: one knee up, the other folded underneath her, hands loose among a pretty mess of seashells, her face turned towards the camera, and behind her the blue sky. Hayaam at someone's wedding, eyes and cheeks modestly aglow beside a gold-encrusted bride. The last, an accidental snap: Hayaam caught unawares, Fruity Pop in hand, before the Frosty-Kreem, hair escaping from her braid and playing in a breeze. Majid knew, he told himself, just what the shots would show. Just as Tahir in his bedroom could dream up his old leg so firmly that its absence in the morning was a shock, did not an old husband know precisely what was gone?

The questions prompted him to open up the dresser drawer and check his memory's sharpness. Had he, with a sinking in his bowels, already known what he would find? It's possible. When Majid slipped the pictures from their sheath, he frowned. He blinked to clear his eyes, gave a shake of his sore head. He brought the pictures close up to his face, one after the other, then held them at arm's length. Confused, he thought, *What happened?* He unfocused his eyes, tightened them again. He felt each hair on his scalp as though it were a needle traveling through his skull.

Was *this* the same old picture? Really? The one at Scallop Bay? Hayaam's dress was *blue,* not violet. Beside her not seashells but stones. And, worse, much worse: rich, still plummy with old colors, the features of that well-known face did not, he thought, look as he expected. Was it humidity, perhaps, which can turn pictures brown? Her cheeks, her jowls, had bloated. The skin was darker than he'd known it. The dear flesh at her round skull—that brow he could recall in sleep, remember with his fingers—had taken on a rubbery look, had blurred along the temple. Was it decay, perhaps, of paper? At the center of himself, Majid hoped it was. Perhaps the photograph was ruined. Look: a watery stain across one eye concealed the bridge of her small nose; the edges of a black spot at her lips had lifted and, just beneath, Majid could see a speck, the blankness, shiny-white, that lurks under emulsion. Could he still see what would have been there, despite the little gap? Could he match what Hayaam in his mind's eye had become with what was left of the old picture? Majid Ghulam tried. He leaned against the dresser and placed a hand on the flat wall. He closed his eyes. He wished. He tried, and he could not.

Who was that woman on the beach? Majid's unphotographic visions of her did not match even what he *could* still fathom from the pictures. How could it have happened that he could not recognize his wife? He asked himself hard questions. Had he grieved Hayaam as she had been? Or had he transformed her himself, so that each remembering of her was, in fact, a violent defacement? Had he replaced Hayaam already, at some lost, incalculable moment several years before? Before even grabbing someone else? And was grabbing Sarie Turner nothing but an echo? An empty move he had already, unknown to himself, made and made again, with faulty grabs at his dead love?

He spent several hours sitting on his bed, looking out into the mirror and trying to imagine young Hayaam as she had been when they first shared that room. Of them both, had she been the heavier? Had he been the stronger of the two? How had Hayaam's hair smelled—was it rose, perhaps gardenia? Had Hayaam's skin, when damp, given off a scent of myrrh, the tartness of a lemon? In his eyes and in the glass, Majid Ghulam saw nothing. He could call no scent into his nostrils. The session gave him headaches. He felt guilty and alone. Ashamed, he hid the photographs between the pages of a book, the book beneath the empty chest. Went down the stairs again.

He would not think of Sarie. He tried instead to focus his attention on the face of his dead wife, but, with a persistence that alarmed him, his own mind conjured up instead Mrs. Turner's throat and thighs and hair and the pink nipples that had stirred him. Intermittently, his thoughts of Sarie broke and Majid thought about his son. Another new, and equally upsetting, theory came to him: Tahir's absent foot and calf and now-truncated knee! It was Tahir, after all, whose appointment with a reeling bus had brought Mrs. Turner in. It was the accident and nothing else that had so churned up the world that Sarie Turner, just like cream and just as pale, had risen to the top. Oh, Majid Ghulam was mixed up! To feel so many things at once can tire a body out! When he wasn't feeling joy, reliving the embrace, or feeling, full of shame, that he'd been grieving a false memory of Hayaam instead of *Hayaam-she-herself,* Majid Ghulam was tortured by the thought that his youngest son's left limb had been traded for cheap pleasure, that the crash on India Street *had brought this lust his way.* Could one be grateful for such gifts?

Oh, nevermind. To each his star! emergent, manly Majid would insist. But older Majid would demur. How could a man who'd doubted God so much, who no longer believed in Divine Plans, all at once presume that certain things were meant to be, the blade of life is hard, etc., but that each moment is the proof of a grand, unfathomable design? How could such a doubting man, falling headlong into a woman who'd appeared when Tahir's leg and missing shoe did not, tell himself that God's work is mysterious and one must simply go ahead? Two white breasts, an open throat, some fur (perhaps, or so he'd heard, a lot, among the women of her tribe) between two legs, that extraordinary quivering, traded for a shin-heel-ankle-calf, for his son's two-footed life? Was this a Godly switch? A European-woman-gift in place of a boy's limb, in place of Hayaam's photographs as they had been the day they'd got them from the shop? *No, no,* gloomy Majid would reproach himself, *no pleasure to be found in someone else's grief.* And he'd resolve to turn away from Sarie, not to let her in. Whatever God had planned for him, whatever bauble of reward for having been so sad so long, Majid wouldn't take. His travails were really far more difficult than Sarie's. Oh, but life persists. A force did work in him, despite it all, and nonetheless, something in his lungs and hips and shoulders pushed him to make do, move forward. Take deep breaths and stand. Time, perhaps? A budding thing? A sign from his own garden?

To his hot confusion Majid attempted to respond by pulling out other items from the past. From behind the dark armoire he took a cardboard box in which he had, at Hayaam's death, set aside two tunics and one pair of loose trousers, keeping them from all the cousins who had taken things away for charity, for poor relations, for the helping-with-the-grief. He wanted, if such a thing were possible, to recall Hayaam as she had really been, before deciding what to do. Perhaps the clothes would help him. *Sight is not the truest sense,* he thought. *Touch and smell may be.* Practicing as he set the old box down, he said: "This is what you wore." He squared his shoulders, bent forward carefully and slowly, peeled the cardboard wings apart, and eyed the folded bundle. He took a long breath through his nose. There was, as he had hoped, a smell, and it rose up and he breathed harder. But it was not a wifely smell. Not once washed since Hayaam's death, the clothes smelled, disheartened Majid thought, like Kikanga dampness, mold. Like things left in the rain.

Nonetheless, the clothing called up something from the shad-ows. As Majid Ghulam pulled the box into the middle of the room and settled on the carpet—could it be?—he felt the air grow thick; a shape appeared beside him. *Could it be?* In the heavy violet of the curtained morning light, Majid sensed an apparition at the corner of his eye. An apparition! He was not entirely surprised. He'd seen things after his wife's death, hadn't he, that no one else could see. Shadows. Birds where there were none. Ancient bearded men in white, sneaking through the dawn. Demons with one human hand and one hand that was wood. At least so people said. Wasn't sadness-madness made of just precisely this? Why not, why not, when he desired it, a presence in the room? *A woman,* Majid thought. Why should he not call up the dead?

Squatting on his heels, hands gone still above the cardboard flaps, which were like doors into the past, Majid held his breath and tried to keep his balance. He felt his chest go tight. He waited. He let the air out of his mouth. He steeled himself. With every blink the shadow took on weight. *This is not unusual,* he thought. *I have been mad and sad. I have been more than dead myself. I have seen all kinds of things.* He prepared himself to look. *All right.* Majid turned his head. Did he see her in his mind or in the space before his hun-gry eyes? Was she really there? No matter, no matter at all. It was, indeed, a woman. A full-sized one, moreover, in a shimmering green dress. With—was it?—Hayaam's almost-shape. Majid sought her face. *All right.* The revenant was real. Could be.

But—was *this* the wife he had been trying to recall? Majid could look carefully at things if he willed himself to do so. He kept very still and tried. Hunched just there beside him, the woman looked, perhaps, as Hayaam's older sister might have. She was heav-ier than Majid's memory of his own happy bride. More *womanly,* in fact. From the base of her round skull a silky rope of hair reached down to the floor. Did Majid feel it, prickling, waspish, like a shiver, too long and yet familiar under his bare feet? He watched. There was no glimmer at the woman's nose, no stud shining in the light. Was *she* widowed, too? His working mouth went dry.

She was not looking at her husband (if that was who he was). Her head was bent over the contents of the box. Majid's eyes, his neck, felt almost frozen, tight. The figure shifted but Majid could not move. He felt no threat from her, no, simply swollen quiet. Everything felt still. This Hayaam-not-Hayaam, biting at her lip, reached out a hooked finger and pulled the cardboard flaps aside. Majid's skin went cold. He felt a bit afraid. But, sensing that *for good or ill* he was in sudden partnership with the woman-shape beside him, propelled by something other than his will, Majid reached into the box. He brought the tunics out and set the sour pile between them.

If Hayaam it was, he thought, braver than expected, then it was time to make a peace. Was that not what he should want? What if he kissed her clothes to show her his respect? Was that not what he should want? To say, "I know to whom these old, sweet things belong, my dear. You were very stylish once. You looked lovely, like a star." Even if she *didn't* look like the Hayaam he thought he'd known. Even if she wasn't his Hayaam at all, but someone who'd been sent, a shade on her behalf. There is an idea in Kikanga and these parts that a supplicant may only be forgiven by the person they have wronged—but that person doesn't always come! Then what is to be done? Majid for a moment closed his eyes against the ghost, and, wishing for a sugary taste—*some sweetness!*—bent to kiss the cloth.

It was the right thing to have done. The way to call up memory, absolutely pure. With the first touch of his lips, beyond the fust and mold, he smelled Hayaam again, this time, Majid knew, *exactly as she'd been,* with no time intervening and no meddling from his unwieldy attempts at remembering what-had-she-been-like. Majid almost yelped. Yes. *There:* a fresh, cool mix of samli, roses, powder, a young woman's pungent (lovely!) sweat. How could he have wondered for a moment about lemon and gardenia when *this,* so clearly her own, was right here in the pockets of the very clothes she'd worn? Exactly as she had been. The precise and veritable-wife-smell made Majid feel faint. He teetered backwards on his heels and, fumbling from the shock, had to steady himself with his elbow on the wooden steps that led to their old bed.

While Majid's eyes were closed, a sound came from the shape. A sound as true as the good smell he'd found under the dust—a sound that had a long, long way to travel, from its source into *this* world. At first there was a sniff. A rumble in the nose. He sensed without needing to see a little shaking in that long tail of black hair. And there it was at last: a giggle. A precise and perfect neither-nudged-nor-turned-by-memory giggle that was, he knew in the crevices of his oldest, surest self, exactly how Hayaam—the real one, the living one, the one who'd gone and died—had laughed. And next? The widower's last win? He found that he had missed *this* giggle, yes, none other. It filled the gaps between his ribs. In a dear and marvelous way, it hurt. She had not come, perhaps, as he remembered; she was not as slender, not as heavy-breasted or light-skinned, as his night pictures had been. Perhaps he'd lost her face forever, the real shape of her limbs. *All right. But she had laughed like this.*

Majid's very skin rippled in relief. For a pulsing, bruising moment, Majid felt that all the grieving had been worth it—yes, he'd missed exactly the right thing. No, he hadn't altered her too much with the years and his forgetting! Was a laugh not grander than a face, an ankle, breast? For sure, a laugh could harbor all the things a person was—their essence. So pleased, so accompanied, by this ghost-Hayaam's high giggle, the smell still wholesome in his throat, he almost felt prepared to undertake nine more years of same. For this nice sound, indeed, and scent. He had meant to reach out to the shadow, to tug on that black braid. Had hoped he could laugh with her. But when his eyes came open in the shadows, he saw nothing. Brown linen, and the pale pool of the floor. Nothing but the room. Majid was alone.

Majid Ghulam remained squatting on the floor for a long time, well past noon, until he couldn't feel his legs. He thought. He squinted. He called out his wife's name. But Hayaam, as she'd not been or had been, did not reappear. *All right.* He paused. He looked at his own hands. He squinted at the windows. He braced himself for what he knew was coming, what he, fearful and delirious, sensed ashiver and arumble at the far-off, unseen brim of a new, convulsed horizon. And it did. It came, tiny and unstoppable, shy, enormous, brave: in his chest a small thing snapped in two and its snapped pieces wiggled. On wobbly legs, Majid stood before the mirror. *I will—,* he thought. He felt all of his teeth swell, his tongue go sharp, then wide. He bit his lower lip and nodded. *I will give these things away.*

He dropped the tunics in a basket. In the morning he would send them to Maria, finally to be washed. He did not need them anymore. Afraid that he would lose his certainty, he reached for an expression that could steady him. *Clothes don't make the man,* he thought, *or woman. Hayaam won't,* he thought, *come back. My old Hayaam is gone.* He walked out of the bedroom. In the parlor where he'd first sat with Mrs. Sarie Turner, beneath the glossy clock, he wept until his mouth hurt.

That night, in the half-gloom of his bed, he thought of Sarie's arms. He slept. He woke up in the dark. The air, after yet another rain, was chill. He stretched his arms above his head and reached his feet right through the baseboard, where, early in their marriage, he and his young bride had with their loving ardor kicked a panel out. He rubbed his toes together as if ridding them of sand. He took a great, deep breath and made his first attempt to firmly lock away an old, known widowed-feeling: a little twinge, a folding near his eyes. He stared at the black wall. He uncurled and curled his fists and, another Majid rising, thought at last: *I will see her again. Her daughter will come to play with Tahir. Tahir's going to walk. He is already sitting up. Habib, Ismail, and Ali will take him to the balcony to sit. The clinic will bring crutches. Maria will give these clothes away. And I will write a poem.*

❧ S e v e n

While Gilbert had a thirst for knowledge, it was not the knowledge of specific living things, or persons in the flesh, that moved him. He was therefore as richly unaware of M. G. Jeevanjee's particulars as he was of any serious changes in his wife. In Gilbert's view, the legless boy's poor father was not more than a local Indian man whose son collided with a bus while Agatha and Sarie—unluckily, indeed!—looked on from the curb. *Unfortunate. Too bad.* But no more and no less. He had other things to think of. Temporarily entranced by a bright hardcover volume called *East Africa Now,* on whose cover robust girls and boys in schoolgear uprooted marigolds with hoes, he was also troubled by an itchy skin condition that was making—he could feel it—advances on his back.

Sarie, in the bedroom, had pulled all her skirts and gowns and blouses from the cupboard. As though invisibles could don them and, rising, bring them suddenly to life, she had arranged them into poses on the floor. She was wondering how she *really* looked with some of these things on and was trying to imagine Mr. Jeevanjee's opinions—as to carwash sleeves, umbrella skirts, and box pleats. Was he fond of frills? What did he think of Sarie Turner, *par exemple,* in that gray dress with the dots? From the parlor Gilbert called. Fingering the yellowed collar of a once-white linen blouse, Sarie paused, wished she had not heard him. Gilbert called again.

When she came out from the bedroom, Gilbert had removed his shirt and vest and stood with his back towards her in a humble pose, as though she were a doctor. "Please," he said. "See if you can't tell me what the devil's going on." She stood beside him and he felt her shadow cool his burning arms. "It's bloody awful, Sarie." He gestured with the top of his round head towards the current volume, spine unbroken on the chair. Sarie watched his bald spot shift, did not look where he meant. "I can't even read."

Sarie was not in the habit (nor had she ever been) of treating Gilbert sweetly. Of treating anyone, perhaps, to specific shows of tenderness at all. But, prepared for ailments of the body, she sometimes cared for him in a practical and reasonable way that was in its application not unlike affection. She knew her husband's body better than she wished to and was, she knew (the Sisters had proclaimed it, like a penance), duty-bound. She kept a bar of sulphur soap for the frequent bouts of dishrag that left even whiter speckles on his already white skin; clove brews for his muscle pains and chronic indigestion (the last to make him vomit, which, without fail, it did); cinnamon to boil for the head colds that made an elephant of Gilbert. Confronted with the skin rash, Sarie felt relieved that she didn't have to look at him full-on and think about his eyes, or hers, or what she might see there. She could focus on his back, which was like the back (Sarie imagined) of every other Englishman on his way into old age: pale, pinkened here and there, flaky where the skin was rough, and, as she had come to think, not exactly ugly. But not precious. About her husband's ailment: Sarie knew exactly what it was.

"This condition," Sarie said, with more enthusiasm than a gentle person should, "will make a red stain like a pine tree up and down the back. You will . . ." Here she searched a moment in the air to grasp the needed words, then spoke with satisfaction. "You will become a little tired, and you will resemble Christmas." She had not seen Christmas trees herself since she was three, but the

Sisters (Angélique?) had drawn pictures for her, and Gilbert, too, had filled her in on rootless trees and baubles. She ran her fingers rather roughly down the pattern on his back and told him that unless he was prepared to spend good money on an ointment, nothing could be done but see the whole thing through. It would go away eventually, as many ailments do. He might go out, she said, in search of ice, which he could rub for solace on his back—and he could save some for their drinking water, which they would all enjoy. Or seek out Aspirin in a packet, which, she thought, she might employ herself. Gilbert rearranged his shirt and turned to look at her. The attention he'd received had made him feel, already, a little less upset, his skin a little cooler. "That's it, then?" He smiled gratefully at her. "Yes," she said. She didn't linger there. She went back into the bedroom, where, except for one white dress with a not-bad quilted feel, she put all the clothes away.

They went again. They couldn't not. She *had* been thinking of his hands. And the sharp smell of his breath, which was somehow hot and sweet at once (fennel, pepper, juice?). Would one kiss become another, and another be a tumble? A wonderful free fall? She'd thought of Sister Angélique again, but each time a bit more slowly, each time with less fear. Would she permit the man to go where none but Gilbert had? Only Mr. Jeevanjee could tell her.

They stepped into the early afternoon. Sarie, anxious, entertained her doubts (fiercely, as one can only do when one suspects, in one's most secret place, that they are all for naught). She wondered: Had she been a fool? Was Mr. Jeevanjee sitting up in Kudra House ashamed? Had he hardened fast against her? Would he refuse to let her in? Would he insult her at the door? Had he lied about his wife? If one of these things happened, Sarie did not know what she would say to Agatha, how she could explain. She looked down at her arms and covered up each elbow with a palm, purse dangling between. As they crossed the roundabout, she panted. When the bus stand, with its smoke and wheeze came into view, Sarie almost wept. Unaware of the wild torrents rushing in her mother, Agatha was cheerful, skipped, dragged her feet and kicked things. Sarie drew a handkerchief from the bosom of her dress and wiped her face with it. By the cane-juice man, she fretted with her hair.

Upstairs, Majid Ghulam, who'd suffered—yes, was suffering softly still—was nonetheless not in any funk. The night before, he'd made, he thought, a kind of peace with Tahir's leg. He'd wondered yet again: Would God really, even at His most wise or absurd, snatch the lower limb from a clever, earnest boy so as to bring the lonesome dad a large and freckled lover? Could these things be related? Perhaps and perhaps not. This was not Majid's business. While Tahir slept, and turned his shoulders now and then to one side or the other, Majid Ghulam decided that perhaps it didn't matter. That mysteries were mysteries, and so forth. He'd moved his fingers lightly over Tahir's bony chest and felt, in the lining of himself, a little worm of hope. He'd said a prayer for Hayaam. Might her soul be in sweetness. And that night he had slept well.

In the morning, on her way to market, Sugra had come by. Sugra: the one cousin who still loved him, bright, round, talkative, and sharp. About Sugra people always said, "Of course *not one of us is perfect,* not even our dear Sugra." But what they meant was that she was not unlike goodness and charity itself. A little brash, a bit too loud, her effect was wonderful and strange, an impression of ebullience and goodwill, of charm, whatever else was true; for everything, *she* could be forgiven. She'd seen Majid through a lot. She would poke at him, she'd tell him to wash up, and say he was a mess. But she would be a blessing. As she always did, she lifted up the gloom, although there was, on that morning, less gloom than she was used to. She had looked at him for a moment from the doorway as if she did not know who he was. "You're looking different," she'd said, and, feeling a bit bare, exposed, he'd said, to shrug it off: "Tahir's feeling better."

She had come up with potatoes and some rice, put them down, and looked at him more closely. She said she'd gone down to the clinic and had not been heard yet. But she reminded him that she did not shy from combat. "If they don't give me crutches soon, I will go to that doctor's house myself." She raised her arms and made a face and jumped and swayed from side to side like a bogeyman, a spirit. "Like this!" She'd made Majid laugh.

That morning Majid did another thing he had not done before: he thanked her specially. He had risen from his seat and squeezed her hand and thanked her. And she had looked at him again as though he were not quite the man she knew, and had pulled her hand away, suspicious. "All right, now. Quit it, please. I'm going." And this, too, had made him laugh. Majid was feeling better. He was trying, yes, for now, as Sugra herself thought he should, to put that grief behind him.

After lunch, he had slept on the blue settee while Tahir, whom Habib and Ismail had carried carefully into the parlor, sat and ate bananas by the window and looked at an old book. While Majid slept, a restful half sleep that did not bring him dreams, he had been conscious most of all beneath his skin of that forward-moving force—which ebbed, oh, yes, and flowed! He'd felt the presence of his son not far from him, and this had made him glad, as if things were going right. He'd woken without visions. He had bathed. As Agatha and Sarie turned the final corner, he felt fresher than a glass of lime juice—giddy, he was hoping, hoping, that Mrs. Turner would come back.

When she saw that he was greeting them more graciously than ever, Sarie, happy, felt a fool. Here the kind man was, perfectly polite—he'd shaved!—and clearly glad they'd come. She tucked her handkerchief into the collar of her dress with her left hand and took Majid Ghulam's fingers with her right. *He wants this!* Her palm curled around his knuckles, settled for a moment. *Il me veut.* Her pale eyelashes fluttered.

It seemed to Majid that her eyes were very bright, the whites of them a little paler than before. And that she'd been breathing hard. Had she been so eager, so desperate, to see him? The thought made him feel tender, brought a pulsing to his throat. As she released his fingers, she bobbed down a little so he should not feel her height. He was touched by the way her scalp showed through her hair, that she was, almost, bowing down to *him*. She reminded Majid for a moment of a schoolgirl, even cousin Sugra, curtsying to the British queen at a Diamond Jubilee. The idea—*little Sarie kneeling*—made him smile.

At the lifting of his lips, Sarie almost swooned. She felt her eyes well up, grow hot. Her knees buckled a bit and she wanted to fall down in relief. But she did not let herself collapse. She sniffed to push the tears back. Her nostrils rippled greatly and her legs went strong again. *Mr. Jeevanjee feels just the same, like me.* She raised her eyebrows and she beamed.

Majid was happily prepared. He had counted out what Sugra had been able to secure for them and sent Habib to the shops for fruit, which is good when one has guests. As soon as Sarie sat, Agatha beside her, he brought out more bananas and a bowl of tangerines. Such kindness! Sarie's blue eyes glowed. Majid, who had thought of everything, turned to Agatha and said, "Take some in to Tahir, won't you? He has things to tell you." Agatha did not need to be told twice. She took three bananas in her hands (one for Tahir, two for her) and three sweet tangerines. Her small bare feet made furry thuddings in the hall. The door to Tahir's room fell open and then narrowed. Majid looked at Sarie.

Now that Agatha was gone, Sarie—having had a tangerine— was calm and fine inside. She settled back into her now-familiar seat and crossed her legs, this time without shame, hoping they looked nice. She said, "What happened here last week—" She stopped.

Moved by a twisting in his bowels and how Sarie's presence made his breath feel thick and slow, Majid prevented her from starting up again by pressing a small banana towards her. "Madam, please." He paused, and tried it out. *"Sarie."* Sarie blinked at him. "There isn't any need," he said. It came out as he had practiced.

She handed him a quarter of her fruit, and, mightily aware of the shape of their two hands, he took it from her seriously. Sarie nodded to herself. *D'accord. Here I am,* she thought. *And here I will repose.*

That afternoon, Majid read out an old poem she had not yet heard; it was about the charming jasmine bush, whose heady blooms enhance the sweetest couplings and bring warm scent to old clothes. Sarie had, it's true, never done a single thing with jasmine; she had never worn it, pressed its flowers into oil, or presented a desired man with a package of its buds tied together in a leaf. She had never left a favored gown to sleep, flowers in its folds. But Majid was not a stranger to the ways that jasmine could push certain things along. He had been married, after all. Though Sarie would not have said so clearly, would not have known exactly what it meant, the poem was an offering, and this much she understood: it gently told her what there was no call to do (panic, worry, flee), and artfully suggested that other needs, for more than fruit and gazes, might at some future date be met. Majid looked at her to witness his effect. Sarie was still flushed, and marveling at the shivers in her limbs. *He has not even touched me.* She raised a hand up to her hair. When he turned towards her, she uncrossed and crossed her legs, put her palms on her big knees, and asked Mr. Jeevanjee—no, *Majid,* please—to read the thing again, from beginning to the end.

❧ II ❧

❦Eight

In the mornings, the sounds of Mansour House awakening rose up to Bibi in her bed. She could hear Issa and Nisreen and the other, darker bibi—Mama Moto, the one who cooked and cleaned. Issa moved around sharp sharp, stepping, sitting, quick and firm like a machine, uttering bright questions ("Are you ready?" "Where's the tea?" "Have you seen my belt?"). Nisreen laughed in answer and moved slowly, shuffling in bare feet. Mama Moto made one-syllable pronouncements, noncommittal, bland. Bibi liked the sound of them, *her* people. She liked knowing they were safe, and hearing them about. And also teacups clashing in the basin, the rattle of boiled water, breakfast being made. But, although it was her habit to wake hungry, she had begun to wait. Morning, she'd heard people say, was the best time for ideas. And she had work to do. She wanted to discover, firmly yes or no, if indeed she had a gift: she was fostering visions.

She hadn't mentioned it to anyone—that convergence in her stitching, with the napkin and the bus—and she was not going to until she was quite sure. Not one of them, she thought, was worthy of her news. Not one of them was really willing, not as Bibi was, to entertain a possibility and thrill to it. They thought she made things up; they thought she was a gossip.

To be fair, Nisreen, in her own measured way, did welcome information. Being the receptionist at pink Kikanga Clinic, she herself was often privy to interesting news, which she sometimes shared with Bibi. But Nisreen dispensed her wares at intervals, dangling them like sweets—more to placate Bibi than to indulge in a shared treat. If Bibi asked her what was new, Nisreen would look up in that vaguely cross-eyed way of hers and shrug, say, "Nothing. The usual, you know. No, nothing I can think." She'd go on folding sheets or picking at her fingernails or polishing her shoes without another word. Bibi had to wait. And then, perhaps, she'd say (as if she'd suddenly remembered), "Oh, well. There *was* something today. Guess *who* came in with a bruise like a brinjal swelling on her face, brought in by an aunt?" Earnest, slow, Nisreen would generously describe the symptoms, how much blood there was, the trimmings of a trauma, but she wouldn't stand for too much guessing about who or what had been behind a punch or slash. While Bibi, caught up like a fish, would twitch and flap and ache, Nisreen would turn away and start combing her hair. Hours later, when Bibi had finally left off asking her for more, she might look up from a book and say, "Oh, yes. Here's a story, maybe. *Who* do you think has gotten pregnant *when?*" And later, much, much later, when Bibi had begun to think, again, *This Nisreen is not made of stuff like mine,* Nisreen might give in, surprise her, saying, "And wasn't Ahmed Shah seen hanging round the paan shop just beside the clinic, overjoyed with his fat self when Salma's husband was away?"

Unreliable, she was. Nisreen might be a good girl, Bibi thought, but her pleasure in such things was idle, unpredictable at best; she didn't live for news, and, more than Bibi cared for, she'd sometimes look away as though she had been wounded and say, "Please. This one I won't believe!" So Bibi shushed herself and did not say: "What if I am a seer?" What if Nisreen laughed, which, not knowing how it cut a person short, she was rather good at doing?

Issa also liked to be informed, but he had ideas of his own about what constituted news. He'd spent too much time in school and not enough in life to think with seriousness of things like signs, ineffable connections. He'd gone out to Kiwingu for a year before marrying Nisreen, hadn't he, to study meteorology, measuring the clouds and speed-clocking the wind, and what was more inimical to her kind of prophecy than *that?* The children, Bibi knew, would think she had gone mad. That she had finally passed the point at which old women could be trusted. Disrespectful, this new youth. "A coincidence, Ma, just luck," she could already hear him say about the bus-and-cloth connection, Issa with that great mustache dolling up his lips. He might suggest she get herself a stand at Mbuyu Mmoja Park, join the charlatans and quacks.

Mama Moto, in a way, was the hardest of the three. She stood up to Bibi, made no bones about it, often told her she was foolish; and sometimes, in the middle of a story, Mama Moto left the room, pretending she had urgent work to do. Bibi wasn't ready for that kind of treatment, not so tender as she was. So she kept it to herself.

In the mornings, after praying, dressing, and securing the remains of her fine hair away from her round face, Bibi, hoping to be entered by the new (she hoped) prophetic spirit of her stitching, got into bed again to lie flat on her back. In her room, spread out like an X, Bibi felt secure. There was nobody to laugh at her, nobody to see. She stared up at the ceiling, seeing not what others might—fine cracks, damp spots by the rafters, or the fan—but rather the dark pools and fine recesses of her embroiderer's mind. Before her inner eyes, Bibi called up patterns. Which one, she had wondered every day, which one ought she to push into the world, and what might it foretell?

Her bread-roll belly rose softly and then fell and rose again while she waited for a pattern to make its outlines known. She kept her eyes as wide as they could be without reaching up with her own hands to peel her eyelids back. Her fingers trailed along the faded cotton sheet, tapping, thrumming, seeking something.

Outside, the clever house crows shuttled and convened along the wires in the courtyard.

Eventually, if what she thought was true, when she had tired of the waiting or grown dizzy from the whirl of that inscrutable potential, something, a real thing that had meaning, would have to slip out from the mass. Colors formed and spilled away. She wondered. For example, what was that pink orb? Was it just a speck of light, the kind that plays behind an eyelid in the sun? Or was it something else? A flower bud? Should she stitch a rose? *Oh, no,* she thought, *definitely not.* A rose! What could a rose portend that a peacock hadn't done? Weren't roses too predictable, like ylang-ylang blooms and jasmine? She was, she realized, slowly losing faith in flowers of all kinds. Flowers called up the hot scent of opened petals, the enticing tightness of closed things, strokes and love and kisses, and Bibi did not want to dwell too long on memories of those.

Love hurt, see? She'd been talking about love with Issa and Nisreen for months now, how love makes homes fill up, how they ought to make a baby, how she wasn't getting any younger and could they please see their way clear? But where had all that gotten her? Nisreen's stomach flat and humpless as a brand-new Danish road, and Issa cringing, banging books, if Bibi brought it up. *And tears,* she thought, *at night.* It wasn't really pleasant, making Nisreen cry.

And there was, too, the other, older thing, which she didn't like to think of but which, in such a childless house, she found herself confronting more often these days. She herself had nobody to squeeze or even think of kissing. *Her* husband, unlike Sarie Turner's or Nisreen's, was buried in a plot that had long been overgrown— and though she never mentioned it (and how upset she was whenever Issa did!), there were three small ones out there, too, who hadn't stayed for long. Shriveled little buds. Flowers, thank you, no. She'd branch out, if you please. Roses were too easy. And the peacock, which she liked, with its potential for a preening and a strut, was, perhaps, something like a has-been—was complete, had been done before.

Now for something else. Hm. Bibi groaned and sighed. How hard it was to tell a veritable vision from a habit, from defaults that float about! What were these nice squiggles? Ah. Elaborate herufi, twined, in pleasing aqua blue. Perhaps a well-designed, inspiring "by the grace of God" to bless a new endeavor? A pretty *Dismilluhi*. Bibi clicked her teeth and sucked air narrowly between them. Why did nothing suit? No, she'd had enough of words. The squiggles thickened, took on the look of leaves. A scroll of ivy, in memory of distant ladies who had taught her how to sew? Bibi almost giggled. She had not made leaves in years. In a way, she would have rather liked to—that rich and creamy green, so deep, the wicked points that, to a needle, were so dear! Botanical, it's true, not so different from flowers. But ivy was a special thing, altogether other. Not to do with love. Ivy?

No. She sighed. As Issa often hastened to remind her, and as so many other things suggested (potholes, Royal Jubilees replaced by Chinese acrobats, the *sarakasi*, agriculture shows, the very layout of her home), it was a different country now. She wouldn't go for ivy. Too British, too much a sign of Empire, too foreign and too green. And alien things should not, as the radio happily announced at morning-noon-and-night, be unduly encouraged to gallivant and prosper where they did not belong. No ivy. It wouldn't be, thought Bibi, seemly. Though she did think there was more to Empire than people these days said. Had it all been bad? Bibi mused a bit. In fact, she thought (though she couldn't ever say such a thing to Issa), she owed Empire a lot. Her stitching gifts, for one.

* * *

Like everybody else, of course, like Mad Majid, and Sarie, Gilbert, and also Mama Moto, Bibi had a past. As a girl in a high and creaky white-washed rag-and-mangrove house that overlooked the sea, Bibi had spent hours locating the special spots from which she could, unseen, be a silent witness. Principally called Kulthum in those days—before age gave her the titles Mama Issa, and then Bibi, shifting what had come before—she'd been, from the start, very skilled at stillness. "Born without a sound," her mother often said. "So quiet! Never a complaint!" For this a mother should be thankful, no? But wait—surprise! A fussless girl, as it turns out, can also bring you down.

Beneath her mother's precious Zurich clock, Kulthum practiced hush. Tamped her breath, stiffened and grew fallow. Motionless as water in a mtungi water-jar, tensed for movement as a scorpion. One-minute-two-minute-three-and-very-nearly-four. Exhale! Even when there was nobody to hide from, Kulthum hid and held her breath. Now and then she fainted and would come to in the dark. It happened frequently that nobody could find her. She acquired a reputation for being absent when there was hard work to be done. "Lazy! Disappeared again! Never home just when we need her." But, almost always, watching and immobile, or knocked out from the looking, Kulthum *was* precisely there—only not quite in the way her tired parents wished.

She practiced under high besera beds, curled up with her toes against the stepladders that led up to the mattress. She peered from low space through the watery light of rooms. She practiced between gunnysacks that smelled sharply of cloves, dozing now and then, sometimes staying for so long that her tender skin turned red from the dried-up buds' sharp heat. She hid along the wall beneath her mother's clothes rack, buried in the hanging pants and cloaks that smelled of basil and wood smoke. Do we need to say it? She laid her eyes on certain things that she ought not have seen.

She saw, for instance, from underneath the bed, her middle sister Nasra weep, two stiff kilua flowers milky in her hands. Kulthum, in whom, even then, facts led to surmise, dreamed up a Busaidy boy whose parents would-not-never have Nasra for a wife. Tragic. Awful. So terrible that Kulthum also wished to cry. Kulthum also saw her father beat the boy who helped them load the cloves into the shop, imagined him a thief. And other things: the kitchen girls skimmed palm-sized heaps of rice from Kulthum's parents' stores; her father counted money in the nighttime and listened to the radio; her mother liked to play before her mirror, moving like a star. For many years Kulthum went unnoticed. She saw but did not say, saw and did not move, almost twitched and didn't. But her own secret was let out one monsoon day when, hiding in her sisters' clothes, pressed tight against the wall, she was bested by her gut.

What little Kulthum saw? A form of human congress. She saw nice Uncle Amal and her oldest sister Zainab gnash and flutter at each other, then fall softly on the bed after clear-thinking Amal had ascertained—mouth pressed to Zainab's outstretched throat, one eye zooming to the latch, free hand flapping at the lintel—that the door was safely closed. Next, Amal covered Zainab's mouth with the hot cup of his palm, and Zainab closed her eyes. They shuddered on the bed so much the glass panes rattled in the frame. Kulthum held her breath for one-two-three-and-almost-four. She tried. But she was stricken not with tears, in the end, and not either with fear, but by a wave of laughter that came up from her stomach and clattered up her throat, then burst out into the room despite the fact that Kulthum—who had felt it coming, who had tried valiantly to stop!—had pressed both hands over her mouth to push the thing back down into the privatest of gullies where it properly belonged.

So *this* is what they did! And *this* is why Amal, who already had a wife (a headstrong, jealous wife whom he kept at Fumaniwa, facing the Seychelles in a great house so she would look the other way), came to visit them so often! And *this* is why her parents had been scrambling to get Zainab a man. As Kulthum laughed and laughed, Amal bounded off the bed, pulled his trousers up, unlatched the door he had so carefully kept shut, fled down-the-hallway-through-the-courtyard-the-back-alley-in-the-rain, not to be seen for months. Not knowing what had happened, Zainab pulled the sheet over her head and shook there for a while; Kulthum crept up to her and peeked under the sheet and tickled Zainab on her breasts and sticky bottom until the two of them were howling on the bed and their mother strode inside to see exactly what was up.

It was thus Zainab and Amal, unwittingly, and the complexities of love, that set Kulthum on a course towards hooks and cloths and thimbles; it was after that, after they had found Zainab a man who could take her far away, that Kulthum's parents ordered their last child to make something of herself. They had decided what. It would get the secretmonger well away, and keep her fingers busy. Even better, it would work the bad girl's brain and keep those greedy eyes of hers fastened to her lap. If she could learn to thread a needle, Kulthum's mother said, their lives would be improved.

And so to the Ladies' Sewing Club—where, on weekday afternoons, qualified white ladies supplemented the daily training in Domestic Arts the girls received in school with additional, decorative instruction—little Kulthum went. The Sewing Club, however, while intended as a punishment, was not entirely so. The stitching did keep Kulthum out of private rooms and kept her eyes in place. But, to everyone's surprise, it also brought her pleasure: she had a talent for it. There was, in Kulthum's sharp and sharper eyes, a roiling swell of patterns that spilled right out of her digits into colored thread and cloth. Things she'd seen before, and things she'd never seen. Flowers, deer (poised, at the white ladies' suggestion, in pale blue fields of snow), peacocks, stippled pheasants, guinea fowl (called *kanga,* because they liked to talk), trumpet flowers, fanlike kadi buds, palm trees (which the tourists liked so much), roses, which were to be expected, daisies now and then, and ivy, ivy, ivy, which the British bought in piles.

Mrs. Harries, with her white, round pillbox hat (like a guy dressed for Ashura, or so some people said), and Mrs. Livery-Jones, plump and always damp, who together manned the thing, approved. Their love of stitchery ran deep, was nationalist, in fact. Both were firm in the conviction that girls who sewed were doing honor to the Queen, communicating with her spirit in some way, mysteriously but certainly acquiring rectitude and rigor. Let men speak of guns and laws! Embroidery, they knew, would lift the natives up. They dreamed a great expansion. Not simply city girls above the Egan Smythe Madrassa, but a huge network of rural Sewing Clubs: country girls in hundreds stitching daisies and cat faces and green leaves into handkerchiefs and shams. African and Asian girls versed in the Domestic Arts, they knew, could turn the world around.

Hands clasped to their pale bosoms, Mesdames Livery-Jones and Harries praised little Kulthum. She was a bright example of precisely what they meant. Oh, they were impressed. She might even go beyond the ideal marriage that was every young girl's hope and attain *her* Independence. "With your quick hands and skills, little Miss Kulthum, you could start a business." Kulthum, unused to kind attention, stitched her thumbs and heart out. What an easy thing of push and pull, pressures that with their rhythm and the way they took possession of her hands made patterns grow along the surface of the cloth so easily she was surprised by hours passing, until Mrs. Harries clapped her hands and led them all in calisthenics to get the blood in motion, turn those narrow girls into the good Imperial subjects they were really meant to be.

At the Ladies' Sewing Club, Kulthum learned to focus her attention on her lap. She made very pretty things. But all that silence, all that focus, had a separate effect: the more she pressed her eyes into her lap, the more the skin behind her neck grew soft and fine-tuned to the world. The more Kulthum performed the thing intended to divert her attention from other people's secrets, the more she sensed with all her other parts when she might catch a scandal at the corner of her eyes or in the tensed skin of her wrist. Out the window once, alerted by a twitching in her knee that coincided with the movement of a bicycle, she saw a stately man, respected for his learning, ease three fingers down a coffee vendor's tin and make off with five slabs of groundnut brittle while the owner looked away. From a shiver at her nape that matched a shift in light, she looked over her shoulder and saw Mrs. Harries dab an unembroidered handkerchief at the corners of her eyes, a letter open in her lap. Later, a tightening beneath the weight of her long braid caused her to see her very own Mrs. Livery-Jones's husband (whose short pants brought his scarlet shins into relief) dart nervous down a certain passage, followed seven minutes later by a slim boy Kulthum knew.

The hours spent attuned to thread and thimbles, intended by her mother as a diet, thus nonetheless made Kulthum far more able than she'd been. When she was done with all the jumping jacks and twists, had packed her tools into a leather satchel that she had won at school ('Made in England'—"*Madein,*" the groundskeeper would say, like a single German word), and had politely said good-bye to Livery-Jones and Harries, Kulthum skipped out of the Egan Smythe Madrassa into the chalky streets, where she filled the stomachs of her eyes with the things that other people did. The Sewing Club kept Kulthum's family safe somehow, but out there in the world, it made her a new force. From the Ladies' Sewing Club, Kulthum-Bibi learned the lesson that presaged her watching in Kikanga and gave her future shape: the best secrets of all, those that you can share, that thrill and bring least harm, belong to people who are not a part of your immediate family. *These* you can discuss.

Older now, in-lawed, widowed, nieced and nephewed to children far inland and one-two in Dubai whom she never saw, Bibi had a lot of time for the things that she was good at. Of the boxy clock that let loose Alpine phrases now and then, and the fans that spun unevenly and did not bring much air, she was often unaware. The only sounds she really heard, clearly and unfailingly (because she loved them both so well, would have traded all the gossiping in China for a grandbaby or two!), were Nisreen's and Issa's voices. Sometimes, too, the clash of pans downstairs and Mama Moto's heavy feet—because Bibi liked to eat, and these sounds signaled meals—and—perhaps because she, too, liked to be alert to glittering things that can be plucked from thickets with an eye, a needle, beak—the hot sound of the house crows flapping in the air. But not very much else.

When she stitched her words and pictures in the mornings and in the afternoons, Bibi didn't even hear the children in the alley or the buses, arumble and ahoot. She was utterly dependent on the shiver at her neck or the trembling of a hidden thing at the corner of her eyes—the secret-love that sometimes made her stop what she was doing and look down into the street to see what she could see. It was this kind of shivering luck that had made her look up from the hanging that was just beginning to read *Al-Fadh . . .* as the *Al-Fadhil*-bearing bus bore down on Mad Majid's little boy. But now, she thought, there was something else at work, as if she herself were being pierced by a great needle, caught up in a tapestry so large and fine that she would never see it all with only her poor eyes. For it wasn't just the bus. What about the peacock spilling from her fingers on the same day Sarie Turner trotted out her daughter in the sunshine and headed for *that house?*

She would open herself up to whatever forces drummed. She would have to try. And, after four long, luckless mornings, which she considered training, Bibi saw, at last, a form emerging from the dark. Rounded, glowing. Could it be a crescent moon, with a little star before it? No. The outline of a skiff? Not either. Tsk, what *was* it? Could it be, she asked herself, a cow? Rounded, with a hump? No, really, not a cow. An animal, but blue, and what should she (*No Banyan, I, no Hindu,* Bibi thought, a little bit mixed-up) do with a blue beast? She breathed a little deeper. When the thing came fully into shape, undeniable and purring, she could see it well, but what she saw she couldn't quite believe. A car. A light blue Morris Oxford. *Just a moment,* Bibi thought. *A taxi?*

She saw it now as clearly as, had her eyes been focused on the world, she would have seen the soft mass of her chest, rumpled in her shift: sharply, fully, as if it had been parked right there in her bedroom, door ajar for Bibi to get in. She watched it for a moment, blinked. How brilliant the thing was—just washed! Perfectly sky blue, the way so many Morris taxis were, with a pale, pale cream-white bonnet. Yes, indeed, a car that Bibi liked, had she been forced to say. A Morris. She had memories of these, oh, yes. Of riding on the seafront in them, of going off to picnics with Nasra and Zainab. And even of a teacher she had had who'd loved his own so much that he had put it on the boat with him when he moved to the mainland. Indeed. A blue Morris with a bonnet. For a moment, Bibi smiled into her memories and thought, *Of course, that is what I will make.* She lolled a moment in relief. The real thing had come through. But then she frowned, and scratched her knees. What could she be foretelling? What could a taxi mean?

Bibi stretched her toes as far as they would go, as if she'd reach a better understanding through the arches of her feet. A taxi. Was she to take a trip? Would they be having guests? She thought about it for a while, even told herself that she might mix two kinds of thread to get that gleaming blue. But something shifted in the room. While she'd started out the morning thinking of herself as famous, special in the holy scheme of things, now that she had a thing before her, Bibi faltered just enough that her enthusiasm waned. It was one thing saying bravely she would take up any vision and another to commit herself to stitching it, in full view of her own household. Of course someone would see her. Of course Nisreen would ask, "What are you stitching now, Bi?" And Mama Moto might hold it in her hands and look at it while Bibi was asleep. *Foolishness,* she thought. *Who do you think you are?* Might it not be sinful to have thought herself so special? *Just an old, old woman who wants a baby in the house. It's a cruel trick.* She wiped a tear from her eye.

A taxi! Who, she thought, would want one? Certainly she didn't, couldn't picture hanging up a Morris stitching on the wall. What words could accompany it? *A wreck can go no farther? Broken things are sweet?* Absurd. Nisreen might frown and ask her what it was about. She could hear Issa telling her, already, that she might as well have made a picture of a rickshaw, a relic of the past. He wouldn't want a Morris, either. Oh, such modern,

modern children. He'd want a Peugeot, a Land Rover, or perhaps a limousine. No, Bibi didn't want to stitch a car. And what would the leaders of the Sewing Club have thought? They had called for birds and flowers, hadn't they? If a person strayed from flora-fauna, they had said, then ships might be all right—for a ship's a clever ocean plant, a bird in a wet sky. But cars? Never once had Livery-Jones or Harries pressed anyone for cars. More recently, of course, like everybody else, Bibi had seen for herself the printed cloths done up with Ferris wheels and lightbulbs, on one even an airplane. But those were all new things. New things for a bright future. A broken-down old Morris, Bibi thought, though she felt a sweetness for it. *Wouldn't that be shabby?*

Bibi frowned, and forced herself back into the world. And though behind her eyelids still that Morris taxi danced, she pushed its form away. She stood, rubbed her armpit absently; the breeze twitched at her hair. She cleared her thickened throat and tried to smile into the city, which she sensed bright and fine and steaming out the open window. Just there, Hisham's Food and Drink. Just there—there, far off but not too far—the light green shape of dusty Kudra House. *No*, she thought, and so suppressed the truest thing she'd seen, *I'll make a pineapple instead.* She wouldn't give it words. She'd make a plain, clear thing. And pineapples were good. "Pineapples," she said aloud, "can only bring a very general, unob-jectionable luck."

By the time Bibi was calling for Nisreen to help her down the stairs, Nisreen was putting on her shoes and Issa was already by the door. Nisreen was slower in the mornings than her husband. She liked breakfast more than he did, but not because she ate a lot; in fact, they were both thin and not as interested in food as (so Bibi told them when she could) normal people should be. Nisreen was slow because she liked to stretch her legs and hold a cup of tea while Mama Moto did the washing up. She liked the smell of porridge, the gentle light of the low rooms. She liked to hear the street begin to hum and clang and toot before she put her feet upon it. Nisreen liked to linger. Issa didn't, never had, not even at the start. He liked, as he often said, "to bring the street the day." When Nisreen woke, her eyes were sour mangoes, sharp and gummy, and her limbs always felt numb. She always woke up wishing that she hadn't, that she could roll over in bed and go to sleep again. But Issa's eyes were always crisper than a rose apple, bright as life itself.

"Come on," Issa was saying. "What if there's another accident out there and you're late answering the phone?" Nisreen looked at him and sighed. She smiled, and tried to slow him down. He was not being unkind, she knew. It was just that he was eager, wallet, briefcase at the ready, the busy world already knocking at his heart. He looked lovely, Nisreen thought. That mustache neat and gleaming, white shirt buttoned up. Efficient. She blamed herself for making Issa late. "Just now, just now," she said. The one leg that had troubled her since childhood felt a little heavy. She balanced herself on her husband's arm to get into her shoes. Issa paused, made sure she wouldn't fall. And Nisreen thought, *He's gentle, yes, I know.* She also thought, as she always did when he was still, and part of him was touching her, that she loved him very much.

They heard Bibi from upstairs, and Issa rolled his eyes. "My mother's also late today," he said. "The both of you, slow-slow." Nisreen squeezed his hand and thought how nice it was when Issa teased her. Sometimes she teased him, "Why don't you go help her?" Bringing Bibi down the stairs could take a while, especially if she had a lot to say. But Mama Moto, who liked being in Mansour

House the best when the two young ones were gone, was already rising from the dishes. She came towards them with her arms out, as if shooing chickens from a yard. "You go on, go on," she said. "Get out. I'll take care of her. You have things to do."

Mama Moto—with her old unsmiling face and her flapping, bony arms—made Nisreen and Issa laugh. Issa held the door, and in a moment they were out of Mansour House and in the yellow day. As they walked, Nisreen thought that she was glad Bibi hadn't been there while she and Issa drank their tea. She felt guilty thinking so, but she was growing tired of Bibi asking how she was, asking with that *look* she had, *A look that begins just below my chin and ends under my skirt.* Bibi used Nisreen's lingering against her. "It means you shouldn't go to work," she'd say, peering at Nisreen over her porridge. "It means that you should lie in bed with your knees up for a while. It's standing up so fast that keeps your belly empty. Leaking, don't you know?" Nisreen had grown tired of trying to explain that standing up and getting dressed and going out to work didn't stop babies from coming. When she tried to argue, Bibi asked, "If it isn't that, my girl, what is it?" And Nisreen wasn't sure.

Nine

After years of hoping vaguely for a turn in his own luck towards the success he felt was due, Gilbert had, despite his dreamy talk, resigned himself to the idea that fortunes did not change. That nothing ever happened. At least not in real life, and surely not in *his*, not at the close, familiar scale where he woke up and ate and slept and opened up a book, then ate and slept again. Out there, elsewhere, great things did occur, of course. One only had to tune in to the VOA or BBC to know so. Independence and Uprisings took place. Colonies disbanded. Wars were won and treaties signed, cities smashed, rebuilt. But as far as he could tell, topplings, accessions, and other transformations primarily took place at the level of the State or of the Natural World (disasters and the like). In History writ large.

In his story writ small, the world moved slow and usual, and nothing ever changed. Indeed, Gilbert thought of *change* as something brought about by Presidents, or War, or by what some called Acts of God. If brought about by men, then it was brought by men who'd *done things* and knew how the world worked. Men, Gilbert thought sadly, other than himself. Unless a person did appear—a knowing Englishman or German who might spot him at the Palm, a history professor who might admiringly look up the modest essays he had published—and offer him a deal, a ready-made solution, nothing, Gilbert felt, could transform his little life. Certainly nothing that originated there, or near him. Much less from within.

Or so Gilbert thought. But as Sarie's visits to the Jeevanjees continued, he began to feel a shift.

He had gotten used to Sarie's presence in his life—*their life*—
which, while by no means ebullient or smacking of rich love, was
in important ways reliable and steady. How long had it been? More
than fifteen years now, more than fifteen years of Sarie in his life.
Sometimes it surprised him, seemed much longer or much shorter
than that. Sometimes Gilbert counted: four years before the end of
Colonies, and eleven after that. And those eleven, endless, slow, not
thrashing with adventure or delight but still not, either, Gilbert
thought, disastrous, were a considerable stretch.

The ordinary tempo was, yes, sometimes interrupted by what
Gilbert called Sarie's "little tantrums" (those days when Sarie
pulled at her own hair and stomped on the red carpet, urging him
to please, *monsieur,* why not get a job), and now and then she
shouted and she snapped and, he felt, damaged him. But he had
gotten used to what he had; it was a constant, known; in that constancy, he had found some comfort. For instance: he was used to
waking up alone but knowing she was in the other room; accustomed, too, from the threshold of that tiny chamber, to watching
Sarie read to their one child, and not stepping inside. He liked to
know that she could be presented with his laundry and that it
would be cared for. That she would make him dinner as expected.
That she could be persuaded now and then to pluck a tune out
with one hand on the broken old piano while he stood behind.
That she would roll her eyes at him sometimes. He had even made
his peace with her recurrent gloom.

With Sarie out so often in the early afternoons, at first he felt at
sea. Her absences surprised him. Now and then he wondered:
what could she be finding in a house he hadn't seen? He pictured
her. Sarie was a woman of good size. Strong-boned. But of all those

burly bones, he thought, not one—*not one!*—contained a deep curiosity or the kind of nimble smarts with which all his limbs and noggin were really rather full. Not Sarie. Unlike the man she'd married, Gilbert thought, she was not an intellectual. For example: she didn't care for books, or History, or Knowledge, or Fascinating Facts. One day—Gilbert winced, remembering—she had even thrown a precious tome by Justus Grand (*The Portuguese in Africa*) down onto the floor and kicked it half across the room to end under the table, so that he had had to fold himself in three to get it back. Why was she insistent, suddenly, on throwing herself so regularly out among the people? Did she expect to learn something that Gilbert didn't know? He had that pamphlet, after all, about Dawoodis, and a recent master's thesis (a commercial history of Ismailis and Ithna'asheris in the town of Vunjamguu) that a man from the local university had once generously passed along. Why should she be on the loose out there in the sun, taking his small daughter to an alien home without good information, which *he* could have found out for her, had Sarie only asked, among his many books?

Part of him was mildly roused. But another part of him excused her daily visits to Jeevanjee and Sons (Gilbert, with what he read about such families, was imagining a Store, an Inc., a Sundries Shop or Co.). He put on a generous hat: *It is,* he thought, smiling, *a little competition. She wants to show that she knows something, too.* He even took some pity on her: she *had* had an exciting time in the mountains of Jilima with the Sisters; living in the city, Gilbert knew, had been difficult for her. But what could he have done? *Poor Sarie, looking for her youth. Let her try,* he thought. *She might learn how Muslims eat.* He smiled. *But she will never understand the reasoning that lies behind it all.*

And yet another part of him, a quiet part, was glad. Sarie's absences exposed him to a different kind of silence. Sarie, if at home, was quiet, this is true. But in another stillness, the one left by her outings, Gilbert found a strange and not unpleasant peace. Sarie's ordinary silence, no matter how maintained or smooth, had a roar and rumble to it. Without Sarie there, the flat was truly, fully still. It seemed to him almost as if the place had never been entirely at rest. Consider: he could read his books and putter without feeling Sarie's eyes upon him. He could put his feet up on the coffee table, not caring how they smelled once he had taken off his socks. He even found that his attention span increased a fraction, so that a book he might have once put down to fetch another in its stead could lie open, cared for, present in his lap much longer than was usual. He didn't feel unhappy. In this other part of him, he didn't *mind* that she went out! How odd! And so he opted not to mind too much what Sarie really did. Something small was changing.

As Bibi, down the road and just around the corner, gathered up supplies for her brown fruit, Sarie told her husband that she and Agatha were going to make another visit. "A good thing for our daughter," she announced, rounding up the peach and lemon sweets that she had bought the day before. "She needs activity and walks." This, though a new concern for Sarie, Gilbert could in no way deny. Agatha, despite the lectures they received sometimes from Council folk—enormous Hazel Towson, most of all—did not go to school. She roamed. She hid in hollow places, sometimes scared her father. He could not but agree that Agatha might benefit from outings. As Sarie said, so plaintively, accusingly, because she liked to blame her husband for anything she could, "She has not even here the easy tree to climb." Sarie expected him to quibble.

But to her surprise: "Indeed," he said. "You're right." And so the two set off.

Once his daughter and his wife had made their way into the courtyard, he opened up the tin they kept in a corner of the kitchen and took out several bills, which he slipped into his pocket. He replaced the tin responsibly, then counted slowly to one hundred to make sure that no one would come back. Oh, he didn't mind this privacy at all! His skin, his limbs even felt good. Satisfied, he pulled on his socks and shoes and organized his hair so that it hid a great part of his scalp. He was going to buy a book.

Gilbert's stepping out into the courtyard, hand in pocket curled around his cash, coincided with the appearance of the Arab from the islands, tired Mr. Suleiman, from the light blue door of his own first-floor flat. Gilbert had just then been about to move with some determination directly towards the street, but now he paused, unhappy. He was not adept with neighbors, not at all. He hoped that Mr. Suleiman was not going to walk, too. What should a person say to an old man like that when one lived beside him? He'd known what to say to Arabs in the courthouse, how to make them wait—but things were different now, and that wouldn't quite do. He didn't like to think about two neighbors taking the same route, not saying a word. Uncomfortable, indeed. It was not, he thought, as if he could ever buy the Arab drinks at the Victorian Palm, or expect the same from him. *Arabs,* Gilbert thought with satisfaction, *are well known not to drink.* Mr. Suleiman, in bright-white robe and fine-stitched cap, fumbling with a cane, frowning at the sandy ground through spectacles done up with silver tape, occupied, thought Gilbert, quite another world. Shy, hoping that the darkness covered him, he hid behind the door.

Ah. It seemed that Mr. Suleiman was not planning a stroll. Instead, the narrow man made his slow way in the opposite direction, tottering towards the plum tree in the corner of the courtyard where the old Morris taxi stood. Once there, he set the walking stick against the fender and peered inside the cab. As Gilbert watched, the old man, half-bent in the sunshine, opened up the driver's door, which, crooked at the hinge, jogged down with a creak. He did not get inside — rested one palm on the frame and cocked his grizzled head. A little breeze picked up his gown and showed a slender bit of unfit, bony leg.

Gilbert shook his head. Watching from the darkness, he felt a little sorry for his neighbor, for the old dead Oxford cab. He thought, *Old men! Nothing works these days!* Perhaps Mr. Suleiman would find what he had come for, turn around, go back into his flat. Should Gilbert hide and wait? But the old man simply stood. A damson fell down from the tree and landed not far from his feet, but still he didn't move. Gilbert sighed. Wondering how long Mr. Suleiman would be there in the sun, communing with his car, he rubbed his fingers at the cash roll in his pocket. He didn't want to wait. *No,* he thought, *I mustn't let him stay me.* So that an onlooker might think he had not seen Mr. Suleiman and was therefore not being impolite at all, he held his breath and turned his head towards the building's wall. Without looking behind him, he marched into the street. *And now, now to find a book!* Released, he headed towards the sea.

As Gilbert walked under the awnings, hiding from the sun, Agatha and Sarie, seated comfortably beneath the fans at Hisham's Food and Drink, were waiting. Ismail and Ali, who now and then helped out a man who ran a shop of largely smuggled goods on Urasimu Road (a Mr. Essajee, who had enjoyed Majid's literary paper and been sad to see it fold), had been encouraged by their father to step their helping up. They'd started working every day, and on some days even took Habib. The boys came home sometimes at lunch but did not stay for long. At Hisham's, Sarie waited.

Agatha sipped passion juice through a red-white pinstriped straw and watched the sweet brews bubbling in their cases at the wall. Sarie ordered ice, the thick kind, kulfi, with cardamom and cream (which the Frostys did not make, which Sarie knew from long ago, Jilima, a cool place by Mukhtar's Drink Emporium), and eyed the clock above the door. Thinking of her husband's library, Sarie estimated that ten days of such treats for herself and her daughter were equal to a medium book, or a pair of heavy pamphlets. *It is my right,* she thought, with a new sort of satisfaction.

She looked down at Agatha. Her single daughter baffled her. She had never been quite certain what to *do* with Agatha, what one did with children (growing up with Sisters had not helped). Though she would not have refused any good things for her child, it wasn't quite that Sarie sought them out. But thinking now and then that Agatha had needs, deserved things, as *she* did, made her Sarie's ally. *We need something, too,* she thought.

Sometimes she made motherly attempts: at Hisham's, she tried giving Agatha a wink, but she was not rewarded. Agatha ignored her, and Sarie turned to the bright clock again, now tapping her heels against the tiles of the scuffed floor. Finally. Time turned. Mr. Jeevanjee would now be by himself—except, of course, for Tahir, who, though he had brought them all together, Sarie thought did not really count. She wiped Agatha's wet mouth with the corner of her dress, pushed their dishes to the edge of the long table, and took her daughter back into the street.

All this Bibi saw from Mansour House, where she was sitting on the balcony. When Hisham's door opened down there, she'd shivered, stopped her needle short. As a cook might keep an eye on cakes that still have some way to rise, she watched the two with care. She'd seen them come and go. She knew they'd gone to Mad Majid's that once. But she wasn't certain yet that this was a routine. She slipped the needle twice into her sheet to keep it safe and nar- rowed her sharp eyes. She saw that Sarie stepped not left but right, and was now taking her daughter up Mahaba Street. If only Bibi could keep track of the European woman's short lavender gown, if she saw them pass that mosque . . . ! Then she'd know that she was right. She watched. Indeed. *Eywah,* Bibi thought. *From there, from there to little Kudra House. Imagine, oh, yes. Yes! But isn't he insane?* She was so happily considering the British woman's fate in Majid Ghulam's house that she did not respond when Mama Moto called her down for lunch. She scooted to the balcony's edge, slipped each arm through a concrete-bounded heart, and, for just a moment, clasped her hands together. Mama Moto called again, but Bibi didn't answer. *Let Mama Moto wait,* she thought. *I've other foods to eat.*

The book stand Gilbert liked the most was managed by a Christian from Fufuka who stayed at the cathedral grounds and took his morning tea with the French and Belgian Sisters. The salesman, proud of his association, often said, *Que la paix soit avec vous* and *Que Dieu vous bénisse,* whether passersby bought books from him or not; he was apt as well to give out blessings in several local tongues, some he'd known himself, and some the Sisters taught. Like Sarie, Gilbert thought, the bookman, too, was given to inscrutable, surprising formulations, but from him these were charming. And also, he had style. The bookman wore a bright green fishing cap high up on his brow, to which he now and then affixed a modest paper bloom. And, even more important, his cho- sen volumes (some missing quite coincidentally from the Mission's well-stuffed shelves) often suited Gilbert. He felt buoyed by that hat, which he could see already, bobbing, from the corner. He felt free, satisfied, and pleased. *Today,* thought Gilbert, *I will make a find.*

Indeed, perhaps the fates colluded here to break a coming blow. Gilbert was in luck. For the price of two kilos of kulfi and a jug of passion juice, or a pair of canvas shoes (so Sarie would have said), he acquired for his collection, dust jacket and all, a rare volume called *The Happy Sons of Sindbad: Years of Arab Seamanship in the Very Bluest Sea,* by a Dutchman named DeFleur. The Christian man, because he liked to satisfy his customers, and also because Gilbert Turner was not any good at bargaining, beamed, too. Gilbert stepped away, new book shiny in his hand. The vendor tipped his hat.

Although the city's Central Post Office rose up just behind the table, Gilbert often visited the bookstand without checking for letters. The one correspondence he engaged in had a proper schedule: once a month, a letter and a wire; he knew when to expect it. Had it not been for *The Happy Sons of Sindbad*—a russet thing whose dust-coat showed an arty ship in ink, asail on a brown sea, and caused Gilbert to scan the harbor line for vessels like the one that graced his book—he wouldn't have gone in at all. On the wide and black-hatched water, Gilbert recognized three ngarawa riggers, the ever-present tugboat, a tanker (run aground and still for many years, like the Morris in their yard), and, hulking and cloud-white, a cruise ship in the distance. No dhows or mtepe ships. Nothing. Gilbert sighed. With no Arabian Sons heave-hoing on the rise, he turned, and there it was, before his open, disappointed eyes: the Post Office, an elaborate rose-columned thing behind a row of pines. Unaware that small acts sometimes bear big fruit, Gilbert registered the pillars and thought: *Let's try, why not, for fun,* and made his way inside.

As he entered that cool space, he felt businesslike and free. He liked going to the Post Office, taking up his key chain and moving past the service windows as though he had a purpose. Not seeking stamps or glue, he did not have to stand in line to face a surly teller with the strangeness that had come, it seemed to him, in the wake of Independence. Checking on his private letterbox, bypassing the queues, Gilbert did not have to feel, as he sometimes did, that he was like a party guest who, having stayed well past the end of things, is still, impolite but helpless, begging for his cake.

With *Sons of Sindbad* tucked beneath his arm, he sailed past the string of people who were waiting to buy stamps or make additions to their Post Accounts. As he sometimes did, he pretended that he was an archaeologist or a sociology professor expecting correspondence from a European college of repute. *Oh, Turner,* he thought gently to himself, imitating tones he heard in Kazansthakis on particularly good days, *you are a delicate and educated man.* The members of an especially long line moved grudgingly apart and made room for him to pass. Feeling wise and gracious, he smiled blandly at the air. Once at the wall of boxes, he located his own with a spare feeling of pride.

Our PO box! he thought. The sight of it reminded him that they *had* made a real place for themselves, he and complicated Sarie — and little Agatha, who shared his pallor, and, he dreamed, might when she grew up also share his love of heavy, wordy books. *Our box, 32.* Other Europeans, the temporary ones, had to get their letters at the Poste Restante, the place for miscellaneous mail that had no significant, no physical, address, no real match in the world. Official visitors, the Finnish engineers, the Chinese acrobatics coaches, German doctors, and the British officers as well (a whole new stash of them, still in charge of things, pretending they were not) picked theirs up at Embassies, forever overseen by gloomy attachés. But this! The Turners' very own. *Our SLP,* he thought, trying (like the nationalist he'd once been, for a time) the local acronym for size—the acronym, because the right words were too hard and he could not remember them without making a mistake. But, nonetheless, *Our little SLP.* And, unexpectedly, to top off Gilbert's pleasure, there was a letter in it.

He knew who it was from. Leaving their own box ajar, Gilbert leaned against the others. He tugged at the left thigh of his woolen trousers, bent one leg and crossed its ankle on its mate. He looked nonchalant and poised. Not from any college, this slender aerogramme. But, still, how nice to get some mail. Gilbert smiled and sighed. *Dear Great-Uncle James has written on a whim.* He thought: *We do light up his days.* The affection he had felt for his new book and for the coolness of the Post Office, for the three ngarawas in the sea, for his little family, spilled out onto the letter, moved across an ocean, a highly charged canal, a blistering blue gulf, some seas, flat lands (Sarie's), a final, choppy channel, to rivers and a brook, and settled on the man who had dropped this missive in the post. Uncle James had really been a savior.

Since Gilbert's postcolonial stash (relatively lavish, for a very little while) had finally expired, the inflows had been small: modest honoraria for some (rather clever, Gilbert thought) written meditations that had been taken by the History Club, and sums he charged occasionally if someone who remembered him wanted their accounts done. Sarie had once tried to give piano lessons, but she wasn't all that good, the students had been few, and Sarie was impatient. She had, as a matter of principle, not been interested in *work.* Hadn't getting married meant she would be cared for? What really kept them going, financed Gilbert's library, put beans and soap and now and then some dresses in their cupboards once the bank account was dry, was a small but regular stipend from Gilbert's only living relative in England: dear old Uncle James.

Uncle James had a special weakness: fond of the Geographical Society, he adored reports from what he called "the regions." As if it were something that a person without extraordinary means could easily take up, like *that,* as a hobby or a wish, Uncle James had wished as a young man to take up exploration. But real life had prevented him. In a family of gardeners, schoolteachers, and clerks, grand-nephew Gilbert Turner had come closer than anyone to braving the frontiers. Still, not *everyone* could say they had an adventurous relation in the wilds of Africa. Particularly one who'd *stayed,* after the great exodus, after all the Kenyans had come back with fear of Mau-Mau in their eyes, after the Ugandans snuck across the borders in such (so thought Great-Uncle James) grand, delicious fear. Not to mention those who bubbled up, more and more these days, from the southern end of that dim continent of blight! A relation who'd *withstood.* How *brave* of Gilbert Turner. And so he had responded to Gilbert's initial, desperate query with alacrity and pride.

His letters were reliably well written. The handwriting, as though he'd slipped a guide sheet beneath the aerogramme to keep his words in line, was always regular and neat. The sameness of these letters was a fundamental part of Gilbert's current life, which Gilbert understood as immutable and steady. As long as Uncle James wrote to them once a month, the Turners' lives would be as regular—not swank, not fine, but predictable and tidy.

He didn't stop to think: this letter was early. But once the tight, sealed thing was spread out in his hands, Gilbert felt the world tilt. This was *not* like all the rest. The words on this blue aerogramme were wrought of thick and angry ink. Gilbert could already see the exclamation marks. Aleap! At every other line! *Exclamation marks.* From a man who dealt in modest commas and light periods, and limited his questions, gentle and polite, to two lines at the end

(*How are the rains this year, then?* or, *Look in on the plains of Mbugakuu, will you, and tell me how they are. It's said they host spectacular migrations*) before signing himself off with an unobtrusive *Fondly,* or a *Yours.* What could have overcome him?

Gilbert felt hot and cold at once. He wished to bring his free hand to his cheek, but first he had to find a place for all of Sindbad's sons. He tried to press the book into the Turners' *SLP,* and couldn't (the box was narrow, small); he thought of holding it under his arm, and then between his thighs, but his arms and legs were weak. With a surge of irritation, he dropped it to the floor—an action which, though he didn't see it, raised some brows among the people who were standing in the line. Rocking slowly back and forth, he restrained the shiny volume with the instep of his shoe. His helpless tongue grew large. He shook.

Uncle James, of all amazing things, was *sending out a warning* (underlined). *I have, I fear, grown impatient* (darker) *with your stipend. After all,* Uncle James explained, *I am now retired* (a heavy period, gouged). Yes, Gilbert knew all that. Uncle James, a man whose hands and eyes and back had dealt in borders, beds, and hedges for over forty years, had in his retirement turned his knobby hands to painting things in oils: not the verdant scapes he'd managed, no, but—seas. *A hobby!* Gilbert thought. He'd even found it sweet. But suddenly it seemed that Uncle James *envisioned a career.* Gilbert, who had started to believe that he and only he could be the center of his uncle's sunset years, was shocked to read that Uncle James was preparing for a *show.* The newborn artist wrote: *I've been painting, as you know, and I am delighted* (softened hand, right here, the letters lighter than the rest) *to announce that I am having some success. But materials for this art, dear Gilbert* (deepening again, and dark) *are prohibitive, and for reasons that you must surely understand*—he did, he did—*not quite within my reach* (this underlined, again). Gilbert's eyes went round. Though he stood very still, he felt as if his face were being slapped, on one cheek then the other. He read on. *I don't suppose you know,* he read, *the cost of Damar varnish or of sable rounds, but they are very* (exclamation) *dear. And* (underlined) *even more so copal* (more exclamations here). Gilbert imagined his old uncle, whom he had not seen in thirty years, now small and hard and mean, in overalls in a dark room, surrounded in the fading light by a fleet of ocean pictures, brackish, sharp-legged easels rearing. The current work, in Gilbert's mind, was just an underpainting, but already it depicted sinking ships. And was that a distant fire, licking angry trees? He blinked. He took, to calm himself, a conscious breath of cool administrative air. His own thoughts were triple-underlined: *An artist? My stipend gone for paints?*

The intent of Uncle James's letter seemed all at once to Gilbert to be gushing like a hemorrhage from a wound that his own trembling fingers could not hope to stanch. He pressed one palm over the sheet and for an instant closed his eyes before looking down again. Unless Gilbert could show, Uncle James was saying now, *that there are reasons* (dash) *let me be perfectly* (in capitals) *explicit* (dash) *that there are* (underlined again) *quite compelling reasons . . .* Gilbert's eyes grew wide. As if he had been stuffed by unseen hands into a sturdy woman's corset, he felt his chest constrict. That "compelling" had been underlined three times caused Gilbert to shiver. His uncle's previous letters had been so regularly sweet, forgettable! So mild! But this feisty uncle was indignant: *Unless there are convincing reasons for you to keep your dear, courageous wife and children in the darkest continent of all, where things, we hear, are bad to worse each day, I will have no choice, dear boy,* (more lines) *but to suspend support.*

His courageous wife and children. Well, Sarie could be brave, indeed. But "children"? Had he, Gilbert wondered, then felt his stomach sink, allowed his uncle to believe that there were two, or three, perhaps, at least one of them a son? He groaned. And perhaps he had even—had he?—allowed his uncle to believe a dreamed-up son was also James, in honor of the man who corresponded so reliably from a cold city by the sea. Ashamed and frightened, he whimpered and read on: *What income I do have cannot be spent so freely on your supper without* (a dash) *hope of returns.* Gilbert found it hard to breathe. *Does he think our lives are easy here?* he thought. *Out here in the . . . colonies?* He stopped himself a moment. There *were* no colonies, not any longer, quite, but didn't Uncle James rather wish there were? And hadn't he imagined himself now and then as just the dashing and besieged adventurer his Uncle James would so have liked to see? Had he not done the man a service?

Gilbert was upset. Was a woman in the thing? A brazen one who bared rouged breasts for the sad old man when he wanted to paint mermaids, a crass, low girl with insalubrious designs on Uncle James's pension? Was his uncle being had? In short: Uncle James requested of his nephew *that some proof of the value of my too-generous support be provided me in your next letter. I suggest a business in which, should I be fully satisfied, I might* (those capitals, again) *perhaps invest. But I shall expect returns.* The skin of Gilbert's brow and cheeks went slick with perspiration. His mouth hung open, closed, and opened, like a fish behind a glass. He felt as though his heart (not pumping, and not thumping, as people said could happen) had simply left his body.

As he stood, a corpulent jaggery-colored man in a well-pressed navy suit stepped towards him, aiming for even-numbered *SLP* 48. He gestured towards the wall, which Gilbert's head and torso now obscured. "Excuse me," the man said. But Gilbert's ears were filled with wind. He stayed. The suited man (this Gilbert did not know) was, in fact, a real university professor. A populist at heart, with strong ideas about hierarchy and the nature of oppression, he had authored several essays on socialism's real, non-European roots and

was not a man to cross. He said again, "Excuse me!" Gilbert, looking up at last, was momentarily confused. The professor's British
accent was more refined and rarefied than any Gilbert could have
aped, in drunkenness or jest. He stared. The suited man stared
back. "Excuse me, *sir,*" this author said, making it quite clear that
he, and not the shivering figure holding to the aerogramme, was
worthy of the title. Gilbert's feet were locked; his spine a spike that
reached the belly of the earth. He did not move aside. Finally, the
professor nudged him roughly with his shoulder and reached out
with some force for the door of his own box.

Still clutching the letter but now, at last, uncoupled from the
floor (his spine dissolved, his frozen feet came free), Gilbert shifted
over, thinking, *That push was accidental.* Surely, Gilbert told himself,
looking down still, unable to focus on his feet or on the tiles, no
violence had been intended? He mustered an "Excuse me!" of his
own, a weak one. He let the big man by, but the historian was not
through. He scowled. Pointed to the volume on the floor. "And by
the way, sir. I say. I say, that" — the socialist professor was referring
to Gilbert's book on seamanship, which Gilbert's shoe had
scuffed — "that is not how one ought to treat a book." Gilbert
looked up at the owner of *SLP* 48 with a feeling of dismay, all his
skin atingle. *Sons of Sindbad,* far less sunny now than their author
had proclaimed, lost most of their charm. Post Office Box
Number 32 was no longer aglow. He closed it. Conscious of the
dark historian's eyes like knives along his back as he bent to take
the book, Gilbert pushed the aerogramme into his pocket, where it
began to boil.

As might have been expected, Gilbert ended up at the Victorian
Palm Hotel, where he ordered what he feared might be the last

beer of his life. As he reread and reread the odious aerogramme, he made the Congo Pilsner last, and called upon his brain. *Think, old man, now think!* He recalled that he had meant to purchase ointment for his back, and this time almost wept: *I can't afford it now!* The thought of looming poverty raised a triple itching in his skin. He sniffed. But with a sense that he was shriveling, growing very small, he did find, in a small place near his heart, the strength to tell himself that he must somehow, somehow, shape up and stand straight. What would the Mastersons and Brickmans think of him, Gilbert asked himself, *like this?*

❧Ten

At Kudra House, Tahir, assisted by the science book, explained to Agatha that planets moved around the sun, and the moon around the earth. "Equinox," he said. She brought a chair into the center of the room and helped him out of bed. "You sit down right here," she said. "I'm going to be the planets."

In the parlor, Majid and his guest had forgone tea. They were shyly sipping water from matching metal cups. Each of them felt hot. Majid Ghulam began to look at her and then away, and then at his own hands. Sarie felt her heart shake. Something had to happen. She couldn't bear staying like this. Taking, perhaps for the first time, her destiny in hand, she touched him on the arm. And next she asked her host if she could look into his bedroom. "I have seen your pleasing balcony," she said. "And also your nice parlor. But *Majid,*" she said, turning her big head slightly towards the hall, "could I—do you think?"

Majid, as if making certain he was where he thought he was, touched his mustache, then his hair. It was happening at last! What movies did not show. What he'd asked dead Hayaam to sanction. He breathed in from his toes up to his hair and brushed his shirtsleeve slowly. "Of course," he said. "Yes, of course you may. Come now." With a shining in his eyes as bright as Sarie's blue, he held her elbow in his palm and ferried her along. "Come *now.*" Majid Ghulam pushed open the door and let Sarie cross the threshold. As shameless as the siren Gilbert had dreamed up for his uncle, she turned down the bent nail on the door frame and enfolded Mad

Majid Ghulam Jeevanjee decidedly into her broad but very tender arms. The pressure was returned, and something in her sang.

The contract, wet, sincere, and cold, was sealed between them quickly, each one crying "Oh!" and "Oh!" as though continually surprised by their joint presence on the bed. Oh! They did it sitting up, not even hidden by a blanket, not even shielded from the green eyes of the room by a drawn mosquito net. The two took on their coupling as if, sitting close together, they had discovered four trapped birds among their clothes and, in a rising frenzy, tried to set them free. Oh! Happy, ragged exhalations! And then, the final ohs, much softer, quiet, still. A fattened, final silence and a series of small shudders, each gentler than the last, a look right in the eyes, no shyness. They rolled quietly apart.

They didn't speak of it. Did not dissect the thing. Sarie's enervated skin gradually grew chill, as damp ground does when the red sun sinks at last. Majid sat beside her. For a long, slow moment, he did not open his eyes. He felt: emptied at the core, as though a cleaning crew had come, removed everything he knew, and hosed his insides down. Sarie felt a tenderness consume her. She waited. At last, Majid Ghulam reached out and gave her thigh an earnest squeeze. Eyelashes aflutter, a bit more formal than Sarie had expected—though she didn't, really, know what to expect at all—Majid Ghulam said, "Thank you." Sarie ran her hand across her forehead from the left side to the right, as though combing back the skin. She smiled at him and tried, as Majid rose, to pull him close to her. She would have liked for him to rest a moment, head upon her shoulder. But Majid squeezed her thigh again and got up from the bed. She watched him fasten his old trousers. At her frown, "I'll come back," he said.

Sarie remained still. Majid gathered up a hair comb and a towel (threadbare, with a faded rosy print), and slipped out of the room.

At first, with Majid gone, Sarie felt alone. She wrapped her arms around herself. Such closeness in a coupling! Such loneliness just after! It was like being given, without notice, extra body parts to manage; growing speedily accustomed from desire to their weight and warmth and style; and next, just when it feels right, suffering a graceless amputation that excises much more than was brought. She heard water tumbling, splashing, from the bathroom, wished that she could see him as he bathed. She wondered, as she would for a long time, what his limbs looked like unclothed.

In the small bedroom's green light, she felt the air around her as a substance. She became aware of dust motes, the wrinkled look of things. She heard the rumble of the street as one hears a distant river, and was glad for the room's height. She thought how far away it seemed—all this—from her own apartment, with its books, Gilbert's favorite chair, his pictures, and the broken, dead piano that took up so much space. Prepared, almost, to see things from it that she had not seen before, she rose to look out of the window into Majid's street.

Out there, three men ferried lengths of wire down the road: road, men, wire, all aglint in the ebbing afternoon. In a shady place along the sidewalk, below a scarlet awning, the man with the pot-belly and slim ankles turned the crank of his cane press and sold a frothy glass to a woman dressed in black who had just come from the market. A boy wove down the street, hawking colored images of Jesus, Parvathi, and the Kabbah tied together with white string. High above the fray, Majid Ghulam's new lover wiped her face and cupped her rugged chin. She stretched her mouth and cheeks, felt her skin go taut. *Majid Ghulam looks from this window every day.* She yawned and reached out for her dress.

Once Majid was fresh again and Sarie's top was buttoned, she called into Tahir's room for Agatha. "Tahir's sitting up now," Agatha announced. He was sitting on the chair still, had liked playing the part of the hot sun while Agatha, now Jupiter, now Mars, revolved. Sarie smiled at them. "Very good," she said. "Come on." Agatha helped him back over to the bed. Majid found a basket, into which he placed four bunches of bananas. "You like these, I think," he said to Sarie's little girl. She did. She thanked him, and Sarie, looking down at her, felt proud. Agatha took charge of the basket. Neck tight with the effort, arms long and stretched against her chest, she held it with both hands and struggled to make sure her feet could move beneath it. Sarie thanked him, too, and said she would be back—then, wondering if she shouldn't have (being clothed again, having been bare only once, brings a special kind of doubt), she added, almost sadly, "If that will be all right." Majid Ghulam smiled, nodded with his eyes, then looked quietly away.

From his bedroom window, he watched Sarie and Agatha make their way down Libya Street. Agatha was tired. She did battle with the basket but refused, with quick shakes of her head, Sarie's efforts to assist her. As Majid trembled at the window, a pair of yellow fruit, plump and bright, no longer than a thumb, spilled out from the basket to wobble in the road. Sarie didn't notice. A bit farther down, she tried to help again, but this time Agatha turned sharply from her and made an ugly face. Sarie, tired, too, made a show of looking up, at anything but Agatha. She meaningfully stared, instead, at the awnings of the hardware stores and tea shops. Agatha continued to make faces, and Sarie, well aware of it, ignored her. Surprised, a little pleased, Majid thought, *Mrs. Turner is still young.*

He felt oddly bereft—not as he had for Hayaam, of course. Death, true love, was something else. A mistress is no wife. But, still, he surely felt relieved of something he had not had time to savor, felt a sweetness-sadness, something like regret. *There* they were, there, the girlish two, receding. There *she* was, the woman who had stroked and pulled at his most private skin. They moved past the white-tiled doorway of R. Tea Shop, became too small for him to see.

From the boys' room he heard Tahir call. He went to him, peeled the sheet back carefully, and lifted him over his shoulder like a carpet. Aware of his son's lightness, he wondered how much the missing length of leg, from calf to toes, might measure on a scale. *Much less than a sack of flour,* Majid thought. *Less than a half-used bolt of cloth.* And yet what a difference it made. How cold his son's skin was. He took him to the bathroom, where, holding his boy by the shoulders, he looked carefully away. As Tahir did his business, Majid thought of Sugra, hoped she'd come back in the morning. Hoped that she would help.

Just before the mosque, Agatha refused once more to be assisted with the basket. Sarie lost her temper. She was feeling late, exposed. *I have done it now,* she thought. *It. La chose. The thing.* The private glow she'd felt had changed, had settled, was now more like a stain. She wondered if Gilbert would look at her and know. To Agatha she said, "Why are you so difficult!" She squeezed her daughter's shoulder with a vigorous hand, to stop her, take the basket from her arms. Agatha wriggled free. "Give me those bananas," Sarie said (did she also, missing his light hands, wish herself to hold what *he* had given, things that came from Majid's house?). She tried again to pull the handles from Agatha's tight grasp and this time gained some ground.

Before the mendicants, Agatha had stopped. Three of them, the regulars, whom they both knew by sight: a tiny woman, head tucked under her arm, sleeping, drooling silver; a man with one eye missing and one blind was propped precariously against the wall like an unrepaired umbrella. His unseeing eye was blue. A second woman, weaving palm fronds on the ground, made snapping sounds with her wet mouth.

Agatha did *not* have a well-developed moral sense. That is, she didn't think, We *have a basket of bananas and* these *people are hungry*. She was no gracious child. But she had a sense of shame and knew for certain that to refuse her mother's predatory fingers there, right there in front of the three beggars, would cause her some embarrassment. The sleeping woman might awake; the blind-eyed man might stare, and the sucking woman with the palm frond in her lap might stick her sharp tongue out. All at once, she gave up the bananas so easily and unexpectedly that Sarie lost her balance, flailed to keep herself and the basket from falling to the ground. "Well!" she said. And watched, abandoned, as Agatha raced ahead to make her own way home.

When Sarie came into the apartment, Agatha sat at the piano, thumping softly at the untuned keys with her left hand, right arm stretched above her like a swaying water plant. Unkindly, without looking up, Agatha asked her mother if she'd dropped any bananas. Sarie grunted. She was sweating. She wished there were a looking glass in that front room, or a window lit up with a darkness that could show her her own face. She smoothed her hair, felt her nose and brow for shine. She held her chin a moment. Then she took a breath, on the airy heels of which there came a Majid-Ghulam-Jeevanjee-shaped pang. *Do I look like a woman who has just been with a lover? Do I smell like love?* She thought for a moment of what love smelled like, sniffed lightly at herself, and hoped instead that she gave off a smell of street and city sweat. She remembered the bananas. *These fruits have a scent*. She filled her fists with them before stepping down the hall.

*   *   *

As she crossed into the bedroom, Gilbert's body jerked. Lying on the bed, socks off, hands over his eyes, Sarie's husband bleated. He was suffering from hiccups. The spasms, having grabbed him by the collar as he left the Palm with Uncle James's letter weighing down his heart, had not yet let him go. Sarie gave her crumpled husband the heavy kind of frown that results from a desire to conceal the tender thing. "What is wrong with you? Gilbert. What is it you have?" Gilbert only moaned.

Sarie said, "What's that silly noise?" Gilbert peered at her between two parted fingers. A cruel hiccup shook him. "Oh, Sarie," Gilbert said, "an awful thing—has happened." He covered both eyes with one hand and with the other searched beneath the pillow for the aerogramme, which he found and held out to his wife. "Read this."

Sarie was suspicious. *He's acting. He wants me to find him sympathetic.* How like her husband to demand all of her attention when she, instead, was the one who needed love. In defense, she set her eyes and cheeks as solidly against her skull as she could manage, made all of herself flat. She could not bear, just then, to find an ailing Gilbert worthy of her kindness. "I do not mean the letter," Sarie said, sitting far away from Gilbert on a stool before the dressing table. She tossed four bright bananas lightly on the bed as if Gilbert were a monkey she was hoping to distract. "*Tiens.* Take these." Gilbert, still covering his face, did not look out to see what she had offered. Sarie sniffed and took up a banana. Mouth full and damp with fruit, she said, "I mean the noise. What is wrong with you?"

A hardness in her voice, so different from the softness and also from the sobbing Gilbert thought that he had wished for, did some tonic work. Something like cold water on a distraught person's face. Gilbert slowly took his hand down from his eyes. Careful, he sat up against the headboard. "Hiccups, Sarie. I have—a case of hiccups." These he demonstrated, ably.

Sarie rolled her eyes. She quickly thought: *A blushing man; a man with rashes on his skin; a man who gets the hiccups. What a husband. Quel mari I have.* But there were some things Sarie could not do. Her nurse's bent prevented her from cruelty. She knew very well that Gilbert's hiccups usually came with other pains that cannot be outdone by clove-brews, salty things or bars of sulphur soap. She thought briefly about sugar, water swallowed backwards, sudden scary noise. "Hiccups, *tiens.* What is it, then, what's wrong?" She considered shocking him by saying, "I have taken on a lover!" but did not. Gilbert, tired, and resentful because he felt in this condition that he merited attention, spoke the next thing rather sharply. "I'd like to tell you why, if you could bring yourself to li—sten."

Sarie, too mixed up just then to feel surprised that Gilbert (who hated, hated, confrontations!) had just accused her of neglect, sniffed again and took the light blue thing from him. She read. As her face changed, Gilbert imagined he could see the fine hairs at her nape and temples stand on end. This pleased him; surely she cared, too. His squawks subsided for a moment. With the sausage of his tongue, he pushed against the twisting in his throat, tried to breathe in, slowly. He remembered that he had not eaten since a modest lunch of beans. "Well?" he said. Briefly safe, he took up a yellow fruit. They might do him good.

Sarie, letter on her lap, examined the pale sheet. She blinked, and bit her lip. Yes, she could see why Gilbert was upset. But, having just come from another bed, she could not support him fully. She had no wish either to soothe him or to make him feel she understood his trouble (their trouble. She wished it to be *his*). As he had been, she was moved by Uncle James's punctuation; she chose to comment on this first. "He is angry! Look at that!" she said,

without moving, without making any gesture to show Gilbert
what she meant. "Yes, look at that." She meant the vividness of it,
the wildness of the writing.

Gilbert felt his wife had missed the point. He moved a little on
the bed. A hiccup came from him. "Did you — did you read it?
The part about — the money." Of course Sarie had. But she wasn't
ready to discuss it. Among the heavy curls and towers of the letters
and the patches of spilt ink, Sarie sought a weapon, and she found
one. *I cannot support your wife and children any longer.* Sarie thought a
moment. She took this very personally. *Children?* Agatha was all
they'd managed, the only one they had. *One* child. Had Gilbert let
the man believe that she had borne a brood? Three children, even
four, and boys, moreover, so Uncle James would send along more
money? Worse, had Gilbert meant to put her through that swollen
business once again? Did he *want* more than one child? What could
that plural mean?

Gilbert hiccupped loudly. His hips and chest rose up in concert
from the bedding in a high, unmanaged jerk. Sarie noticed that her
husband's feet, high-arched, fat-toed, landed sideways on the sheet
like two fleshy letters C. He jerked again, again. Each hiccup
yanked his big toes towards him in a spasm, thrust the eight remaining digits back. She wondered if he knew how strange, how
ridiculous, his feet looked. "Gilbert," she said, loudly, leaning forward, a banana in her hand. She wished he would stop moving.
"Gilbert!" The sharpness of her voice did still him. Breath free for
a moment, Gilbert, hoping once again for gentleness and wondering if he'd get it, peeked out rather gingerly between a forefinger
and thumb. A soft bleat came from his lips. *"Au pluriel?"* she said.
When Sarie spoke to him in French, Gilbert knew that she was
moving back from him, receding, looking at the world from a van-
tage point he could not share — one from which he and every-

thing he stood for was foreign and disdained. "Gilbert." She poked
her husband's trousered leg with the unpeeled part of her banana.
"You told him we had children, *au pluriel?*"

Once he'd woken the next day, Gilbert, struggling still with
pockets of trapped air, unsure of his breath, went nonetheless directly to the Frosty-Kreem, where, he thought, he might be
treated kindly. Because it was a Saturday, the place was overrun; he
had to wait outside. The air was bland and silky, swollen and too
warm. The morning light glowed dull. In the grayish gloom, behind twenty-seven boys and girls who formed a thick, unruly line
outside the door, he waited on the pavement for over half an
hour. Several pairs of parents—women in approaching middle
age, broad-torsoed in their shining weekend wear, mustachioed
men with canes—watched their offspring proudly. An older man
with spectacles and the refined mien of a schoolmaster laughed
kindly with the daring ones who jockeyed for positions closest to
the door. Schoolboys in short-pants, girls in colored dresses made
of knees and elbows, they jostled one another, shrieked. Gilbert
stood behind them trying to look stern, arms folded on his chest.
But he was tortured, still, ungallantly, by sporadic closures of his
throat.

Near him, a lean boy with early stubble on his cheeks and a
comely curve in his oiled hair announced that he felt rich enough
this Saturday to purchase something other than a cone ("An Italian
cup! Pink and brown and white!"). A round girl with fifty-two
small braids huddled on her scalp (Gilbert counted, to pass time)
pointed the boy out to her companion; they frowned in his direction. Someone said, "Thinks he is a Jeevanjee! A Topan! *Arre baba!*"
and a tiny boy in short-pants who had been attempting to sneak

past Gilbert in the line paused in his attempt to let his mouth fall open at the sound of so much change.

A Jeevanjee. Gilbert felt oppressed. So much glee, children with new coins hard and bright in their hot hands, so much noise, so much Saturday behavior! He scanned the young, thrilled crowd; its members, he was suddenly, bitterly, quite sure, had more funds than he could even dream. *Millionaires and capitalists,* he thought. *Each and every one.* His gaze settled on a parent in a dark blue tailored suit whose neatly combed mustache gleamed bluish like wet silk. The man raised a soft, clean hand up in the air against a band of flies (which scattered!); at his wrist a gold watch shone. And Gilbert, lost, abandoned by the world, said quietly between his teeth: "Parasites, each one."

His stomach hurt. Desperate for Sarie's company, for talk, for something kind to make him feel less fear, he had been hiccupping all night. But Sarie's sleep had been so firm that when he tapped her three times on the shoulder, on each occasion offering a new term of endearment ("Sarie-love?" "Dear?" "Sweetheart?"), she had not even groaned, or pushed his hand away.

When he finally made it to the door and stepped into the Frosty-Kreem, he was, as always, startled by the coolness of the place and by how sound was different there. Though the customers were tightly packed and many, their voices came out muffled, and this softness was principally due to one of the Frosty-Kreem's two defining features: a herd of multicolored animals—plush, crocheted, and furry—that hung down from the ceiling. Yellow monkeys, red and orange kittens, polka-dotted donkeys, a dozen vivid zebras, mute themselves, suckled at the people sounds. The clash and clink of spoons on bowls, the drizzle of cold coins, the trilling of the metal bell, had a weird, dry softness to them. Behind the scarlet counter, Kazansthakis, dispensing chocolate and vanilla cones with what looked like eight quick hands, was plush and soft himself. *A bear,* thought Gilbert idly. *My friend would be a bear.* The Frosty King did not speak to him, but he was sensitive to changes in the air—to *grown-ups* in a room—and he noted Gilbert's presence the moment he came in. He'd deftly slipped a cone to Mrs. Frosty (a pink one, for a change) and asked her please to place it into Gilbert Turner's hands so he'd have something to do.

Behind the door, pressed against the wall, Gilbert folded— *Like an aerogramme,* he thought—each time a set of boys and girls came in and each time a set went out. He hiccupped, hiccupped, still. With each attempt to press the cone against his mouth, his insides tightened and his jagged throat shut down. Some children noticed him and stared, elbowed one another. Their close attention was difficult for Gilbert to withstand because (and this was feature two) the Frosty-Kreem's four walls each boasted a mirror. A single laughing child was therefore 4, or 16, 64, 256, a staggering, incalculable repetition beneath the breeding toys. He saw himself, himself, himself, and them, and them, and them, the back of Mr. Frosty's head as well as its red front, again, again, again. The reflections made him dizzy. Against them all, Gilbert closed his eyes. By the time the rush died down and Kazansthakis stopped to wipe the counter, Gilbert's ice cream, uneaten for the spasms, had melted thickly all across his hands. His pale brown eyes were red.

It was Mrs. Frosty who gave Gilbert the push. He told her almost everything. The threat. How he needed but could not imagine having an idea for a business, something for his selfish Uncle James, to keep the money coming. How he couldn't, couldn't, no, how it was all beyond him and how he couldn't face it, did not know what to do. Mrs. Frosty smiled. Child of Polish prisoners of war, she had a few ideas about emerging from misfortune. Seated on a leather stool, rag in hand, eyes bright, Mrs. Frosty said to Gilbert: "Agreeing to a change is hard. You will feel that you are getting your fat feet into a pair of shoes that doesn't fit."

With Mr. Frosty's love of talk, and her hours turning cream, it wasn't often that she got to tell anybody anything. She didn't care for most of Mr. Frosty's friends—the French couple (too pious!) and the Danish engineers (she thought of them as boys, so arrogant and careless!). But there was something about Mr. Turner, who always looked like a lost thing though he had seen (she thought) so much—something about Gilbert that could turn her talking on. *This man,* she thought, *likes to listen.* Well. He liked listening to *her.* She was always very gentle.

" 'Shoes?' " The Frosty King brought Gilbert a washcloth for his hands and patted Gilbert's back when a hiccup snapped his throat. "What does Mrs. Frosty tell you of the shoes?" He set to straightening the plush green monkeys and a tiger that had, in all of the excitement, clung to one another. "Don't listen to my husband, Mr. Turner," Mrs. Frosty said. "*He* can't remember how it happened. He's forgotten all my work." The Frosty King blinked absently at her, smacked Gilbert on the back, and slid away into the storage room to check on their reserves.

"What you have to do," said Mrs. Frosty—golden eyebrows arched, generous torso settling nicely on the Bakelite before him, "is to make a working plan. An idea for the uncle." Mrs. Frosty's voice was clear and high and warm. Gilbert was aware of her reflection in the walls. He managed not to see himself; instead, he saw an army, a regiment of brave and handsome women, buxom, kind, determined only to help *him.* Mrs. Frosty and her loving twins and triplets. She spoke wisely again, smiling all the while.

"You need an idea. But here's what you must do." She pressed her hands against the counter and stretched her fingers out. Leaned in conspiratorially and said, "If you want a last thing from your uncle, Mr. Turner, you must make it sound . . . like smashing!" She slapped the Bakelite. He started. "Smashing!" she said. "Like a fortune." She leaned in. "Believe that something very big, so big, is going to happen. Surely going to. Because *you* will make it so."

When she half closed her pale eyes, Gilbert saw the roundness, the smoothness of her eyelids, and was moved. He closed his own eyes for a moment, and there he had a vision. He saw plump, delightful Mrs. Frosty unpin her coffee-colored hair and stretch her thick arms towards the Frosty King on an evening filled with moonlight and the ruby shine of leaves. He saw Kazansthakis look up from his account books and move towards Mrs. Frosty like a long, unhurried, and inevitable train. How safe those two must be! What he saw in the temperate space behind his eyes—the certainty in her, reaching for her man, the able tilt of Mr. Frosty's arms—inspired Gilbert Turner. When the breathing, warmer, living Mrs. Frosty placed her hand on his, her touch was like a shock. Gilbert came back to the Frosty-Kreem and looked at her again. He blinked. "Believe in it," she said. She lowered her round voice. "That's how I make Mr. Frosty do all the things I want."

A strand of hair had snuck out from her bun to make an s-shape at her throat. Gilbert's hand went damp. She said, "You know what I mean." And Gilbert thought he did. "Think big." He moved his hand from hers and uncurled his thick fingers. Yes. He felt a good deal better. While Mrs. Frosty tugged at her soiled apron and put her hair where it belonged, he breathed in and he breathed out. He opened his mouth wide and waited, but no cruel hiccup came. *Believe in it,* he thought.

Kazansthakis came back into the parlor and gave Gilbert some ice cream to take home. "Pistachio Promenade," the Frosty King announced. And then, on seeing that the wobbly guest was leaving, said, with a pout: "So soon?" He would have asked about the boy, the mystery father, and what Gilbert had learned; he'd been hoping for a story to wrap up the afternoon. But Gilbert, apparently recovered, said, "I really ought to go," and Kazansthakis sighed, looked elaborately dejected, which Gilbert appreciated more than he could say. Mrs. Frosty stepped towards him and squeezed his suddenly firm arm. "You'll see," she said. "You will think of something." He felt her sweet breath on his face and briefly thought of cherries. "And now," she said, "you must hurry home." She gestured to the bag he held. "Before it melts again."

Eleven

Gilbert returned to Mchanganyiko Street with a vigor in his step. The ice cream box was heavy at his wrist, but he felt anchored by its weight. He liked to think of it, frozen at the heart but softening, its slickening exterior. The visit had renewed him: Mrs. Frosty, saying, "Believe that it can happen!" and the theatric Frosty King, so sad to see him leave. The city streets looked sweet. In Gilbert's tender state, the house crows shifting back and forth along the sagging power lines seemed remarkable and fine. The boys on bicycles—who made road crossings a danger, who hooted now and then at white men because they were no longer what they'd been and hooting was no crime—seemed charming as they never had: full of derring-do. Gilbert, moving, so he thought, towards some derring-do himself, tried a hearty smile. Waiting patiently for an opening among them, he thought as older people cannot help themselves but think (of younger ones, as to the vagaries of life): *They have no idea.*

He didn't, either, curse the cars. In fact, he took some time to look at them, which he very rarely did, or did only to grunt and wish that they were few. The flattish Fiats and arched Mercedeses, fussing, gurgling, others tat-tat-tatting uncertainly along and others all ajerk, didn't bother him at all. They caused him neither envy nor a headache. These cars were not new; used and dented, imported long ago and left, they were relics, like the house crows, and thus seemed oddly noble. For once he didn't think of them as *traffic,* meant to splatter him with mud or fill his chest with fumes.

Instead, he felt a playful sympathy for them. They'd been left behind, like him. *These old things have suffered!* He found himself admiring chrome—still shining—the variously styled grilles, the ample silhouettes. There an Austin, here a Ford, far off a wheezing Scout, a (once spectacular) Bel Air, at last, a Land Rover, moving like a box. Marveling at their aweless, resolute procession, he briefly felt as if he were participating in the motions of something greater than himself. Taking valiant breaths of dieseled air, he noticed, perhaps for the first time, that even city fumes could not suppress the hardy tang of sea. What had Mrs. Frosty done to him? What a fresh mood he was in!

After crossing each wide road, Gilbert looked around. The city appeared gracious, welcoming—*munificent,* he thought. At every curb, he found that he was smiling. At Seafront Road and Freedom Street, on the roundabout that held the sober, nearly life-sized statue of a shiny native soldier bent over a gun, Gilbert tipped his head and closed his eyes in homage to the fortitude of men. He thought of Mrs. Frosty's hair, her bosom. How very kind she was. Because all women he considered (when he did) led Gilbert to Sarie, who somehow was the measure of all things, he saw in his mind Sarie's throat, her back (still muscular, he thought), her still-nice brawny legs . . . though he and she were growing—weren't they?—old. He imagined himself resting on her chest, stroking her long neck. What if he were to come up with, as Mrs. Frosty had suggested, a really big idea? What if he, relying on himself at last, developed an idea and then put it to work? Perhaps, he thought, perhaps! What would Sarie think of him? What would life be like? What would the Thorntons, with their jet-setting carnations, and the super ex-colonials in the well-tiled mansions, think?

Gilbert was aware of feeling light, of feeling nearly good—and as he approached their crumbling complex, he was momentarily confronted with something in himself that was so near to happiness he was reluctant to go up. Could he go first to the Palm? His mood was bright but fragile. Perhaps these feelings were a sham, would fade the moment he got home. Would Sarie laugh at him again? Would she remind him of the rash along his back? Would his hiccups return? He stopped a moment on the pavement, stretched his fingers, wound his wrists. Would Sarie tease him for the little lies he'd told Great-Uncle James, for the boys he said they'd had? But, still beaming, Gilbert opted to be brave. He and Sarie might not be, he told himself, *a proper king and queen,* but the Pistachio Promenade would surely not survive a stroll back to the harbor for a beer. *Which, old man,* he told himself, *you'll be having plenty of, once the business is in place. If Uncle James is pleased. Which he must—he will—be. Yes, of course he will.*

He marched into the courtyard, to their block, and up three flights of steps. On the way, he let himself envision a good future in which he took Sarie to the shore at Scallop Bay for picnics, perhaps across the channel to those low and sparkling islands for a swimming afternoon. *She might like that,* Gilbert thought. He even, briefly, considered little Agatha: *We'll order books from England!* They'd been right to teach her; she did like to read. There was something sweet in that, the image of a father giving his girl-child a book. He nodded to himself. In the better life he was imagining, he would drink whatever drink he pleased, and stand his friends to more. Oh, he hoped Sarie would be kind. He'd been through so much! But when Gilbert reached the landing, his heart sank to his heels: he could hear, as if the mighty woman had been holding to his collar and shouting in his face, Jim Towson's great wife.

Sarie opened the front door and lunged at Gilbert with both arms. Her freckled skin was flushed. Her hair—never tightly bound, mind you, but, still—was severely out of place. She was in a panic. "Gilbert, you are here!" she said brightly, loudly, like a person in a play. She pulled him past the threshold. "Look!" she said. "It's wonderful, *n'est-ce pas?*" It wasn't wonderful at all; Sarie didn't mean it. It was horrid. It was part of their life here by which both of them felt harmed. But what was she to say? "Mrs. Hazel is here, too." Gilbert loosed his arms from Sarie's grasp and winced. *Why now?* he thought. *Why now?*

Hazel Towson, British Council volunteer, founder of Auxiliaries, though the time for them was past, was the kind of woman who, some persist in thinking, does well in the tropics. Energetically committed to the doing of good works, convinced that Europeans had a reputation to uphold, she could not leave well enough alone. Hazel, as she never failed to mention, came from people who'd had farms. Good, hardworking stock. A Woman with Her Head on Straight. And muscles. A Daughter of the Soil. As such, Hazel Towson had Ideas about what people like herself—what Europeans— were, and these she did her energetic best to implement. The Turners were a challenge to her vision.

Hazel, here's the rub, did not like to see a European (as she put it) *uninvolved*. Nor did she like to see them shabby. Shabbiness in Europeans, Hazel Towson knew, was the result of laxity and lack— lack of fortitude, ambition; a failure on their part to *recognize* them- selves. Degeneracy. Shabbiness, Hazel believed, was foreign. Without confronting their own nature as it should be and accepting it— without *self-actualization*—Europeans in the tropics could get lost. Risked not counting any longer. Inattention to one's duty would result (the Turners, case in point) in only downward spirals, fraught with shame and poverty, and, probably, disease. The way out of downward spirals, Hazel thought, the fuel for upward ones, was action, and more of it. For all her brethren in these parts, she knew, there was a special place; and, she knew this in her bones, it was Hazel's destined work to find out what it was and—with enthusiasm, grace, and a firm and knowing hand—steer the lost ones towards it.

Hazel had of course attended several garden parties at which Gilbert Turner's wife had spoken of her past and, like the others, had thought Sarie starkly out of turn. But she had not reacted exactly like the rest. She had coughed and shuddered once or twice for show, but *she,* unlike the other ladies (towards each of whom she exercised a lucid pity for their respective failings), knew strength when she saw it.

In Hazel's murky but determined view, Sarie had not started out with the same benefits, the pedigree, that Hazel herself had, and on top of that had languished far too long in hopes of matrimonial ease. Women of her class were, however, not meant for such leisure, waiting to be cared for without using their hands. A wealthy woman might, a person who was delicate and fine, who could expect to be looked after. But Sarie Turner was not fine. Sarie Turner, Hazel knew, was deeply in the wrong about who she thought she was. Look at those big arms! Those feet! She was meant to *work!* With the proper attitude, and practice, Hazel knew, something in the woman could be fierce and maybe even fine. Something Could Be Done.

Hazel thought that Sarie should return to nursing natives. Not for pay, of course; fine or not, white women had to be above that. This time as a *volunteer.* Sarie should be *charitable* and *active,* and everything would change. For it was energy, not money—*devotion,* and not pay—that would swing the Turners' fortunes. Oh, Hazel understood the ruin loans could bring. Money was, she knew, what Sarie Turner wanted and what Gilbert Turner was unable to provide, but it wouldn't help these two. If a person just behaved as was their lot, could accept the *spirit* that History bequeathed them, the dust would settle in their favor. And there was also this: while Hazel Towson always publicly deferred to men, she knew very well that it was women, not the colonels or the adjuncts or the dashing attachés, who upheld the real standards. Who kept things going right. And look at Gilbert Turner. A perfect sorry mess! Sarie Turner was thus for Hazel Towson a precious, urgent charge.

As Gilbert stood—his inner self collapsing—on the threshold of his home and passed the softening parcel to his wife, Hazel, who'd been speaking as he came, went on without a pause. Yes, Hazel knew he had arrived, and she would eventually greet him. But she had begun a little speech, and—as moral women should—would end it, undeterred. ". . . national crises like the one we face" —she meant Independence— "require strength from each of us."

Sarie, leading Gilbert to the sofa by a shirtsleeve, nodded blankly, and said, "Yes." Gilbert held out a limp hand, which Hazel, speaking all the while, took up and brandished with the strength of seven men. "We must all do our part," she said. While Hazel pumped his fragile hand, Gilbert felt, from the strong set of her shoulders, a ferocious energy: the shove of clamping dams, iodine campaigns, the rousing force of speeches made through loudspeakers that functioned. The vigor of another world he would have once liked open to him, the world that kept him wishing for the Club at Scallop Bay. But before Hazel Towson, everything in him recoiled. Mrs. Hazel Towson (never Mrs. Jim, as other wives had been: Mrs. Gerald Brickman, Mrs. Osgood Hill) was the skirted incarnation of the District Officers whose strength had made him quake—a woman with a vision, *many* visions, and a pointed disapproval for men like Gilbert Turner. He knew that Hazel Towson thought he'd lost his place in History because he lacked the stomach. *She thinks,* he told himself defensively, *that I'm holding Sarie back.* And here he surreptitiously recalled the pleasure he had felt with Mrs. Frosty, with the house crows and the cycle-boys, the cars. *Little does she know,* he thought, *that I'm about to make my mark.* When Hazel finally fixed her eyes on him and smiled, her mighty teeth appeared to him as large and square as tombstones.

Having seated herself handsomely in Gilbert's favorite chair, Hazel now addressed him. It was sometimes best to fill the husband in. In her fierce and even boom, she explained, as she had to Sarie, that her Brave Women's Auxiliary was presently engaged in an attempt to vaccinate each native infant in the country against a regiment of ills. She'd come to enlist Sarie. Gilbert's hot ears withered. He tried to look away but found, as usual, that Hazel Towson's gaze was difficult to shake. "Oh, very nice, very nice," he said. "I'm sure." When Sarie sat beside him on the sofa, he was grateful for her weight. Hazel talked and talked, and Sarie, prompting, pinched him now and then. "Oh, yes, I see," he said. And, "My, how grand."

Though they kept a modest box of Nanjis in the kitchen, Sarie, Gilbert noticed, had not offered her guest biscuits. Aware that Mrs. Towson might later advertise the absence of sweet things in the Turner household to people whose business it was not, he nonetheless privately approved. *We'll have to buckle down,* he thought, *until our ship comes in.* Hazel paused to catch her breath. A fly landed on her shoulder and she squashed it. The motion made him shiver. *Oh, why, why,* he asked himself, *did she have to come today?* She was inauspicious on all days, a cloud, a force to be escaped. But to have Hazel Towson pop up from the suburbs on this very day, after he'd felt really good and hopeful, briefly —*to have her come to talk about our destiny*—seemed a dangerous sign. He told himself he would pretend she wasn't really there. He might leave the room, he thought. But Sarie wouldn't let him.

In a momentary stillness, Sarie tried to say her piece. "Gilbert!" She wanted him to help her. Wide-eyed, putting on the gentle voice that meant she thought Hazel was a fool, Sarie laid her hand on Gilbert's knee and said, "Mrs. Hazel, Gilbert, thinks that I must stick needles in the babies!" She shook her head in wonder. "Help me, now. What can I say to that?" Gilbert shivered, ached, recalled the garden parties, and felt torn sharply in two between Hazel Towson and his wife. *Needles in the babies! What will she say next?* But, unable to name it, he also recalled painfully that he'd once been in love. *Sarie needs assistance from me,* Gilbert thought. *She's depending on her man.*

Mrs. Towson coughed. "Not quite that, I'm sure," she said. "Your Sarie, Mr. Turner . . . I must say. We're not indiscriminate, you know. And Sarie knows this, too. She's teasing. As we all know she does. *Vaccines. Syringes.* We'd simply like her help. Her presence, now and then. *With all of her experience.*" Hazel Towson looked at Sarie as a disappointed parent does a child who refuses to perform in the presence of fine guests. "Perhaps, we thought, Sarie could give us all a talk. Improve herself, you know. Help *us.* She does *know* about nursing, doesn't she?" Here Mrs. Towson was deploying a secondary strategy that she knew as You Must Win Over the Man. She thought she would recall for Gilbert the very thing that had always pained him most: "We've always heard it told." It was a little challenge: defend your wife by pushing her to join, or I will bring up her faux pas again, and I shall be relentless.

Bending to remove his shoes (though Sarie, wishing he would not, jammed her elbow in his side), Gilbert tried to stall. His skin itched. "Through the hospitals, I suppose?" he said. Sarie, disappointed, rose to offer Mrs. Towson a refill of her tea. Both to tea and Gilbert's question, Hazel said, "Oh, no, no, no, my dears." She pushed the cup away with a forceful outstretched finger. "Not through the hospitals, I'm sure. Thank you very much." Sitting up again, feet free, his head passing not far from Mrs. Towson's knees and arms, Gilbert thought she smelled a little like manure. Like a fresh field in rural England. Rich and dark and loamy. Hazel waited until he'd sat up and Sarie had stood still. "Hospitals." She leaned towards him and smiled. "What do *they* know about children?"

When Sarie rolled her eyes at Gilbert, it was not because she had deep faith in hospitals or governments or because she cared that her big guest had refused another drink. She didn't mind if Hazel Towson overlooked others' expertise or made decisions on her own, without consulting anyone but the British Council's ladies. She didn't know if vaccinations were really valuable at all and, what's more, didn't care to argue. What irritated Sarie was something rather complicated that neither Sarie's guest nor husband really understood.

Firstly, as a mission girl, a woman with a past, she felt herself more interesting than all the Council women, and resented their intrusions. Their ease and confidence, their skill at being *ladies,* at once silenced her completely and brought out her very worst behavior. Among them she felt huge, ungainly, stupid, and, uncomfortably, much better than them all.

Moreover, she didn't wish to be involved with women who would see almost right away that she herself was in possession of much less than they were. Where she had rubber thongs, they had Bata pumps and European brogues—beaten up and worn, indeed, but costly, bearing up yet to the march and tick of time. While they cleverly acquired chocolate bars, Danish butter biscuits, and boxed vanilla sugar, Sarie stuck to Nanjis and to gummy turbinado. They smelled of perfumes purchased in a shop, while Sarie smelled occasionally like talcum, and more often like herself. She also knew her teeth were not what they had been. No, no, she couldn't face them—feeling herself better than them all and being poorer than each one was an awful combination. The only use she had for the British Council was for the children's books, which Agatha demanded. From them she wanted nothing else. Sarie understood what Hazel Towson didn't: it was money brought on good behavior, not the other way around.

But Gilbert's shaken inner man had rallied by this time and wished to show himself. If Hazel Towson could choose this very day to visit them, he would choose this day to battle her. He would take up arms. What her husband said pleased Sarie, though she was as surprised by it as Mrs. Towson was. "I'm sure that's very valuable," he said. "Very valuable, indeed, dear Mrs. Hazel. But . . ." Here Gilbert looked at Sarie and placed his hand flat on her knee. "Sarie is too busy at the moment, I believe, to be of any help. She has, excuse us, won't you, some serious things now that require her attention."

For once, Hazel Towson did not know what to say. She had expected that, as had occurred in other households, the husband would give in and push his wife to do what she was told, what propriety required. She took no pleasure in surprises. But, she thought, was she not Hazel Towson? She tugged her big white shirtfront down, checked her buttoned cuffs, and leaned forward in her seat. She was not finished yet. "Busy? What could be more serious, Mr. Turner, if I may, than curing native children?" Something in her tone suggested that native children were at risk of terrible diseases from which only she herself, with Sarie at her side, could save them. Her words echoed in his mind, and he had a sudden, lurching vision of dark skins laid out beside a woodshed; he even smelled sharp salt. Hazel Towson frightened him. *Perhaps,* it struck him suddenly, *she's too much like a man.*

Sarie, for her part, did not find Hazel Towson particularly masculine. But she did not enjoy her attitude. She was used to Gilbert, too, tendering opinions about what she ought to do, and to disregarding them when she found them too restrictive. But Hazel Towson, Sarie thought, didn't have the right. *As if she can tell me what to do. As if she knows what happens here.* She even thought, forgetting for a moment Mr. Jeevanjee's real shape and turning him into a weapon, *She has no idea that I am thinking of a man who is not at all my husband.* Then, wishing she had not combined Mrs. Hazel Towson and the (sweet!) form she had just clutched, she tried to see with her mind's eye the very delicate plum color that outlined Majid Ghulam's upper lip. She managed, and she shivered.

Gilbert wondered how explicit he could be in front of Mrs. Hazel. Speaking of a plan too soon might sour things. He didn't, after all, have a real idea. He only knew that he was going to try to have one. But he also thought that mentioning an imminent success might loosen Hazel's grip. *If I mention it again,* he thought, *it will almost be true.* Also: *I'd like to see her face.* "We can't quite tell you at the moment, Mrs. Towson, but Sarie and I—"With a look at Sarie that Hazel Towson would recall later with distaste (something like *devotion*), Gilbert said the words that would, instead of freeing them from Hazel, have the opposite effect. But there was a momentary victory. "Sarie and I," Gilbert said, "are preparing for a change." He lingered so on Sarie's face (thinking, *A business! Yes, we're going to make a start!*) that, although she was absolutely wrong, Mrs. Towson thought she understood.

The horror of it balled up in her throat. Her eyes boggled in her head. *Could it be?* she thought. *My God. Isn't Sarie quite past that?* She became violently embarrassed. "I see," she said at last. And Sarie, who had not yet understood, looked from guest to husband. Hazel Towson's big eyes remained wide. A hardy sniff shuttled through her nose. She crossed and uncrossed her squat legs beneath her khaki skirt. She wound her ankles round and round like propellers on a plane; she cleared her sinewy throat.

She had had a shock. But, equal, as she liked to say, to the most terrible of crises, she took Sarie's hand in hers and dutifully, even kindly, gave it a quick squeeze. "How wonderful," she said. Sarie wished to pull her hand away but sensed that she should not. When Hazel dropped her eyes to Sarie's chest and lap, and asked, in a near whisper, "But, dear, is it wise? So late? You're not exactly *young,*" Sarie slowly saw. She blinked. She restrained a little laugh by squeezing back at Hazel's hand, harder than was right—which made Hazel feel that Sarie was in more dire need of her support than she had hitherto imagined. "Oh, my dear," she said, and shot Gilbert a nasty glance as if to say: *Men. Look at what you've done.* She then turned back to Sarie. "Another child? Right now? Oh, Sarie, are you sure? It isn't a mistake?" In Hazel's view, sex among the indigenes was one thing—in fact, having plenty of opinions, she could discuss it at some length—but in her set, the set that she imagined and kept attempting to bring into firm being, couplings between Europeans over forty, and moreover between poor ones like the Turners, were another thing entirely. Better left in silence. Hazel had been given a surprise that was beyond the pale of what she could anticipate; she was disappointed in herself, and this made her, for a moment, weak.

Although he'd won in the short term, and although this was a first, Gilbert for a moment was displeased. *Not a child,* he wished to say, *no, not at all. A business.* He had wanted to be heard just as he'd intended. But Sarie took another tack. She looked down at her knees and clung to Hazel's hand. "I know," she said. "I know." And to keep him from correcting her, she kicked Gilbert in the shin. She didn't want their plans—even if they had none—open yet to scrutiny. Let Hazel Towson be embarrassed, let her feel distaste at the very thought of mating among people of their age. *What would she think of Majid!*

Sarie closed her eyes and leaned back into the couch. If she could make love with a man she barely knew and conceal it from her husband, could she not also let Mrs. Hazel Towson think exactly as she pleased? A pregnant woman, Sarie thought, couldn't *volunteer.*

Gilbert wanted Hazel out. And there was still a little happiness in him that had not been plucked out, a tiny sense that he *could* do things. He stood up and made it clear that it was time for her to go. "Well. That's right," he said. "Sarie needs her rest. Exactly." He felt stronger. "I'm sure you understand." Hazel, caught off balance, let herself be led. Gilbert walked her to the door.

"I won't get up," said Sarie. "This heat!" She had never before had the upper hand with Hazel, was feeling rather shrill. She gestured at her hips and looked sweetly at her guest as if to say, *You know that pregnancy is trying.* "Oh. Oh, yes," said Hazel. "Don't get up, my dear. Of course." On the landing, Hazel shook her head. *A pregnancy! At Sarie's advanced age!* But she couldn't leave entirely outdone. If she did not have pride, what did she? She gathered up her spirits. Pregnancy or no, a decent woman ought still attend *some* functions, at least until she *showed.* She poked her head back inside the Turners' flat, holding to the doorknob with both hands, oddly like a girl. "Next Friday, Sarie. There's a luncheon, don't you know. You might think of coming down, if you're not feeling awful. You could do that, at least." Sarie moaned a little from her seat. "Perhaps!" she said, and waved.

Gilbert closed the door and Sarie laughed. A little strangely, Gilbert thought, but, still—here was his own Sarie laughing at something *they* had done together. "Oh, wonderful," she said. "Wonderful!" And Gilbert, shy, covered his mouth with both hands, then said, muffled, "Yes, I suppose so. Wonderful, indeed." As though she really were carrying a child, Sarie struggled to get up. Recalling what he'd said—*a change*—she wiped her mouth and went to stand beside him. She looked him in the eye.

"'A change,' you said? Something very serious? Gilbert?" Sarie frowned into his face and tugged hard at his shirt. "Were you playing? Did you mean it? You are having an idea?" Could he have thought of something just one day after the letter? So soon after the fact?

"Not quite yet, no, dear," he said. He plucked her hand away and laid it on the sofa. "But we're about to, aren't we? Something's going to happen. We'll find something to say." Sarie, unsure of her husband, followed him into the kitchen. Would he hide anything from her? She was partially put out. She had also had the thought that she might beat him to it, might have to, after all, because *she,* not he, was strong. She reassured herself: *Of course not. When he's thought something, I will know.* She knew *him,* after all.

Gilbert pulled a spoon from a low drawer and held it in the air a moment as though it were a wand. "Let's have some ice cream first, now, shall we?" She couldn't turn that down. Watching Sarie eat, pale hair over her face, Gilbert felt a twitching at his heart. A desire to be competent in a way he felt the men at the Victorian Palm all were. He'd come through again. He'd please her. He'd decide on an idea and present it to her, fully formed, impeccable, and grand.

Later she followed him into the bedroom. Perhaps because she had recently been held by a nice man and wished to share her joy somehow, and because they'd triumphed, for the moment, over beastly Hazel Towson, she agreed to rub her husband's feet. *Poor*

Gilbert, Sarie thought. *How difficult his life is. Uncle James's letter really was not kind.* Gilbert sighed into the pillow and let Sarie pull his toes. He felt the world recede. He slipped in and out of consciousness. Everything would be all right. He'd come up with something, and Sarie would be happy. Sarie dug her fingernails into the soft part of his soles. He giggled and he sighed. He almost fell asleep. Outside a hot green flash released a downpour and filled the room with air.

While Gilbert softened on the bed and the sound of rain grew large, Sarie started thinking. She was not pregnant with a baby, no, but she did feel something growing. Was there not a small thing, an unknown, at work now in their lives? Something that might cause—who knew—a satisfying swell? New life? Certainly the recent feelings she had had, that all kinds of things were possible, had to do with Mr. Jeevanjee, with going out into the world. But what if they also had to do, as in an aftershock or echo, with surly Uncle James? She thought about her life. What a wild conjunction of events! There might be love, and money, too! They *would* soon be making money, Sarie thought, because they had no choice. The urgency of it, while she sat comfortable in the bedroom, thrilled her.

She let her mind move from one thing to another as Gilbert's limbs went still: Majid Ghulam, who had whispered in her ear, who had pronounced her name as though it were that of a country; the aerogramme with its invigorating dare; horrid Mrs. Hazel; Gilbert's new excitement! She couldn't think about everything at once. So very much had happened! She'd focus on the business first, and then, and then, she'd stop and close her eyes and think about the way that Mr. Jeevanjee had held her shoulders still as he pushed himself inside her, and how the world had spun.

First things first. A business. The Turners needed an idea. And could she not, if asked, be brimming with ideas? What if she came up with something? What if she showed Gilbert that she could think as well as he believed he could? Hadn't she been fine, succeeded with the Jeevanjees? Taken a hard thing upon herself? Been faced with a hurt boy, assisted him, then later marched down to the clinic and discovered where he lived? Had she not changed the texture of her days with a little bit of verve, some action? She'd show Gilbert, Sarie thought. She would make her value known. Oh, yes, she would think of something.

What might the Turners do? At first, eyes closed, to get warmed up, she tried imagining lighthearted, decorative things. She giggled. What about . . . what about . . . ladies' gowns made out of ribbon, which (thanks to Amélie) she knew how to stitch? She had made a blue one once, which as it happened she'd put on the first evening that Gilbert and his Magistrate had spent at the Jilima Mission. What better to get Gilbert and herself firmly out of danger than the very type of dress she had been wearing when he'd been smitten by her youth? Sarie yawned, cracked her neck and hands. She looked down at sleeping Gilbert. *Non, non, c'est bête,* she thought. A silly, funny thought. Who, in these great times, had the cash to spare for something so adorable and frivolous as a whole gown made of ribbon? The business must move capital, and lots of it to boot. Offer people what they could afford, something that they needed. She gave up on the ribbons. She bit down on her lip and tatted idly at the covers. What else might they do? A restaurant, perhaps? Waffles, which, as she had heard but could not remember seeing, people ate in Belgium? No, no, Sarie was no cook. The very notion tired her, made her want to bathe. And who wanted waffles here? She closed her eyes and waited.

A business. Uncle James was requesting something large. Did he have any idea, any clue at all, about how things really were? There was no real business to speak of, not for ordinary people, what with high-minded officials declaring left and right that business was un-patriotic and only for the few. The Frosty-Kreem and Hisham's Food and Drink, thought Sarie, had been permitted to remain, but with a lot of dealing. Perhaps even Hisham's, like the shops on Urasimu Road, was not owned any longer by those who had put it into place; shop doors were government property now, required friends up high. A business in a shop! No, it would not be possible, thought Sarie, to acquire all the permits, to sneak and slide beneath the eyes of officers and Ministers and spokespeople and spies. They could not have a storefront. And Gilbert, Sarie thought, this time without any satisfaction, Gilbert was a nobody. *Mrs. Hazel's right. Poor Gilbert,* Sarie thought. *Without me he is lost.* She would have to think of it herself. But what was the perfect thing?

While Gilbert set to snoring and the evening sky spread out, Sarie's real idea came, and when it did, it took hold with the clarity of answers on a math test, with the stillness of a mountain range re-vealed by shifting clouds. It was a floodlight in her brain. And once Sarie had had it, she was on her way. In the deepest recess of her chest, in the lining of her stomach, Sarie knew what they would do. *If I'm worth anything, du tout, this is what we shall make. Of course,* she thought, *bien sûr!* Without pausing to shake Gilbert and alert him to her brilliance, or even let him in on the ground floor, to say, "My dear, what do you think of that?" Sarie took a mental step that she would later find rather tricky to undo. She understood that native crafts would save them.

C'est ça, she almost said aloud. *Nous vendrons les souvenirs. For people unlike us who have great things to remember.* Surely now in England there were proud, imperial dreamers crippled with nostal-gia who would give up all their teeth and more for a Makonde statuette, or a basket from the Lakes? All those men who'd eaten at the clubhouse, who'd hosted garden parties and taken long safaris with their wives to snap pictures of the hippos? The men Gilbert had been certain smelled of History and more? Wouldn't they like a reminder? So many of them had run off in a hurry, giving all their clothes away, selling furniture for songs. *They will like,* thought Sarie, *to have some items when they tell their friends the stories. Like the show and tell.* If only they had statuettes, how much more people would listen!

Oh, she could see it clearly—a business for the times. A business that would not require a shop-front or a local clientele. A business that could sneak and curl and shiver along the tricky mangrove coasts. *What if,* thought Sarie, *we can borrow someone's ship and do it from Nairobi?* She didn't worry about details or the fact that they knew no one. She was swept up in her vision. Yes, she could already see small crates packed tight with dark, emaciated figures, shipped efficiently far northwards, to be bought by portly, eloquent, discriminating men (like slavery, indeed, she thought with some surprise, but without such blood and terror; a revision, rather, yes, for better, modern days). She imagined other boxes filled with baskets made of fibrous, tightened stuff that would give a scent of Africa, for ladies to set out on dining tables, to display their finer fruits; or velvets from Kasai to line a gracious hall. Perhaps even Uncle James could sell them from his house! Didn't *he* want souvenirs of things he'd never done?

Sarie almost laughed. Only two days into the news and, already, see how she had solved it. The export of such things would put her on the move. She might be central to a traffic of this sort, off on journeys to the west, to railway towns and harbors where artisans might live. She still had contacts, surely—one or two White Fathers or some Jesuits, languishing in ruins. They'd remember her and point her in the right direction. *They'd* collected masks. And by now each one of them must have published a great book, a wise compendium of all the local ways. They must know where the best trinkets were hidden! She thought about Jilima. What if Betty had not returned to Texas, was still living at the Baptist Mission selling eggs and knitting children's hats? Sarie even thought she'd like to see Betty most of all. "I've slept with a local man," she'd say, "but, I think, don't worry" —she felt the hairs along her scalp each give a little tremble— "that it might be like love." Betty would listen in amazement. Then she would talk about it with Clothilde and Amélie. Sarie would tell them they looked young, and all of them would thank her. She might find news of Angélique, learn what really happened. She might even find her. They'd have a cup of tea.

Sarie smiled into the room. How different life seemed, after little Tahir's accident, after those amazing visits to his home, after holding—oh!—Majid Ghulam Jeevanjee, after Uncle James's letter, even after Mrs. Hazel's (here she giggled right out loud, smacked her sleeping husband lightly on the rump) great mistake about what had set to work in Sarie's nether parts. She felt, indeed, at the very heart of things. Perceived. She even wished that Uncle James had pushed them like this many years before. *We could have had ideas from the start! We have been rotting, pourrissant! So lazy. Missing what was just before our eyes.*

In her new excitement, she did very briefly try waking Gilbert up. She pressed her biggest toenail into Gilbert's sloppy calf and tapped softly at his shoulder. She tickled Gilbert's chin with two light fingertips and crooned. But Gilbert only gave out a great sigh and a wiggle of his feet. If she had woken him just then, let him see the brightness in her eyes, shown him she was serious, things might have turned out differently. But Sarie let him sleep. And, upon a second thought, she decided that she wouldn't tell him right away.

Later, he would see how wise she was. Feeling sure and glad, she thought about her lover. *Perhaps,* she thought, *I will take Majid Ghulam with me to the highlands. We shall together purchase knives.*

What Sarie didn't know, what she could not expect, was that her familiar Gilbert—soft, a reader, shy, and in general amenable to her commands when she could not fulfill his—would from his own dreaming pull another Gilbert. From the rhythm of massage, from the pressing of her fingernails at his yielding flesh, perhaps from his own agitated skin, a little boy in his old head clambered to an attic, where he found and opened up a box, looked in it, and felt glee. As outside the green rain battered the flat roofs and chilled the steaming roads, Gilbert, all his knots undone, was changing, and was being given, in a dream, an idea of his own.

❦ Twelve

Bibi spent the evening with Issa and Nisreen. They listened to the news from England, and later to the Germans: in Egypt things were changing, in South Africa they weren't, and, somewhere on the border, there were more rumbles of War. But the news did not intrude too much on the loveliness of things. In her hands, the pineapple was growing. The pineapple, thought Bibi, had been a good idea. She hadn't done the taxi. Wouldn't. Even if it *was* a herald, she wasn't yet prepared to say so openly at home. At the moment she regarded the idea of her prophet-self with affectionate amusement. Though she had been too shy to take it up, she did feel, at least, that she had weathered that first dare with grace: "Thought you were a seer, eh? A person who can *know things?* Well, my dear, stitch *that!*"

She hadn't, was not strong enough quite yet. But she was happy with her second choice. The pineapple, she told herself, though likely not a cosmic gift—did not portend a person, for example, giving on the inside and prickly on the out, or a tangy glass to drink—was just the thing to stitch. It would grant her the appearance of an ordinary woman (no mad lady making cabs) and also reassure her that, even if she couldn't tell the future, even if she'd chosen, knowingly, to turn the other way, she was clever with a needle.

The small pineapple pleased her. She liked the sharp thing's shape, the way the fruit was jagged, hard, how it was dangerous from too close up but how from a little distance it could look soft and round. The pineapple she stitched, in brown and yellow thread from a jersey she'd convinced Mama Moto to give up in exchange for some old shoes, was ripe, ready to be plucked. A grown thing. But Bibi also liked to think about how such fruits began: humble nut-sized promises concealed in scarlet folds, held intimate and safe by red and rosy spines. *Like babies,* Bibi thought.

When Bibi thought of babies—which she often did, she really couldn't help it—she felt happy and then sad, then happy once again. Such sweetness in considering new life! She thought about the new life *she* had made, her very own success: there he was, strong and stunning Issa, huddled by the radio with a serious look she liked to think he'd gotten from his mother, the look she'd had as little Kulthum at the Ladies' Sewing Club, which had so impressed her teachers. *He'll always know he came from me,* she thought. *Just look at that nice face.*

As she often did, Bibi found herself recalling Issa's absent brothers, all dead far too young. Her marriage, her first house, the troubles with her belly, the secrets she'd uncovered and had shared with cousins and some aunts—those things stayed quite vague. What she really did remember from those years were the faces of the babies she had lost, and these, like Issa's, she was sure, had been just like her own. But tiny, wrinkled. Too young. Fruitlets, quickly gone from her. When she saw her own reflection in the mirror in her bedroom, Bibi thought about the lost children a lot. She was getting old; her face was getting smaller. She was shrinking. It was easy thinking those lost sons had looked like her, when she herself was growing smaller every day. *We're all babies, in the end,* she thought. The idea made her smile. It also made her eyes tight, brought a perfect kind of sweetness, hovering on tears but hovering only, because the parlor with her Issa in it and his hardworking Nisreen, and the soft sound of the radio, felt so comfortable and right. Bibi let the pineapple slip down onto her lap and stretched her tired fingers. Her hands ached. It would be nice to go to bed. Oh, but not quite yet, not yet. How lovely evenings were! There was so much to think about at home, when she could bear it, when she let all the outside news go still, when she forgot about Kikanga—when she remembered exactly where she was, and who lived right there with her, and who *would* be beside her to the very end.

She sighed, and smoothed the white cloth she'd been stitching out over her lap. *Babies.* Oh, perhaps everything had babies hiding in it, a little army of soft bodies, just waiting to be thought about and brought into the world! Babies in a fruit, babies among flowers, babies everywhere. *Poor silly Nisreen!* Bibi looked a little sadly at her, feeling all the love she had in her gather in her chest. Nisreen, stretched out—so small!—on the bright sofa, was not listening any longer to the news, though when the broadcast had begun she'd paid very close attention, giving frowns and clucks about Johannesburg and Cairo whenever Issa made a fist or shook his thinking head. Now Nisreen was sinking into sleep; her heavy glasses had dropped down from her eyes, lenses at an angle, just above her mouth. Watching Issa's wife stretched out like that, and feeling all the sweetness-sadness of the nighttime at her shoulders like a cloak, Bibi wished again that Nisreen would swell up.

What a thin girl Issa'd taken on! "For smarts!" That was what he'd said. A girl who'd studied hard, had been apprenticed in a pharmacy. A girl with glasses on! How Bibi had argued. She knew several nice girls who'd studied in a pharmacy—for one, Ilham Masoud, who was beautiful and strong and who had stopped her studies when she married; Salma Ali also had studied medicine a while, found it couldn't hold her. And how could she forget? There was Majid Ghulam's cousin, too, and hadn't he been on her mind? Of course, of course, charming little Sugra, who had even known Nisreen. And Sugra was now married, and as far as Bibi knew, *her* husband didn't make her work for others, potion-smarts or no. Now *there* was an example. Wasn't Sugra blooming, fat and round with babies at her breast and back, doing many interesting things that did not ruin one's eyes?

"Aren't *you* smart enough alone?" Bibi had asked Issa at his suggestion of Nisreen. "Don't you know smarts above mean nothing down below? Neck down, I mean to say?" But Issa had insisted, and when a mother loves a son so much, what is there to do? In the end, Bibi had to tell the truth: she liked Nisreen, she did. How could one not love a girl who did almost everything one asked? Who could fail to be impressed by a person who could solve the word games on the radio and read poems out loud?   ·

But glasses meant poor eyesight, didn't they? From studying too much! Which brought gray hair, too, as it had to Bibi's boy. Hadn't Issa's hair gone quite white at the edges from all that looking at the clouds and checking how-much-rainwater-has-fallen in the calibrated cups? He'd come back from the meteorological institute almost, almost, an old man! And where were the girl's breasts? What hips could the girl claim? *A baby would get stuck in there, no room to move around. Come out narrow like a twig, would snap in any wind!* And, *She limps,* she thought, *a hobbling child we'd get, if we got one at all. When she thinks too hard her eyes cross. If these two had a child,* Bibi concluded—because when the thing a person wants is nowhere to be seen, it's useful to decide that thing was never good—*we'd get a blind boy with bad knees. Or even get a girl!*

Issa grunted at the radio, and Bibi, frowning, turned her thoughts to him. When she tired of blaming one, she set out towards the other. Couldn't he keep at it? He thought too much, indeed, but in men that's not a threat to things, not always. Issa, she was sure, was perfectly all right. Could function. Yes, of course he could. Who'd dare think otherwise? One small look at Issa was enough to make her glad again, and proud. *Look at that big man!* she thought. *What hands!* As his mother looked on tenderly, Issa leaned in towards the radio and propped his ankle on his knee, holding it for balance. *How the boy can concentrate,* thought Bibi. *Like a dog on a lost chicken, like a shark on an old man!*

"What's that they are saying?" Bibi asked. Issa didn't hear her. "*Weh!* Issa!" She wished that he would look up from the radio and explain the news to her, not because she cared for details, but because she liked it when he spoke. And it seemed to her that he did not speak very much these days. "What's going on out there?" Bibi asked again. Issa's head came up. He raised his eyebrows at her. "What's that, Ma?" He gave an absent nod and turned the volume up.

The broadcast finally ended. The nation's plodding anthem wheezed into the air. Issa turned the radio off before the band could finish. Nisreen, pulled away from sleep by sudden stillness in the room, stretched her arms and caught her glasses as they fell. She sat up and smiled. Issa bent to fold the newspaper. He yawned and rubbed his eyes.

Nisreen said, "I thought it was morning." Bibi turned to look at her and her hard thoughts slipped away. Nisreen did look sweet, half-woken. And if she'd just stop wearing glasses, well, her big eyes were not bad. *And look,* thought Bibi, *how she does love my Issa.*

Nisreen, those eyes on her husband, did, indeed, look soft; but Issa didn't notice. He was looking at his trouser leg, straightening a cuff. *Nisreen wants what's right,* thought Bibi, *despite that nothing-chest!* Nisreen folded up her glasses and ran her fingers through the hair that had got loose from her twist. She waited. *If I were Issa,* Bibi thought, *I'd make a sign right now, and lead her to the bed. What if tonight's the night?* she thought. *What if she's really ready? What if—* she looked down at her pineapple—*this one's a sign, too?* Bibi thought she would go first. *If I leave them by themselves, Issa will look over at his wife and see what I just saw. His loins will be stirred up.*

Bibi folded her new pineapple in half and, with a satisfying stab, fixed her needle to it. "I'm going now," she said. She got up from her seat and held the wall for balance. She shook her head at Nisreen's silent offer to help her to her room. Issa said, "Ma, are you sure? Can you get into bed?" and Bibi showed him that she could by taking one big step herself. Nisreen told her to sleep well.

Believing that if she thought what she was thinking hard enough, he'd do exactly as she wished, Bibi gave her son a look. He was made of the same stuff as she was, after all. She'd held him in her womb! How could there not be deep communication? Her eyes stayed focused on him even as she reached the doorway and stepped out onto the landing. *Make Nisreen a baby,* Bibi thought. *Put something in her pot.*

But when she lay down in her bed and listened, hoping she would hear what one *should* hear, she only heard Nisreen's soft shuffle down the hall and Issa telling her good night, he still had paperwork work to do. Bibi shook her head and turned over on her side. How difficult it was with such a modern, studious pair. Did she not prod enough? Did they not understand how important children were? How things that start like nuts and grow in scarlet worlds grow up to feed a person's heart? *That's it,* she thought. Perhaps she'd stitch a heart once the pineapple was done. Hearts were loud and clear these days, what with bright talk of romance and those movies from the West. A heart. What if *that* swelled his loins up, to flood poor Nisreen's gate?

There was no heart in the morning. Bibi's fingers wouldn't move. She had stitched too long the night before, and when she woke up the next day, her hands were cramped and stiff. They hurt. She couldn't stitch a thing. And that pineapple she'd worked so hard on wasn't even done!

Mama Moto gave Bibi some uji in a bowl so she wouldn't strain her hands with bread or tricky fruit. When Nisreen came into the kitchen, Bibi looked her over. If Issa and Nisreen had done the thing she'd hoped, love would show on Nisreen's face. She'd look fresh and clean and especially well bathed. But Nisreen, neatly dressed and spectacled, was plain Nisreen again—not as she'd been for a moment on the sofa when she woke—and was already talking like a person whose head is full of busy-city-thought. Nisreen said that she would ask the doctors at the clinic for an ointment and bring home spinach if she could. Issa, looking like a businessman—*the important man he was*—asked Mama Moto please to bring a rope bed to the balcony so Bibi could lie down. And next the two of them slipped out the door into the world, walking side by side, but with, thought Bibi, a space growing between them: a space she felt was mirrored in her chest, as though her ribs were parting ways.

Once they'd gone, Bibi settled on the balcony. How early Issa and Nisreen got up! Out there, Bibi thought, Kikanga was only just coming awake. But she also felt a bit of pride. *Early birds,* she thought, as Mrs. Harries had so liked to say. *Going for the worm.* They *did* take care of her, and nicely. Comfortable on the rope bed, Bibi didn't think so hard about the babies, or *the* baby, the one she hoped would form inside Nisreen at any moment now. The balcony was Bibi's place to think of other things. There were other things to look at—things that, at first glance at least, didn't always have to do with women swelling up.

Getting ready for the day, the street displayed for Bibi's benefit its morning passersby. Mango-men prepared their tables, organizing salt and chili-pepper bowls, sharpening their knives; litter-women stretched their backs and rubbed at their thin necks before getting down to work; the boys on cycles and on foot called out to one another; a chain of little girls in white and blue, with satchels, moved past like a colored snake to catch a city bus; five Bohora ladies in light gowns, big purses heavy at their arms, ambled towards the market. Bibi sighed. She watched. Got ready to take note.

In the street and in the windows of the houses just across the road, she looked for faces she might know. Down there, Kirit Tanna, shirttails loose over his trousers, shouted at a dark boy from the alley, demanding the day's water. Abrahman Ferozi, old and gowned, was heading out already to the corner coffee stand, where he'd argue about Pakistan and Zionists and Russia, the price of coffee beans and oil, until, at noon, heart apatter and exhausted, he'd give a little boy some sweets to get him safely home. Mama Ndiambongo, gray and hunchbacked, swept the courtyard at what had once been Lydia House. Behind two dusty flame trees, the New Purnima Snack was almost, almost, open. She could see Vijay Mehta rolling up his sleeves, bend to start fryers.

Bibi's fingers hurt and Nisreen wasn't pregnant, but overall, life was not so bad. Nevermind about the maybe-meaning of her threads or the problems in her household. The pineapple was just a pineapple today. Out here on the balcony, she had a country of her own. It would be good to have a rest. Bibi felt serene. Nothing there just yet, nothing to perk up her secret-seeking sense. She rubbed her fingers in her lap and thought about Majid Ghulam, poor old widowed Ghuji, and how sad his fortunes were. She wondered, too, about that European woman with bare legs, who now regularly stepped into Hisham's Food and Drink with the little girl beside her and, upon stepping out again, didn't head back home.

Mama Moto came out of the parlor with a bowl of lentil broth and a brand-new red clay burner to place under the rope bed—onion skins and basil, to soothe Bibi's old hands. Bibi spread her skirts apart and let Mama Moto slide the burner right below her bottom. Bibi, as she sometimes did when there was little going on and nothing to be stitched, told Mama Moto to stay with her a moment. She had something to say.

Mama Moto, Bibi thought, was a serious woman, too. They were not so far apart in age. And they'd been together for as long as Bibi could recall living in Kikanga, all her married life and after. She'd been hired by Bibi's husband, who, as proper husbands did, understood that wives needed some help. How right he'd been to do it, Bibi thought. She and Mama Moto had lived together through some of the same things: the arrival of the radio, ration cards and blackouts, electricity and taps, the golden times of Hollywood, freedom, revolution and kung fu, Independence, telephones, motherhood, and age. They'd see television soon.

Each of them had an only son: Bibi's darling Issa, and Mama Moto's Idi—born not long after Bibi's final child was washed and wrapped and buried, but in his own way brave, successful just as Issa was, if in a less official world. People called him Moto (and it had come back to his mother, and her new name had stuck) because with his hot hands he pilfered things, because his goods were hot, and because now and then he vanished, like a fire's rising smoke. *Mama Moto's Moto is a thief,* thought Bibi, *but human shapes are many. God gives each a star.* She'd long stopped teasing Mama Moto for her child's escapades. She tried to call him Idi sometimes and not Moto, to show she understood that he was not all spark and flame. And it was true he'd lately grown so able at his trade that he got caught only rarely, was really rather cool. But names don't disappear. Mama Moto didn't steal, in any case. She was temperate and upright. *She's almost like my sister,* Bibi sometimes thought.

When Bibi told her stories, Mama Moto listened. She also learned things on her own. If Mama Moto gave out what she knew, she was most often direct; she didn't spin things into tales that had to be unraveled before Bibi could decide exactly what was what. Mama Moto was not, at heart, a gossip; and while this troubled Bibi in Nisreen, in Mama Moto it was a posture she approved of. Mama Moto was reliable and, thought Bibi, truthful, in a way many other people weren't. She named her sources when she could, did not take things on faith. And because Mama Moto's social world was different from Bibi's, because she didn't care too personally about the Jeevanjees and the Hafizes, the Tannas or the Mehtas, Bibi, if she was uncertain or bored, could make a story up and Mama Moto might accept it. She was also, Bibi didn't like to say but often thought with pleasure now and then, easy to make fun of. Bibi thus began: "What do you know, Ma, about the white woman who lives around the corner? That white Mrs. Turner?" Mama Moto set the soup down and looked up. Her knees creaked as she rose.

Despite Bibi's now-and-then great love for her, Mama Moto didn't feel as close to Bibi as Bibi did to her. Though she had never once pointed them out, she was more attuned to the differences between them. There was, for instance, the fact that Issa had an office for his business and Idi's office was the street; that Issa had four neckties and Idi, she thought, only one; that, Freedom notwithstanding, Issa could walk into almost any shop and be given some credit, and other things besides. That the two loved and only boys were not exactly friends. And that this state of affairs was due not to any difference in their brains (which Mama Moto thought were equal, at the very least) but History, which was never really just; and that Mama Moto slept downstairs in a corner on the floor, while Bibi, coddled, lay on her besera in a high up, breezy room; and so on and so on and so forth, though Mama Moto didn't like to say. But at the same time it was also true that she didn't dislike Bibi; sometimes she even loved her. They'd been together for so long that she was used to her. And she was glad to have a job. They did sometimes have fun. And although Bibi thought *she* always had the upper hand, Mama Moto had some methods, too, for achieving satisfaction.

Mama Moto rubbed her long, long fingers up across her face, over her long skull, and pinched her narrow neck to soothe where it was sore. She pulled her working cloth tight around her shoulders, then, screwing up her lips, looked out at the New Purnima Snack. "That woman?" Mama Moto curled her nostrils and furrowed her high brow. Mama Moto, as it happened, knew far more than Bibi did about Mrs. Sarie Turner, and Majid Jeevanjee. But she was not ready to say. She lied: "Nothing, Bi. She is a white woman, that's all."

Bibi understood without needing to be told that Mama Moto knew more than she said. "Come on, Ma. Tell us what you've heard." Balanced on her arms and feet at each wooden end of the rope bed, Bibi lifted up her chest and hips and pulled her dress up so the smoke would reach her better. She gave a hollow grunt and settled down again while Mama Moto sniffed the morning air and peered across the way into Salma's open window, where a pale blue curtain shrugged.

Mama Moto sighed. "You think I get out to hear things, with all the work I do?"

Bibi let her wrist hang in the air and shook it back and forth. "Ah-ahh," she said. "Listen to you, just! As if *your* life was hard. You run up and down the stairs as if you were a girl!"

Mama Moto laughed. "You think I have time to go outside and listen at the walls, with your washing to be done?" Bibi plucked her tongue quick from the roof of her wet mouth and made a clucking sound. Things were warming up. Still considering the curtains, Mama Moto said, "All right. All right. I'll tell you something new. Idi says she goes to look in on that boy. The one from your own accident. Those Indians. Up on Libya Street."

Bibi was surprised. It wasn't often that news came to her through Idi. "Moto?" Bibi said, and Mama Moto frowned. "How does Moto know?" Mama Moto pressed her lips together and set her shoulders straight. "My *Idi's* a good boy," she said. "He knows what's about."

Bibi sniffed, said, "Heh." The two were silent for a while. Mama Moto checked the onion skins and righted Bibi's pillow. "So?" said Bibi. "What does *Idi* say?" Saying "Idi" helped her. Mollified, Mama Moto almost smiled. She rubbed her ear, got ready. "Not much," she said. "She must be bringing him some medicines for pain. Just like I bring you. You know, I heard that white lady's a doctor." Sometimes, to get Bibi excited, Mama Moto said the opposite of what she knew to be true.

Bibi bent to take the little bowl of stew, which smelled, she thought, much better than those onion skins. "Medicines, eh? Do they stink like what you bring me?" Bibi made a face and set the bowl back down. She plucked at Mama Moto's dress to get all of her attention. Here was Bibi's talk, getting off the ground: "Look at me, *I'll* tell you." Bibi's eyes grew small. "I'll tell you what medicine she's taking over there!"

Mama Moto did her best to look as blank as the flat floor, but, in this case of the Jeevanjees, she was at least one up on Bibi. What Mama Moto knew, she'd gotten almost from the source. But she wasn't going to say all that, not right away, at least. She liked how Bibi's mind worked. She said: "Tell me then, why don't you? Mrs. I'm-a-teacher-on-the-balcony. Mrs. I-know-all. Quit your bragging now and tell me how it is." Bibi liked it when Mama Moto teased her. It made her feel much younger. She waited for a little more, and Mama Moto gave it to her: "Come on now, old lady. Let it out or your sour mouth will pop. I'm not living at the Mountain Top Hotel, you know. No one brings *me* breakfast. I've all your work to do."

Bibi nodded and then grinned, her little mouth as open as could be. "Brings him medicines, you say?" She held the bowl close to her mouth with the heels of her bent hands. She drank up all the soup. "Medicines, you say?"

Mama Moto took the bowl from her and shook the last drops out into the street. Mama Moto knew Bibi was guessing, that she might have ideas, but that she didn't really know. "Medicines. That's right. That's exactly what I said."

Bibi coughed and spit. She gestured broadly with her arms, looked up into the sun as if she had an audience in the sky, and said, "Remedies!" Round eyes hard like coins. "Doctor?" And now, loudly, so that someone on the street might easily have heard, "Doctor. Ha! I'll tell you what she's fixing." And announced that she had known before anybody else that Majid Ghulam Jeevanjee (a peacock, after all) had recently convinced that sunburnt, freckled woman to spread apart her legs and give him British juice — which, as everyone has heard, is potent, and exciting.

Repeat: Cities don't split people up so much as bring them all together. Which is why Mama Moto, though she said nothing to Bibi, was aware not only of the news at work in Majid Ghulam's heart, but of who his downstairs neighbor was. Here is how it went.

Sour Maria had a story, too. She was not a city girl. She'd been in Vunjamguu two years, had moved in with her brother, who'd come out well before she did. He'd done six months at the Secretarial College for Government Assistants and then secured his future with a rare and steady post at the National Tourist Board, shelving maps and postcards. When the Housing people did their famous reclamatory work, the whole first floor of grandiose Kudra House, for the people's revolution, went to this humble man. Maria's brother had moved in not long after Majid's two had fled for London and Toronto, leaving poor Ghuji behind. He had treated that first floor as if there were nothing just above it. He'd done his very best to ignore Majid, and Hayaam, and all the growing boys, and lived his own life rather quietly. Incurious—a good citizen, he was—Maria's brother was uninterested in Asians, who, as far as he could see, had gotten where they were by stealing other people's things. He had not made any mark with Majid Ghulam Jeevanjee, had not stirred when Hayaam died; nor had he interfered when Mr. M. G. Jeevanjee became Mad and Sad Majid. But Maria was quite different.

Soon after Maria came, her brother took a wife and went to live with her (her people had a larger house a little out of town, and her mother, unable to walk, needed help at home). But who in their right mind could willingly give up a little city flat? He did not provide the Tourist Board with his new address, and he left his sister there to settle in so firmly that no one could uproot her or take the flat away. Maria, respectful and obedient, promised that she'd spend a lot of time at church, not speak to men in private, and wouldn't ever get in trouble.

By herself, and young, Maria needed patrons. And so, in addition to the selling of sweet buns in the morning and the evening, by which if she was clever she could meet most of her needs, she did things for the Jeevanjees in exchange for Majid Ghulam's—she thought—power to protect her from any thing or person that could harm her in the street. She washed their clothing, made them tea, and kept the courtyard clean. Sometimes she cooked meals. And, although they didn't know it, she also prayed for them; because she prayed for them, she monitored their progress.

She approved, at base, of Mr. Jeevanjee, and even his wild sons. As time went by, in fact, she cared for him quite fiercely, the way a young girl might for an uncle she admires. She was not like her brother; in her view, Mad Majid was a person who had suffered and who needed her somehow. As she would say to anyone who'd listen, anyone who had bad feelings about Asians: unlike the bindi-sporting Hindus who cared so much for gold, and unlike the Goans, who all whined about cathedrals and gave up their rare earnings for new steeples, at least the Jeevanjees believed, without much fuss, in God. *They are as good,* Maria thought, *as any Asians get.* She especially thought this because Mr. Jeevanjee did not joke with her about how she went to Church, or ask her to stop singing hymns and modern gospel tunes when she was working in the courtyard. He was uncivil only, thought Maria, to those who told him how to be, and this Maria wouldn't dare, not openly, at least. If that Ismail or Ali teased her and he heard, he shouted and the boys left her alone. He was not actively unkind to her, and in return, Maria felt protective.

Because Maria was often home during the week (selling sweet buns in the mornings and only sometimes before sunset), she knew exactly when Sarie Turner came and exactly when she left. Maria did the washing for the boys, and she sometimes sat with Tahir, who had at her prompting also told her that when Mrs. Turner visited, he didn't always hear much talking from the parlor. That they had gone into his father's room. Maria had not pushed him further, but she had taken note.

It is important to recall that Maria was not simply a good girl with a basic faith in God; she had been reborn. At the Emmanuel Revival Tabernacle House, off Mbuyu Mmoja Park, Maria spent her weekends reading and rereading the Good News. Anxious about Evil, she was thus equipped to know what was innocent and wise. Sarie Turner, she could tell, was neither of those things. Did she not always come when Mr. Jeevanjee was by himself, but for his newly crippled son? Did Mr. Jeevanjee not look newly bathed at the white woman's departure? Maria knew all about loose women, women who tripped men up with lust, then killed them in their sleep because they wanted power. Mr. Jeevanjee, she'd known almost from the first, was in the clutches of a viper.

If she saw Mrs. Turner coming down the alleyway when she was working in the courtyard, Maria made a kissing noise between her lips, looked away from her, and spit. She wished that she could talk with Mr. Jeevanjee and urge him to slow down, to *think,* and consider his own God. Four wives notwithstanding, Allah had no soft spot for adultery, of this she was sure. But say such things?— she couldn't. Unlike her big brother, Maria felt the Jeevanjees might throw her out if she spoke her thoughts too clearly. They were Asians, after all. But how she wished to put her two pence in! Sarie Turner's lack of morals and the way that she was leading Mr. Jeevanjee to Hell were two of right-thinking Maria's principal concerns, and they took up a good deal of her time. But Maria did not have a simply one-track mind; no, she worked on several fronts. Another thing she thought about was the upcoming salvation she was planning of a boy who would, if she did not act fast, become a viper, too. Maria was in love.

Beside the Emmanuel Revival Tabernacle House at Mbuyu Mmoja Park, there grew a certain mango tree under which Kikanga's ruffians met: slit-eyed boys with open-collared shirts and necklaces that shone, sunglasses to shield their roaming eyes—boys who milled around. Boys, Maria thought, who were dangerous and sly and in need of the Good Lord. While some of them, Maria understood, were well beyond the reach of one so recently rebaptized as herself, she also knew (impulsively and therefore with some certitude) that there was hope for that band's leader. The handsome one: a boy named Idi Moto. Idi Moto could be saved, Maria knew, because, despite the less-than-legal things he liked to do, he cared about his mother. Mothers, children—the sweetest ties that bind! How could a girl not be reassured by a boy who thought about his ma and stole nice gifts for her? Oh! A boy whose name meant flame and fire was too much to leave alone.

For his part, Idi Moto was observant. While Bibi's Issa might get by with noticing the signs in obvious news that was spoken on the radio or decreed by his superiors, Idi Moto, in order to survive, had learned, in subtle ways, not to miss a thing. "That Issa might read papers and reports," he often told his mother, "but I can read a person." And so he could identify targets for his tricks, and other folk whose weaknesses might help him: policemen who were idle, night-watchmen who took long naps, or tea girls who liked gifts. Idi was astute. In his private, sensual life, he mostly liked to fool with eager girls or knowing women who could improve his technique. But he also liked a challenge, chaste and unformed lovelies whose plump hearts were abrim, who thought they couldn't fall. He therefore liked Maria. When she came out of Meetings and sat beside him on a bench, he let Maria talk—for talk and jokes and gossip from a girl, with boys like Idi Moto, cannot but lead directly to the language of the heart. So Maria told him all the things that made her mad and sad, and Idi Moto stroked her thumbs and earlobes when she got carried away.

Thus juicy news does fly. While he fingered her warm neck,

Maria warned her maybe-man about the ways of women. And spilled the beans on Sarie. And went on and on and on. And was only interrupted in her speech when Idi, looking at his fancy watch and working down his hair, said he had to go; had promised, he said sweetly, to look in on his ma. But how nice of her to sit and talk with him so long. Maria squeezed his hand, let go, and, with a tingling in her throat and eyes, told him he was blessed.

❦Thirteen

Sarie woke up with a start, as though her heart had skipped. Inside her, locked tight in her chest, the warm red shape at work reminded her of Majid. Outside her, Gilbert slept. She nudged the pillow up to hide his head from view. He felt her move and sighed. Against her husband's flank, the mirror (already aglow with city light), the heavy dresser, and the door, Sarie closed her eyes and thought about her lover: a poet, a man with serious wounds, kissing her at last! Though she tried to feel again as she had with Majid's lips upon her, and as she had before she woke—tried remembering the hot point of his tongue—she could not manage it completely. Could not see him, quite. Something in her, Sarie thought, had shifted, and she was not certain what. Slow, perplexed, aiming with her stretching to put herself in order, Sarie stiffened all her toes and cracked her neck into the pillow. Between what went on outside of her, at the surface of her skin, and what sat immobile, locked away inside of her, she discovered a new gap. As though those limbs she felt, spreading from her joints—hers, of course, not anybody else's—were a little foreign to her. As she brought her hands up to her face and touched her own warm cheeks, ran her fingers through her matted hair, she had, throughout, the odd impression that she was being touched by someone other than herself. As though, indeed, there were two Saries, not one.

And, somehow, it was true. From that morning on—perhaps presaged by Uncle James's letter, or by Hazel Towson's visit, when

she had laughed so hard, or by the new idea that had come, or perhaps it didn't matter what or when—from that morning on, Sarie
occupied two times, two separate dimensions, as if she had two
lives: one that bloomed in darkness, in a secret, thrilling present
teetering on the lost edge of the past; and one that begged for
light, that gestured, urgent, from a summoning future. In the present, which filled her from the inside, there was Kudra House with
its swollen, stolen hours, the fluttering on Majid Ghulam's bed, a
sharp and visceral excitement, a man for whom she was—she
knew it—extraordinary, new. And in the other life, the one she felt
outside her, there stood another Sarie, palms damp but future-
bound, prepared to make an entrance. *Change,* she thought. A business. Ideas to be had. The present stood for Majid. And the future?
Well, Sarie wasn't sure.

Could these worlds, this present and the not-yet-given future,
move along together? *Could they?* This was the hard thing, the per-
ilous confusion: as certainly as she had felt she should attend to little Tahir when he fell down in the road, Sarie felt required—but
by two things, not one: by her present lover, what it meant to be
held tightly by a man, and also by Great-Uncle James's push. Each
needed all of her attention, all her energy and care. At once. There
was no other way. How was she to do it? Not to anything specific,
but to it all, whatever it would be, *D'accord,* she thought, agreed.
She'd be doubled if she must. She'd juggle and not fall. *I am a brave
woman,* Sarie thought. *I am very strong.* And appearing single and
contained, though inside she was split, she got up out of bed.

Finding water in the pipes, Sarie filled up all their buckets and
put the kettle on. As she moved, despite the many different forces
she felt welling up inside and around her, she noted that her muscles functioned well. But she overfilled the buckets, spilled water
on the floor. Bending with a cloth, she thought, *C'est ça. Je suis dis-*

traite, distracted. And she found that this was strange: what, since marrying Gilbert Turner and agreeing to *this* life, to moving to *this* flat, to mothering *that* child, had there ever been that could *distract* her? So many things at once! Sarie laughed out loud. The sound of her own voice, thankfully unchanged, had a steadying effect.

Looking out the window, she pushed the slats of glass apart to let in a little air. Through the gum and grime, she saw the street fill up. A well-dressed man holding a clean but battered briefcase paused to check his watch. Moved on. A drunkard with long locks and short pants teetered at the curb. A litter-woman stooped to poke a cardboard square. A watchman called a coffee salesman to his perch along a wall and drank three cups in a row. She heard engines come to life. So much, inside and out! She felt for a moment overwhelmed, and the quality of that emotion, the very fullness of it, made Sarie feel—let's say it—young, and also ripe, brimming with potential, ready to be plucked. And had she not *been* plucked? Had she not already undertaken something unexpected? Taken on a lover? Had Uncle James not suddenly provoked Gilbert into action, and her, too? Had Hazel Towson not surmised the unlikeliest of things? Oh, there *was* a tingling in her. Anything could happen. Looking at the street, which was filling, too, with sunlight, Sarie felt, tinily at first, but soon with greater certainty, a desire to go out. To be out there and to walk, and walk and walk and *think*. She remembered her idea, fixed her mind to it. The *souvenirs!* she almost said out loud. *I'll think about just that.*

Should she tell Gilbert her plan before leaving the flat? Was it still a good idea? How prescient she had felt the day before, how clearly she had seen it. She'd felt it with an unmatched absoluteness while Gilbert was asleep. Would she be as certain once he was awake? How would he react? Was she ready to divulge it? *No,* she thought. *I'll keep it quiet for a day. I will think the new thing through.*

She would take a walk with Agatha, stretch her stranger's arms and legs, and *ponder*. She buttered bread for Gilbert and covered up the plate with a warped round wire net. In the bedroom, where her husband snored alone, she put on a pink dress. With a rubber band and pencil, she fixed her hair a bun. She stepped into her daughter's room to wake her. "Come on," she said, "we're going for a walk."

At Mbuyu Mmoja Park, soothsayers in dozens had set up all their wares. Maasai ladies seated on the ground waved cardboard sheets over special roots and powders, to keep the flies away. Shambaa men in kanzu gowns sat on metal buckets or on logs behind their wooden tables, cloudy bottles in long rows like dominoes before them. Island boys on bicycles with coolers offered Popsicles and water. At all edges of the park, buses stopped, and started.

Sarie walked with new assurance, yellow purse swinging in the air. Beside her, Agatha swung her arms to match. Sporadically she kicked at things—pebbles, bits of leather—but didn't say a word. Sarie was relieved; how easily, how kindly, Agatha went along with her whenever she went out. *A good child,* Sarie thought. She patted Agatha's shoulder and surveyed the world around her; it felt oddly open, large. She stopped before a small display of woven baskets and wooden spoons in pairs. *A sign,* she thought. She bit down on her lip, said, "Hmm," and ably repulsed the wrinkled man who lifted those wares towards her. A little farther on, another man, in natty pants, transformed guavas into neckties and pulled watches out of mangoes. A squatting youth sold goatskin seats and pale long-handled knives. Sarie looked at everything.

They walked right through a game of football played by quick boys with a fat ball made of twine on a torn and pitted field. At the grounds of Emmanuel Revival, wall posters depicted a pink and piglike man with too much orange hair; beneath his face, the caption: *Brother Ewald Matting Sheds His Light and Heals! Come All and Be Saved!* Agatha raised her arm to point, and Sarie absently reminded her that pointing was for apes.

They let the park recede, Agatha tripping now and then on her own feet, and Sarie feeling proud. They passed but did not stop before several city landmarks: the Cooperatives Association, the local Library (which they did not frequent), the House for State Statistics, and the New People's Museum. They crossed another road, from which Sarie could make out in the distance the weed-filled, rubbled graveyard that held the dust of British men who'd fought in several Wars. The busy central part of Vunjamguu receded, and they found themselves not far from the old Yacht Club, before the Gymkhana, where, many years before, an animated Sarie had spilled tea on her shoes.

Beneath a crimson frangipani, a peacock tottered on the rudder of its tail. Agatha stood still and memorized him, in order to tell Tahir. In the distance, past a low white house with a fresh veranda painted red, in a far-off world that, light and flat, was enveloped in a haze, Agatha and Sarie saw a horse, and Sarie paused a moment so that Agatha could watch. While Agatha took mental notes (brown with a white spot, small man on its back, waving a long stick), soft, distinguished laughter burst out from the house, and Sarie pictured for a moment British knives and forks aclatter on pretty Scottish plates.

As they stood, a Fiat rolled into the driveway just behind them, scattering white stones. Sarie didn't wait to see what kind of people would get out, who was heading in. She pushed Agatha ahead. Behind them, great skirts rustled softly, and well-oiled car doors slammed. At the overgrown Botanical Gardens (no longer as well managed, as botanical, as they'd once been), Agatha finally got tired, asked where they were going. Sarie hadn't known, not really. But when Agatha posed the question and Sarie looked around her, she saw their steps had not been aimless. She'd been guided by an intellect wiser than her own. *Forcément.* She perceived their co-ordinates exactly. *Of course. That's where I must go.* This time Sarie raised her hand and pointed, straight ahead. "There," she said. "That's it." The Mountain Top Hotel.

In Gilbert's early days, the Mountain Top Hotel had been among the gracious hubs of European life: explorers (real ones, not like Uncle James's vision of his nephew), politicians, planters, airmen, colonels, and their ladies (some quite modest and some painted, others more like men) had convened there on the weekends after lunch at the Marina Gilbert mourned. Settlers from the hills, officers fresh from the hinterland, had rented rooms, where they would sleep beneath cool fans and eat familiar breakfasts brought to them without a sound by chambermaids and waiters so endearing and so dutiful that they were never seen. From the Mountain Top Hotel, important people, royalty, had made off for safaris with delicious picnic lunches packed by unseen cooks. Others, more ambitious, had scaled enormous mountains and flown champagne to the peak. They'd photographed it all: their black-and-white mementos had once lined the hotel walls.

After Independence, the place had been transformed. What had once been just three stories high, in coral rag and timber web, had burst up from the ground renewed—an imposing concrete block, fourteen floors that overlooked the sea. Built with Chinese and German money, it had swelled into an edifice, a monument to freedom. Along the roof, the hotel's name appeared in thick black letters more than ten feet high. On some nights, the neon outline of a mountain's snowy crest flashed red, then gold, then green.

It also had, these days, a different clientele. Socialists in suits discussed redistribution and the need for people's power with high-ranking members of the Cabinet. Thinkers—historians and economists—were invited to expound progressive theories over filling five-course meals. Southern revolutionaries, outlawed in their homes, held conferences in the twelfth-floor meeting rooms and wrote things down in code.

The photographs of British mountaineers and ladies in broad hats had been replaced by portraits of good men—one of whom, headed for another mountaintop, had not so long ago been killed in Memphis, U.S.A., and others who, fists raised to the sky, had risked everything they had for goodness in the future. The chambermaids and waiters had stayed on, but they had been infused with nervy brightness, a visibility that scared off many of the ex-colonials who had moved to Scallop Bay: these domestics spoke, and freely.

It was thus, in some important ways, much more glamorous than it had ever been. Downstairs there was a restaurant, open to the public, in which people of all kinds were permitted to associate and where soft drinks were sold, as well as cornmeal pap, poppy cake, and cheese. Daring women from the British Council sometimes went, to say they'd seen the world. A swimming pool somewhere, concealed by a high regiment of upright ashok trees; inside, with a high view of the ocean, for hotel guests alone, a well-stocked, glinting bar.

Sarie had not been inside the Mountain Top Hotel in years. But she knew that crafts were sold there. All the real hotels had gift shops, and that's where she would go. She would get a feeling for the kinds of goods that she and Gilbert might explore. How intrepid Sarie felt! Investigative and efficient. She pulled Agatha along, and, dismissing the two doormen (who had seen them coming, who had already raised their caps), they spun together through the Mountain Top's one revolving door. Walking tall, Sarie pretended not to see the guests: African dignitaries in starched dark green or rosy suits, bright pens winking at their pockets as they made toasts by the window; some European ladies from abroad in fashionable soft dresses sipping tea on leather sofas beneath a few remaining posters of rhinos and giraffes; a big white man in creased safari gear—that Mr. Remington, perhaps. They walked right by the bellboy (a man, really, an old, gray man in a red fez, back straight as a pole). They walked right past them all, *As if,* thought Sarie proudly, *we were going to a room.*

The souvenir shop, which had stayed intact and in place as the hotel was rebuilt (even fired-up reformers pick up trinkets for their children), was not much larger than the Turners' parlor, but it was stacked and filled to overflowing with exactly what she'd come to see. Moving through the doorway, Sarie coughed. The man who owned the place, sallow, wrinkled in a short-sleeved light brown shirt that did nothing for his arms, looked up and nodded vaguely. In a long, exhausted voice, he said, "When you want to buy, you ask me." He went back to filling up a scrapbook with interesting stamps.

Sarie didn't greet him. There was too much to take in. Her big blue eyes were hungry. Could she see them all? She steadied herself with a hand on a low shelf. Her stomach hurt. Indeed, she felt nearly sick. Here were wooden and carved things from every region in the country, and even from elsewhere. Sarie lurched and shivered. Was *this* what hovered at her skin and waited to be known? Her eyes adjusted to the light, and in that hazy, variegated shine, Sarie sensed the future.

The sallow man, she saw, dealt in items of all kinds: not simply statuettes and baskets, but gifts and memorabilia that Sarie, musing in the bedroom, had not yet considered. Bracelets made of jade; soapstone candlesticks and plates; arrows (neatly labeled *Poison* in typed print); walking sticks in green and scarlet paint; carved, dark busts of grizzled men and those of fresh young girls (men from brow to throat, girls from head to chest); the cured, weird feet of elephants and zebras; studded boxes from the islands; carpets; silver rings expressly left unpolished to seem older than they were; copper armbands from Rhodesia; beaded straps from Swaziland; neck rings from Uganda. *Jewelry!* she thought. How many, many items she could put into one box if only she thought small. There were also wooden animals in sets, wildebeest and boks of various shapes, lions, hippos, too. Oh! Sarie's stomach settled.

While Agatha picked up a giraffe and made it walk along a shelf, Sarie fingered necklaces and jade. She eyed the tiny gems whose blue, she was aware, was precious, mined only in these hills. *Yes,* she thought. *Potential.* They would work their way through statuettes and jewelry to stones, once they could afford it. Oh, she would have a lot to say to Gilbert! He would be impressed. She was peering at a case of fine transparent stones, imagining the rare and airy sounds of Gilbert's admiration, when she had to close her eyes and groan because a real sound had intruded. Oh, would she *always* be there? Behind her, unmistakable and bright, came Mrs. Hazel's voice.

"Sarie, dear! Hoo!" Hazel wore a polyester sundress printed top to bottom with loud deep purple flowers, black belt tight around her. Her lips were painted red. She looked, thought Sarie, shocking. Where were her ordinary clothes? Whenever Hazel showed at the Mchanganyiko flat, she wore white blouses and khaki, long brown skirts, and big, brown, scratched-up shoes. She came dressed like a farmer. Even at the garden parties, Sarie had never before witnessed Hazel in such color. And nevermind in lipstick!

Sarie was surprised. She felt oddly betrayed. It made Sarie think that Hazel, on her visits to the flat, thought of it as *labor,* that she intentionally dressed down. And, even more unsettling, that Hazel had, perhaps—though Sarie had the honesty to think, *As, moi-même, I do, too*—another, secret life that she liked to keep from them. At the Mountain Top Hotel, at the coast resorts, perhaps even in the high-walled homes of Scallop Bay, Hazel Towson *bloomed.* Sarie had the feeling that, just as she'd been caught by Hazel, Hazel, too, had been uncomfortably revealed. The duplicities abounding made Sarie feel more patient than she would have otherwise. And careful.

"I was just here having lunch." Hazel ran her hand across her belly with an appreciative, soft sigh, as if the food inside that gut were made of down feathers and gold. "That cornmeal, and a pretty little stew. Local food, you know." Sarie thought that she had never seen the woman's hands so gentle, Mrs. Hazel so beatific, so full and satisfied. Yet wasn't Hazel Towson *hard?* Sarie's knees felt cold. Did *everyone* have double lives?

Sarie clutched her purse and nodded. Hazel stepped in close and smiled, peering at her as though through a magnifying lens, as though she, too, had just discovered something. "Then I thought: is it? It can't be. Not *here.* Not at the Mountain Top Hotel." She gestured with her shoulders at the shop, the neat tiles of the lobby, and the buzzing ceiling lights. "But then it was. It was. And look, Sarie!" Hazel patted Sarie's arm as if to show her what Sarie didn't know. Looked at her as though she might, one day, right there, ask Sarie to lunch. "I'm right. It's you, just as I suspected."

Sarie blinked at Hazel's hand. While she didn't like the word "suspected," part of her did warm to the approval she could sense in Mrs. Hazel's voice. And the sound of *Yes, it's you.* Hadn't she been a little less than sure, herself? *Yes, yes. It is me,* she answered silently. She smiled a little, shy, hoping Mrs. Hazel would not ask too many questions. Hazel Towson *was* persistent; surely, even softened by a meal and with a gloss on her thin lips, she could still sniff out a secret. While Agatha watched her mother from behind an ebony woman with a basket on her head (taller than she was), Hazel, softening even more, spoke the next thing quietly: "How's it been, my dear?" She moved her eyes to Sarie's hips, then back up to her face. "You know."

Sarie looked away and almost, almost, blushed. "Oh . . ." Sarie shook her head. "Mrs. Hazel." Hazel thought that Sarie was finally being prim, patted her to show that she approved. "Nevermind. I'm glad to see you're better." Sarie nodded, and, quite truthfully, she said, "Yes. I am. Yes, I really am."

She was. She did not know what she would say if Hazel asked her why she'd come across her so far from Kikanga, of all places at the Mountain Top Hotel. But women with a vision often fill things in. Hazel had ideas of her own. "Stones," she said, "are such a good investment." In fact, she'd bought stones here for fledgling children, too. Most recently for a grandniece who'd come into the world three months before, in Devon. Although she was thinking, *Where on earth will Sarie find the money?* she felt called upon to be polite and kind: Sarie did seem to be coming round, at last; and though the rubber band and pencil really wouldn't do, that pink dress was all right. At least she was exhibiting the right kind of desire. Hazel added, "Small ones can be quite affordable." She cast a skeptical and knowing eye at the gray man behind the counter. "If you can bargain with them." The salesman snapped his stamp book shut and frowned. He looked into a drawer. Hazel patted

Sarie's hand. No, it didn't matter if Sarie Turner had no money for the stones. Desire mattered most.

In the silence that came next, Sarie sensed that Hazel wanted something from her, a reward for being gracious. It was one thing staring Hazel down in the safety of her own apartment on Mchanganyiko Street—but here at the Mountain Top Hotel, where Hazel and not Sarie seemed to be in charge, Sarie felt unsure. "Stones," she said. *"Bien sûr."*

Hazel nodded, pleased. Maybe it did take something shocking, like a baby at her age, to set Sarie Turner straight. "That's wonderful." She was satisfied, for now. So, turning on her heel, she waved. And said, "You *will* be there on Friday, won't you? For our meeting, as we said."

Relieved that Mrs. Hazel was going on her way, Sarie said yes very quickly. *"Absolument.* Yes, Mrs. Hazel. Yes, I will be there." To vaccinate the babies. Indeed, what could be more important? "I will come," she said. "Yes, yes." Hazel Towson smiled. They would talk more about the stones in a few days, and of course, disease.

Sarie, peering out into the parking lot between two shelves of soapstone boxes, the clever lids of which concealed a frog to show a snake, noted with some awe that Hazel Towson climbed into a taxi. She took her daughter's hand. She was ready to go, too. She'd seen enough to know that she was thinking the right thing. And Mrs. Hazel had confirmed it. What she'd said about the stones, that they were a good investment! That's what they would do, eventually. Start out with the crafts and end up with the stones. She and Gilbert would do far better in the end than even this shopkeeper had, she thought. Oh, yes, they'd outdo this little shop with *exports.* She smirked a little, pleasantly. They'd make themselves a fortune. On the way back home, she thought about what she'd say to Gilbert. And how grateful he would be.

*   *   *

Gilbert was not the sort of man who recalls with any clarity what he has dreamed of in the night. Nor did he put any stock in images that, now and then, inexplicable and strange, did nag him when he had come awake. He'd often claimed, in fact, whenever Sarie talked about the things that came to her in sleep—face creams, porcelain bedpans, spears, or shining pairs of shoes—that he never, ever dreamed; as though the nighttime nothingness he swore by made him wise. In the void of his own sleep, he'd found a kind of pride. *His* dreams, if one could call them that, came to him during the day, when his faculties were sharp, when he was in control. *My little hopes,* he called them, as when he told Kazansthakis that he'd like to be in business or wished to spend his old age by the sea. But it hit him as he tied the final shoelace and stood up. Something *had* come in the night. Something sleek and smooth, disturbing and familiar.

Unlike Bibi, with her roses, pineapples, and taxis, unlike Majid, with the things he saw in half-light, and also unlike Sarie, who could recount her dreams with a remarkable precision that Gilbert found exhausting, he didn't quite know what he'd seen. What had come to him as he was bending down, aware of a little itching in his back and a pain along his hip, was more specifically a feeling. Something he'd once known. Or something that would come. Absurd. What kind of thought was that? He jiggled the heels of his hands against his ears to shake it off, cleared his throat, and made his way downstairs.

In the sandy courtyard that was the stomach of their building sat, as always, the quiet Morris Oxford, shapely, smooth, and still. The damson fruits had left dark marks on the boot, like pepper or like mud. *Mr. Suleiman's taxi,* Gilbert thought. He had seen it

many times, of course. And just the other day. But—was there . . .
something different? Perhaps. Perhaps indeed there was. Gilbert
looked at it, in fact, as though he never had before. It was regal,
really. Handsome. Quite a vehicle, he thought. That blue paint, so
durable, was also pleasant to behold. Not unlike a sky. Gilbert
cocked his head. Felt quiet. Unnerved and transfixed. What was
tugging at his throat, the corners of his eyes? What was stirring in
him? Looking at the Morris still, Gilbert noted how its trimmings
shimmered in the sun, how clean the windows were, the hubcaps,
too, their spokes, despite the city dust. Did Mr. Suleiman polish it
at night?

He sniffed. He narrowed his brown eyes and tapped his closed
mouth with two fingers. And, vaguely but more surely with each
step, he sensed that whatever had awoken while he slept had had to
do . . . with cars. *With cars!* Gilbert almost laughed. How very, very
odd. He cocked his head again. He cracked a knuckle in his
pocket, took a step towards the street. And swore that with a drink
(to fuel the thinking process, finances be damned), seated at the
Palm, he'd mull the feeling over before turning to the plan. *The
plan,* he thought. He pulled up his loose trousers and, vigorous,
rubbed his forearms. He threw back his head and felt a springing in
his stride. Perhaps! *What if?* he thought. Indeed. *What could be more
manly?* Here Gilbert thought of Sarie, smiled: *Something for the cars.*

At first, Kazansthakis thought Gilbert was mad. While he could be
counted on for stories and peculiar facts and was not bad to drink
with, Gilbert was in Mr. Frosty's estimation perfectly incapable of
doing anything demanding or original himself. It was the place of
men like Gilbert Turner, Kazansthakis thought, to endure the
strange new times in a not undignified, but permanent, poverty—

never reaching, voicing a discomforting desire, or asking, for too much. He had no business making business. The very thought, Kazansthakis found, to his surprise, was nearly—just—offensive.

Men like Gilbert had a special place in History's bright march: they served as a reminder, Mr. Frosty thought, of what had been the case and wasn't any longer. Empires, he thought, were fueled by men who couldn't do much and whose prime task was to provide the bulk. Foot soldiers, like Gilbert. Yes. Gilbert was the very stuff of over-rule: not too bright, a little dreamy, interesting in his own idle, silly way, but, all told, rather weak. He was not bold, he lacked imagination, was not meant for center stage; he was brick, not mortar. And when Independence came—when loosed from those who might have led him—Gilbert had, exactly as required, shrunk, dried up, and gotten used to struggle. And from that struggle, Kazansthakis thought, he could never rise. He hung on, as others like him did, a barnacle, affixed by unknown glue to the changing world's new walls; but he was not—as the Frosty King had said himself!—a *doer*.

The colonials who had made it — the Greenleafs, Remingtons, and those who lived in Scallop Bay—would have been great men anywhere, Kazansthakis thought. They would always rise above. Their very greatness as the members of a Nation, emissaries of the Colonizing Power, was due in part but in part only to men like Gilbert Turner, who, through meaningless and boring, necessary acts, propped up the flash and flare: pushed papers around, organized the books, and never once complained too seriously or wanted what they couldn't have. With Empires disbanded, the Thorntons and the Greenleafs could take care of themselves. Gilbert Turner, Kazansthakis thought, could not. He ought, a silent casualty, politely take his tiny place and not attempt a project that would only cause him pain.

With two Congo Pilsners in him, frothy, cool, and sharp, however, his mood began to turn. There *was* something new in Gilbert. A weird, intriguing gleam in those watery brown eyes. He was remarkably persistent. Kazansthakis softened. "What exactly, Gilbert Turner, are you thinking? For . . ." He stopped himself from wincing. "For the *cars?*" Well, Gilbert didn't know, exactly. It was enough for him just then to have determined on the way out to the Palm that he had indeed, perhaps, as a red-faced, pudgy boy in England, acquired as a hand-me-down a modest set of toys in the shape of such contraptions. Though he could not know, and perhaps had never known, their makes or precise models, he did recall—the more he thought about it and the more he drank—he did recall, with a ferocity that so shook Kazansthakis he ordered three more beers at once, that the little cars had thrilled him. Gilbert was quite drunk. "I loved them, Mr. Frosty!"

Gilbert may or may not have owned such items as a boy. But he was certain of his story. "I loved them and abandoned them. I forgot," said Gilbert—were there tears in his eyes?—"how very much they mattered." Gilbert was suddenly amenable to the explanations Kazansthakis liked. He'd read too many books, perhaps, got tangled up in them, and forgotten who was who. He began to think symbolically, to entertain theories of fate, and the connectedness of things. "I was unfaithful to them, don't you see?" he said, knocking a great glass off balance and retrieving it—surprising himself most of all—with uncharacteristic grace. "I forgot all about my childhood!" Kazansthakis watched him, noncommittal, slightly worried for his friend but awed by his insistence. "This thing with Uncle James." Gilbert belched. "It's meant to put me on my feet. Return me"—this he said more softly—"to my forgotten glory."

The Frosty King had never seen his friend in such a confused state. Glory? Mr. Turner had had glory? Best forgotten if he had!

Perhaps he had a fever. In his drunkenness, Gilbert for his part experienced his own mind as oddly sharp, uncharacteristically perceptive. "I'm not ill, Mr. Frosty," Gilbert said, and hackles rose in him for the first time in what might have been a hundred thousand years. His throat itched with it, and his back. He felt certain and afraid. As though a deed had just been done. "No, I say. I'm absolutely serious. I'm not only a thinker, you should know." And though he did not know at all what the *thing* was, he said, with a breaking in his voice, "I'm going to try this thing."

Kazansthakis watched his friend. Nodded to the waiter to bring another round. Indeed. Well. "You're certain, Mr. Gilbert?" He rubbed his round, red chin. "One hundred percent, then?"

If Gilbert had stopped to ask himself this question, had not been so drunk, and had not been so—admit, it, yes—*offended* by the Frosty King's response, he might have answered differently. He might have, as the Gilbert of the weeks and months before would have, stepped away from his own statement and said, "No, no, Mr. Frosty. Just a little joke, I suppose. I didn't really mean it." Or, "You're right. I'd best forget it, don't you think?" But these things he did not. The hubbub of the Palm—soft, rising in small waves, the tinny skittering of feet and cups and bowls—and the look on Mr. Frosty's face (surprise, curiosity, an unexpected glow) spurred him on. So such decisions take. He needed to confirm it, say, "Yes, I am. I have always, always. Thought highly of engines. You know, cars," he said, "and things."

The Frosty King was not entirely convinced that Gilbert had really had a motor-love as a small boy. It was the very first he'd heard of it, and they'd been meeting there for years. When had Gilbert ever sympathized with Mr. Frosty over the difficulties he endured supplying his own Fiat? Had they ever spoken wisely about OPEC, the ups and downs of fuel? The crises? Had they ever talked about the buses that the Soviets had brought in? No, he did not believe his friend. But he was swayed by something else. By Mrs. Frosty, truth be told, who had rubbed his neck and back, kissed him hotly on the ear, and said, "Poor, poor, Mr. Turner. Can't you try to help?" And also, yes, by the fierce red look on Gilbert's face, a kind of shame and fury, an excitement, something that could, perhaps—yes, why not, why not, if it did not portend disaster?— be transformed into joy. *So what if people changed their spots?* he thought. Perhaps this world was made for that. Oil prices were stable once again. He could not think of any trouble rising, other than another war on the far border, and wars were good—weren't they?—for a certain kind of business. People used their cars, and most of them were old. The buses broke down all the time. *Why not?* he thought. Indeed. This shift, this sudden news—he thought: *It's just like in a movie.* The dawning of adventure. So he stopped shaking his head and raised his glass to Gilbert.

Gilbert sensed the change in Kazansthakis, and it stilled him. He sighed, felt the roll of his own gut settling nicely at the high edge of his trousers. He dug his hips into his seat, puffed out his pounding chest, expanded, spread his weight over the crooked metal chair. Beyond them, in a busy wind, white clouds came and went.

When the Frosty King said, "Spare parts, then? Is that where you are going?" Gilbert, had he owned and worn a hat, would have thrown it in the air. Exactly. Spare parts, absolutely. He felt as if the world around him had come to an invigorating stop. And, in a moment, Kazansthakis, who did like a little play—especially when it involved outsmarting the smart (who liked to put men behind bars or at least extract from them large sums for putting into motion plans for things like this)—made a few suggestions, said he'd like to help. "Fun!" he said. "We're going to have some fun! Spare parts, my dear Mr. Gilbert. Have another drink. To spares!"

"To spares!" said Gilbert Turner. In the wet and dizzy moments that ensued, Kazansthakis drinking with both fists and Gilbert, belching, struggling to keep up, the Frosty King suddenly recalled a man he knew who now worked at the airport. And wasn't there a woman he'd once tried to kiss (a single weakness, one small moment, about which Mrs. Frosty didn't know—and thank God it hadn't worked) who still harbored a small flame for him and now wielded at the Customs Office a much-desired stamp? What about, oh, yes, the Frenchman from the airlines who frequented the Frosty Kreem for scoops of sweet vanilla? And that other person, too, very, very local, who had liked pistachio in his youth and who was now, if Kazansthakis was correct, the Minister of Trade? The Frosty King did have a motor of his own, and he was often worried about spark plugs, brake shoes, baseplates, and the like. By his fifth order of drink, the Frosty King was hopeful and, indeed, violently, irreversibly impressed by Mr. Gilbert Turner.

"I will find things out for you," Kazansthakis said. "Do it, Mr. Gilbert." He stood. He shook Gilbert's hand with both of his, meaningfully, with respect, as if sealing something private, as though Gilbert Turner were a new, important man. Someone to be reckoned with. A Greenleaf or a Thornton! "The sky's the limit!" Kazansthakis said. He gave Gilbert a wink before skipping down the stairs.

Gilbert returned home with hubcaps spinning in his mind. "Spare parts," he said under his breath, repeating it until the two words might mean almost nothing, or be the meaning of the world.

By the following evening, a secret competition thrilled the tiles and carpet of the Turners' old apartment. Gilbert paced and Sarie skulked. Each made notes beneath their fingers in the air, and, when colliding in the parlor, each turned from the other to hunt down the scraps of paper on which each had tried out sums. Though neither of them knew it, skinny statues, jewels, and woven bags were warring in the parlor against pistons, calipers, and fly-wheels. They each had an Idea.

Sarie, however, was the more honest of the two. One day over lunch, she told her husband of the plan. "What do you think about it, eh?" she'd asked. "The crafts? For the big men who have gone back to their home? For people like your uncle?" Gilbert pushed his rice away and found himself contemplating Sarie with a kindness in his heart. In his visions of the future, Gilbert had begun, without so much as trying, designing for himself a slightly mythic spouse: a sweet one, a docile one who would admire him. So inspired by his talks with Kazansthakis, charged, excited, he felt himself becoming, in his own estimation, something like a businessman. And didn't businessmen have charming, pretty wives who listened? He wasn't really being cruel.

If Sarie had ever said to him at an attentive moment, about someone else, "That person doesn't look," or, "That person doesn't listen," he would have said, "You're right. Awful, yes, just awful," because he himself had often felt that no one looked at him or heard him. He didn't do it meanly. It was just that he had his little hopes, and he did like his daydreams. But Gilbert's dreams, just then, were taking on all kinds of lucid shape. That evening in the kitchen, he found it hard to tell which woman was real and which woman he was just coming to sense would spring fully into being once the business plan was firm. When Sarie told him her idea, as a good man ought to handle a good wife, he decided to be tender, and took care not to be dismissive.

"Why, certainly," he said. "A good idea, dear." And though he didn't press her and didn't ask for details about what she'd already sorted out, Sarie smiled at him over her teacup. It was not the full response she'd hoped for, but she was trying to be patient. The thing had been decided, had it not? She could wait, and would. *Men like Gilbert,* Sarie thought, *need time for bright news to sink in.* "All right. We'll talk about it soon." She rose up from her chair so surely and so happily that it looked to Gilbert for a moment as if she had just burst up from the ground, a sudden tree, a fleshy woman-geyser. He refocused his eyes. "Oh, yes, my dear. We'll discuss it at great length." And then he turned back to his little paper, where he scribbled with his pen. "I am sorting *les détails,* you know," she said, and Gilbert, a little bit impressed, thought, as he sometimes did, *My Sarie can speak French,* and murmured, "Yes, of course, I'm sure."

Sarie was relieved. She'd won. She'd had their idea. And Gilbert, she believed, would in good time come around. *He will need to soothe himself at first, because he hasn't thought of anything and he will owe to me success.* She'd give his manly pride some room. Gilbert, thankful for her silence, began to write down what the Frosty King had told him (spark plugs, Germany or Japan; fan belts, France or England; flywheels, Emirates; and shipments, island ports and airports). It occurred to him as he wrote, *flywheels,* that he could not remember, exactly, what Sarie had just said. *Baskets? Hm.*

As he wrote, and wrote, and wrote, an illuminated world emerged before his eyes, one of his own making, and he grew increasingly intent on keeping all specifics from her until everything was right. He'd reveal nothing to Sarie, to his wife—*My helpmeet*—until he'd seen Kazansthakis one more time and gotten his approval. He'd meet up with the Frosty King for some final talk and be ready in the end to compose a reassuring letter to great old Uncle James. Or perhaps, he thought, seduced by the idea of presenting

her with (what was it people said?) a great *fait accompli,* he'd wait a
little longer, until Uncle James had been so mightily impressed that
everything was set. *Then,* he thought, *I'll tell Sarie what I've done.*
Gilbert wanted, shall we say, to impress the woman he had married, the mother of his child, just as, he thought, he had once done
in his youth. Had he not been fine then, a promising young man?
And had she not been darling? He was sprouting, bit by bit, a certain kind of wing.

In the meantime, unimpeded by someone else's sharper mind,
advice, or realism, Sarie's visions soared. How clever she was! How
amazing that she had in all those years of living in the city, of sitting
with her child, of cringing at the thought of garden parties and of
functions, not thought even once about going into business, of setting, so to speak, up shop. She'd spent years sitting at home, moving
slow through rooms, wiping things, folding and unfolding washed
and dirty clothes. She'd only had one child, and late—and for this
Sarie was glad, grateful for whatever it had been that had kept her
insides free. But free for *what?* she asked herself, feeling now that
she must hurry. She'd had so much *time!*

Lots of people started businesses, so it seemed to her. Even, no,
especially, in the Jilima highlands (*Where, in some way,* Sarie
thought, *I am really from*). Men sold everything they could, transformed trash into commodities (rubber tires for molding into
shoes, beaten tin for making mixing spoons and lamps), and
women, too, did things. Women sold tomatoes, onions, woven fans,
and carpets; they fashioned brooms from twigs, and ladles from
palm husks. In Sarie's new conception of herself, she, lost child, little Belgian girl, had grown up at the breast of enterprise, suckling
acumen and savvy from everyone she knew. She began to think
more deeply of herself. Of how she'd come to be, of who she
might become. And in that other part of her, the part that she had

felt so still and quiet when she woke from her idea, she thought about Majid Ghulam, whom she hadn't seen for several days. But, oh, how she wished to share her thoughts with him! How she missed her other man! She'd go, she thought. She'd go see him alone, and revel in their limbs.

Fourteen

After bathing, wet hair dark, Majid Ghulam took up the little scrap of mirror Ali kept stored on the sill. Ismail and Ali thought a lot about their looks. They battled over hair oil and pomades; they each owned a comb. Ismail had recently acquired aftershave, a dark brown, slick concoction with a sharp metallic scent. Inspired by his brothers, Habib, too, sometimes checked for acne in the glass. But Jeevanjee had not ever, not since Hayaam's death, and not since what was like her second death (the wraith; a living woman's body; his brand-new filling-out), really taken stock. *And yet*, he thought, remembering a poem, *there comes sunlight on the ruins*. Another: *Peacock males do strut*. What did he look like this morning?

The slender shard, broken in the sideways shape of a lateen, felt light between his fingers. Like a person holding a soft creature, examining its fluff and checking it for fleas, he held the mirror with his palm and brought it to his face. No fleas, indeed, but a hard-lined face and some rather sagging skin. His eyelids seemed enormous. He rubbed a flake of white stuff from his upper lip and assessed his thin mustache; it was tufted, not as neatly shaped as a dapper man would like. But he could find some scissors, or a better blade.

At first conscious of the effort, then with greater courage, he smiled into the glass. It didn't matter so much what he looked like. He knew that eyes and mouths and skin and hair, and the cut of a mustache, weren't all there was to romance. He knew that manner, bearing, mattered almost more. It was poems taught him that. He'd often written long and hard about the way a person walked, the sway of certain feet, the shape of shoulders tensed. The way a cherished voice can pump the smitten heart. He'd once known something about love. He'd always had, he told himself, a sense of deeper things. Of spirit. Sarie Turner's recent, unexpected absence had given him the chance to think: How should he understand it? Was it romance? Was it love? Majid wasn't sure.

He thought of how, the other day, Sarie Turner had dissolved beneath him on the bed, how she had met his limbs with kindness and with, he thought, a need that was something like his own. How, resting her head in the very heat of things, upon his shoulder, she had bitten at his skin and caused him a sharp pain. He'd felt a recognition. Was that it? Was that the source of pleasure? That something in tall, hard Sarie Turner felt like something in himself? Perhaps Sarie, too, had sorrows in her life, things she couldn't speak of, that had ruined everything, turned her plans around and given her thick jolts that she had never wished for. Perhaps she too had long been torn from how it should have been. She was an orphan, after all, and she did not, except for her small flat, Majid thought, really have a home. What if they were, together for a moment, on the edge of a rebirth? Each to find new things?

He did like to think of love, of being in love, feeling love. He hadn't, in so long. And yet how thrilling it could be! He had wanted only, in those first days after the eager battle on his bed, for her to keep coming to his house, and touch him as she had. His skin shook with it, his legs and back and chest. How grand it was to feel a woman in his arms. Hayaam lurked no longer in the corners of his sleep. He could look in on Tahir without guilt. He didn't know if Sarie Turner was the end of things—if she was what the feeling that he had (lambent change, a freshness!) meant,

or if she was more like a signal, a signpost on the road. He didn't
know what his boys knew or if they had suspicions. And he didn't
care, even if Maria, with her strutting and her scowling, was issuing
a judgment. He didn't want to know. Shutting many questions out,
Majid wished just this: to bask. Lust had made him strong, determined. And virility had brought another sense, a slowly growing
feeling that he, Majid Ghulam Jeevanjee, might have some things
to choose from and that he might stage, at a not-too-far-off date, a
bright reentry to the world he'd left so long ago for grief.

Sugra came that morning. He knew she'd come before she called
to him to say that she'd arrived. The metal doors below gave out a
squeak and bang. He heard the thump of Sugra's feet, then Sugra
shouting to Maria, to say "Hello, hello!" He walked slowly down
the hall and greeted her from the top of the dim stairs. "Come up!
Oh, I am glad that you have come."

   At the bottom of the steps, Sugra placed her elbows at her hips
and peered at him through the fust in an exaggerated way. Majid
had surprised her. "Glad? You are, are you? Glad? What? Can you
say that again?" Sugra's voice was loud. Sometimes, Majid thought,
she hollered. And on some days he lacked the strength to please
her. But he didn't mind saying it again, not today, when he was
feeling brave. "I'm glad, I'm glad," he said. He took a step towards
her. "Have you heard me now?" Sugra cocked her head and
waited. Something in her cousin surely was ashift, and though she
did not know the cause, she had decided to be gratified to see it.
"Say it one more time."

   Majid laughed at her despite himself and heard his laughter
echo on the walls. He found that he was not only laughing at his
cousin, but also at his laughter. He teased her. "I cannot believe the

sun can rise when you are still asleep. Your husband must have sunglasses; your children all must squint. I am so glad to see you I feel I've not been glad before." By this time, Sugra was halfway up the stairs. She brought her face close to his and frowned. She twisted up her mouth and raised an eyebrow, steep. "Who's this?" she asked. "Who's this man I see?"

This was a bit too much for him. Majid looked away, moved back up the stairs. Glad. How long had it been? A silence passed, and sobered him. He led her to the kitchen. She straightened her long dress and looked down at her bag. More seriously, she said, "Ghuji. You are sounding like a poet. What is happening to you?" Majid swallowed, turned away from her and asked, "Have you been to the clinic?"

He had not gone himself. He'd promised Tahir that he would, that he would secure crutches, and that he would personally hurl any doctor who was slow to give an answer out the nearest window. But everyone who'd heard him—the aunts, the older boys, and his smallest son—had known he did not have it in him. He hadn't left the neighborhood for as long as they recalled; he never left the house. When he'd made the promise, Sugra, from across the room, had given him a gentle look. She had raised her hand and pressed her fingertips just slightly to her chest, bent her head a little, before turning away to offer someone sweets. He had known that she would do it. Get the crutches for his boy. She was the type to make connections, after all, to remember people's names. And she'd once studied with the doctors, long ago. If anyone could get something tricky done, she could.

Sugra had been trying. She'd gone down to the clinic now three times. "The first time, that big doctor was not in. The second time he was, and he did all the dancing-dancing that a good doctor should do. 'Yes-yes,' he said. 'I promise you.' We'll see. It's because he's scared of *you*, you know, that he said he'd do his best. 'Mad Majid!' he is thinking."

Sometimes Sugra's forthrightness could startle him, make him feel that she was seeing things in him that he would have rather hidden. Other people didn't say, "I see that you are changing," for example, or "People think you're mad." But Sugra let a person know. She was looking at him still, and Majid turned away. She shook the dust out of her skirt. "What—what happened this time?" he asked. She was now considering her sleeves. "This time," she said, "I went into the reception and saw a girl I went to school with. She works there; what do you think of that? I go in to get crutches and instead I see a friend. She's married now. No kids."

He was thinking about Tahir's missing leg—not as an event, not quite as a condition, but in a concrete sense, as an absent limb. He thought about the thigh that ended in a stump, the emptiness below it. Very briefly, he thought about the shoe. Sugra looked at him again and saw that any glumness he had lost was welling up again.

"Oh, Ghuji!" Sugra said. She had liked his teasing! Wished he would stay bright. "It's not the end of things." Sugra's round face shrank a little. It was hard work visiting a cousin who'd been gloomy for so long. It would have been easier for her if Ghuji hadn't teased her, hadn't seemed, somehow, to be edging out of grief. Having laughed with him, after sorrow for so long, it was harder not to wish that he'd be really glad again. She took steps towards Tahir's room. Majid, helpless, shuffled after. "Come on," Sugra said. "I've heard Habib is working on a cane. For in between, so at least your boy can move." Majid blinked at her. Sugra shook her head and groaned. "I mean, until the crazy doctors give us something nice."

*   *   *

In the afternoon, Sarie made her way to Kudra House alone. She was, she'd said to Gilbert, to meet with Hazel Towson for a British Council Luncheon, followed by a lecture on the Public Health Campaign, and afterwards a tea. And couldn't Gilbert see his way to watching Agatha awhile? Gilbert had said, "Sarie, no. Not really? You're not going to *that?*" He'd laughed. "I thought it was a joke!" But Sarie said she'd promised, and Gilbert finally shrugged. No matter what he really thought of great big Mrs. Hazel, no matter how she made him feel, he thought: if they were going to have a business, come into real money, it couldn't hurt for Sarie to have some proper lady friends. Why should Sarie not get used to being close to all of that, get ready to step in? Once they *were* in business, he'd be more than equal to Jim Towson's brash wife; he could look her in the eye, say, "No," or, "I don't think so," and not feel terror in his heart. And so could Sarie, yes.

"All right," he said, still scribbling. Sarie was already at the door and about to move into the stairwell when Gilbert raised his head. He'd almost forgotten. "But what will you tell her about . . ." He gestured to his stomach. "You know. The baby." He looked shyly away. Sarie frowned a moment, then pretended she was thinking. She'd forgotten, too. But she knew what Gilbert didn't: she was not going to attend any British Council do. "Something, I am sure," she said. And Gilbert, thinking of spare parts again, did not ask her what.

Outside, the earnest, jovial sun was the color of a lemon. A light breeze tickled the high buildings, and the hot swath of the sea was the happy kind of bluish-green that is reported here to keep bad luck at bay. Sarie walked to Kudra House with a frothing in her heart. She felt as though she hadn't seen her new man in a year. So very much had happened!

On Mchanganyiko Street, Sarie's stride was easy. She did not worry that she would be seen. She thought, without knowing who "them" was: *Let them all see me!* And she held her head up high. Something about those four days, her walking in the park and that productive visit to the Mountain Top Hotel, made Sarie hope she *would* be noticed and remarked upon. She felt present, happy with the air, prepared to notice things, and, why not, to be noticed, too.

She passed the narrow paan shops and the green-mango-chili stalls and thought how sharp they smelled. As usual, on Mosque Street, the mendicants were out; the weaving woman registered her passing with a pause. Before the man with one blind eye, Sarie, feeling generous, dropped a shilling on the sheet. He blinked, and shifted slightly. On Mahaba Street, Sarie stopped before the window of the New Purnima Snack. Kachoris! How hot and good they smelled.

As Sarie moved along, she felt exceptionally alert. How busy and how nicely colored this day seemed to be. The soft blue of the sky; such bright doorways and trees! She craned her neck to see the high fronts of the old houses: at one, thick plants on the roof; at another, four pink windows, shut. At the balcony of a blue mansion, Sarie noticed an old woman looking down and almost smiled at her. On Libya Street, Sarie walked more quickly. She passed the hardware men, mechanics, mamantilie women who sold red beans by the ladle, cane-juice-coffee-oatmeal men, little boys, and bus touts, and felt part of a great pattern—in motion and ashift. Everyone, she thought, yes, everyone, had business to take care of, lots to think about and do. Her purse bounced lightly at her side; the rubber heels of her kandambili shoes snapped hard against the bottoms of her feet; her own fresh cadence pleased her. Oh, how big the new world was! And how unthinkable, how lucky, that she was going to see her lover on her own (she almost hugged herself), that she had one at all.

Once beyond the metal doors, Sarie was relieved not to see Maria right away. It was one thing not minding how she looked, out there, on Mosque Street and on Libya. But in Kudra House's alley, Sarie was unsure of Maria. When upstairs with tea or sweets, Maria did not seem like a threat, no, was simply Majid's house girl. But if Sarie saw Maria by herself, out here in the courtyard, she had the sharp, unpleasant feeling that she was being weighed. Maria made her nervous. She could hear Maria on the other side of Kudra House, running water from the tap. Not in sight. Occupied elsewhere. *Today I am so lucky,* Sarie thought. She closed her eyes, sighed with her mouth open in a tickled, private way, and stopped for just a moment at the threshold. Next, to bring her heartbeat back to center, she held her breath and counted slowly to sixteen. Then, both hands curled over its mouth, she pressed her purse tight against her stomach and walked up those cool stairs. She felt almost pretty. To bring some color out, she bit her lip with her top teeth until she could feel the lower ridge come near to popping through the flesh.

On the second-to-last stair, she called out *"Hodi,"* in the local manner. Once. The parrot's cry rang out, "Who? Who?" There was no other answer. *Hm. Has Majid not heard my voice?* Sarie stepped inside, confused. Where was he? *"Hodi!"* Twice. Surely he would come and greet her, pull her towards him and squeeze deeply at her fingers. Sarie could see the shadow of the parrot's cage swaying clearly on the wall, marking out the pattern of the talking bird's excitement. "Guests now! Guests now! Guests!" Remembering Maria down below, she called out rather formally: "Hallo, Mr. Jeevanjee!" Then, with tenderness, a lightness in her heart, she called out more softly: "Majid? Majid?" The caged bird had gone quiet. Majid did not answer.

Is he not at home? Sarie felt a pang, a momentary sinking, called again; and then (relief!) Majid Ghulam's clear voice rang out from far back in the house. It said: "Come in! Come in! You're welcome." Sarie thought how different his way of speaking was from Gilbert's, how much more in charge of words he was. He said, voice steady, "Come in all the way, please, until you are inside." She set her purse down on the settee, checked her hair with happy hands, and smoothed out her short dress. She stepped with ease out of her negligible shoes and slid them with her toes to rest beside Majid's leather sandals and a pair of worn-out cleats shared by Ali and Habib. Affectionate, she thought: *Their shoes.*

"Majid?" She was aware as she pronounced his name that it had become one among the sweetest, softest sounds that Sarie-in-the-present could imagine (others: night wind through the leaves of plantain groves, her footsteps on the ground). Passing, for the first time unaccompanied, beyond the coffee table and down into the hall, Sarie felt, without quite knowing how, that she had undergone a subtle alteration. What new status, whether she had slipped up or down the scale of honor, she could not decide. Was she from here on in to simply saunter up the stairs and step through the blue parlor, dispensing with hallos and welcome-welcome please? The idea of it thrilled her.

She came out on the high balcony and saw her lover squatting. Huddled at the end of the veranda, Majid was examining the henna seedling in its rusted metal tin. He looked, she thought (and she approved), like a nurse about to give a patient a massage, assessing the stiff limbs before making a first move. He tugged lightly at the thickening stem, then patted at the earth with both his palms spread out. With a wave of his ten fingers he sprinkled water near the roots. Satisfied, he urged her to come near. Eyes encouraging and nice, he nodded. "You aren't a guest here anymore." Sarie shivered, thankful. All her doubts were gone. It didn't matter if she came to see him every day or only now and then. He'd greet her, she thought, just like this, any time she chose.

When he did get up, Majid brought a slender forearm to his brow and sent his trousers properly back down his thin legs with a tugging at each thigh. He bent forward and unrolled the tattered cuffs, which had come up to his knees. Sarie held her hand towards him, but he pointed out that his was dark with soil. She touched his wrist instead. He blinked at her. Sarie's face was open, sunlit. She felt very, very tall, indeed, as though her weight were concentrated in a mass that hung far above her skull, balanced on the distant needles of her feet. His smile made her feel dizzy.

Majid held the blue door open for her. She looked meaningfully towards him as she passed, leaned very slightly in. He moved into the kitchen, beckoned. Sarie watched him wash his fingers, palms, and wrists with a stub of laundry soap. Then, thumb and finger on her elbow, he ferried her into his room. "Tahir is asleep," he said. Majid closed his eyes and placed, by way of explanation, both of his clean hands flat against her chest. And so, before everything else, they riffled through each other's clothes. The dress, which she had so nicely straightened in the stairwell, fell, at her insistence, from her body to the floor. Majid kept his shirt on.

He smiled lightly while they did the thing—not at her, exactly, but at the room, himself, and at their moistly urgent stew. It pleased him that she frowned, that she tugged and plucked at him as though she were very busy drowning and did not especially desire to be saved. That she seemed, he thought, *A wild one.* He pressed himself against her with a certainty he recognized: it was the same sureness he'd felt, years and years before, when choosing the right word. When slipping commas into place.

*   *   *

Afterwards, Sarie wanted to stay naked for a lovely little while. When Majid held her dress out, Sarie shook her head. He set it down, instead, upon a chair, and patted Sarie's arm before going down the hall. She rested on his rumpled bed and waited for him to come out from the bathroom, clean, shirtsleeves long again and fastened at the cuffs. She plucked idly at a kapok tuft that had come creeping through a small tear in the mattress, and squinted at the window. Between the wooden shutters, the afternoon was soft.

Sarie also listened, idly, for sounds from Tahir's room. As Majid was pouring water from a ladle down his chest across the hall, Sarie heard, from the other side, the side that held the boys' room, something that sounded like a shuffle, a stretching in the dark. How many things a person feels in the midst of an affair that has not yet firmly taken shape, or ended! She sat up with a gasp, as though with Agatha's absence, too, she were more naked than ever, more at risk of something: *His boy is awake!* She lurched forward for her dress, imagining that Tahir might come bursting through the doorway, finger pointed at her heart. She had almost reached her dress when she had a second thought. She listened, listened. There was nothing. Then she calmed herself with a tinny, awkward laugh. *He is not walking on his own yet. No one has got crutches.* Tahir's new condition, Sarie thought, held a few advantages for them. *Even if he is awake, if he tries to leave the bedroom, he will hop and hop; then he will fall and be in need of help. A fall must make a loud noise.* She yawned, too; then, stretching out her arms, determined that if Tahir was astir—her very will would force him back to sleep. She wanted to be happy.

When Majid, trousers traded for a blue seruni cloth, came back and closed the door behind him, Sarie rolled onto her stomach and crossed her ankles in the air. She patted at the rumpled sheet, but Majid smiled and shook his head. "In a moment, Sarie. Wait." He moved away, and as Sarie's feet described fine circles in the air, he sat down at his desk. He pulled a pencil from a drawer and opened up a notebook she had never seen. She wondered, *Will he write me a poem?* She watched him in the mirror.

Majid, whose body had just lain with hers, who could still faintly smell her talcum and her other, rougher scents on the surface of his skin despite his recent bath, *was* writing her a poem. Or, a poem about her. *This,* he thought, *is what she's bringing me.* The pencil moved, slowly at first, jagged. He looked up into the mirror for a moment. Saw Sarie watching him. *How pale she is,* he thought. *How big.* She *was* big, much bigger than he was, and Majid, eyes resting for a moment on her jutting hip, then moving up her muscled arm, felt awe. He wrote: *Above the quiet sea, a giant moon has shown.* He stopped. In the mirror, Sarie smiled at him. She wanted him to write a good one, then come to sit beside her, read it while she rested her great head on his knees. "Is it for me?" she asked. Majid smiled but didn't answer. Sarie watched his head and back, the slight bobbing of his shoulders as the pencil scratched and stopped. She wondered, *Shall I tell him now about Great-Uncle James?* No, she'd wait, she thought. She liked feeling, when with him, that nothing else could matter, that what went on *out there,* with Gilbert, meant nothing at all. Telling him would change things, shift a balance. She didn't want to, yet. She'd linger.

Sarie stretched her legs, ran her toes along the panes in the high board. *How pretty those panes are.* A peacock, lotus flowers, waves. Some of them were missing. Majid was still hunched over his notebook, frowning, shaking his bent head. Now and then he brought the pencil to his mouth. Sarie looked at her own legs, then arms, next at her smart lover, then at her legs again. She felt slow and long. This was nice, this quiet after making love. This sitting in a room while a good man wrote a poem. She thought Majid looked handsome, and that the part of his face she could still see in the mirror looked feverish, intense. Sweetly, as she might have thought of Agatha if the girl had been a boy, she wanted to protect him.

The thought she had surprised her: *He is not as strong as I am. These things he feels could kill him.* And Sarie almost laughed. How strange that she should feel that way about a man. And then, she thought, *Not so.* Had she not felt this way about young Gilbert Turner, too, once she had been married, once she'd seen him bare? That *she,* not he, could withstand anything to come? That *she* had bones, not he?

Majid was writing on: *Along the shore her sizely jewels are treasures for the poor.* Yes, the poem was for Sarie, somehow. At least it was for the Sarie he was thinking of just then, who was bringing him new life. When he looked up at her reflection, Majid's face was bright. The lines around his eyes were slack with gratitude, contentment. Sarie's wish to shield him sharpened and grew teeth. No, she would not tell him, yet, about planning for a business. She reached out for her dress. *It might,* she thought, *upset him.* His job, Sarie thought, was to write, and write, and write.

"It's late," she said. It was. The light outside the window had acquired a greenish cast, gone deep. Sarie rose, and Majid put down his pencil. "Don't stop writing," Sarie said. She came to stand behind him and touched him on the shoulder. "Just please if you can zip my dress." He reached out from his seat and brought the zipper up, pausing, as she bent, to touch her tousled hair.

"The clasp," she said. "Please you must also close the clasp." Majid's fingers flailed and stumbled at her nape, tried twice, and managed on the third. Sarie thought, but did not say, *I do not trust my husband to close my dresses for me without making a tear. But my lover, yes, my lover, is another sort of man.* She didn't let him walk her down the stairs. "You write," she said. Majid took her hand and squeezed it. "You'll read it to me next time."

Once Sarie was gone, Majid rose up from the dresser and went into the hall. He stepped into the boys' room. In the dimness, Tahir was an ashy shape, small beneath the sheets. A thin arm dangled to the floor. Something in Majid, a tiny anxious thing, plucked once at his heart. *"It isn't the world's end,"* he thought. *That's what Sugra said.* He tried to feel that this was true. And Sugra's visit, Sarie's (holding her! her legs!), and the poem, and the softness he could despite it all feel rising now and then from unexpected places—in the bathroom, on the balcony, sometimes in the very air itself—helped Majid to think that Tahir would be fine. *Patience,* that was all. He touched Tahir on the forehead, said a little prayer. From the hallway he could hear Maria. There she was, banging loudly at a pot—bang! bang!—just as Sarie must have crossed into the street. The parrot, waking, let out a vivid shriek that sounded like the slamming of a door.

Sarie walked home from Kudra House still feeling slow and thoughtful. She'd stayed rather late. The street was coming quiet. Her thongs flipped lightly on the ground, a dull thud underfoot. She could hear her steps, her sighs, and also heard her hands as they brushed against her dress. Her legs felt very long. On Libya Street the cane-juice man had locked away the grinder in the empty hardware shop from which he rented space. Flecks and sprigs of cane flesh glowed pale along the curb. From behind the boarded doors, Sarie sensed the presence of the press, which was painted blue, which had (she could see in her mind's new and eager eye) an ornate metal wheel. Sarie stopped there for a moment, then moved again, cool beneath the awnings. From nowhere, everywhere, from beneath her flip-flop feet, there rose the sweet and heavy under-smell of sewage. Sarie took it in. She wanted to smell everything: cane and gasoline, and even rotting things, and talcum, and the heat of Majid's chest. So many details, suddenly, so many things to feel!

To such an inundation, Sarie was unused. So much had hap-pened in one week that Sarie was surprised she still knew the way home. The sky—after all, a city sky that she had known for years and should have felt was hers—seemed lush and suddenly like powder. Ponderous and feathery, brittle, delicate, and grand. The house crows were gray flashes in the hidden wings of things—sometimes a swift rustle, sometimes a hard caw. The houses, too, which she had known a little while in other, better days, looked older and more secretive than she had ever thought them. She wondered to herself if she was seeing things through the eyes of love or through her lover's eyes. The second (ever practical) she discarded as a physical impossibility. But, without for all that being certain she knew what it was, she liked the first one: love.

Heading for the roundabout, where she would make a turn and start towards the water, Sarie said something to herself for the first time, because this was an afternoon of firsts: *When I was young, I did not expect to live here until I became old. But here,* thought Sarie, noticing for the first time that the trees in front of the old mosque were not mango trees at all but another sort of rich and green, thick thing, *I am.* Next, *I will be here forever. And this*—with a bit of drama, now a sigh, an exhalation whose temperature exactly matched the air outside her mouth—*is where I am going to die.*

She experienced a moment of surprise, a shock. *When I am very old,* she thought, *I will remember Mr. Jeevanjee. Perhaps,* she thought, *perhaps I will still know him.* In the evening street, Sarie felt an overdue, a much-belated, orphan's pang. In her soft, loose state, unfolded as she was by her secret man's caresses, and perhaps by having been beside—as she saw him—a *poet,* it struck her, years after the fact, that her parents were both dead.

In Jilima, Sarie had thought more than once that when she became old enough, she would go back to Belgium and would learn, properly this time, how to be a nurse. But she hadn't. She had been, it struck her, passive about things. It would not have been simple to go back. There was no one left to see. After the War's end, there had been too much to do, renew, expand, recover; the Sisters, to whom she'd grown accustomed, seemed to feel themselves in the middle of the future. They were busy planting vegetables, building a new hut. They'd studded the two cows. And they themselves had no idea how to take her home. They'd waited without saying so for this: a husband, for someone else to show her what to do. It was easier to stay. Sarie grew up and grew tall, and when the Magistrate's assistant hit a donkey with the car and came to them for help, she was, it seemed to everyone, ready to be wed.

She had thought (in the vague, mild way that she had long been used to thinking) that she might end up in England with her husband. He was British, after all, and wouldn't he, as British people did, long somehow for old, familiar things? Know what his home was? Europeans, Sarie had once heard, didn't die in Africa unless killed in native wars, or by terrible diseases, or unless they were, as the Jilima Sisters had all been, inexplicable, for good or ill, and determined to remain.

But when other expatriates packed up, made steamer reservations, and held their final dos, and Gilbert Turner, longing to be different, afraid of failure back at home, had gone running in the opposite direction, dug himself right in, Sarie, unperturbed, had exchanged one future for another with a few words from a husband. "If we are to be resting here," she said, "I will take back all the blouses which I was going to give away." How full of accidents life was! She'd simply plucked her blouses from the box she had prepared and set them on the shelf. She hadn't asked herself, or him, a thing.

At home on Mchanganyiko Street, Gilbert was asleep, but he was shaken by the sound of Sarie's voice as, finding Agatha alone on the dark steps, she told her to wash up. He yawned, stretched his pale, short fingers in the air. He heard Sarie opening the door and thought, not entirely awake, confused, *How simple marriage is.* He was proud of Sarie for attending that long luncheon. He felt sympathetic towards her, tender. *How she must have suffered.* He made up his mind to ask her what the ladies at the Council had to say, if Hazel Towson had proposed anything outlandish, whether she had thought to bring back any cake. He wasn't sure that he would tell her that he had spent the afternoon composing the most important letter of his life. Or that, once the thing was done, he had taken Agatha for ice cream at the Parlor, where he had given the blue envelope to Mr. Frosty, who would give it to a steward who was flying to Dubai and on to London the next day. *Not quite yet,* he thought. *It will be like a gift.* He'd surprise her with it all once he'd had an answer.

Sarie, loosened by her walk, and feeling—because making love can do this—that her body was uniquely suited to affection of all kinds, stepped into the bedroom and touched Gilbert on the shoulder. The openness and gratitude she felt for Mr. Jeevanjee, her Majid, spilled out also onto Gilbert. She had—and though it disconcerted her, she gave over to it the way one gives in to a swoon—the same desire to protect him that she had had at Kudra House, for Majid Ghulam Jeevanjee and his sudden little verse. Gilbert touched her hand with his and laid his cheek upon it. Sarie pressed her fingers down, released them. She felt able, well, and proud. In charge of both her men.

❧ III ❧

Fifteen

And so. In the days between Gilbert's sending of the letter and the receipt of Uncle James's reply, there was a certain stillness: the surface of the world a smooth expanse, nothing to disturb it but the future's unknown shade and twitch. Bibi, keeping when she could an eye on Issa and Nisreen, nursed her aching fingers. Majid simmered quietly. Gilbert's back itched intermittently and seemed, sporadically, to show signs of improvement.

Sarie, laboring in secret, continued to feel doubled. She liked her private self increasingly, was enamored of the person brought out by her walks to Libya Street and by Majid's (now tender and now furious) investigative hands. In Kudra House's parlor and in Majid's cool, damp room, it was sometimes for Sarie as if time itself, come to rest on vast, oblivious haunches, were nodding, happy, in the sun. That present self, which was Majid's and her own, was prospering, and it pleased her. Squinting as though from a glare, she did also think about the other one, the self-on-the-horizon. That self occupied the future, and Sarie vaguely understood it as belonging rather to a public—or to Gilbert, Agatha, and even Hazel Towson. To customers, accountants. She was hazily excited about the things she felt were coming; in that audience, surely, Majid also sat (*Where would he go,* she thought, *unless he was to die? He lives so close to me!*), but she could not either fathom *Majid's Sarie* at the same time as she envisioned *the Sarie that moved forward,* into other days.

In that future life, did they still meet, like *this,* or had they learned another style of being? Did they still take off their clothes? Did they go out to the balcony to feel the city's air? The future gave her headaches. She couldn't see it clearly. And because it so confused her, she didn't tell Majid about her plans or Uncle James's letter. She made no mention of the export business, volunteered no news about the husband she was fooling, and kept her daydreams about visiting Jilima with Majid—on a train, in search of baskets, knives—mostly to herself. Though dream of this she did: Majid on a hilltop, beckoning to her; Majid close beside her in a taxi, slipping a warm hand between the treasured trinkets and her thighs; Majid bringing breakfast to their table at a state-run coffee shop; Majid naked in the empty, freeing rooms of far-off, strange hotels.

Without the special mix of attributes that made her who she was—that combination of great strength, curious inattention to the things that milled around her, and an insatiable desire (for Majid, for the wonder of her own splayed limbs beneath another body, for a house her legal, chairbound man could not, she thought, imagine)—she would not have been as equal to the task of simultaneously administering to each separated self. Such projects are hard; she struggled, but Sarie was no weakling. She became accustomed to the quivering between her present and her future, which was like a wall between her insides and the outside of her skin; to waiting without knowing for what Uncle James would say; now and then to thinking deeply of the changes he might bring, and wishing them intensely—just as she grew capable at once of forgetting Uncle James and Gilbert, and even little Agatha, completely while Majid removed her clothes. Perhaps when things were set, when everything was sure, she would regale her lover with a tale about how useful, independent-minded, she had been. Tell him something to amuse him. Tickle his thin arms and talk about Dodoma knives and oval heads from Zambia. But until then she would protect with all her might the winsome, fragile steadiness of those private afternoons.

Majid, for his part, grew a little easier about lolling on the bed with her after they had tussled, letting her go cool while he left his hands to wander at her throat or spine. In between her visits, he finished three new poems, their completion punctuated by his lover's step. He, too, felt a gap between the present and the future—and, more importantly for him, between the *past,* this present, and, less clear and less certain, what might be to come.

To keeping some things to himself, he was as attached as she. He didn't tell her that the grieving-for-his-wife had shifted with her coming (he'd told no one—*whom could he?*—about Hayaam's visitation, could not speak of it at all), that he felt himself released, or that he was sure this newness hinged in part on Sarie, on the very fact of her; or that sometimes as he held her he experienced his own hands as he never had before: as variable and interesting. What strength! What gentleness! What ferocity, right *here.* He never mentioned Tahir. He didn't talk about the practicalities of life: he never spoke of Sugra's visits, how she brought him money, sometimes of her own and sometimes from his brothers, who trusted her far more than they did him; that he wondered what they'd do for food once Maria found a man; that he'd sent Habib to buy a notebook; that he now wrote every day; that he still thought of *that shoe,* had dreams of sending Tahir to a well-run private school. When Sarie came, they only talked a little, and they kissed, and he pulled off her clothes. But he thought of these things all the time: *I am writing once again. I am no longer Mad. And at any moment now, my boy will learn to walk. Something's going to happen. Perhaps I won't be Sad.* And so while he held Sarie tightly, shuddering successfully at each one of her visits—thinking, sometimes, *Passion!*—he was also cognizant of something else, an even greater wave preparing to engulf him: a wave that might propel him to a smooth and breezy shore, the pale contours of which he could, as yet, not fathom.

When she went to Kudra House, without or with her child, Sarie didn't say to Gilbert any longer that she was going for a visit to the father of the boy who'd lost a leg to the big bus. She allowed Gilbert to think she had moved on to other things for which he would have felt, she thought, his habitual disdain. She said vague words to him, about the British Council, about getting books for Agatha, even about nonexistent teas with Mrs. Hazel's friends. She mentioned baskets now and then, and soapstone men and frogs, and Gilbert would look up from his books and smile pleasantly at her, as though she'd been particularly clever. "We'll see," he'd say, and reach out for her hand. He had by now understood that Sarie did have an idea, that it had to do with trinkets. But he didn't take it seriously. He'd show her what ideas were, he thought, when the thing had come out right. It amused him, charmed him, that she thought she could help. It *moved* Gilbert, in fact, and made him all the more determined to do well, to show her that she needn't worry, that she herself need not make any contributions. His desire to surprise her with a ready-made, impeccable solution that could not fail to charm and to impress, to bring about relief, was firm. He neither disabused her of her vision nor explained the truth to her. How *glad* Sarie would be that she had him to rely on, that he would, at last, take proper care of her.

When Agatha did accompany her mother, she still spent time with Tahir, who was getting better. He talked about the crutches, which were going to be more suitable, correct, he told her, than the stick Habib had found. He told her how his favorite aunt came by to make sure he was well; he described for her the way Aunt

Sugra laughed, the little jokes she told, and how she brought him sweetmeats she had made for him herself. Agatha, who didn't have relations whom she knew, attempted to describe her father's old great-uncle James. "He's been alive for years," she said. "He doesn't bring me things."

Tahir let Agatha run her hands over his stump. He moved it up and down for her like a lever or the tail on a slow dog. To the hollow sound of Agatha's applause, he sometimes took up Habib's cane—another stump, a hard, curved piece of driftwood, knob larger than his hands—and, palms fastened to the wall, the bedstead, or the dresser, hobbled round the room. He admitted now that it did hurt, sometimes, in the empty air where his shin and foot had been. Agatha was glad to know that things you couldn't see could harm you. She smacked at the ghost leg to see if Tahir winced. They were finished with the science primer, which (Tahir with assurance, and Agatha, less skilled, following along) they had read aloud. They had imagined many things: the known and unknown planets, the peculiar sucking dance of water down northern, southern, and also equatorial drains; and considered how a rubber ball can both be heavy with inertia and elastic, bouncing more and more. For a while, they had nothing else to look at, and they talked. In exchange for stories Tahir had heard Sugra tell or had gotten from Maria, Agatha, sitting at the far end of the bed beside the leg that wasn't anymore, explained to Tahir what her father did at home.

On a Sunday visit to the book stand, Gilbert learned that the Christian man in the green hat had set a book aside for him. A blue one called *Shambala,* which set out the history and nature of a kingdom not too far from the sea. "A book that is exactly right for

you! God bless, God bless! In the name of heaven, this I knew that
you would like! *Mungu akujali!*" The book vendor was ready, so he
said, to sell it very cheaply. But, while a previous Gilbert might
have taken pleasure in the busy man's attention, he felt, instead, resentful. *Right for me?* How could the man pretend to know the sort
of books he liked? He seemed to have decided that Gilbert was
one way and only one just as, Gilbert thought, he was becoming
something else. *I'm a different man now.* He'd said, "No!" and had refused to take it home, even for a song.

He'd found a truer thing and purchased it: a sturdy plastic-
covered text that promised to inform him of everything a man like
him—an *ordinary* man—should know about the workings of a
motorcar. It was a not-too-ancient guide to the mechanics of the
engine, a do-it-yourself manual published in a city called West
Lowell, USA. The vendor looked at him, perplexed, but Gilbert
only smiled. *Imagine that,* he thought. *It may have been right here for
months, and without your new idea, you never would have seen it! Who've
you been for all this time, old man? Tell me that, just who?* He'd wished
just for a moment that Mrs. Frosty, pretty and admiring, had been
there to see him choose. He squared his stoop and held his head up
high. He tipped a nonexistent hat to great old Uncle James and
winked at passersby.

Agatha told Tahir that her father had moved his studies (so she
called them, and they were) from the parlor to the kitchen table.
There, sweating with the effort—because engines, he was finding,
were somewhat different from peoples (though, in a way, accord-
ing to this author they had customs and beliefs, apparently, as
well)—he read the *Everyman's Car Handbook,* trying to achieve the
same demeanor he had mastered with the other, older books: that

of a knowledgeable reader, cool in his good judgment. It worked. He mimicked that old self so well, in fact, that Sarie didn't see what he was reading. Native marriages, she thought. Or farming by the shore. She was annoyed, however, by Gilbert's recent habit of sitting in the kitchen, where the light was always good, and where she went to be alone.

"My mother doesn't like it," Agatha told Tahir. She reproduced Sarie's rolling eyes and the shaking of her arms high above her head to show Tahir how her mother tried to press her father back into the parlor, where, Sarie had said, "a man like you belongs."

Gilbert would not have told a soul—not Sarie, and least of all the Frosty King—how different it was to be reading about calipers and carburetor plates, the resurfacing of flywheels, instead of irrigation, rituals, and kings. To Agatha, he seemed capably and energetically at work. He frowned and wiped his brow, sometimes nodding in amazement. He examined every picture and, in pencil, listed all the words he wished to practice and recall.

On Gilbert's rather fancy pad—which he had purchased at the Government Stationers (once known as V. N. Chandra Books but taken over in the fray)—each leaf of pale, translucent paper showed a light ink drawing of an animal, like a watermark, far away on the savanna in a soft and subtle brown. Agatha's father had shown them all to her: giraffe, lion, warthog, waterbuck, and eland, and a charming, slender, small one, too, that he had called a dik-dik.

When Gilbert showed them to her, Agatha had asked him where "the real ones" could be found. Gilbert had looked up from his handbook, open to a segment about cylinders, and laughed, relieved he had, for this at least, an answer. "Right here in this country, silly girl. Where *do* you think we live?" (He did like, sometimes, to talk with Agatha. She made him nervous, as her mother did; but she didn't contradict him, didn't mind his tone. Would only raise

her voice in protest if he was really in the way.) When she had si-
dled up to him, fingers edging towards the picture as he wrote,
Gilbert had felt uncomfortably aware of the smell that came from
her—very different from his, from Sarie's, very like a child's, like
milk and like hot sand.

But when she stared at him in answer, he realized that Agatha
had no reason at all to know where dik-diks lived. He softened.
She'd never been there, had she? She'd never left the city. The
thought made him momentarily ashamed of his own fatherhood:
Have I been good at all? He didn't like to think of it, didn't like to
wonder if he had gone about it the wrong way. Where were models, after all? There were none. Fatherhood and marriage, Gilbert
sometimes told himself, were simply states of being, things a man
lived through. There wasn't any reason to consider such natural
conditions as if they were campaigns or things to be assessed. A
person simply *was.* Gilbert tapped his pencil on the page. He didn't
like it when his daughter looked at him so closely, made him feel
that he should say something, that he ought to ask her questions.
He frowned and sent her to the courtyard. "Go and play now.
Leave me be." And Agatha had gone—*glided,* more like, it had almost seemed to him, as though his daughter had no feet. Then he
had looked down at the warthog on whose horn tip he had written the word "idle," and the warthog made him think.

Once, when he was just beginning and did not have his own
desk, Gilbert had been taken to a wild place called Kimbuga by a
traveling Circuit Judge whose regular driver and assistant had with
no notice fallen ill. The Judge, a man named Hewett, had requested a replacement. Gilbert, just a clerk then, taking files from
one person to another, had been spotted in the hallway. The Court
Secretary, potbellied, red-faced, ever-present pocket watch drag-
ging down his shirt, had not even blinked. "Take Turner," he had

said immediately, and, with two scarlet fingers, flicked a small thing from his chest. "We won't miss him today."

Without apology or thanks, Judge Hewett had given him a leather case to hold and, like a chief or king, had preceded Gilbert down the back steps of the courthouse to the parking lot, not once turning around to make sure he was there. Gilbert had felt small and even a bit angry. He had blushed, of course he had. But once they'd left the city, were progressing down the bumpy road, he had felt himself expanding, buffeted by wind. *I'm driving to the regions,* he had thought. *With the Circuit Judge, out into the wild.*

Gilbert balanced the wood pencil with his thumb, closed his eyes and tried to see Kimbuga as it had been that day. With Gilbert at the wheel of the new Land Rover, the rugged road arattle beneath them as they went, Hewett, as men like him were wont to do, had told Gilbert of his exploits. The one Gilbert recalled most often was about hunting in the south, how one day near Twavuma the Circuit Judge had saved a porter boy from being eaten by a leopard. He had waited patiently until the beast was almost on the child, while all around him natives prayed and howled. "I let him get *this* close," he said, tapping with a finger on his cheek, just below his eye. "To fool him." While the boy put up a fuss, Hewett, knowing what a decent man should do, had pulled the loyal trigger—shot the spotted beast right in its soft neck. Hewett shrugged, a proud smile at his lips. "That's how you do it, you know. You wait. I got him in my sights, let the thing get close, and then I did the job. Just once. Once is all it takes if you know what you're about. What a pelt he made!"

Gilbert, shaken, asked about the boy. Oh, he'd burst right into tears, of course. Wet himself, the Circuit Judge was sure. Had wept and hidden in the bushes, shaking like a flag. It had taken three of Hewett's older lads to calm him down and to convince the sorry boy that he had *not at all* been shot and was not close to death. That he was as unmarred as they were and as ebulliently alive as the shattered beast was not. Hewett's laugh, too large for the Land Rover, had bounced along the glass and nudged at Gilbert's legs. "Thought *he'd* been shot, you see. Couldn't tell the difference between his own self and a damned beast!" Hewett said. "That's their trouble, don't you know. Afs," he added, "haven't any nerves."

While admittedly admiring of the High Court Secretaries and Circuit Judges of the world, Gilbert had experienced an uncomfortable and unexpected solidarity with that weeping porter boy. Did he himself not often feel mistreated? Indeed, it had occurred to Gilbert then that, just as *he* was, Africans were neglected rather often, too. Shuddering, he tried to picture himself in a helmet, sweating, his exposed skin swarmed by mosquitoes, tsetse flies, and gnats, holding to a leather case for a superior, interrupted by a leopard. Would he not have—also weeping—run?

He had parked the car beside a thorn tree. He hadn't felt an intimate affection for the vehicle that day, nothing more than pleasure in the drive; but now that he was on his way to starting up a business that would keep such old things fresh, Gilbert thought about the Land Rover's square bulk with the giddiness and thrill of the professional car man he now was, every day, becoming. He dropped the pencil on the table in approval and rocked back in his chair: That Rover. *Brave old thing!* he thought.

He'd followed Hewett to the tiny district courthouse, where, so it seemed to him, not much was going on. In the veld beyond the whitewashed compound, Gilbert caught a glimpse of motion and had himself gone still: his arm hairs rose and prickled, his ankles turned to ice. *Leopards,* he was thinking. But the movements, once Gilbert could bear to look again, more closely, had been rich and dappled; not threatening, but calm. Giraffes, a pair of them, on the horizon. Nice-looking, ambling things. So slow.

Hewett, who had marched ahead, as was his privilege, finally turned around and called for Gilbert to catch up. "Come on, then, Turner. Never seen a 'raffe before? They're the women of the wild, old man. Just waiting for a heart attack, they are, no pump or muscle in 'em. Bear up! We haven't got all day." Gilbert pulled himself from them just as a human woman in dark cloths emerged from the small courthouse and curtsied. He remembered that efficient bobbing of her knees very clearly, too. Practiced, elegant, discreet. *Giraffelike,* he had thought. She had straightened herself up, and then she'd stood there, watching.

Hewett's voice had torn right through the air. Pushing on, he said, "Bagged a pair last year." His boots made bulky sounds on the stony, still-damp earth. "Heads mounted on the wall." Hewett gave Gilbert a very manly grin. "I like to tell my missus if she gets too smart with me, I'll put her up beside them. Have you a wife yet, Turner?" Gilbert hadn't answered. When they reached the court-house patio, the woman made a sound and slipped into the shadows. Hewett pulled his case from Gilbert's hands without so much as a thank-you and made him wait at the reception while, in a room Gilbert didn't see, he and a respected colleague set an urgent matter right.

In Kikanga, in the kitchen, Gilbert thought, *Well. 'Raffes.* He got the pencil back into position. Shyly, with something like a fondness, he remembered Agatha's question, wondered where she'd gone. *If Uncle James comes through for us, I will take my women on a trip. In time we, too, will have a car. A Land Rover, indeed. I'll show Agatha a dik-dik.*

Tahir had not seen giraffes, or dik-diks, either, but he was sure that Aunt Yasmina had, that in Mombasa beasts were in attendance, mating in the trees and sometimes strolling down the street, watching, waiting, for a weak one to split off from the herd. "If you go out to the shop just once after dark," he said, "they'll eat you alive." Agatha made a doubting face. He was sitting up. She said, "I don't believe you." She liked not believing Tahir. It made him swear to things. "*Haki ya Mungu,* it's God's truth," he said. Tahir flicked his wrist so that his index finger snapped along the length of the next digit, loud and sharp and clean. "A lion will tear your legs off and get working on your arms." He said this with such earnestness that Agatha thought, *He knows what legs torn off are like. Maybe he means it, maybe it's true.*

Of what went on in the other bedroom during her visits to the Jeevanjees, Agatha knew nothing. Tahir, who could feel his father changing, something broiling in his father's skin that was communicated through his fingers when he touched Tahir at night, was not certain what he knew. Maria, however, thought she knew exactly, and did her best to tell him. When she came up now and then with washing, she sat in the boys' room awhile and told a tale or two, which she would end with prayer, kneeling by the bed.

She'd told Tahir that not only was a serpent suckling at the breast of Kudra House itself, but that swine should be cast out. Like lepers, demons, locusts. Like a hundred plagues. Her analogies confused him. She asked Tahir to pray with her, as always hoping that he would but knowing he would not. He had shaken his head no and laughed and, as Ali sometimes did (*Mshenzi, weh!*), had called her a barbarian. Maria had smiled very knowingly and surely, lovingly, indeed, and risen from the floor. "You have lots to learn, you." Then she put on a voice the way the Elders did. "Pride comes before a fall, my child." She kept her eyes on him as she folded up a bedsheet she had taken from the line. "No better than a pig. That British woman-snake."

Tahir was not interested in either swine or locusts, very much, but he liked considering snakes. He imagined one fastened to his chest, where there were two slowly growing nipples for a slithering beast to choose. He wondered how such a thing would feel. He might frighten Agatha with an account of how it happened. How a snake can wrap itself around you, for example, and make your very life come gasping from your mouth. In the end, he did tell Agatha what snakes can do, but he kept what Maria thought about her mother wisely to himself.

Majid, though he suspected that Maria had ideas, took a special pleasure in believing that what took place on Sarie Turner's visits was a secret from them all. Picturing the several cousins he had left, and also old Rahman (whom he'd harmed so much that day), and even dear Sugra, Majid thought, *What would they all say if they knew that crazy Jeevanjee has got himself a woman? Or that I've written some new poems? That I need yet another notebook, as I haven't done in years?* He wasn't ready to find out. He liked how good he felt, and that there was no one there to see it but his mistress. Long, pale Sarie Turner. Dear Mrs. Turner, with her own secret life. Whom could Sarie tell?

❦ Sixteen

Bibi, whose hurting hands were not yet loose enough to take on a new stitching, kept firm watch on Kikanga and witnessed several things. For one, she spotted Mad Majid's little cousin Sugra, whom she had not seen since a wedding long ago, walking down the street. *That* Sugra, yes. The one and very same, the Sugra she had held up to her son as the real example of a fiancée when he'd proposed Nisreen. Seeing Sugra gave Bibi a boost. Hadn't she just thought of her the other day, when looking at her Issa? Were her mere thoughts conjurings? Had she *predicted* Sugra?

Bibi watched her closely. *Strange,* she thought. The way a person was remembered, used as an example, was sometimes different from what that person was when you saw them in the flesh. When Bibi was unhappy with Nisreen, she told her that she acted too much like a bush baby, too shy, that she startled far too easily, could be frozen by a stare; and when Bibi said these things to her, she sometimes thought of Sugra, who, surely, walked with confidence and could look trouble in the eye.

But seeing Sugra now brought a little shock. Unlike poor Nisreen, Sugra barreled, strode, did not have a careful walk, looked a little too indifferent, Bibi was surprised to think, to the others in her path. Of course, Sugra wasn't lame, as Nisreen was, but, still, wasn't there, Bibi thought protectively, an *elegance* to Nisreen's wary limp? Sugra, from this height, did look nicely round. And she was finely dressed, in lavender, in a long loose dress that modestly suggested but did not emphasize too much her heavy-breasted top. Yet why in such a rush? Bibi paused. Treading with such power, marching at such speed!

The more she thought about Majid's cousin Sugra, the more she watched her move, the more Bibi started to remember what she had forgotten, the kinds of things one does forget about people whom one doesn't often see. *Look at that! She's frowning!* For all her love of drama and her skill at telling tales, at imitating keenly this person or that, Bibi liked reserve, restraint, when a person was in public. And what could be more public than this brash Kikanga street? Little Sugra Jeevanjee, far too grown to do so—*a proper woman now*—was striding down the road with her eyes steady on the ground and a grimace on her face. As though it didn't matter, not at all, what anybody thought! Bibi stretched her toes and yawned. It was pleasant to compare a person walking down the street to someone in one's family. Yes, she sometimes wished Nisreen would spill what news she had more quickly than she did. *But Nisreen doesn't show the world her onions. Nisreen knows what's private.* Bibi closed her eyes and sighed. When she looked again, Sugra had gone on, in the direction, Bibi thought, of Libya Street or Mbuyu Mmoja Park. How nice to feel protective: *My Nisreen's refined.*

The other thing she noticed: Sarie Turner's visits to the Jeevanjees—unless she'd started taking other routes (*and would a British woman understand what alleys could be for?*)—were now slowing down. She didn't pass by Hisham's every day, and sometimes Bibi spent entire afternoons without once seeing the woman and the girl. Twice a week or so, instead of every day. This meant, thought Bibi, that something between Majid Ghulam Jeevanjee and that woman in the too-small dresses must have been resolved. *You don't need panic-panic-daily-time, or even too-short skirts, if something's been agreed.* They were settling, she supposed, into a routine.

Routines were good, she thought. Knowing just what to expect, reassured by the appearance of that thing just when you knew that it was due, and knowing it would come again—now *that* was a real pleasure. *But,* she thought, stretching her poor hands, *there's also need for change.* In fact, just as she was comforted by Sarie's slowing down and by how used to Nisreen and Issa's wakings-up and sleepings she now was, she also wondered how, and whether, anything could change. She *did* want things to change, some of them, at least.

On the balcony, where the old rope bed had now become a fixture, Bibi closed her eyes and hoped that she might soon be up again to stitching. Though she had rejected it so firmly, that Morris Oxford niggled at her. She'd dreamed about it twice. How strange to have a taxi in her head. Had it really been intended? She'd been so resistant! Had she been right to let it go? From downstairs she heard Mama Moto cooking. With a smile, the kind of smile a person has when certain that if hunger strikes there are good things to eat, Bibi napped a little. In her drowse she turned away from the blue taxi and asked for something new. *Tell me what to stitch once my fingers have come right,* she whispered to whatever spirits were in charge of things like this—then also, to be safe, to God, Keeper of the Cosmos.

When Bibi saw what clearly was an envelope, a pink one, fringed in dark blue stripes interlaced with red, she ground her teeth and moaned. *See what happens when you ask? Naam, naam, naam. All right. Indeed. Succumb.* She'd go ahead, and properly. She waited for the envelope to come into clear focus. Yes, there it was. An envelope either sent from, or going, far away. She saw the airmail motto clearly: in these parts, in the local tongue, it said, quite literally, *by bird.* She smiled, and experienced no surprise at all when, outside, house crows gave a call.

An envelope. What was it going to mean? Would a cousin write from England? Visit from Dubai? Was there going to be a death? A marriage? Had someone she'd forgotten decided they remembered *her?* Mrs. Harries, Mrs. Livery-Jones, asking how the stitchery had fared, had little Kulthum ever started up a business of her own? Her old teacher Mr. Suleiman, who had told her she would not amount to much but who, she knew, had been charmed by her bright eyes, and who had given her a ride sometimes in his nice taxicab? *A taxi cab.* She shuddered. *This.* A second test. The envelope: could it be from dead Uncle Amal's last and happiest wife? From a friend Issa had made once when he was far away? Well, Bibi didn't know, but once she got her mind around it and decided that she could not go back on her word, the envelope in her mind's eye made her feel that good things might be along, if she could only wait. The sign of an announcement? Something that she didn't know showing it was there? She sat up slowly and prepared to go into the bedroom, where she kept a lot of woven things she could unravel for her stitching. The envelope. Pink, she'd need. And blue.

{❀}Seventeen

The following day, Nisreen went to work as usual. She walked in Issa's company down to Seafront Road. The two of them had tea. Next, he brought her back up India Street and left her at the clinic. They parted as they always did: she unlocked the front doors, and Issa watched her enter, then went on back towards the ocean, where his own office was. At reception, Nisreen slipped out of her shoes. She watered the three croton plants and wiped their concrete pots. Sharpened up her pencil and looked idly at her files. Things were just the same, she tried to tell herself, as they had always been. Weren't they?

Nisreen's shoulders hurt. Her eyes stung. But she did try to be brave. *Weren't* things just the same? Wasn't Issa gentle, the sea exactly where it always was, still as large and blue? Weren't the parkside casuarinas shifting loosely in the wind, as high, slim pines should do, and hadn't her sweet tea tasted as it ever did, too milky and too hot? But though she tried to make a mental list of all the things that *were* none other than what they'd always been, Nisreen had the feeling—one that had been lurking there for months—that she herself was not.

Nisreen was not blind, despite her failing eyes, and neither was she deaf. And just because she limped, a little, well, it didn't mean she couldn't feel the ground beneath her feet. And though she didn't think that Issa minded, didn't think he cared as much as Bibi did about the flatness of her stomach and the smallness of her breasts, she herself was tired. She felt sad. *A person must fall down,* she thought, *if they're pushed and pushed enough.* It wore on her, Bibi's poking at her stomach as though fingers through a cloth could bring about conception, frowning at her chest as if a glare could call up milk. Sometimes Issa told her, "It will happen when it happens. Nevermind my mother." But would it really? When? Nisreen wasn't hard enough not to be upset, and she was too obedient not to wish that she could do exactly what was wanted, what old Bibi asked. And when Bibi had, the night before, just going up to bed, winked and pointed at her own ancient loins as if Nisreen did not know where anything began, Nisreen had gone into the store-room, where she'd stayed for a long time and cried, until Issa broke open the door and pulled her, shaking, out. At her desk in the clinic, Nisreen rested her sore head on her hands and wished she were in her bed.

When something finally happened, Nisreen had been sitting motionless for a long time, not even dangling her feet. She hadn't taken up that knife-sharp pencil once, not to doodle, not to write down any messages, and not to poke neat holes in patterns through any scrap of paper. Things went like this till noon. No one had come in at all. *Nobody,* it seemed to her, *needs help here but me.* She had sat there by herself, immobile, wishing she were other than she was, wishing Bibi would be quiet. Nisreen sat so still that things in her felt silenced, too, and she wondered if a person could forget what speaking would be like, or moving, if they sat still long enough. And so when Sugra Jeevanjee—plump, great-eyed, and pretty in a long, flowing green dress—appeared before her, Nisreen almost shrieked.

They hadn't talked much the last time, had simply said, "Hello," "How wonderful!" and, "You are looking well," and Sugra had been late for something: she had been more like a pleasant flash that came and disappeared, caught briefly by Nisreen as she spun and rushed away. But this time when she saw her, Nisreen felt that Sugra had *arrived* and that she was going to stop.

Sugra had not stepped off the sunlit street, as she had the last time, but came from behind the wide door that said *Private* holding two great crutches in her arms, in front of her, as men in films sometimes hold bouquets or big gifts for their loves, and she was smiling hugely. She had stepped into reception not carefully or slowly, as patients do, or orderlies with fragile things to hold, but sharply, all at once. To sad Nisreen, Sugra's popping through the doors so brightly, having gotten what she'd come for, what she'd been asking for, for weeks, seemed almost like a sign. Something in the air went sweet and lingered, had the aura of success. Nisreen tensed her wrists against the counter. Rose and stretched her toes along the floor. Crutches, after all. *There's help for crippled things,* she thought. *There must be.*

Stepping towards Nisreen, Sugra gave her old schoolmate such a lovely look—a look that said, "There's no one else I'd rather come upon like *this* than *you, just as you are*"—that Nisreen for a moment felt that Sugra had been sent along precisely to help her. Perhaps her gloominess, her wishing, had themselves sent Sugra down—nevermind the crutches she'd been asking for back there for weeks, since that little boy got hit. Nisreen dried her face with a long sleeve and, starting softly but with some effort ending with a smile, said, "Oh, Sugra, you have got them!"

While Sugra's greetings washed over Nisreen's ears, too rapid to be followed, Nisreen thought: *Sugra, who might have been a nurse. How odd it is that things turned out this way.* It was true. Their destinies might really have been switched. That lovely time spent studying medicine together in a high hall outside of town! Taking buses, eating fried muhogo chips beside a narrow river, going home with books! That time of only being girls! Sugra had been able, much more so than the others. Gifted. Much more expert than Nisreen. *Could have been a doctor!* And yet, Nisreen had ended closer to a medicine chest than Sugra, saw syringes every day. Counted up thermometers sometimes, put pillboxes away. Wasn't *that* surprising? Nisreen had married Issa, who wanted her to work ("Use the brain God gave her," as he had said to Bibi); Sugra, to everyone's surprise, had taken on a man who wanted her at home tending to his children, and only made allowances for his wife to run about if she was bettering his reputation by helping her relations, neighbors, and the poor, entirely for free. *Husbands,* Nisreen thought. It seemed to her just then that it was husbands, and not wives, who made any difference at all. She didn't like to think what life would be if Issa kept her home.

When Sugra finally paused, Nisreen took both her hands and squeezed them. "I'm so glad," Nisreen said, and Sugra, through the crutches she still held in her arms, said, "Yes, oh, yes. Me, too!" And then, because her mission was accomplished and Sugra liked to celebrate, she said, "It's nearly lunchtime, after all. We haven't had a chance to talk. Can't you get away and walk a bit with me?" Nisreen wished to cry again. Of course. Sugra'd come to save her.

Because Nisreen never asked for much, an orderly agreed to watch her place behind the counter for a while. Nisreen took up her purse and head scarf, and next was squinting in the bright midmorning light, walking beside Sugra, who at first held to the crutches sideways, like a package, then brought them apart and held them at her side, one each—talking all the while—as though some other, busy part of her were wondering precisely how the things were used. *How like Sugra,* Nisreen thought, *not to ask to have them brought, not to have them wrapped, not to hide what she is holding.* Other people did, Nisreen herself would have. Most people thought one should.

Here's what some hoped to dislike in Sugra but could not, because she was so kind: Sugra, open, fearless, clear, did not like concealment. It struck Nisreen as odd, again, that it was *she,* not Sugra, who had a job at the reception — Sugra, who didn't mind what people knew as long as it was nearly, nearly, true or so elaborately and fantastically false that it couldn't really hurt. Bubbling, knife-sharp, charming Sugra, who had such skill for talk.

If Sugra hadn't been so kind and so good-looking, Nisreen might have been embarrassed to be walking close to her, this portly beauty holding to the crutches for everyone to see. But Sugra could preempt all criticism with her laughter and good cheer. Could make people feel fine. When Sugra turned to her to say, "And your glasses make you look so thoughtful, yes, like someone at a College," Nisreen blushed, was charmed, forgot she had a limp; she felt she wouldn't mind what Sugra did in public. It was good just to be with her.

In a moment, Sugra was talking about Majid. "Oh! He's not so bad anymore, not so as you'd feel sorry." She paused to put a hand on Nisreen's arm and looked into her eyes. "You know they call him Mad Majid, now, don't you?" That was in Sugra's manner, too, a fairness, making certain everyone was well equipped and would appreciate whatever story was to come. Nisreen nodded, bit back a passing impulse to mention Issa's mother, say, "Oh, yes, I know it all," and Sugra moved along. "Three years ago that accident would have destroyed the man completely. But slowly-slowly. Drip by drop! He has changed. He's only sad, now, not so mad. I haven't heard him shout in . . . oh, four years, I should say." They walked up India Street and farther on to Mosque Street. A boy was selling tangerines; mendicants looked on.

The talking put a bit of distance between Nisreen and her sadness. Sugra's green dress made a *swish-swish* as they walked, and the crutches scraped the ground. Nisreen closed her eyes and opened them again, blinking at the colors in the day. She licked the backsides of her teeth and squinted at the sky. It was good to be outside. Sugra paused, grew quiet for a moment; and Nisreen, who had been lulled by Sugra's talk, almost missed a step. Quiet still, Sugra touched Nisreen lightly on the arm. Nisreen stopped and turned. Sugra's face was tight. Nisreen could hear her breathe. "Tahir," Sugra asked. "Did you see him come in?"

Bibi hadn't asked her, had felt too sure that *she'd* discovered him to think that anyone would have something to add. Not even Issa'd asked. But of course Nisreen *had* seen him brought in. *Poor one,* she had thought. And though the news was sad, being asked made Nisreen feel a lightening inside her. It was good for her to talk. She *wanted* to. And next Nisreen was telling Sugra—a bit eagerly, perhaps, too clumsy with her timid change of mood—about how Tahir Majid Jeevanjee had looked when they had brought him in. How terrible. How they'd brought the leg inside before the boy, and how Nisreen had known from looking at it—how short it was, the foot that did not seem a grown-up's—that the limb was once a child's. How she had never seen a person coming in, in parts that way before. How when his living body followed, the little boy was pale, a sort of gummy green. His whimpering had filled the hallways with a heat. How it had made Nisreen feel afraid of wishing for herself. How could it be borne, to see a broken boy like that, and know that he was yours? How she had thought, and then immediately unthought, *It's good Hayaam is dead.*

They had stopped beneath an awning. Sugra pulled Nisreen towards her in the shade. Her nice eyes grew a shimmer; her bright face looked blue. Nisreen wondered if she'd said too much. Didn't know if she should put a hand on her friend's arm. If she should say some more, or stop. Then Sugra seemed not to be listening anymore. She interrupted her. "He's the best of them, you know." Sugra looked at her own feet, then up, away from her companion. "That Tahir. Really, really good." Nisreen bit her lip. Sugra turned towards her again and took up Nisreen's hand. She squeezed it, hard, to show she was all right.

They walked. Nisreen had never seen Sugra really soft, or crushed, before. It wouldn't have occurred to her that Sugra, glowing, funny Sugra, *could* be sad, like this. Sugra talked a little less. She focused on the crutches, setting their ends down beside her and pressing with her weight, just lightly, each time she took a step. She sniffed. Plumped her weighty chest. "It won't be so hard as that. I'll show him. This." She paused on the left crutch and delicately lifted up one foot. "And this." She set the next foot down and followed with the crutch. "Like this." It was not quite the right way, but Nisreen didn't say so. *Strange,* she thought. *It's me now who must do the cheering-up.* It occurred to Nisreen, too—an odd thought, one that she had never had—that perhaps Sugra and Majid Ghulam Jeevanjee had been cut from the same cloth. *If Sugra got unhappy,* Nisreen thought, *desperately unhappy, would she short-circuit, too?* Weren't laughing-laughing and such friendliness just the underside of vast hostility and tears? Weren't they both unstable, in a way? *And what if it were me?*

At Libya Street, Sugra made as if to turn. But Nisreen, thinking about sadness, and that she ought somehow return the kindness she felt Sugra had done her by appearing at exactly the right time, had the germ of an idea. Yes, they'd come this way for a reason. Taking on a shadow of her friend's ordinary brightness, borrowing from her, she said how nice it was to have seen Sugra these days; and if she was taking, after all, a break from work, which she so rarely did, it might at least be special. Wouldn't it be sweet to go up to the Park and have a fruit ice in the shade?

*   *   *

Mbuyu Mmoja Park, with its avenues of bushes, benches, and dry fountains, was shimmering and busy. The men who transformed neckties into guavas and briefcases to baskets were holding their best shows, entertaining groups of children and adults who were also taking breaks from offices and school. At the edges of the crowd, young men sold crackling dubbed cassettes of country music from the U.S.A. and Germany, rally songs for youth, local church recitals, and qasidas from Malaysia. Coffee vendors clicked their cups and litter women rose and bent and men with palm brooms swept. The Emmanuel Revival Tabernacle House, with its pretty, shady grounds, was milling with the faithful. Boys rode by on bicycles, trailing boxy freezers filled with fruity ice. Beneath three ancient flame trees, at one remove from all the buzz and hum, the doctors from the islands tended to their patients; roots and powders passed discreetly from proffered hand to hand.

Sugra and Nisreen found a cement bench beneath a frangipani, the pink flowers of which, Sugra told her friend, reminded her of sweets. Nisreen stopped a cycling boy and bought four orange pops. Each of them ate two. The freshness tugged Nisreen and Sugra from their sorrows—Sugra a bit faster, because she was resilient, and Nisreen rather jaggedly; but with each gritty lick and swallow, Nisreen was more certain that leaving work at noon had been a good idea, that Issa needn't know, that she'd done the right thing. That there might be a pattern to this day, that her tears had been a wet but necessary step towards something in particular. That ending here, at Mbuyu Mmoja Park, just might be significant.

Sugra told old stories they both knew from their bright student days. As she spoke, Nisreen thought about how she'd heard Bibi say to Issa that Sugra was a woman and that Nisreen was not. She didn't think this jealously. She pondered. In some ways it seemed true: how Sugra, with a lightness, pleasure, that Nisreen didn't have, took other people's news to heart; how Sugra swelled with kids (was it two, now? three or four?). Oh, yes, for Bibi, Nisreen thought, tongue flat at her teeth then in farthest corners of her mouth, Sugra would be fine. Nisreen smiled. *But Bibi doesn't have her. She only has me.*

At one o'clock, muezzins made their calls. Sugra tossed the fruit-ice wrappers to the side and rubbed her hands with sand, picked the crutches from the bench. The heavy skirts of her green dress shifted as she stood, rippled in the light. Nisreen walked with Sugra to the far edge of the park. At the curb, she hovered. Sugra, who had stepped into the road, looked at her in surprise. "You're not going back to work?" Nisreen's limping leg was hurting just a little. Her glasses had slipped far down her nose from heat, twin distorting orbs at rest almost on her cheeks. But Nisreen felt determined. Hadn't Sugra been so brash as to walk five blocks with crutches at her arms, as though she were a cripple? She looked around her with increasing certainty. "Not yet," Nisreen said, mouth set. She pushed her glasses up, looked firmly at her friend. "There's something I should do."

Sugra understood when certain limits had been reached. She herself had crutches to deliver. "All right, then," Sugra said.

"Till soon, God willing, yes?" Nisreen squeezed her school friend's hand, then raised her own up to her mouth and kissed it with a happy snap, a sweetness at her lips. Sugra did the same. "God willing, yes, oh, yes."

As Sugra and the crutches crossed the busy road, headed off to Libya Street, Nisreen nodded to herself. *For sure, my business is with God.* She spun on her good heel and, confidence inspired, made her way towards the children and the magic men, one of whom, as she arrived, announced that he was going to call a monkey from a yellow bar of soap. Just beyond that magical assembly, Nisreen saw another: flame trees, bottles, white gowns glowing in the sun.

Although it wasn't Saturday or Sunday, Maria, having made a special trip, was waiting just outside of the Emmanuel Revival Tabernacle House. Brother Ewald Matting, the ruddy man from Texas, U.S.A., had spoken every weekend for a month to eager audiences so large, so vocal and impassioned, that not all of them could hear. His success had been complete. The healings and salvations he had brought about (a daily 40-Healing cap) had not satisfied demand. Seekers? In Vunjamguu, a surfeit, yes, a glut. From the kindness of his corn- and pork-fed heart, Brother Ewald, just back from a soul-search in the highlands, had thus returned for extra days in that seaside town: Vunjamguu, whose people, he had said, were special and made all of him feel warm.

Maria was among those who, when Brother Ewald had first come, had had to sit outside the meeting hall, perched on a high wall above the heads of taller worshippers who'd filled up the church grounds. She hadn't heard him well nor even really seen him. But having caught the highlights from the lucky few who'd gotten there so early they had found seats in the front, she was not about to let him leave for Texas (via Ghana) without trying one more time to get a decent look. So she had oiled her arms and legs, put on the violet gown, tightly done her hair, left the Jeevanjees to their own Tuesday selves, and gone out for some grace.

The meeting was at three. She got there so early that the Tabernacle doors were not even open. And she was further pleased to note, beside her favorite tree, the very boy she dreamed of. He'd come just as he'd promised! Seated happily beside him, she let handsome Idi Moto stroke her arm and back, while she tried to think of new ways to convince him that Brother Ewald Matting was a man worth listening to, a man who brought salvation. Wouldn't he come with her and sit nicely through it all? While Idi Moto played with her hot hands, Maria scanned the park for a glimpse of Brother Ewald. She was so wound up about the meeting she had come for that even Idi started looking at the passersby, the crowds, wondering how the famous preacher looked. He thought it would be nice to spot him first, then take Maria's arm and say, "There! Just there! Is that the man you mean?" Maria's pleasure, if not her drive for his Salvation, was steadily infectious. Moreover, perhaps he'd learn something today that he could use for profit, or something small that would amuse his ma. Indeed, did he not recognize a face or two, a racketeering nod, the posture of a figure by the toilets—or, yes, perhaps even a slim and limping figure there, or there, or there?

Gilbert, hoping for another manual, perhaps, and also for a letter, was making for the harbor. On the way, he thought about the methods Kazansthakis had suggested of smuggling spare parts into the country. He considered, at first, the most extreme of ways. Just for fun, Gilbert imagined: hushed negotiations with dark men on wet ships made of wood, tethered among mangroves, nocturnal meetings at a lonely border post where the air, adrone with fabled insects, would be humid, cling to him like a coat. At the thought of such adventure, Gilbert smiled. *Surely, I won't do that myself?* An assistant would, not he. A lackey. Like the coastal kingpins, Gilbert thought, he would have retainers. Wouldn't he? He reveled for a moment, then remembered that he was, as yet—if it was to be at all—entirely alone. He frowned. Thinking practically was hard.

Head awhirr, he moved forward in a daze. But as he passed the mirrored doors of the People's Bank, he tripped on his own feet. He stopped. With the air of someone who can't hear very well but knows that something, somewhere, is reaching out to him, Gilbert looked around. Yes. "Hoo-hoo!" Standing on the stairs, big backside reflected in the doors behind her so that she looked to be arriving and departing all at once, Hazel Towson called to Gilbert with a wave. Her voice, indeed, her very being on the steps, was bright, and loud, and shrill. *Hoo-hoo.* "Hoo-hoo!" she said. "Oh. Hello there! Mr. Turner!" Gilbert's insides curdled. Oh, didn't she just—didn't she just have a way of being there when one really didn't want her?

With Hazel on the steps above him and his own feet on the sidewalk, Gilbert found himself looking right into her buttoned, heaving chest; his first thought was that Hazel was not simply personally colossal but physically enormous. Huge. Even bigger than before. Had she grown since her last visit? What a formidable woman Jim Towson's Hazel was! How able Hazel was to transform a person's day! Gilbert would have tripped on his own feet again had she not placed her square hand on his arm. "Be careful, now," she said. "Goodness knows the sidewalks aren't what they once were." Capably holding Gilbert up, she stepped down to his level, where he was relieved to find that, no, he hadn't shrunk, nor had she really grown. He was instead confronted with her ruddy, horsey face at the level, as it should be, of his eyes. Hazel Towson looked back at the bank. "Coming for some money, are you?" She smiled at him with her great teeth, and Gilbert blinked at her. He wished to scratch his back, to rearrange his trousers, but did not.

"No, no," he said, leaning, still, though he didn't want to, on her arm. Hazel Towson ably ascertained that he could stand, and let go of him gently. He found his wobbly footing. "Well," she said. "I shouldn't think so." She reached up to her head, smoothed her big brown bun. "To the Post, then?" When she fixed her narrowed eyes on him, Gilbert had the feeling that she looked at him as a person might a small and helpless, unloved thing—a lizard or a bird—who has been tricked into a corner.

"Expecting something? Sending something off?" She smiled. Gilbert felt her breath and with it sensed a pointed shriveling in his gut. His nervous bowels shifted and he squeezed his legs together. It was true that he had nearly told her, that first day, had almost, with daring and enthusiasm, said, *We're going to start a business.* But now, with the any-day potential of Uncle James's answer at the forefront of his mind, he didn't want to say. He didn't want to ruin it. *If Hazel Towson knew,* he thought, *she'd laugh, she'd jump for joy. She'd tell me I was sweet. That I was coming round.* "No," he said. "No, no."

As Hazel spoke again, Gilbert noticed that, as though not trusting him to answer on his own, as if giving him some options, she ended every statement with a question. "You're just walking for a lark?"

Gilbert had always been aware of something fierce at work in Hazel Towson's manner, but on that afternoon he felt her powers trebled. Indeed, it was as though, if she kept going, she might hit on the right answer, say, "Hoping your relation has agreed to send you one last wire? For the business you've been dreaming?" Before her he was helpless. Pinned by her acuity, he would have to nod, and say, "Well. Why, yes. Yes, how did you know?" And that wouldn't do at all. He clenched his stomach like a fist and pressed his teeth together. "No, no," he said. He tried to step a bit away from her but found it hard to do.

To every side of him, unyielding streams of people headed in and out of buildings and competed for the buses. Far beyond them, he could see the ocean, undisturbed, slate blue and indifferent. He gave its distant vastness a mildly desperate look, thinking that the ocean didn't care about Jim Towson's wife, or even Uncle James, or him, for that matter, at all. How lovely it would be to be like that, to heave, to move away unblamed for being impolite, not being good enough. To be, simply, far away.

Hazel, talkative, for sure, but not blind to other people, *did* perceive his wretched look. How disconsolate expectant men could be! Understanding, so she thought, she patted Gilbert's arm. "You're out clearing your head, of course, I see. Come to rest your mind and give Sarie some peace." Gilbert took the opportunity to nod, to step away from her a bit. "That's right," he said. "Er, yes." Hazel felt, again, that she alone knew exactly what was what. What would people do without her to lay out for their perusal the conditions that impelled them? But it was a nice exasperation, comforting to her. What a lucky woman. She smiled at Gilbert Turner, and more kindly, conspiratorially, she said, "I do understand, you know. I've been there myself." She too looked at the sea, as if for confirmation, as if that enormous body were not different from hers. "A woman who's expecting isn't always easy to be near, now, is she?"

Woman who's expecting. Mother-to-be. Gilbert felt his skin burn in the sun. He'd nearly forgotten all about his and Sarie's baby! At the idea of the baby, the little subterfuge that had prevented him from spilling all the news, the *real* news, Gilbert blushed, blushed brightly. And Hazel knew that she was right. How powerful she was. With just a little sympathy, she thought, a man would open, like a book.

She smiled once more, leaning closer in so that Gilbert smelled that scent again, of rich earth and manure. Surely nothing bottled could provide that kind of fragrance—What would such a thing be called? Settler Days, or Empire's Green Time? She didn't any longer have a thing to do with farms. Whence *did* that smell arise? Hazel Towson seemed to him all bust and heave and muscle, a prodigious figure on the prow of a great ship, undisturbed by swelling tides or squalls. She closed her eyes a moment, as if taking in the spray, then fixed him with a look. "I could say a lot about such things, Mr. Turner. My mother—" Here Hazel gave her hand-bag a coy tap, as though—he winced—she'd trapped the woman there. "My mother couldn't bear the smell of liver the whole time she was down. My sisters"—the buckle of her purse aglint— "both ate butterscotch like mad. Couldn't get enough. And you couldn't say a word, or look at them cross-eyed, without their bursting into tears. Like babies. Like the babies they were making." Hazel's voice had softened at this last. She tapped Gilbert on the forearm with something not unlike approval, gently.

She might not be sanctioning the pregnancy, no, certainly not that; indeed, Hazel thought repeatedly, *At her age! How is it even possible?* But there was nothing cruel in her; she could see what people needed. Once trouble had arrived and could not be sent back, there was nothing for it, one made the best of things, faced the facts head-on. Gilbert Turner, Hazel thought, was in need of under-standing. For his part, Gilbert, impressionable, susceptible to certain kinds of women, had a vision: an enormous farmer's wife hurling liver from a window; behind her, two whopping, swollen girls fought bitterly for sweets. He blinked, felt hot. How far away the sea was!

When Hazel suddenly fell quiet, Gilbert felt required by the moment, that he should pay attention. Indeed, Gilbert had the odd impression that, despite her blustery talk, her questions, nothing had been said yet—that the stories and the sympathy had, rather, been a pretext, a prelude to what she'd really meant to say. He waited. "Sarie," Hazel said at last. Then, with surprising force she pulled away from him, stepped back onto the lowest step of the People's National Bank as though to see him clearly. Or, he thought, to make certain he saw *her.* From a height, with Gilbert's eyes meeting her throat, Hazel said the following: "She must be having a hard time. And *that's* why she didn't come that Friday. So unfortunate, you know. We were all expecting her, and we wondered how she was. Poor Sarie, we all thought. In fact, we were afraid that something had gone very wrong," she said. "That there had been, you know . . ." Hazel's round, protruding eyes grew rounder and protruded even more. Had Gilbert not been looking up into her face, he would not have understood what she said next, because Hazel's energetic voice dropped away completely as she mouthed the final words: "An accident."

Gilbert, covered by her shadow, shivered. *Friday? A luncheon? An accident?* For an instant, he felt hot and cold, and hot, and Hazel's face was red, like meat, her tight hair was slick gold. The skin of his worn back went brittle and then slack. Hazel leaned towards him and away. Gilbert gave his head a shake and frowned, then everything was usual again, and Hazel, turning up the volume, averred that she, herself, of course, would be very much taken aback if there *was* something wrong with Sarie, because Sarie was so *strong.* And more than that, she'd seen her, hadn't she, with her own eyes a few days before the meeting. Let's see, where was that? Oh, yes, at the Mountain Top Hotel. And wasn't she robust? "So I'm supposing, Mr. Turner, that everything's as right as rain, then. Just as it should be. Our Sarie's a brave girl, and she is perfectly all right. Am I right? I am right, aren't I, eh? I must be."

On the far blue slice of sea, a tiny dhow showed up; it bobbed and bobbed and dipped. As Gilbert watched it with one eye, he felt himself come loose from Hazel Towson. *Sweet ships, those,* he thought. And felt something that had flattened in him struggling to rise. Was it? Yes. He recalled the splendid sons of Sindbad. Bearded, full of song. The book he had purchased then set down. So long ago, it seemed. Had he even read that volume's inside flap? Perused even the foreword, the acknowledgments, at all? Making for the harbor, the ship swelled a bit in size, and Gilbert found his feet. He echoed Hazel's words, but curt. "Oh, yes. A strong girl. Brave. Just fine. Thank you, Mrs. Towson," Gilbert said. "I'm sure." He was thinking about mangroves. Hazel's face receded. He couldn't hear exactly what she said; nor was he aware, precisely, of his own replies. Things like, perhaps: *Oh, yes. I'll tell her that I saw you, certainly*. Rather like the ebbing of a song, each word softer than the last. Wobbling but determined, he found an opening in the crowd, turned away from her, and finally slipped free.

He was so relieved to be in motion, to be smelling other bodies now, and, still, the scent of sea he had discovered not so long ago in the city's swelling air, that he did not mull over or weigh what Hazel had revealed. He did think, briefly, *So what if Sarie didn't go?* That ship was getting bigger, and Gilbert had an urge to walk towards the harbor to get a better look, to meet it. He felt tired of Hazel Towson; he even cheered for Sarie. *Good for her, to let that woman down.* And when he thought about the Mountain Top Hotel, he smiled. When had Sarie gone there? Why had she not told him? *Why the Mountain Top Hotel?* Oh, she did do silly things sometimes. He laughed, feeling oddly tender. Had she more imagination than he'd known? *Sarie must be dreaming, too,* he thought, *of how our lives will be, once I've sorted this thing out. Once I have a business.* Jewels, was it? He'd buy his woman jewels, he thought, and more. And where *had* he put that book, which he'd bought on *that day?*

As he walked, picking up again the thread of happiness that had wound around his legs and chest, then spun him like a top when he'd first started out, Gilbert thought that in the evening he would make, for fun, just fun, an inventory of all the things he'd buy for Sarie once spare parts were getting from his stores to those who needed them the most. Once he'd found his place in . . . History. He paused a moment with this thought because, he realized, he did not mean, for once, that old, old History of grand safari tales and hatted men with exploits, but a new one, an invigorating History, for a new land on the up. *An economic History,* he thought. *When I have made my mark.* He was so enthralled by the idea of this future that he quite forgot where he'd been headed when Hazel had appeared, and instead of visiting the Post Office, instead of sighting dhows from the seashore, Gilbert found himself nursing a warm pint at the Victorian Palm Hotel, where he watched the light of day sink into the sighing, trembling sea. He scratched his shoulders now and then, shifted in his shirt. But the itching didn't stir him. He was thinking of the sky, how neat it was at the horizon. *As neat,* he thought, *as our new life will be.*

Eighteen

When Sarie and Agatha went again to Kudra House—
Agatha triumphant that her mother had, this time,
permitted her to come—things did not go as expected. As they
stepped into the courtyard, Maria was just coming down the stairs,
holding in both arms a bulging printed cloth filled with upstairs
laundry. At last! Maria—who knew what Sarie didn't—could not
quite believe her luck. Wasn't this a chance? Had she finally been
rewarded for her steadfastness and prayers? She slowed at the last
step and smiled, and Sarie, thinking, *She has never smiled like this!*
grew wary. Standing on the threshold, Maria said, "Hallo. Welcome,
Mrs. Turner." She blocked the entrance firmly, did not move aside.

Sarie raised a hand up to her throat. She swallowed. What was
happening here? Unhappy, she said, "Thank you," and tentatively
made as if to go up. But Maria, not giving an inch, grasped her
bundle tightly. She tilted her head to the side. "You want to go up,
isn't it?" Her choir voice was sweet. How terrible the girl was,
Sarie thought, standing there like that, between Sarie and her man.
Sarie frowned, stepped back into the alley and reached for Agatha's
hand. Who did she think she was? "Don't you want to go upstairs?"
Maria said again. Oh, she seemed to swell up in the doorway, girl
and bundle, head scarf, as if doubling in size to conceal the stairs
behind her. "Up?" Maria pointed with a finger, to the sky. Sarie
wavered and fell silent. Squeezed her daughter's fingers with such
fear that Agatha cried out and snapped her hand away.

Sarie rallied. "Of course I'm going up." Maria, having tugged one of her plump feet from her blue thongs, leaned her shoulder on the lintel for support. Deliberate, she gave an ostentatious point and flex of chubby, able toe, then rested her bare sole on the surface of her shoe. It was a fine display of comfort, of her right to be exactly where she was, of her feeling that, indeed, *she ought to have a say.* She looked down at Sarie's pale, long feet, then, leisurely, at the pomelo-sized knees that showed below the frayed hem of the white visitor's dress. Her eyes at Sarie's face again, ashine, she shook her head almost sadly and let out the following news: Ismail, Ali, and Habib were hard at work at Mr. Essajee's Emporium. There was no one to meet her. No one there to watch her little girl. Tahir was not well, after all, not well enough to host her. What *would* she find upstairs? Oh, Maria didn't know. Because? Oh, yes. Well. *Majid Ghulam had gone out.* "You see, you see. Bwana Jeevanjee's not here."

Sarie thought Maria must be joking. Not here? Not here? *Awful girl!* "Pardon? *S'il vous plaît?* What do you mean?" Sarie asked. She took a step towards Maria, came so close she felt the edge of the fat bundle graze her thumping chest. Maria didn't budge. Sarie's hot heart clenched, unclenched, and jumped. *He's gone?* She could not quite believe it. "What?" she said, more softly.

"Not here," Maria said, more firmly. "I say, Bwana Jeevanjee's not here. Gone out. Won't be back today, oh, no." She drew her foot, as if it were a tongue, across the length of her own sandal, played the blue thing with her toes.

In the alley, Sarie faltered. Had she feared this all along? Had she shored up the walls around the present stillness to prevent exactly this? Had she encouraged all the poetry to make quite sure that he would know her value and *not do a thing like this?* Majid out. *Out?* What could he be doing? Sarie's head was spinning. What could the man *need* out there? What had he gone for? She could not hold Maria's gaze. Agatha, irritated, twitched. Sarie sought her hand again and caught it firmly up in hers.

As Maria watched her, Sarie thought about what she had seen from Majid's bedroom window once. Men huddled under buses, fiddling with tools. The cane-juice maker, busy at his press. A world. Was *that* where he had gone? Was he milling in that world *she* did not know? Oh, Sarie wished to act. It was hard to be observed so closely by a house girl. She let go of Agatha's hand and, to put up against Maria a united front, tried to put her arm around her daughter's shoulder. But Agatha, who had desires of her own, sprang up from her place and, abandoning her mother in one energetic thrust, pushed herself very quickly between Maria and the wall and went skipping—Sarie heard but could not see—up the stairs beyond.

Betrayed by her child, alone before Maria, Sarie was doubly upset. But being doubly upset just then redoubled Sarie's strength. She could not let Maria win. As though she had remembered suddenly, had been foolish to forget—*what had she been thinking*—she tried a little laugh. "Of course! Of course he has gone out. I forgot, you see. He told me this last week. That he would not be here." Maria was unmoved. Sarie said, as though Maria were really, really stupid, "I did not *expect* to see him. But I have to go upstairs."

But Maria was not finished. Something in her had finally been set free. She was going to speak—on behalf of good women everywhere, in service of the Truth (if not the truth, exactly). "Well, I have tried to stop you, Mrs. Turner. Go on. Go up, just. *He's* gone. But *our lady* is upstairs." Then, like a fighter who goes slack to trick a great opponent, Maria moved at once out of the dark doorway, down into the alley where Sarie, shaking, stood. "Go see her, the lady of the house." The stairwell loomed as Maria, generous hips asway, started towards the courtyard. Sarie looked as though she had been hit.

Maria could not quite repress a giggle, a hurrah. *A Jezebel. A harlot. A painted she-demon born and raised in Sodom. Mungu am-samehe, nothing but a viper.* Maria felt so wonderful that she kept right on saying things as she proceded towards the taps. Had not Brother Ewald called them soldiers, free to use all arms? "She's very beautiful, you know. We love her! Bwana's favorite lady."

Though she herself felt frozen as a fruit ice, Sarie's feet pro-pelled her. *A lady? The lady of the house? Qu'est-ce que ça veut dire?* Her legs shot her up the stairwell like a rocket and right into the parlor, where, shocked, enraged, she found her daughter sitting comfortably on the settee while a lovely woman dressed in green taught Tahir how to walk.

Sarie's heart fell from its cradle, clattered through her stomach, and zoomed down to her feet. She nearly fainted from it. The boy was standing up. What's more, he was in the midst of taking a great step. *He's walking all around, won't need any help.* The sight of it—the woman in the dress (plump, fine-faced, bright-eyed, capable, and *shapely!*) and the crippled boy on crutches—was too much, and twofold. How could she not have known before, considered what would happen? How would Majid have any time now, how would they find silence? When could she come by? And, worst of all, just then, slicing at her gut: *Who* was this new woman? What was she doing *here?*

Without waiting for a welcome—indeed, it seemed to her that she had arrived unnoticed, that no one saw her, or that if they had, not one among them cared—she moved, invisible, towards the settee and sat down. The coffee table, she could see, had been pushed back to its ordinary place, too close to the seats for her to stretch her legs. She thought that she might cry. But she was wrong, of course; she was too large not to be seen. Tahir had looked up but hadn't nodded at her; rightly so, for his efforts were elsewhere. Agatha, it's true, ignored her, but this, too, from a child, is a luxurious sign of notice. Sugra did pay heed. But she was in the midst of something urgent; she wanted first to make quite sure that Tahir was all right. She'd been saying, "Come to Auntie, now, just a little farther, show me what you know." And Tahir wobbled, moved. Went to stand beside her. And then, and only then, Sugra reached for Sarie's hand, for Sarie, who had collapsed on the blue seat and who needed, Sugra knew the moment that she looked, all of her attention. Sugra understood who this must be. It pleased her. And while Tahir leaned against her, she smiled a great, warm smile so bright it deepened the nut color of her pleasant, open face and made her eyes look light, cream-green like her dress.

Sarie, trembling, took the woman's hand. But a heat licked at her throat. Who was this? Who was this upstairs-going-*lady* about whom she'd not known? What was she doing *here?* How could this have happened? Had Majid thought so little of her? Had he been fooling with this other woman all along, bathing after holding Sarie only to move on and pollute himself—crudely, coarsely, she was sure—with another woman's limbs? Sugra's sweetness didn't help. It was, thought Sarie, *A distraction, subterfuge.* Sarie was unnerved, yes, at last, just as Gilbert had predicted: well out of her depth. Her teeth felt furred and warm.

Sugra, still holding Sarie's hand, nudged Tahir from her side. She looked across at Sarie as one does at an accomplice—as though surely Sarie cared and was delighted that Tahir was, after so long, finally standing up. "Is that all you can do? And with guests here! Can't you do it harder?" Sarie took her hand back and, feeling slightly sick, sat looking at the boy, the woman, and the room.

With his only foot, Tahir took a step. He propelled his shoulders straight ahead, nudged both crutches forward, then pressed his full weight down. The abbreviated leg, suspended like a cluster of bananas on a tree, hung loosely from his hip. When Tahir put his good leg down, the half-leg—like an echo or a recoil—swung forwards and then back. Sugra clapped her hands. "So, my little man, you can do it after all. Again, yes, now, please—or?"

Agatha, supportive of her allies when it mattered, applauded from her seat. When she said, "Yes, you must do it again!" Sarie felt betrayed. But she decided to join in. They'd been through this together, after all. "That's right," she said. "Do it for your friend!" she said. "And for me. For your Mrs. Turner!" Her voice rang oddly in the air. She could not say his name. Agatha continued to ignore her. Tahir, concentrating, didn't answer. Sugra's smile was kind, but at that moment Sarie feared her. She felt distinctly separate from everyone, even from her child. As if confronted by a family, a threesome: Tahir, Agatha, and the-green-dressed-woman-with-the-smile, the *lady of the house.* And on the settee, like an extra limb, huddled in the corner, all alone, Mrs. Gilbert Turner. Sarie felt demoted. *We love her,* she heard Maria say again. *She's so beautiful. Bwana's favorite lady.* Her throat hurt. Her bowels shifted, continents adrift; the soles of her feet burned.

Without meaning to, she winced. Sugra saw her from the corner of an eye. She patted Tahir's arm and sent him to his room. Not everyone was as interested as she—*though they should be,* Sugra thought—in little Tahir's legs. "Take your friend along, will you?" she said. "Show her how you put your crutches by the bed so you can reach them by yourself." The children slipped away, Tahir struggling bravely and Agatha excited, giving praises as they went. The women were alone.

Sitting in the chair Majid Ghulam had taken that first day, just beneath the clock, Sugra looked benevolently at Sarie and said, of all things, "I'm so glad you have come." What perverted twist was this? Sarie had no idea what to do, what could be expected of her. Or, indeed, what she could expect. Majid's *lady*. Could her lover have deceived her? She thought about the Kuria cattleman and about Angélique. Had that thief been faithful? Had Angélique gone, too, to where her lover lived, and found he had a mistress or some wives; that he did, in the end, love cattle more than he loved her? Her eyes roamed over the coffee table and the floor, her legs, as if looking for a clue. She felt Sugra waiting, watching her. Did not know where to look. She scratched her wrists, wound her ankles round and round. *At least I,* she thought, *told him of my husband. I told him about Gilbert. I told him nearly all.*

Sugra knew of Mrs. Turner's visits, how since the accident on India Street she'd come almost every day with her little girl in tow. She'd heard about it from the aunts and from people in the storefronts whose wandering eyes were keen. She'd also heard it from the boy. She respected her for it. Was grateful. So rare, these days, for strangers to be gentle more than once! In Tahir's version, Sarie's energetic daughter sat beside him on the bed feeding him bananas or reading from a book while her mother sat with Majid, demure in the front room. Sugra, who thought that, like her cousin, Mrs. Turner was a widow, who had heard no mention of a husband, had, actually, hoped that they did do more than talk. She had thought (since no one in their family would have him) that Majid might find pleasure there. Weren't British women known for starting up affairs? And hadn't Ghuji seemed much braver recently than he had in a long time? Smelled a little sweeter? She could see that Mrs. Turner was unhappy. She said, "You expected to see Majid, eh? You came to see my cousin?" Sarie didn't speak, was watching, waiting, thinking, trying to stay calm. Sugra attempted to encourage her. "I have heard about your visiting, you see."

Sarie focused on this last. It was not the best thing to have said. Now Sarie imagined Majid telling all to someone else, to someone he loved better. Laughing. A jealous woman would be easier, she thought. But the more Sarie looked at Sugra, the more she felt that Sugra had nothing to fear. Only a woman who is perfectly secure can treat a rival kindly, after all. Sarie felt confused, said nothing. Something in the woman's face was tender. Sugra seemed *concerned*.

Sugra, for her part, was beginning to feel certain: the British woman came for more than tea. She cocked her head and gently said, "He's gone out. I am as surprised as you." Sarie paused, sniffed. Rethought things a little. *Could a rival be so calm?* Sugra looked at Sarie sideways across the coffee table and touched her hand again, inviting her to join her in soft talk about Majid. "All of us have worried so for him, you know." She lowered her voice. "Since the children's mother died. May she be in peace. It altered him completely. He's been lost. Has Majid told you this? It's good he has a friend."

All of us. Sarie felt as she had the first day, the first time she'd entered Tahir's room after the accident and had thought about the aunts. The women who made visits, came with cakes, and with no feelings of trespass watched the sick boy sleep. She felt again that she did not belong, that she stood uncertain on the margins of an unfamiliar world where she might make mistakes. As Gilbert had done far more than imply. She tried to slow her heart. *Wait a little.* She bit down on her lip and nodded slowly. "You are Majid's *cousin?*" She could not meet Sugra's gaze. Her fingers fluttered at the hem of her white dress.

Yes, Sugra knew a sweetheart's longing when she heard it. She almost laughed out loud. After so much widowed love and sorrow, how *natural,* how wonderful, that Ghuji would be subject in the end again to *really masculine* desires. She could also tell when a woman thought that someone else had slipped into a bed. *How silly!* The parrot cried out from the kitchen. Sugra clapped her hands down on her thighs, let out a pretty giggle. "Yes!" she said. "My *husband* lets me visit Ghuji now and then, you know, because we were children here together. Ghuji is my cousin, like a brother. I look in on the children when I can. It's hard once you are married!"

It took Sarie a moment to understand that Sugra's "Ghuji" was her very own Majid. This woman—not a *lady,* after all, perhaps; perhaps a relative who had a husband of her own—knew her Majid by a nickname. As children do, as people who are raised together. *A brother,* Sarie thought, embarrassed. Oh, that terrible Maria! Had she been playing games? From the wild mix of emotions that were twisting in her belly and sending heat into her face, a tear had escaped. She squeezed it from her eye with a deep frown, as though something else—dust, an unknown thing, an insect—had caused it to appear. She batted at her face. Relief? Yes, oh, yes, relief. Her Majid, her poetic lover-man, could not have a lady. *Only me,* she thought. Finally, she looked across at Sugra. She did not care if her voice shook. "Will he be back today?"

Sugra shrugged and smiled. "Well, now, *that* no one can say. Today Majid has surprised us. Who knows when he will come? But, look. Why don't we have tea? I will call down for Maria."

That she was on the verge of reenacting with his cousin what she had done with Majid Jeevanjee on that first day gave Sarie a chill. And thinking of Maria made her angry—*elle m'a joué un tour!* she thought. No, she did not want to stay. And was furthermore surprised by what she *did* want: to be safe at home again. With Agatha in bed and Gilbert reading in the parlor. With the things she understood, and no strangers to see her. She could not have tea with Sugra, wished she'd never come. "No. No, thank you. Please," she said. "I can't." Sarie got up roughly, feeling as she pushed the table back that a skin was falling from her. She called loudly out for Agatha and, without waiting for her, hurried down the stairs.

Around the corner, deeply satisfied, Maria turned the taps and slapped at soaking things. Sugra leaned out of the window, looking sweetly down: "It was good to meet you, Mrs. Turner! Welcome, welcome. When will you come back?"

For Majid, the day Sarie met Sugra was the day he fell out of the past, through the unexpected now (which had never been as still for him as it had been for his lover), and into something that, while not quite yet a future, was absolutely new. It was the day, he would later recall, that he'd come back to life. That morning, Majid had woken early, bathed, and, for the first time in many years, since not long after Tahir's birth, which was also Hayaam's death, said prayers at a mosque. He did not choose the grandiose masjid he had frequented in the past, the towered place beyond Mbuyu Mmoja Park, where he could count on seeing people he'd once known and been close to, people who had grown up with Hayaam or loved her. That, he was not certain he could bear. Majid had started small. He walked out to the mosque that gave the name to Mosque Street, the high, white, crenellated thing around the corner from his house, the mosque whose prayer call had taught the parrot almost all the words it knew.

Majid understood the value of small signs, the first slow, tender steps. *It doesn't matter where I go,* he thought. *It's the going-out at all.*

Any mosque, any mosque, would do—and better, really, not to go to the old place, the *real* place, right away. Wouldn't it be easier, if this was really a fresh start, to go first to a little world where he was not well known? He entered the gates bravely, gave each mendicant a coin.

At the white-tiled water tanks just inside the walls, Majid washed his hands and feet with other city men, exchanging simple greetings, acknowledging their presence, nodding as he should. Majid didn't know it, but the first to say hello was the very coffee salesman whose coals had toppled when the *Al-Fadhil*-bearing bus had borne down on his son. The coffee salesman, to whom most men of Majid's age and pedigree looked very much alike, didn't know it, either, though something in Majid made the man feel kind. They asked after each other's families and smiled afterwards, sincerely. Whatever happened outside of the gates, however split up and on-what-side-of-what-fence, it was good to be together.

In the cool, high, vaulted space, Majid prayed with thirty sleepy men, standing, bowing, touching his bare forehead to the floor mat, where, with a little wave of pleasure, he noted the bare toes of the men ahead of him. How soft and silly men's feet were when seen from underneath. How every man's were different! Knobby, slender, stunted, bruised, fine, long, or very small. But also, yes, how very much the same. Just toes on sleepy feet. The synchronic standing, bowing, rising, the way he felt alone and not alone, all of that joint motion and joint stillness, soothed him. *Amin, amin.* His own worship ended, Majid walked out slowly to the steps. Before he left, he turned towards the mirhab. Other men were still arriving. Some sat down and stretched their legs along the thick layers of palm mats, opened books and read. Still others curled up in the corners, thinking they might sleep. Majid, who had stayed inside the rooms of Kudra House for so many private years, felt shy. At last, he found his shoes among the dozens at the door. Pausing at the steps, he straightened up his cap as men continued milling, washing, entering and going on their way. Of course such things went on! But how he had forgotten.

Afterwards, he was glad that no one knew him. That no one there was close enough to what he had once been to say, to themselves or to another, "Look, it's Majid Ghulam Jeevanjee, crazy Mad Majid, who couldn't grieve his wife and go on with his life. A-laa? I thought he was dead." Because just then Majid felt anything but dead, and not entirely crazy. As he'd walked out into the morning, the air had seemed particularly fresh. He'd looked up Mosque Street and then down, and thought: *I know each end of this. To Libya. And beyond that to the park. On the other side, the sea.* A litter woman passed him and he smiled, not at her, exactly—in fact, she didn't see him, bent over as she was, seeking husks and crumpled bits of tin—but at the thought of her. At the thought of people who rose before the dawn and *did* things. He'd once risen early, too, each day; had had a sense of duty, worked at things. Looking at Kikanga, Majid felt ashamed and proud at the same time. Ashamed at how hard other people worked, and proud, proud that he had come. The feeling made him think about the Bata shoe that Tahir had never gotten back, the shoe whose loss he'd felt so keenly, and the doctor who had said, "What's a shoe, *yakhe*, in the face of life and death?" He wondered where it was, but this wondering did not, he found, upset him as it had. Perhaps the doctor had a point. What if life *was* bigger? *Those doctors*, Majid thought. *Maybe they work hard.*

He'd been about to turn up Mosque Street, heading home because he didn't know what else to do, when something oddly reminiscent of Hayaam made him stop and stand still at the corner. Not a vision, not Hayaam herself, nor the woman-like-and-not-like-her who had sat beside him in the bedroom and looked at those old clothes on that painful, painful day. Nothing so outlined or so firm, but a soft sensation in the corner of his eyes, at the edges of his skin. Out of reach, but *there*. As if in this great world he was not really alone. The impression that he was accompanied by something other than himself brought into relief, and altered, how the shuffling of feet and sandals sounded on the street, a bit of how the light looked. Just behind his shoulder, he thought that he heard Hayaam laugh—that good laugh, the one he had remembered right—and the laughter in his ears commingled with a shiver at his skin, a freshness in his sight. He saw a pinkness in the air and in the sky, a gildedness to things; felt buoyed by the shapes that moved around him. Blessed. And so, shy and new, loose and fine from his ankles to his elbows, from his neck to the skin of his wide brow, Majid turned away from home and headed towards the sea.

Not thinking anymore about whom he might see on his way, who might see him or might whisper, say, "There goes Mad Majid," he had walked down India Street in the direction of the sea. And he had stopped at the corner of Mahaba, *Where,* he thought, *it happened.* Where Tahir lost his leg. The aunts had done this. Come to look. Yasmina had gone back to Kudra House after her first pilgrimage in elaborate hysteria, describing the great puddles of blood—their little Tahir's!—that must have dyed the road. How a person could still *tell* that an accident had happened, even once the rain had washed that blood away; how that road gave her the shakes every time she passed, made her angel-hairs perk up. Even Sugra said she'd stopped there, looking into the store windows of Hisham's Food and Drink, and wondered, thought about, how little Tahir must have felt, what he had been doing when the rattling bus came down. Majid had not done it. *Just a road,* he'd thought. *Another road where somebody has suffered.* He hadn't gone so far as to say what he did feel: *So what, so what? Nothing for us but sorrow. Why go seek it out?*

But the intersection jarred him. He felt a little bus-crash in his gut, a pulling in his arms as if the very air itself were urging him to stand where his own Tahir had. To cross the road and pause, tilt his head and close his eyes, think of shooting at a crow. Imagine. What *had* Tahir been thinking? But Majid went no further. Awakening, Majid might be, but he was not like the aunts. *Let the inside stay inside,* he thought. *The knife of life is sharp; we take the blade but must not ever flinch.* And while his chest and belly quivered at the thought of little Tahir being crushed by a big bus, Majid's two legs held him steady, and he swallowed. Did not look away. *That's where it all happened,* Majid thought. *And this is where I am. All right.* The most important thing, he thought, was walking, without muttering or shouting, without glaring meanly at any passersby, without feeling that at any moment he might weep. The most important thing was being equal to it all.

He'd thought to pause at Hisham's Food and Drink, where the aunts had gone to get the news from Iqbal when Tahir's leg first fell, and where, long ago, Hayaam had liked the ices. That would itself be a poem, no? Going to the very place where so much news—about his little son and even, surely, in the past, about his own craziness and grief—had been made up and tossed into the world. But he was not quite ready for all that. One day, yes, sometime, but not yet. Hisham's was too bright.

However, thinking about Hisham's—cutlass patties, ices, eggs embedded in potatoes, almond sweets—decided him to eat. He passed A. Tea Shop and Tea Shop J., named for Alibhai and Jaffar, and chose not to go in. He crossed the street away from Habib's Restaurant, where the bajia mix was sweet. All of them too known, he thought. Majid, who had hurled himself so firmly into the broad, consuming jaws of sadness for so long, was now, instead, emerging, and willing to be tender with, at last, himself. He'd stick to places in which he would not elicit any detailed memory, friendly or unkind, where he would not have a presence. He turned along Mahaba Street and settled on the New Purnima Snack, where, in the long shade of the flame trees, three ancient island men sold cinnamon and cloves.

The Purnima was just right. There was old Vijay Mehta— whom he'd only known by sight and to whom he had, as far as he recalled, not done grievous harm: black hair dyed as ever, mustache as trim and neat, bent over the fryers. There was the bright calendar, the plastic flowers poking from the cracks—pink and yellow, tangerine. There was the blue table, the old sink by the mirrored wall. Majid sat far in the corner, by the window near the taps. A gloomy waiter came to him, and Majid, smoothly, in one phrase, ordered up a large plate of jalebis and a cup of milky tea.

What, he wondered, had come over him? How tasty the air smelled! How fine the Mehta elders looked, smoking narrow cigarettes and waiting for the peppers and the chutneys to be brought for their kachori! How charming Mrs. M. looked, chatting at the till in her workaday brown sari! For just a moment—the space of a long swallow or a restful closing of the eyes—Majid felt as happy as he had when Ismail was born and as light as he had been when Sarie Turner (so *he* remembered it just then) bared her breasts for him so suddenly and willingly in the blue, surprising hall and reached out for his arms. *Sarie,* Majid thought, guiltily at first. What if she'd expected him? *What if she has come?* The Mehtas' ageless man shuffled over in a white coat like a doctor's and set down Majid's tea. The jalebis would be right along, he said. Majid thought: *Jalebis. Fryers all asteam. Old men who make certain there is sugar to be had.* Something in him swelled, and Majid forgot Sarie. He could just then not bear to feel himself in any way relied upon, by anyone. Did not want to feel responsible at all. *Well. If I have missed her,* Majid thought, *she is sure to come again.*

Bibi had been trying to perceive for several minutes exactly what Salma Hafiz and her husband—or another man, yes, wouldn't that be better?—were doing in the bedroom she could just vaguely make out between the curtains that hung across the way (light green, were they, with a rice or barley print?). Had Salma's husband's trip into the highlands really been so smooth, successful, quick? *Has he come back so soon?* Bibi's neck was strained, her head pushed forward from her chest. If she could, she would have sent her head all the way across the street, like a telescope or wire. Her neck, she thought, amused, would have been just like a bridge from her balcony to Salma's. She could look under the bed, check the cups for dirt. Identify that print. She wished her body were as large as any building, so she could twist and turn and reach and witness everything that happened. Her eyes would be like windows. *I'd be Big Kikanga Bibi!* Bibi laughed, felt light.

The pale curtain whisked and dangled, and Bibi couldn't tell if that dark square was emptiness beyond, or Salma's dress, or the turned head of a man, moving in the room. But she didn't mind so much just then. Sometimes it was the seeking, and also the not knowing, that gave her the most pleasure. She finally gave up. It didn't matter, in the end, what Salma Hafiz really did. Because Bibi was working out the envelope, and remembering the Ladies' Sewing Club, where blue was meant for boys. And because the night before, as she'd gone up to bed, had she or had she not heard some loving laughter and a thump from Nisreen and Issa's room?

She'd been about to turn back to the envelope, which was coming along nicely, when she caught sight of Mad Majid Ghulam. When Bibi spotted Majid stepping out alone, and not simply stepping down from Libya, but coming *up* from India Street, as though he'd been on a trip into the city—perhaps down to the docks! or to see about a permit!—she sat up with a gasp and let her stitching fall. There he was. Crazed old bad-luck Jeevanjee, alive as Mama Moto or Nisreen. And whereas she could crane her neck and peer and squint and didn't care if people saw when she was spying on poor Salma or on Mama Ndiambongo, upon seeing Mad Majid, Bibi felt that she should make herself as small as she could be. She blushed. She felt a swelling in her skin. She felt, indeed, as if she were seeing with her own very naked eyes a man about whose heft she'd had a pulsing, sexy dream. Or a long-admired movie star appearing from the blue. Unprepared, caught out and excited. *There is old Majid!* Bibi clutched the stitching to her chest and pressed her face against the grate. She placed her round chin carefully between the panels of a heart. Where had Majid been? And where could he be going?

He looked, thought Bibi, much, much younger than she had been thinking he would look. Had her eyes gone bad? Could she trust what they were seeing? Look how his hips swaggered, just a little, how his head was high and undisturbed in the busy morning air! He was a little gray around the ears, it's true, but that was not important. Who was not, these days? He looked, she thought, *Attractive*. Not poorly preserved. *He's left his crumbling house!* she thought. And then: *Where is Mama Moto? This I'll tell Nisreen.* She watched Majid look about, a little like a cat deciding whether it should cross, or leap, or sit, and fastened her eyes to him as he moved, finally, with a confidence she would never have surmised, into the New Purnima Snack. There she saw, she thought, Majid

Ghulam Jeevanjee say something to handsome Mr. Mehta, greet the busy Mrs., and take a table by the sink. Her old fingers twitched. A thing like a trapped bird went wild behind her eyes. Change quivered all around. *At last,* she thought, *new times bring new things.* But, oh, how hard it was to know exactly *when,* or *what,* and *what it meant,* if one was stuck at home and on a balcony, no less. What was Majid *doing?*

The unfinished envelope felt hot beneath her hands. *Majid Ghulam Jeevanjee has stepped from Kudra House. He is ordering kachori.* Well, she was wrong about what Majid had gone to eat. At the New Purnima Snack the jalebis arrived, and Majid thought he'd not tasted anything so sweet in a hundred million years. Not since Independence. But she was right that things were moving, new things, shaking in the air. She was so excited about having witnessed unhinged, widowed, short-circuited, and wicked Mad Sad Majid Ghulam Jeevanjee walk into the Purnima that when Sarie passed with Agatha ahead of her, Bibi didn't see.

❧Nineteen

Sarie's visit to Majid's, the strange meeting with Sugra, left her troubled and bewildered. Sarie was upset—in part about Maria, about Sugra, and the possibility that Majid lived a wider life—but also in a comprehensive way that placed many things in doubt. Unsettling: for the first time in her life, Sarie felt consciously uncertain of her judgment. Accustomed to assuming, as many of the Sisters had about themselves, and as Gilbert always did, that what she believed she saw was the same as what there was, Sarie had never thought herself a person who was sometimes right and sometimes wrong about the layout of the world. But now she was confused. She was sure Maria meant to harm her. But she wondered about Sugra. *Was* Sugra just a cousin? Was she Majid's lover? If she wasn't, *had* she been—before, or after his wife died? What were cousins, in the end? Didn't Jeevanjees and many others in these parts go with cousins above all? Had the late, unnamed Mrs. Majid not in all likelihood been a father's brother's child or another close relation? Was Sugra really married to a man who was *not* Majid Ghulam, and did she only come, as she had said, "to bring our Tahir legs"?

How *kind* Sugra had been, how it had seemed that Sugra wanted most of all for Sarie to be welcome. Could one trust in kindness, really? Or was kindness nothing more than the greatest trick of all? Hovering by the windows at Mchanganyiko Street, Sarie rubbed her lips and face and wondered what was true. Maria was a thorn. And Sugra, well . . . Sugra, no matter how she'd twisted Sarie's heart, wasn't the worst thing. *This* was: where had Majid gone? Had he not thought that Sarie might visit him that day, as she often did? Did she not occur to him? Had he not *hoped* she'd come? *Had he*—and here the little verses did not seem as lovely as they had, contained in Majid's rooms—*gone out to write a poem?* Did Sarie not matter at all?

She didn't go again for quite some days, though Agatha— loyal, Sarie thought, to Tahir in a way she was not to her mother—cried and stamped her feet. She would miss the changes in his walk, she said; she wouldn't see him win. Sarie remained firm. "No, no, no," she said, though Agatha did threaten, said she'd throw herself under the cars her mother warned about each day, that she'd run into the street. "I'll go lie under that taxi! I'll look for a big bus!" But Sarie was entrenched. "Then go," she said. "See if you can move me!"

She walked slowly in the flat, washed things she had left un-washed for months—the insides of the cabinets, slats of glass on the hinged windows, the bathroom's high, wide sill, the round drain on the floor. The present was no longer what she had thought it was. She did not know what was true. And so what of the future? What was going to happen? What *had* Gilbert written to old Great-Uncle James? Write, he had, she thought, though he hadn't told her, hadn't answered, even when she'd asked; had sim-ply looked at her in that irritating, absent, beaming way. Had the letter reached its aim? How had Gilbert introduced the idea of the business? Would Uncle James agree? In a far-off English place, had their fates been sealed? When she tired of her husband's smiles and pressed him, Gilbert shook his head and put a finger to his lips. Or tried to kiss her on the cheek. Said things like, "Let's not talk until it's real," and "Later, later, dear. Once we've gotten a reply." And, "Trust me, Sarie, please." Was he doing what she thought? Would he fail, again? Would this man she had accepted years ago bring ruin on them all?

She had liked the feeling that the present would go on, like this, forever, but now it wore her down. She thought about the baskets and the spears she'd seen at the Mountain Top Hotel. The jewels. Such sparkling, colored things! Such comforting, dear trinkets. As if to will the business and her future into being, she focused on them, thought: *Arrows, bracelets, stones.* She saw them clearly in her mind. Oh, if she could step into that future, Sarie thought, the present, so unknowable, suddenly, couldn't cause her grief. She worried about Gilbert's silence, then told herself she shouldn't. She wanted, and she did not want, to know. And so she told herself: *Gilbert has been quiet because he wants to be so certain we are fine before we really start. He does not want me to hope. When he has an answer, he will want to talk. We'll discuss it all. I will try to wait.*

But not knowing made her anxious. She went to find her husband, who was dozing on the sofa. "Gilbert?" Gilbert grunted in his sleep. She sat down at the piano. "Gilbert."

He was dreaming about Fiats and about Hungarian buses. The sound of her voice stirred him. "Mm?" he said.

Sarie plucked a note from the piano. Two. "Gilbert." The dream-sights disappeared. Sarie said, to herself, almost, but to her husband, too, and loud enough to pull him out of sleep, "It's going to be all right, isn't it? Isn't it? It *is*." Gilbert stretched his legs, pushed his toes against the pillows. "What?" He opened both his eyes, just barely, peering at his wife beneath a folded arm. "The business," Sarie said, voice softer now, as though she was afraid. "The baskets and the sculptures."

Gilbert smiled at her in half sleep. "Come," he said. He unfolded one arm, he beckoned, and was pleasantly surprised when Sarie came towards him. *She seems a bit worn,* he thought. *And tired.*

All this waiting and the worrying have my little Sarie down. Sarie knelt beside him. He could hear her breathing, shallow, saw a flutter at her eyes. He was touched. *My dear.* He thought again how pleased Sarie would be if Uncle James agreed and when he told her what he'd planned. How she would see that cars were far better than statues, much more sturdy and exciting than gaudy souvenirs; that they shouldn't (Gilbert almost laughed, thinking of how Sarie spoke) *put their eggs in baskets.* When he placed a hand on Sarie's shoulder and looked into her face, she didn't flinch, or push his hand away. Gilbert felt confirmed. *See how she needs me.* "It's going to be all right," he said. "You'll see."

Sarie fixed her eyes on his, tugged with one hand at his shirt. "You will go to look?" she asked. "You'll go to find the Post?" Oh, he would be her soldier, would defend her, life and limb. "Indeed, my dear. Indeed. And if there's no letter today, I will go again to-morrow. And the next day, and the next."

He yawned. It was time, wasn't it, that Uncle James replied? He'd go out in the afternoon. Gilbert took hold of Sarie's fingers, closed his eyes again. He thought about Judge Hewett and Kimbuga. And giraffes. In a moment he'd have *really* woken up, feeling fine; and perhaps, perhaps, once he ventured out, there would be a letter. Lolling, Gilbert sighed. Sarie took her hand from his, sniffed at it, and, sadly, wiped it on her dress. She went back to the piano. Without thinking, Sarie did what she had not done in years, what she had not liked doing, and what the Sisters had always said would save her, if she would only try: she bent her head and prayed.

At last. On the Thursday when it happened, Gilbert had the wherewithal to close the Post Box door and step out from the wall

so that any men could reach their letters without having to push
Gilbert around as that historian had once done. Tearing at the
aerogramme (all blue, not pink, with *Airmail* stamped in English),
he felt a little sick. He'd grown, admit, accustomed to the waiting.
To the sense of possibility. To maybe yes or no, a feeling of perhaps.
"Perhaps" was easier than other things, of course. Easier than certainty. And pleasant. Maybe yes and maybe no: all maybes, nothing
to confront. Gilbert's mouth went dry. His fingers shook a bit. That
letter held the future, everything; could hold, he thought, obscurity
or greatness, a decision—between a life and something else, something too familiar, worse. He took a deep, deep breath and told
himself to think about the sea—the one thing, Gilbert thought, he
really shared with Uncle James. Each man by a shore, each aware
that on the unknown side of dangerous waters there lay all sorts of
potential. A great, blue kind of peace. *I'm ready.*

Feeling deft for once, he worked the complicated creases without tearing the paper. He smoothed the light thing out and closed
his eyes before determining to look. His knees knocked. He felt a
coldness at his spine, a tingling; as if a smaller version of himself,
coiled and tight, hands across its ears and eyes, had hidden there,
prepared to fall or cry so that, should the letter bear bad news, his
larger self would not. But as he opened his eyes slowly, the bigger,
life-sized Gilbert, too, small one notwithstanding, almost, almost,
wept.

Dearest Gilbert, Uncle James began. *I see you have grown up!
Thank you for your prompt and, shall I say, inspiring, response to my last
letter. I have considered your proposal.* Gilbert closed his eyes again.
Could he bear to read on? The letter trembled in his hand. The
huddled little man at the base of Gilbert's spine stretched his arms
in wonder. Gilbert read a little farther, felt something like a song.
You have gone some distance towards restoring, or securing, rather, my confi-

dence in you. Some of us, it seems, take longer to mature than others but shape up after all. And for you it is high time. I grant you my—provisional—approval. I will wire necessary funds. But, dear Gilbert, be forewarned that without certain proof of progress I cannot be relied upon to furnish further monies, and that, following this wire, I will discontinue your allowance. Any future wires are to be treated as investments. Do recall, as I explained in my last letter, that I shall expect returns. I have paints to buy.

Had he been a looser man, Gilbert would have jumped for joy or hooted. Instead, he hugged the aerogramme tightly to his chest and rubbed his hands across it as he walked, blindly, to the street. *Further monies.* How stuffy Uncle James had grown! How pompous! But how dear! Oh, yes, it was going to be all right. Just as he'd told Sarie. He had intended after stopping for the post to pass by the Victorian Palm to look for Kazansthakis. But this was news for Sarie, wasn't it? For Sarie, first of all. *Let Kazansthakis wait!* Feeling like a husband, Gilbert hurried home to number 2, where Agatha and Sarie, bent over the *Adventures,* were reading about pirates.

Sarie took one look at him and knew. Oh, some things did turn out! Nevermind Majid Ghulam's Sugra. Nevermind her lover's absence. She'd work it all out later. She took in Gilbert's blush, the glitter in his eyes. Gilbert, speechless, nodded on the threshold. Without stopping to think, impelled by her relief, Sarie hurried towards her husband and thrust her arms around him. Small in her embrace, Gilbert, shocked, mouth muzzled by her shoulder, muttered, gasping, "Yes. Great-Uncle James agreed." Sarie, seeing trays of precious stones, crates abrim with bracelets, spun around the parlor with her only legal man clutched tightly to her chest. Gilbert, like an inexperienced girl in the hands of a good dancer, felt his two feet leave the floor. Just as he had held the letter, Sarie lunged and lurched, pressed him hard against her breasts, and cooed into his ears.

She's happy! Gilbert thought, and because he could not recall the last time Sarie had held on to him with so much strength and focus—or indeed, if she had ever done so—he let her squeeze and turn him until he felt a little dizzy. "Sarie, Sarie, stop!" he said.

He pulled himself away while Sarie laughed out loud. She jumped into the air and landed with a hearty, solid *thunk* on the red settee, where she kicked her feet before her like a swimmer. "Oh, Gilbert!" Sarie said. "You wrote him a nice letter! We must thank your uncle James."

Steadying himself at the piano, still undone from the surprise of Sarie's—so impulsive!—arms, he beamed. "It worked, my dear, it worked." Gilbert wiped the sweat from his bare brow and stood there, panting, trying to collect himself again. Agatha, who had retreated to the kitchen while her mother pulled her father up into the air and made circles with him on the floor, looked warily into the parlor and wondered what had happened.

Hands flat on her thighs, knees bent, like a diver at a pool, Sarie asked, "What shall we do now?" She was imagining Gilbert and herself bent over the kitchen table, Gilbert's notepad at the ready, pencil in the air. Gilbert listening to her, writing what she told him to. She imagined herself shining. But Gilbert tucked his shirt into his trousers and adjusted his old belt. "I think," he said, "that I'll go see Kazansthakis." Wasn't that what he'd intended from the start? Shouldn't he be there right now, on the patio of the Palm, waiting for a toast? Kazansthakis, after all, together with the little dream, Gilbert's little hope, was the reason for this plan—the brains, so far, behind Gilbert's new idea. The Frosty King would know exactly what to do. Oh, he'd go there right away.

It was not what she had hoped. But Sarie held her tongue. She did think, *He should stay right here and make the plan with me,* but she also felt, magnanimous, that she should grant her husband a little space for joy. For feeling that he'd done something important. As he had. With Majid she had learned the place of intermittent silences, and she had also come to see that certain questions were right on, and others were too quick. Why not treat her Gilbert to a little kindness, too? *It's true,* she thought. Kazansthakis had been in business for a while, had lived through Independence, and the parlor was aboom. He would have some contacts, too. Why should she imagine selfishly that she would be this thing's only heart? Why not be generous, for once? "All right," she said, adjusting. "Mr. Frosty will help us with the baskets, then. He will give us counsels." Proud of her own kindness, Sarie nodded at her husband, then bent to rearrange the crocheted headrests on the chairs.

"The what?" asked Gilbert, already heading for the door. He had quite forgotten. Had she not held to him so well, so beautifully, when she'd first heard the news, he might have loosed a laugh. He didn't. No, a wave of tenderness engulfed him. "The baskets? Oh, Sarie!" His fingers lingered on the doorknob; his heart beat warmly in his chest. Poor big-boned, helpless, misguided, funny, darling Sarie. Would she not give up? Her persistence charmed him fiercely. "Yes, yes," he said. "Of course he will. The Frosty King, indeed!" As he left, before Sarie could dissuade him or push him from herself, he grabbed her face with both his hands and planted on her damp, soft, open mouth a loud and smacking kiss.

He did not find the Frosty King at the Victorian Palm. Instead, he drank with Göethe Bienheureux (who talked about his sausages) and bought a Danish engineer a drink. The engineer, impressed by Gilbert's tenure in the country, was thrilled by Gilbert's anecdotes. "It's an honor," the man said. Gilbert talked about the Sikh shrines on the railway, and the King of Kudra's wives. He also named the disparate places where body parts reputed to belong to Dr. David Livingstone had been diversely laid to rest. The engineer applauded. "Not really? You don't say? I'll remember that one, sir," he said, "so I can tell my friends."

❧Twenty

In its part of the city (beside the Old Empire Cinema, just by the new harbor, and not far, either, from the People's Bank, the Post Office, the dead clubhouse, and the Court), the Frosty-Kreem was a significant attraction. All kinds of people went there on a sunny day and had done so for years, and others, when it rained, sought shelter and dessert. At the Frosty-Kreem, Kazansthakis saw, coming in for cold things after hot lunches of stew, smartly done-up office men with lipsticked women on their arms; independent ladies ordering fancy sundaes, ateeter on high heels; saw ministers, officials, people from the Customs Office, others from the Bank. In the afternoons, schoolchildren in groups came — a crush of blue or green topped with white and satchels; boys with tender Adam's apples, girls with hardening limbs. He saw the stalwart Vunjamguu types who, after Independence, had had nowhere to go, and also the new immigrants, the people who had once lived on the islands, and their children. A few of these were Europeans, teachers, most of all: a bony, quiet woman who had run a Sewing Program (once Livery-Jones had died), a now-wrinkled Mr. Pursewarden, who had taught literature out there and now wrote poems over chocolate mounds with nuts; and also solemn Mr. Suleiman, who the Frostys knew had suffered, had had narrow escapes, and who, though he had once driven a cab, was sometimes brought on foot by nieces, not for ice cream but for shakes.

Others were old residents whose families had built the firmer parts of town. Among them, Theosophists and Hindus, Sikhs and

Catholics, too. Others from the offices: the girl who worked, he thought, reception at the corner clinic, and her husband, the meteorologist with a mustache, who did something in town. Evening moviegoers, who could fill him in on what had happened on the screen if he couldn't get away and see it for himself; and also the expatriates, the fresh post-Independence folk who gave the place new life. ("The expats," he would say, while Mrs. Frosty rolled her eyes at him. "Their wives don't pat them anymore!") There were Danes and Swedes and Finns, serious men who tirelessly initiated roads, the plans for which had been drawn up in countries full of snow; doctors, German and Chinese, who bemoaned the state of things; some inscrutable geologists. He also saw a good deal of the airline people: Hans, the German, with his lean wife Greta and two fat boys who liked strawberry ice; a never-married Dutchman (Jan?) with pearly, vacant eyes who ordered huge banana splits but did not like whipped cream. And, of course, most regular, the family from France.

Xavier and Madame Celeste, a small and shapely couple with four anxious little girls, came, almost without fail, every other afternoon. Xavier had no real taste for ice cream, but he liked to talk with Kazansthakis while his girls sat by the window, where they pointed shamelessly at people on the other side of that clean glass with motions of their spoons. They liked vanilla scoops awash in chocolate sauce, which Madame Celeste, with a nervous giggle and a flash of creamy teeth, always very loudly called "a Negro in a shirt." Indeed, while outside poorer folk bought orange ices from the cyclists when they could, or only dreamed of sharbat, juice, and yogurt shakes that they could not afford, in safer circles the Frosty-Kreem was central, and Kazansthakis knew it. If he listened closely while he worked, he could acquire new connections, and could stay as up-to-date as nearly anyone in power, or more. And though he didn't like to do it, he could ask for favors now and then. In the wake of Gilbert Turner's outlandish proposal, at the urging of his wife, Kazansthakis had put out a single feeler to help things come out right.

The Air France troop came into the parlor, as expected, on a Thursday afternoon. Casting nervous glances at the Frosty King, his wife, and his own hands, Xavier had waited by the register until the girls, with Madame Celeste presiding, were seated at the window. Impatient, tugging at his sleeves, he watched Kazansthakis for a while, until he had no choice but to go through with what he'd come for. He slicked down his light hair; moving closer in, he raised his arms so that the counter's edge was tucked into his armpits. His hands reached out to Mr. Frosty. Kazansthakis, occupied, saw the air man wink and wondered whether Xavier had something in his eye. "Are you all right?" he asked. Xavier crooked his finger. "Kazansthakis," he said in a whisper. "Those things you wanted, *mon ami*." Kazansthakis wiped red syrup from his hands and frowned. Xavier looked lugubrious. "What you asked me for. They've come."

"Ah?" At first, thinking about cones and sprinkles, the Frosty King did not understand. He rubbed idly at a silver scoop, checked his white apron for stains. "Hmm?"

Xavier brought his head so low that the counter glass fogged up with his breath. "Those things you wanted."

Kazansthakis, who had so many things to keep track of, couldn't think what Xavier meant. He looked the Frenchman in the eye and waited. A sigh was building in his mouth, a tapping in his foot. Xavier brought his face even closer to the Frosty King's. He cast a glance over his shoulder at the girls, and Kazansthakis for a moment thought that Xavier, who'd gone red, might be suffering from sunstroke or be about to tell the Frosty King his latest dirty joke. "The spark plugs!" Xavier whispered.

Kazansthakis stilled his raised foot in mid-tap and brought it down around his other ankle, like a serpent at a tree. He squeezed the unsighed sigh back down into his throat. "Ah," he said. "Ah. Hah." The spark plugs. He remembered now. The Air France flight had come in on the Monday. "Ah, hah. Very good."

Xavier, whose whisper had the sound of sand, said he would go get them. He gestured, like a mime, *They are in the car.* "I'll be back," he said. Kazansthakis rolled his eyes, thinking that unless Xavier grew accustomed to acting more discreetly, he'd not call on him again. How could a secret be a secret if one treated it so strangely? "So go," he said. "You think they're good to me out there?"

He stepped away from Xavier and attended to a schoolgirl who'd come in with a little less than the right change. "Just this once," he said to her, though he didn't really mean it. While the Frosty King scooped lemon ice into a cone, Xavier went out to his Citroën and came back with a box that bore the label *Fins Pâtés de France.* Mrs. Frosty, who'd come out from the storeroom, said she loved pâté and showed him where to put it.

The next day, the Frosty King stepped out of his parlor and, unaccompanied, excited, yes, despite himself, headed for Kikanga. What he held was too important to hang on to, too interesting to take to the Victorian Palm without knowing for certain that Gilbert would be there. He'd put Gilbert Turner down, it's true, had never thought he'd do a single interesting thing—but now that Uncle James had come so brightly through, what if the plan worked?

Hoping that no police or party chairman on the prowl would stop to ask him how or who he was, or where he might be going (or, indeed, *what was in the box*), the Frosty King stuck close to the buildings. He did not much care for sun. He infrequently took walks so far from his own shop. He hated, hated, sweat. But he wanted very much to see—was looking forward to!—Gilbert Turner's face when he showed him what he had.

Upstairs, in number 2, Sarie was staring out the window and biting at her lip. Gilbert, at the kitchen table, sat looking at a picture in *The Everyman's Car Handbook:* a watercolor image, delicate and soft, showed a man in steel-blue coveralls scratching at his head with one pink hand while a spotted dog lay loyal at his feet. More attracted by the painting of the man than by the efficient diagram of a standard carburetor on the facing page, Gilbert found his own pink fingers moving to his head. When Sarie, passing close to him, tried to look over his shoulder, he'd said, "Not quite yet, my dear. Not yet," and covered up the picture. She'd drummed her fingers on the table, bored her worried eyes into his naked brow for almost a full minute, then turned her back to him.

When Kazansthakis came, she was pleasant and polite. Like her husband, she believed in Mr. and Mrs. Frosty. She thought, *He's come to help, give us some advice.* Gilbert stood to greet the Frosty King. Without asking what it was, or understanding that it was meant for him, Gilbert took the package. Sarie shook Mr. Frosty's hand. She asked after Mrs. Frosty, and Kazansthakis winked. "She's fine, just fine, Mrs. Turner. But she asks after you, and you we do not see."

Sarie smiled at him, felt that she could trust him. Wished to please him, very much. "I will make you grenadine!" she said, which was special, rare, and of which they were almost out. She slipped into the kitchen feeling, hoping, that at any moment now, the quivering in her stomach might go still. The Frosty King must make everything come right. Gilbert would shape up at last, speak out and *get going*.

Gilbert didn't understand at first. While Kazansthakis described circles in the air to loose his shoulders from the walk, Gilbert said, "What's all this, then?" Kazansthakis pursed his lips and sent his nose to one side of his face, looking for a moment like a trickster at Mbuyu Mmoja Park. "You shall see, my friend!" Kazansthakis cracked his knuckles, rubbed his chest, and grunted. "A gift. Something I am giving you. For your grand and new beginning." Kazansthakis raised his brow; he winked.

Gilbert, mesmerized, watched as Kazansthakis pulled a handsome pocketknife from his belt loop, knelt, and sliced the box lid's lips. The cardboard flaps came open like a double door, and Kazansthakis motioned with his head that Gilbert ought to come and see.

Gilbert did not like to kneel or squat. His legs, he'd often felt, were not designed for such an awkward, native posture. But the Frosty King was waiting on the floor. Gilbert, one elbow propped on a splayed knee, tried to look as comfortable as he could; he kept losing his balance. Holding himself up with a palm flat on the carpet, he looked into the box.

With all his reading and his notes, Gilbert should have known exactly what they were. Cylindrical. A dull, flat-headed tip. They looked almost familiar, yes. Did not the pink man have some? A central, bulbous bolt extending into porcelain. *What are they?* Gilbert frowned. *I've seen these things before.* Five regular, fine grooves. The Frosty King, at Gilbert's curious silence, took on the air of a highly trained magician who has pulled a rabbit from a tiny hat but hears no audience clap. "Turner!" he said. "Well? Turner. Tell me what you think."

To please the Frosty King, Gilbert said, "Oh!" and, "Ah." Wobbling on his heels, uncomfortable, he waited for knowledge to descend.

Kazansthakis was not fooled. He sighed. "Oh, Mr. Turner, what *will* we make of you?" he finally said. "You are a dreamer from the start, with your hair high in the clouds. Look again, my friend. Look hard. I got them from Japan!" Kazansthakis parted the brown flaps and held them firmly down.

Gilbert wished the Frosty King would give him just a moment, just some time to think. Feeling small and trapped, he reached out towards the box and placed his hands inside. The shiny necks felt cool and smooth and round. He knew what these things were, he did. But what could they be called?

The Frosty King went on in disbelief: "You must be joking, man," he said. Gilbert was horridly ashamed. Would the Frosty King abandon him, disgusted? His face went deeply red. He sensed a headache rise; his scalp twitched. Kazansthakis sat back on his heels. His voice was not *too* hard. "Oh, Mr. Turner. Too many storybooks for you, I think! You can't see a single thing that isn't written down."

Gilbert raised a little cylinder into the air and peered up at its gleam. *Longer than my thumb,* he thought. He struggled, closed his eyes. *I know,* he thought, *I know.* It was important that he say the correct thing. What would Kazansthakis think if he couldn't name them—these items that (this much he understood) were intended for the business? But, yes. The answer came to him. He pulled on his friend's arm; his tugging caused the Frosty King to lose his balance and land rolling on his back. "Yes, of course!" At last! "They're spark plugs!" Oh, he *had* learned something after all, from that marvelous, valuable book. He was laughing, on the floor.

"They're spark plugs," Gilbert said again, and Kazansthakis

rolled over and hugged him. "That they are, my friend!" Gilbert felt as tightly held as when he had come home from the Post Office and Sarie'd swung him round. But in Kazansthakis's strong, thick arms, he felt a certitude he hadn't in his wife, a wave of manly pleasure. That he was not alone.

"Spark plugs!" *It's going to work!* he thought. The car handbook was difficult, indeed, but with such a friend as this—! The Frosty King *would* help him. He *would* learn what each thing was, in time. And wouldn't people shopping for spare parts themselves explain exactly what they needed? *They* would tell him what was what. And he would write it down and find it. Gilbert hid his face in the crook of Kazansthakis's shoulder, where the Frosty King was moist and rich from his long walk. The Frosty King was ticklish, and Gilbert's breath there made him giggle; next, spark plug burning in his hand, Gilbert giggled, too.

When Sarie came out from the kitchen and said, "What are you men doing?" Gilbert, in his happiness, thought that she was lovely. The most magnificent thing on earth. So beautiful! Blond and rosy, graceful! So deserving of his love! He was laughing, still, and happy. "Look!" he said. "Look what he has brought us! *Spark plugs!*" Sarie looked suspicious, wary of the happiness collecting in her husband and also in the Frosty King, who, still giving the odd giggle, was looking Gilbert over with a proud, approving look, shaking his big head as though Gilbert had performed an admirable feat.

"Spark plugs?" Sarie frowned. She set down the tray she'd come with, approached them. Softly, Sarie said, "But, Mr. Frosty, why? Do you mean for our business?"

Something in her shifted from one foot to the other. Sarie, who had welcomed him so freely, sensed something go dark and felt suddenly indignant—for herself and for her husband. *How like the*

Frostys to imagine they know best, she thought. How like them to act without permission. Who did they think they were? Spark plugs? What for, what for? The front parlor seemed to shimmer. "You have committed a mistake," she said. "Though of course this is very nice of you to think. But has my husband not explained?"

Kazansthakis did not rise. With a dainty flourish and a bow, he reached over to the table and took his grenadine. He sipped, licked his upper lip. "Thank you, Mrs. Turner." He raised the glass, which glinted in the light. And, thinking that she, perhaps not unlike her husband, was a little *slow,* revealed what Gilbert had not thought to, what Gilbert had been saving up for last. "I have brought your husband, this Automotive Turner, his first box of spare parts." He held the glass up in the air as if making a toast. "To get the business going. Spark plugs. My little gift to you." He twitched his generous lips, a moue. "Do we like those apples, eh? What do you say to that?"

Sarie blinked. Something bad and odd had happened to her eyesight. What room was she in? Where was she, exactly? And how tall? What *size* was Sarie Turner? Those two men on the floor seemed very far away. Small. *Apples.* What was Mr. Frosty saying? Indeed, which one was Mr. Frosty? Which one was Mr. Turner? She saw spots before her eyes, she did. The room shook. They were both still on the floor. They clucked. They scratched at things. *Like chickens,* Sarie thought. "Spare parts? But, Mr. Frosty—" Sarie gave Gilbert a pleading look. "We are going to sell the baskets. And the souvenirs. Gilbert? We were going to discuss it." She touched her wrist lightly to her forehead, left her hand there for a moment, bare palm out, like a miner's lamp. "What *should* we need sparks *for?*" Below her, the two men's outer edges, their red skins, faded and dissolved; they swelled, and filled the room. She shrank. She found it difficult to breathe.

"Mrs. Turner?" "Sarie?" "Dear?" "Madame!" She couldn't hear

them properly. Their heavy voices came to her as if through a long, dry metal drum. She held on to the doorjamb and reached out for the piano, feeling that her legs had grown so long she might not manage to sit down without some clumsiness, a fall. And she could not bear to fall.

"Spark plugs?" Sarie heard her own voice rise. "Why spark plugs for our baskets? For the *souvenirs?*"

The men came into focus once again, but they looked tighter, harder, more compact, than they had before. She looked from Gilbert to the Frosty King. She decided that she did not want to sit. *I will stand right here over them,* she thought, *until they tell me what it means.*

A stillness took hold of the parlor. Both men stopped their laughing as though, without any warning, someone in the wings had flipped a little switch. What were her eyes doing? Gilbert and the Frosty King seemed to Sarie suddenly immovable and heavy. Two man-sized balls of lead. The Frosty King's red face was taken over by a hotly mixed expression: something like embarrassment, for Sarie, and something like annoyance, for poor dreaming, dreaming, silly, truthless Gilbert Turner. Gilbert, who still thought Sarie was the finest-looking woman he had ever seen, didn't realize how serious it all was. He made as if to stand; said, "Sarie, look at it. Just look." He held out his open palm, where the single plug was shining. But his wife was like a statue.

The Frosty King had stopped looking at Sarie and was eyeing Gilbert strangely. He said, very softly, "Gilbert. Gilbert." Kazansthakis wanted to restrain him. He laid two fingers on Gilbert's outstretched arm like a person looking for a pulse, someone guiding a blind man. This visit to the Turners' had not turned out exactly as he'd hoped. "You didn't tell your wife?"

Gilbert, silenced in mid-chuckle, turned back to his friend. It had not turned out as Gilbert had expected, either. He didn't know exactly where to look. He sniffed. All at once, his face felt very bare, too naked. Why was the Frosty King staring at him so? Why wasn't Sarie coming down to join them, laugh with them, to see the treasures in the box? Weren't they just like jewels? Weren't they just another form of trinket?

Half to Kazansthakis, half to his still wife, he said: "It was a surprise! I was going to surprise her." To Sarie he said, "I was going to surprise you."

The rest happened very quickly. The Frosty King stood up, downed his grenadine in a single gulp, wiped his mouth with his own hand, and excused himself to Sarie. "Please come to the Frosty-Kreem sometime. My wife does ask for you." He patted Gilbert on the back to give him strength for what he imagined was to come and, without waiting to be shown down to the courtyard, slipped into the stairwell, muttering, " 'Surprise!' "

Upstairs, loosed, Sarie had one of her *little tantrums* — though it was much, much greater than any in the past. Indeed, she took the news, it seemed to Gilbert, disproportionately hard. Had she really thought that he was seriously at work considering what she'd suggested lightly only once? Or twice? What was it, souvenirs? Was it knives or stones? What had she really said? Not much, he thought. No, she hadn't told him anything. She'd only made suggestions, after all, for what was to be *his* business. Why *was* she so upset? Would he not be in business principally for *her,* for *Agatha,* for *them?*

But Sarie shouted at him. She threw the empty glass hard against the wall and shouted even harder when the clear thing failed to shatter. She called him names in French. And eventually, she cried. She ran into the bedroom, where she slammed the door and curled up on the bed. *Spare parts,* Sarie thought. And she said it to herself over and again until she couldn't hear it anymore, could not cry any longer, and finally fell asleep.

Outside, it was growing dark. In the silver light, farther down the road, before going to the movies, young men took young women to the Frosty-Kreem, where Mrs. Frosty was still waiting for her husband and, resentful, was counting up the scoops she'd doled so she could tell her man exactly what she'd done while he was doing God-knows-what-and-where. In Mansour House, Bibi was stitching up the envelope with a sense of great things on the way. Nisreen woke up from a nap, came quietly into the living room, and switched the lightbulb on to safeguard Bibi's eyes. Farther down, in a different sort of dusk, Majid stood on his balcony watering the jasmine. He had finished that new poem, called it: *Early on the Avenues.* His skin felt warm, and he began to think of Sarie, hoping she'd come soon. He was sorry to have missed her, wondered idly how she had seemed to Sugra, what Sugra had thought. He heard Tahir in the parlor, moving, felt a lightness in his heart. Like a father and a man.

Alone in his front room, Gilbert was exhausted. He was, he told himself, a small ngarawa rigger that has weathered a great gale and must now recall its bearings. He closed the spark-plug box and pushed it up against the bookshelf, feeling that without intending to he had done Sarie a great wrong. Shy, afraid, like a person stepping from a fragile house after a quake, he went into the bedroom, where he kissed his wife's closed eyes and noticed they were damp. He lay beside her fully dressed, listened to her breathe. She still looked pretty to him, even in her sleep. A big, brave, muscled girl. Outside, in Kikanga and beyond, buses heaved and rattled in and out of town.

*   *   *

Sarie stayed in bed for three long, deadly quiet days, rising to drink water and to pee only when she thought that Gilbert wouldn't see her. Agatha sat silently beside her on the floor and tried (although she couldn't really) to read a novel she had found under the bed, a thriller that Sarie had attempted, left, and forgotten to return. Gilbert, cowed first by Sarie's rage, then by the heady silence, came in now and then, wishing and not wishing that she would come awake. He didn't know what he would say. He didn't bring her anything. He didn't know what his wife needed, and, though he asked himself again, again, he had no idea, really, still, what had happened in the parlor.

At first when Gilbert came to Sarie's side, she had had the energy, the temper, to turn away from him. And though he wished she wouldn't, he had been slightly reassured by it, this usual angry sign. On the second day, she stopped moving at all. If he came in and spoke to her, she simply looked ahead of her, right up at the ceiling, never—so it seemed to Gilbert—even blinking. Once, she turned her face just slightly so that she was almost looking at him. But she wasn't really looking, not at him, or anything. Her blue eyes were enormous, and Gilbert walked away, backwards, feeling that she might stab or pierce him with that aimless gaze if he should turn his back. *All this for a small misunderstanding,* Gilbert thought, amazed. *All this for a basket.* Sensing that the Frosty King, who knew and loved his own Mrs. Frosty with such ability and grace, expected Gilbert to take care of his own household for a while, he did not go out to the Palm. Kazansthakis, Gilbert felt, had not approved of what he'd seen.

He sought refuge in the books he had, for a whole month now, abandoned. The splendid *Sons of Sindbad.* He sat down, even put his legs up on the table, but quickly found that the new book could not hold him. It was too enmeshed in *this* whole story, in the recent past, the *now*, in his hopes for the bright future. *The Clove Tree*, an account of silviculture in the islands, which he *had* read, several times, because it was so clear, fared a little better. Like *The Everyman's Car Handbook*, this volume had photographs and drawings, and a list: things that could endanger a clove crop and those that could enhance it. Diseases and their cures.

Afterwards, he went into the bedroom. Sarie's stubborn silence, her refusal to take food, and her inability to speak made Gilbert feel afraid. He also felt dismissive now and then. *Good God*. But the stillness that had overtaken Sarie and held her in its grip had also furnished Gilbert's wife with a kind of special charm. *She's weak,* he thought. *She requires all of my attention.* In the mirror, he could see that he looked pink and that Sarie had gone sallow. She was losing weight. Her long face was growing longer. How small she looked among those dirty, twisted sheets! When Gilbert laced his fingers in the damp mat of her hair, which smelled, she let him, and she began to cry.

Later, in the quiet, Gilbert thought about what Hazel Towson had said before the Bank, about Sarie not having arrived somewhere. Perhaps Sarie had been a little off, already, for a while. *She's got a hard life,* he thought with sympathy. *I haven't done my best.* And then, though it was quite impossible, *What if she's pregnant after all?* The thought, which he pushed aside as promptly as he'd had it, made him nonetheless feel warm. He smiled into her scalp. Far more injured than either of them knew, she let out a wail. "Sarie, Sarie, dear," he said. "I'll take care of you."

🕸Twenty-one

Whom the Frosty King saw Gilbert next, he did not mention Sarie. He had, it seemed, decided to assume that Gilbert Turner must be man enough to handle his own home, and the only thing he'd said had been encouraging and kind: "Once you've gotten moving, Turner, things will be A-Okay and Tip Top." He had winked, bought his friend a beer, and Gilbert had felt forgiven for an error—one that he, in fact, still did not quite understand to *be* one, and that he had, in any case, not at all intended. But he did not resent the Frosty King for thinking he'd been wrong: he liked feeling forgiven. Also, he did love Mr. Frosty and admired him too much to call up any anger or to argue with him about what wives ought to be told. And, he thought, more-over, *If Sarie were like other women, then, yes, I might have told her. But she isn't. Look at her, in bed like a stone. She isn't really normal.*

Believing that she was unlike any other woman and that only he clearly understood how unbalanced she was, he didn't put a lot of stock in the Frosty King's reaction. Much more comforting and meaningful was that the Frosty King had also generously forgiven Gilbert for not knowing right away what the packaged things were called. *Friendship,* Gilbert thought.

Kazansthakis, for his part, felt that once you undertook a thing it was foolish to turn back (he had in his own life tried a great many odd things, knew the value of continual adjustment, and understood that people didn't often know a lot until they learned things on the way, because they had no choice). He was also implicated now in Gilbert's little business: he had relied for Gilbert's benefit on some very valuable connections. There was, therefore, pride at work in what he said—he couldn't live with failure, not even from a distance, and if Gilbert Turner failed, Mr. Frosty didn't think he could envision endless evenings at the Palm again, things as they had been. He would, he knew, leave the man behind. And so he hoped that Gilbert would succeed.

He offered reassurance: Gilbert, in the Frosty King's opinion, need not know in depth how motors really worked to be an adequate purveyor of their parts. He urged Gilbert to keep at it, to be more theoretical, to operate instead in the kingdom of *ideas* and not get lost in details. "It's not the nuts and bolts of it, my friend," Mr. Frosty said, restraining a *ha-hah,* "it is knowing how to move things. *Management* is key. How *do* you think the British did it for so long?" Gilbert liked the sound of that. It relieved him of the fear of letting slip how little he had learned. It let him think the difficulties he had had—with memorizing names, with understanding how cars actually moved—were not a sign of weakness. No, they were certain proof that his role was more important than he'd thought: *I am no mere mechanic, then. I'm the man in charge.* He thought about the history makers, the colonialists, and Empire. And these thoughts gave him freedom. Strangely, this not-needing to know unexpectedly achieved for him what the notepad and the handbook hadn't: it brought engines to life.

In the days of Sarie's breakdown, Gilbert's mind grew sharp. He allowed himself to take some pleasure in his own imagination. His mind conjured engines up for him, bright ones, rusted ones, big ones, small ones, engines of all kinds, and set them whirring in his ears. He focused on the parts he thought that he could name, saw fan belts busily afan, radiators radiating, agleam in a pale light. Could picture pistons dancing. And the names refracted, became other words: *Pistons, pistols, crystals; radiators, aviators; fan belts, sand belts, sand.* He thought seriously of horsepower, considered wagon trains and steeds, saw cowboys, Kazakhs, Sultans, and the might of Nordic men. In a kind of play, delirium, he understood at last—in a way that did not cause him pain—that every wire had a place and that for all time this was true, whether he knew well or did not which wire went where. Releasing himself from the need to know exactly how things worked, he felt their beauty rise. Their inner elegance or turmoil didn't matter. Their overall effectiveness, their magic general movement, took resolutely hold and drew him. Their mystery, indeed. Confident in his affection, Gilbert grew increasingly enamored of them—cars and parts and smoke, the smells, their secret, complex sounds. Engines. He forgot to hate his ignorance and learned instead what felt to him to be a manly, royal secret. He needn't be an expert to make a business work. He was not proposing to *fix* engines, after all, only to procure their little needs, their sundries. He was not, as Kazansthakis said, "about to build a car."

When not lolling at the Palm discussing *matters* with his friend, and now and then impressing engineers with tales, Gilbert spent his time beside his wife as she slept and cried, or in the kitchen, where Agatha, fending for herself, ate buttered bread and looked out of the window. He felt a swelling in himself. A transformation, joy. Through his rounds—hotel, home, and back—Gilbert understood: all the years of office work, the rubber stamps and papers, the move into Kikanga, the sitting in the parlor with his library at hand, had been nothing but a pause, a long, slow interim that had begun with Independence, and ended on the day that Uncle James's letter showed up in his box. An important hibernation. Time and history's gestation, giving birth, at last, to a grown-up Gilbert Turner. He felt more alive than he could remember feeling since the first days of his marriage (five days in a borrowed coastal villa, Sarie vivid, furious, on the bed). Even Sarie's silence helped him. Ensured his victory, in fact. It seemed to him, indeed, as if he could, as he never had before, hear his own heart speak.

There was only one more thing, and it had Gilbert stumped. Kazansthakis, who had made some subtle inquiries and who knew, thought Gilbert, how a business should be run, urged his friend one evening at the Palm to bring someone else in. To take on, as Kazansthakis put it, "an adviser." "A partner, like. A Tonto to your Ranger. A fast horse to your cowboy." At first Gilbert had (amazed, in awe!) thought the Frosty King was making him an offer, the sort he'd dreamed of for so long. Could it be? That he had been coming to the Palm for years, eyeing all the others hopefully, when he might have, all that time, simply focused his desires on the man he met so regularly, the most faithful of his friends, the one who spoke his name? That the Frosty King had wanted him like that, exactly as he wanted to be wanted, truly, all along? "A partner?" Gilbert said. He looked down at the table, sure that he was blushing. The skin of his back tingled. He ran his thumb along the cracked rim of his glass. "But aren't you . . . ? Aren't you busy with the parlor?"

The Frosty King was shocked. He intended no such thing. He was shocked and then upset. It was quite beyond him how Gilbert could have had the madness and the nerve to conjure this scenario. There was a moment's pause. Gilbert's open face. The scrape of someone's chair. A glass set down too quickly. Then the Frosty King laughed loudly, a bit too hard, perhaps. "Not me, you fool! *You* need an *assistant*."

To show he was not hurt, Gilbert nodded, blinked three or four times, and then laughed, too, though not quite sure at what. He told the Frosty King that it had been a joke. "I know, old man," he said, puffing out his chest even as his ears felt suddenly on fire.

"And you know I wouldn't have you. You're always at the pictures. Your head's in the freezer." He took a sip of Congo Pilsner and looked out at the sea. To appear consumed by serious thoughts, he frowned. What did Kazansthakis mean?

Kazansthakis did not want Gilbert to lose heart, but his own networks were far too precious to him to risk them all at once. On a dubious plan, no less. On the daydream of an inefficient man. The spark plugs had been a special, one-time gift. A trial. A favor he'd called in. And Xavier, without some recompense, would not do it again. He reached across the table and patted Gilbert's hand—Gilbert, who had lost his footing, who was staring at the sea and wondering how to look as though nothing could harm him.

The Frosty King took hold of Gilbert's fingers and squeezed mightily at them. "Listen." Gilbert did. "This is what I mean: for things to really work," he said, "you'll need a local man." Gilbert, though he felt a headache threatening and that almost-healed old itch ahover at his back, regained a bit of his composure. He prepared to listen, bravely. But he was afraid of what he'd hear.

Still pinching Gilbert's knuckles, so that Gilbert had to give him all of his attention, Kazansthakis said: "You need someone who knows other places in the city. Who knows everything there is. Someone with connections. Someone who knows people we do not. And someone you can trust. You can't," said Mr. Frosty, "do this by yourself. How will you find custom?"

A girl brought him his soup. He let go of Gilbert's hand. The pressure he'd exerted had, just as he had wanted, the effect of stemming what the Frosty King had feared might be a burst of sobs, a breakdown. At the release of his sore fingers, Gilbert held his glass between his palms and tried to take deep breaths, succeeded. Now assured that Gilbert Turner was not going to crack up, Kazansthakis

turned towards his steaming broth, slurping as he spoke. "You"—
slurp-slurp, and a wave of the thin spoon—"must bring the capital"—*slurp-slurp*—"and your partner find the means."

Gilbert had not spoken. Watching Kazansthakis—so healthy
and so broad!—so certain of himself, bent over the bowl, so prosperous in the sunset—it seemed to Gilbert for a moment that
everything he'd hoped for might now be at risk. He felt foolish.
Oh, why were his moods so inconstant? How could a person feel
so confident one moment, so bare and lost the next? How could a
grown man feel so suddenly that he might begin to cry? He
looked at Kazansthakis but he did not respond. He pressed his lips
together. *Why has he not said this before?*

The old Gilbert in him threatened to come back, to say, "Oh,
I'll just scrap the thing. Try another project." Even, "Souvenirs, perhaps." Yes, he very nearly thought: *What about the baskets?* But he
couldn't let that old Gilbert return. What would Mr. Frosty say,
Mrs. Frosty think? No. Attached to his fresh life, the new Gilbert
stepped up: *A moment, please. You're now too far along.* This new
Gilbert—the one Gilbert esteemed—was made, he told himself,
entirely of iron. He had come this far and he would not turn back.
He would not let himself fail. *All right.* Kazansthakis was his men-
tor, *knew things.* And this wise, emboldened Gilbert had to be prepared to do whatever he was told. And so the Gilberts—new and
old, ashift—listened.

"Gilbert," said the Frosty King, "what you need are some
friends."

The Frosty King explained: Gilbert's job was to give orders
and to pay for what came through. But for someone to give orders, they need people nearby who will carry out the things that
must be done. People who would know things that Gilbert
Turner didn't. At first, at least, someone who could get him cus-

tomers, who would have more precise ideas about acquiring parts from this place or from that. Someone who—here the ancient Gilbert cringed and the new one puffed and roared—someone who was *local.*

Gilbert knew the Frosty King was right. He shook but didn't show it. He hadn't any friends. And he had thought that Kazansthakis knew. But if he didn't, didn't know, Gilbert did not want him to, did not want to say it. To show he understood, he nodded and he smiled "You're right. I see. I should have thought of it myself. A partner. A really local man." Gilbert paused to order two kebabs and another round of beer. He looked sagely at his hero. Dishonesty, he was coming to suspect, was not unconnected to certainty and pride. He thought he'd try it out. He lied. "I have just the man." Once spoken, as it goes, the lie almost came true. He curled his upper lip and turned to face the sea. "That's right," he said. "I have someone in mind."

Kazansthakis, who had expected arguments, complaints, or that terrible timidity Gilbert so frequently displayed, was pleasantly surprised. The evening was so sweet, after all, the twinkling lights of fishing boats already making patterns by the shore. The Frosty King finished his kebabs, didn't press for details, finished his last beer. And next, aware that it was *he* this time, rising from his seat, and not the other way around, Gilbert rose, and said that Sarie would be waiting. Kazansthakis, as if Gilbert, right before his eyes, were becoming a real man, turned his lips down, tipped his head up, leading with the chin, and gave a single nod. Gilbert Turner, yes, might be shaping up. "Heigh-ho, then," he said without to-do. "Give her my regards." Gilbert nodded back, and Kazansthakis softened. Making two thumbs-up with his fists high as Gilbert tucked his chair in, the Frosty King gave his friend a smile. "It's going to be all right," he said. "Great guns! That's the way to go."

On the way back home, Gilbert wondered what to do. Wondered how to make it work. It was true. He needed what the Frosty King called "networks," and "connections." He was ashamed that he had none. Great guns! And yet, when they'd first moved to Kikanga, hadn't he said all kinds of things about fitting with the locals? About melding with the scene, rejecting all the folk who'd moved to Scallop Bay, the way wealth separated people so that some felt so much better than everybody else? Hadn't he so recently recalled Judge Hewett and his porter? The frightened native boy with a leopard at his throat? He'd believed in all of that, he had. It was just that, as a reader—*As a thinker!*—he had been content to let Kikanga swell around him, while he read.

He'd been lazy, hadn't he? He hadn't made new friends. He didn't speak the language. But he'd let the Frosty King believe all kinds of things about the wisdom and the virtue of moving to Kikanga, of taking up a government-owned flat, of throwing in his lot with locals. The new nation! As he had done with Uncle James, old-new Gilbert thought, he'd let untruths take hold. It was time to turn untruths into fact. To live up to his story. How Mrs. Hazel Towson would have loved him at that moment! Yes, he would come right in the end.

He walked slowly in the dark. He passed Mchanganyiko Street and chose not to go down it. Soon he found that he was wandering. He walked and walked, past the mosque, past high Mansour House, past the busy roundabout, and ended at the buses, not far from Libya Street. The answer came to him as he neared Mbuyu Mmoja Park. He recalled what Kazansthakis had once said, about accidents fastening the wounded to those who'd seen them fall.

Of course the man was not his friend, exactly, but wasn't he quite close to him somehow? Linked to him through Sarie? As the call to prayer spilled from all the loudspeakers at once, he thought:

What about that Jeevanjee? Sarie's little friend? Wasn't the mysterious Mr. Jeevanjee as local as one got, for an Asian in these parts? And wasn't (here Bibi might have sucked her cheeks in and said, *Blood's not everything, you'll see*) every Asian man an expert at doing things with money? He most likely had a shop or two already, had smuggled scores of things into the country and sold them at great profit. And wouldn't Sarie be relieved to know she *had* been helpful in the end?

Twenty-two

In the Mchanganyiko flat, Sarie was astir. She'd been awake for hours, limbs thick with a dull tingle, eyes fixed on the ceiling, sightless, hot. In the early afternoon, though the deadened parts of her might have stayed that way forever, her body tired of it. She rolled onto her side. Her legs deposited her feet onto the cold floor with a hollow thud. Her shoulders pulled her up. Sarie sat there for a moment, hands loose by her knees, before rising, struggling, as though pulled up by the hair. Standing at the mirror, naked, she felt dizzy, full of enervated blood that has been sluggish for too long.

Looking at herself, uncertain what she saw, she listened for her breath. Her mind was not quite clear. Fingertips lightly pressing on the dresser, and swaying back and forth because her balance was not good, she tried to catalog events. But something wasn't right. Time, for one, was different: it was as if none had passed at all, not between discovering Majid's absence from his house and Mr. Frosty's visit, and not between her lying down and getting up, as if everything that had brought her fall about had taken place at once, and as if she, though standing, were falling through the air and had been falling, for an interminable moment, well beyond the reach of clocks, sunsets, dawns, or movements of the moon. Time heals things, Sarie knew. Time takes pain away. She did not feel at all well, and therefore time stood still.

She willed herself to understand what had taken place. She couldn't, not at first. The people who had harmed her—Maria,

Majid, Sugra, Gilbert, and the Frosty King—she conceived of as one person, causing one complex collapse; she felt their effects simultaneously, as one intolerable wound. Her body ached so cruelly that Sarie, facing herself in the glass, was not convinced she wouldn't, if she checked all of her flesh, find signs of the disaster. But how unmarked her skin was, how unbleeding and unbruised! The trouble was elsewhere.

She wished to be methodical. Eyes shut, she tried distinguishing between them, husband, lover, woman, enemy, and friend; between the afternoon at Kudra House and (afterwards? before?) the noontime shock of Mr. Frosty with his plugs, arriving in her home. She brought her fingers to her brow and focused on Majid. She tried to help herself. *He did not know we were coming. He did not do this to hurt me. He wants very much to see me. Had he known I was coming . . .* She said Majid's name a few more times, softly, in several different ways, thinking how her Agatha sometimes requested little songs to help her from a dream or to distract her from an illness: "Majid, Majid, Majid Ghulam, Majid Jeevanjee, Majid Ghulam Jeevanjee. M. G. J. and"—what she herself had never said but knew that others did—"and Ghuji." The sound of her voice helped. She pressed her thumbs against her eyelids, waited for the coiling and uncoiling of the livid golds and reds she knew would rise up there. She listened to her hair. She thought next about the spark plugs. She could see these clearly and they hurt her. But she pressed her teeth together. She tried to see, again, Gilbert on the carpet, bright thing in his hand.

The next thought came to her because she couldn't face the rest. A tiny one at first, it was a bit of her old self, for, if not resilient, then what was she? *Well, so we could begin. We could begin the thing with spares. And later . . .* Her long legs almost gave, she almost fell back on the bed, but her knees snapped into place. *No.* She could not reframe the thing, tell herself that she was still all right. Such enthusiasm would be false. *Branching out,* from car parts into baskets, as if souvenirs had been a second, new idea, instead of Sarie's first, would not be a branching out at all, not from Sarie's tree. All the wrong way round. But if not that, then what? She let her eyes come open and looked down at her feet. If she was to live at all, she thought, she could not enfold her husband's vision and pretend that it was hers, couldn't think of it that way.

She must erase the first idea, what had come to *her.* Forget everything she had envisaged, say it hadn't happened: that she had never stood before the Gymkhana looking at a horse, or pulled Agatha behind her into the Mountain Top Hotel, that she had never peered at gems that winked behind a glass. That she had never rubbed her husband's feet and thought herself his savior. She must: *Forget, forget, dismiss.* But thinking was too hard, and noting so specifically what she should forget was rather like remembering, the opposite of what she had to do.

She raised her eyes again and tried to see herself. *I'm yellow,* Sarie thought. Her teeth were caked, rough, filthy. She ran her hands along her throat and ribs. Her hips. She felt her bones protrude. Her tears welled up again. *I'm old,* she thought. *I'm old.* She heard Gilbert coming up the stairs. She didn't wish, just then, for anyone to see her—Gilbert least of all—so very, very bare. So sallow. She reached out for the nearest thing; and, meanly, it was Gilbert's dirty robe, which he'd left over the chair. How close it felt, how thick.

Gilbert was surprised to see her standing. He came up to her and kissed her. "Sarie, dear." He tried to hold her hand. Sarie didn't flinch. She didn't pull away from him; she didn't, either, take his hand in hers. Gilbert raised his fingers in the air; they hovered, fluttered, near her head. He would have liked to stroke her cheek, but

Sarie's look—red eyes, mouth closed, confused—persuaded him he shouldn't. *Too soon,* he thought. *Not yet.* He smiled at her and sighed. The sight of his tall wife in his robe—too short for her legs, but, still—was touching. "Don't you look nice, love? How do you feel?" he said. He wondered if the color suited her. Didn't lovers sometimes wear each other's clothes? He had heard (or had he read?) somewhere that local men slept in colored cloths they borrowed from their women, mistresses and wives, to demonstrate their love? Was this what Sarie meant? To say she cared for him, though she found it hard to speak?

Sarie, long-stilled blood now coursing to her feet, felt a sinking in her chest. She leaned without intending to towards Gilbert, and he did, at last, clumsy, eager, dart in to rest his lips a moment on her cheek. He spoke because he didn't know what else to do—he'd mastered Sarie silent in the bed, but Sarie standing, still upset, looking so worn out, made him a bit nervous. "You know, dear, I think I have an idea." He sat down behind her.

At the word "idea," Sarie felt a curdling in her throat. She turned and gazed at him as if at a geological formation that rose up far away, a mountain. *An idea.* Her gums hurt. She saw once again all of *her* ideas, how certain she had been about the trinkets and the baskets and the long Dodoma knives, the bright blue shards of stone. She felt foolish in a way she hadn't felt before—not when ladies at the garden parties had dropped their drinks in horror at her talk, not when Gilbert told her shoes were too expensive, and not when he had so heartlessly insisted that women, if you please, can make or break a man.

She felt tremendously outdone, and stupid, which was worse. She didn't want to hear Gilbert's idea, but she didn't either have the strength to move or cover up her ears. When Gilbert asked her if he could please be introduced to Jeevanjee, who might be just the man to help, Sarie looked at him as though he'd asked her to perform a crazy kind of sex. But she was not entirely surprised. "Your friend Mr. J.," he said. Why should the world not topple?

It hurt her to hear Majid Ghulam's name in Gilbert's clumsy mouth. "You know," her husband said, "the Jeevanjee you've gotten friendly with. The father of that boy." Sarie heard a ringing in the thickened air and watched as her old husband came in and out of focus not far from her face. Though her eyes had cleared enough to see that he was not a mountain, Sarie saw instead an insect, a knobbed creature, a lizard, on the bed. *The Jeevanjee.* It sounded like a joke, the name of a small animal, something foreign, quaint. Gilbert's eyeballs seemed to swell and shrink and spin.

She didn't say a word. She sank down on the bed, not beside her husband, whose feet were on the floor, who *sat,* like a man explaining things, but beyond him, where she lay, knees curled into her chest, while Gilbert talked and talked about how useful it would be for him—"for *us*"—to put his head together with the head of an experienced businessman like this M.G., whom she had so providentially got to know and like. "You *do* like him, don't you? He's *all right?*" he asked. He turned around to take up one of her hands. "Have you seen him recently?" Sarie made a fist. Looking sweetly down, Gilbert clutched the furled mass tightly, as if, like an envelope that he could open, it might conceal a prize.

As they sat on the bed, Agatha appeared. She hovered in the doorway, made a testing sound. Gilbert looked towards her. "See?" he said. "Your mother's gotten up." Agatha did not come in. "Look, Sarie." Gilbert, for once emboldened by the presence of his daughter, raised a hand to Sarie's face and firmly pulled her chin towards the door. Sarie looked. She thought, *What does the child want?* She did not reach out to her. Agatha, as she often did, kept still. She'd been in the courtyard scouring the ground. There were pebbles in the pockets of her dress. "Come on," Gilbert said. He found he wanted very much for Agatha to be there, near them on the bed. It would have made him feel a little better. *We're a family,* he thought. And Sarie wouldn't cry in front of Agatha; with Agatha, Sarie was robust.

They both turned away from him at once: Sarie lay back down, and Agatha, looking down into a pocket, twisted a thin ankle, bent a knee, unbent it. "I'm going back outside," she said. And Agatha was gone. They heard her close the door, and then her feet quick on the stairs.

He had not let go of Sarie's hand. He thought her fist felt looser, and began stroking her thumb. Beneath Gilbert's spotted skin, where unseen blood and flesh were throbbing with new highways, traffic jams, the wreck and shine of speeding things, Sarie felt the story change. She suddenly *could* think, and what she thought about was this: her lover's back and toes and ankles and the flavor of his mouth. At last she opened her closed hand and, hoping idly they would break, squeezed her husband's fingers. Gilbert thought he understood the fierceness of her grip. Yes, he felt Sarie's love for him return. He sighed. He lay down on the bed beside her, eyes full no longer of her face but of things that only he could see: the future, years ahead, when things had really changed, a legal business with a sign, an office, and a girl to make the tea. He knew she had agreed. "You're wonderful," he said, and kissed her on the brow.

He nestled his own tired head into the pillow. "It could be like this," he said, and he went on, painted her a picture. When he'd finished talking, Sarie took his robe off, handed it to him, and strode into the bathroom, where she stayed for a long time. Cold in Vunjamguu's sharp water, adding to it her own tears until she couldn't anymore, she sat by herself in the dark. Eventually, chill and made of stone, Sarie heard Gilbert go out and felt her strength return.

She made up her mind. Because the hardships and the sadness that swelled and moved inside her were too difficult to think of with precision, Sarie, with a monumental shove against and through her weakened skin, stepped outside of her body to give herself advice. She thought instead of what somebody else, looking at her from a distance, someone with a sense of History, might tell her. She wondered what Clothilde would do, or Sister Bénédicte. What Angélique might say. She thought of Betty, too. But the voice she heard, the one she gave a sound to, was Mrs. Hazel Towson's. *You are middle-aged. You are past your prime, and Belgian. You are the mother of a daughter. And you also have a husband.* That she didn't want one, or the other, really, was well besides the point. That she *liked* her short, pale dresses, for all their stains and wear, did not matter at all.

She'd been foolish from the start. How blind she'd been, and silly, thinking she could have two lives, one that moved in time and one that didn't, ever. How *meaningless* she'd been. Gilbert's business— this business in which she, apparently, had no business being—this business, she could clearly see, was more important than anything she might have learned about herself or someone else, or life, or love, at gloomy Kudra House. More important and concrete than whatever Majid Ghulam might want or whatever Sarie might have been, so vaguely, so desirously, attempting. She'd end it. She'd end it then and there and not set eyes, if she could help it, on Majid Ghulam again. Well, she would have to, she supposed, if she did what Gilbert wished. But even then, if she had to greet him on occasion, ask him mildly how things were or inquire about his boys, he would be Mr. Jeevanjee again, that old Mr. J. Perhaps, as Gilbert had called him when she had been in bed, once she'd forgotten everything and become somebody else, the second Sarie with no first, he would simply be "M.G." She did make one decision, the only one, she thought, that still belonged to her: *Foolish I have been, peut-être. But I will not be ashamed.*

❦Twenty-three

On her final visit to the pale green house on Libya Street, Sarie wore a very old but flattering yellow gown that made her hair look bright. From Mchanganyiko to Mahaba and to Mosque and Libya streets, she bit her lips to make her mouth look sharp. She dug her fingernails into the pillows of her palms to make sure her blood was moving. She willed her headache to grow stronger, to keep her heart in line.

In the courtyard, she saw Tahir with his crutches, an entirely strange boy, showing off his moves to a giggling, encouraging Maria, who did not even look up when the alley doors came open and Sarie passed them by. They both glowed, she thought: Tahir nothing like the fallen child she'd spoken to while life poured out of him, but thicker, more substantial, than she'd known, and Maria's skin was sugary and shiny, like a date's. The bald cat stepped towards her. Shyly, briefly, it touched its round head to her feet. She did not bend to pet it. Without announcing her arrival or waiting to be called, she walked right up the steps.

The three big boys were out. Majid, as she'd hoped, was up there by himself, in the bedroom working on a verse. She didn't knock. The door fell open silently. She sat down on the bed, where she could face the mirror. In the watery, browning glass, she watched him. Majid at first did not see her, and Sarie—who was finding that premature nostalgia could serve well as a defense— thought, dramatically, *So a poet looks at work!*

Hidden by a shadow from the open window's shutters, Majid's

face was undefined and dark. The skin of Majid's neck and back and the slope of his thin shoulder, in contrast, seemed to Sarie unusually pale. He held the pencil to his mouth, pressing with a knuckle at his lips. *M.G.*, she thought. The name was uttered at the surface of her mind, not in any secret place. Did not cause her any pain she could distinguish from the pounding at her brow. She felt removed from him and also from herself. As though what would happen in this room would happen elsewhere, not to her, and not to him. To others—*Mrs. Gilbert Turner and Majid Ghulam Jeevanjee, a businessman*—whom she might recall someday. She felt cold a moment, rubbed her arms with heavy hands. She concentrated on Majid Ghulam, M.G., the brand-new Mr. J. She watched him shake his head over a word he had just written. His tongue slipped out, slipped back. She thought, unmoved, *I have licked that tongue. That tongue has licked me.* Majid looked at Sarie once, then twice, then put the pencil down. He turned happily around. "You're here!" he said.

"A poem?" Sarie asked. Majid didn't answer right away. He said instead that he was very glad to see her. She'd stayed away so long! Dear Sarie. He had missed her. When she did not come back after the day that he'd gone out, he'd thought that she was angry with him, that she wouldn't come again. "I'm so glad you have come," he said, and he stretched his arms towards her. There was a lilting in his voice. He *had* thought about her, her presence and her body. His limbs had missed her, missed how willingly and seriously she gave herself, missed that eager drowning look. He came to sit beside her.

Sarie, focused on her mission, didn't say, *I miss you all the time.* She said again, "You are working on a poem?"

Majid smiled, wiped his hands against his shirt as if he had been working on a car, on a mechanical endeavor instead of on a verse.

"Yes." His voice was shy and proud. Sarie asked if he would read it. "Later," he told her, "when it's really done." They sat silent for a moment, until Majid pressed his side against her shoulder and slipped a hand between her legs. "Why have you stayed away so long?"

Sarie didn't move away. Like a person taking up a favored sweet before starting a diet, *I'll enjoy this now,* she thought. He kissed her neck and bit it, laughed. Sarie let him move her limbs, let him spread her thighs and lift one knee up above his own. She let him take hold of one breast through her gown; palping, rubbing, at her chest. He even tried to tickle her. But he could see Sarie was cool. "What is it?" Did she seem a little thinner, this big woman who had become almost like a fixture in his mind and house? Were her freckles brighter? Thinking she was playing, he slipped two fingers down into the collar of her dress, palm cupped as if he hoped to scoop a wriggling thing from water. He stroked her, but she didn't move towards him. "Come, come, Mrs. Turner"—he sometimes called her that, in play—"tell me what it is. What is happening with you?"

Sarie had not known how she would feel upon being close to him again. She had tried to steel herself along the way, had imagined simply sitting in the parlor with him, legs pushed up against the coffee table, explaining how things were. Making her proposal. Not once taking off her clothes or leaning in to kiss him. But she had bypassed the parlor; here she was in Majid's bedroom, and there he was, asking rather kindly what had kept her from him and could he come in please. She didn't feel relaxed by it. But there *was,* she realized, something she did want, that she could take from him.

Let the business wait. With a hooked forefinger and thumb, she grasped Majid Ghulam's chin, and with her other fingers pulled his lower lip down before crushing, with a ferocity Majid had never felt in her, her great teeth against his. He let her. Sarie trembled everywhere. She panted, grunted at him. She kissed him. She wiped the inside of Majid's open mouth with the breadth of her wet tongue. She licked his skin below his nose and sucked hard at his chin.

Majid struggled with her. *What is this?* He wanted at the very least, as Sarie had insisted that she liked, to stop and take her clothes off, give her time to fold her panties in a square and lay them on the floor before he rubbed himself against her. But Sarie didn't let him. She pinned his arms behind him, forced him backwards on the bed. *Much too fast! Not like this!* He yelped. But in this he had no say. She rose up mightily and straddled him, knees tight at his small waist. Majid Ghulam was trapped. He watched her in amazement. She pulled his trousers off completely and tore open his shirt. His hands rose up to touch her—*soothe her slow her down*—but she batted at them, fought them off. He protested, and she pushed him down again. Baffled, cold, he watched. She was terrible, a storm. How heavy, long, she was, how very tall and white. She smelled like city dust, like oil, the peels of unfamiliar fruit.

Majid didn't move, did not know what to do—did he want her? Did he not? He didn't have the leisure to decide. Towering above him, with one finger flexed and a challenge in her eye, Sarie moved her underclothing just slightly to the side, just enough for what she wanted. She clamped his hips with her big knees and shoved him upwards on the mattress. His head hit the wooden bed board, hard. "Do it," Sarie said. She pulled his skull to hers, and when, confused, he kissed her, she bit him on the cheek. And he pushed himself inside of her more fiercely than he ever had into any willing woman, even his Hayaam. Groaning, Sarie clutched the wall. She shouted. Majid Ghulam labored there until he felt his very lungs and heart would pop.

Afterwards, when he finally slipped from her, Sarie fell beside him, and he felt his limbs go free. He shuddered. Experienced a desire both to hold and stroke his lover and to cry or shout at what she'd made them do. *What now?* She turned away from him to face the wall. Majid pressed his fingers on her spine, releasing, pressing down again, as though patting earth around a plant or tapping on a counter. Sarie didn't look at him. How quiet the room was. Majid sat up and she let him. He asked her to sit, too. She didn't. She brought one hand to his thigh and pressed her mouth into the pillow. Looking down at her, Majid rearranged her panties. Pulled her dress over her hips. He stepped into his trousers and put them on again without rising from the bed. He waited while she shook.

Sarie finally spoke. "My husband's uncle has agreed to send him money, and we will begin a business." *Her husband.* Majid bent towards her, pressed his chin against her scalp. He watched her in the mirror, petted her back slowly, until she finally turned around. Sat up. "Oh, *Majid*," Sarie said.

Majid watched his lover's double in the glass rest her head against his shoulder. What was happening between them? What was changing in this room? Was that a bruise now forming on his cheek? Had he bruised her, too? A little breeze came in; the central page of his new notebook stood up straight, then slowly fell again. *Mrs. Turner is going into business.* He didn't know quite what she meant, but he was glad for her, of course. "When you are in business, Sarie Turner, will your husband need you always? Will you be too occupied to visit me instead?"

The air seemed regular again. But he also felt another thing.

Was it a kind of ache? Was she leaving him behind? What lay in wait for him, if Sarie became wealthy, *Once*, he thought, *once all of this ends?* He hadn't thought of ends before, not clearly. He'd been caught up in beginnings. But what would happen when she went back to her husband, Mr. Turner, *Gilbert?* It struck Majid that Sarie must, sometime. He felt kindly, sweetly sad. Yes, even wistful, though she wasn't gone. What would he do then?

When she told him about Gilbert and the spare-parts business plan, that Gilbert wished to meet him, Majid was, at first, incredulous. He didn't want to hear it. But Sarie, head still hurting, digging at her palms with her fingernails again, would not be deterred. She talked and talked and talked until Majid felt—just as he had felt her push him down onto the bed, just as he had felt her bite him—an awful logic taking hold. A force swelling from her eyes, her arms, and even from that boiling place between her legs, to settle on his shoulders like a coat, transform him. He touched her as she spoke, as if he could find the source of Sarie's talking with his hands and stop it, gently roll and tamp it down with a forefinger and thumb. She let him press himself around and into and all over her while she repeated like a little song that there was no other way. That it was the best thing, for him, and for herself. That the accident had brought them all together so a new thing could be formed.

"You shouldn't do this," Majid said, "not for me."

But Sarie shook her head even as she finally responded to his hands and wrapped her arms around him, very tenderly this time. "We need you, Majid. It is not all for you."

He stopped saying no, and Sarie, for a moment, felt a bit like her old self again. She giggled in relief.

Majid held her, stroked her hair, and she kissed him as she had when the thing between them had just got off the ground, as though approaching from a distance. Majid held her elbows lightly with his hands, as if he did not know them. But in the midst of their leave-taking, Sarie left a mark on Majid's throat with her strong teeth. Darker than the stain she'd left upon his cheek, it was a bruise that would turn black. She hoped that mark would stay. That when Majid came to tea and met her husband in her home, she could look at it and not feel so afraid.

Majid did not get up to bathe, did not get up to see her hurry down the alleyway and out into the street. Feeling that the world had given a great lurch and stopped, was hovering midspin, he closed his eyes and slept. Maria, stripping coconuts of hair on a straw mat while Tahir, worn from his exertions, dozed and stretched beside her, watched Sarie Turner leaving from a corner in the courtyard. Sarie didn't greet her, and Maria didn't speak.

Outside in the sun, Sarie nodded at the thoroughfares: Libya, Mosque, Mahaba. And just there, off towards the seafront, a short and narrow thing, was India Street, by Hisham's Food and Drink, where it had all begun. She said this to herself: *Nothing, nothing, nothing, there's nothing here at all.* She didn't go straight home. No. She walked along the harbor, passing the Victorian Palm, the Court House, and the Gymkhana. She went up a little farther and turned to look just once at the Mountain Top Hotel. Farther down, where a low, neat fence held a rich and well-cut froth of fine white bougainvillea, Sarie strode into an office. At the British Council, she wrote a number down and left behind a letter.

Twenty-four

When Majid came back from that first tea with Sarie Turner and her husband, the neighborhood was dark. The electricity was gone. In the steady light of a Dietz lamp, he found Sugra in the parlor reading an old novel. His walk home had made him lonely. Slipping off his shoes, he thought, *How faithful Sugra is.*

The air smelled very slightly of rose powder. Majid sighed. Sugra's smell made him think of plenty, the possibility of which he'd glimpsed that very afternoon. He thought again about what he would do if he had any funds: books for his last son, a pigeon coop, some good trees for the courtyard, perhaps eventually a paper once again. And other things besides.

Sugra looked up from her book and welcomed him. "And so? You're never home these days! I'll have to stop my visits. There's no one here to see. Your boy is always walking. One day I'll come up and even Tahir will be gone." Majid thought how pleasant it was to be teased like that, in a gentle woman's voice. And how sly and brave she was to think ahead, of Tahir in the world. "Come on, come on, Ghuji-with-the-secret. Where is it you've been?" Teasing, Majid thought, was a central part of love. He thought about how Sarie Turner had done many things for him, had seen him at his barest. She'd petted him and smiled at him and held his hands in hers. But had she ever teased him?

He went to sit beside her. "I've been to a tea."

Sugra closed the book and set it on the table. She looked at him with interest. A tea! She liked the thought of that. Her father, in his day, accompanied by Majid's, had gone to one or two; and so had even, at least once, her mother. Not much good for ladies, it was said, white women with their arms as bare as day but with their hands in gloves the way a doctor's were, and all that mixing with the bachelors. Oh, but for the men! In other days, an invitation to a tea might have portended, yes, inestimable things. The Aga Khan, Sugra was sure, had also been to many. Had even drunk champagne and chatted with great men. So had the brilliant Topans and some dozen Jeevanjees. Was a tea what it once was? "Ghuji, how exciting! With your English woman-friend? Tell me all about it." Oh, Majid *was* getting better, surely.

Majid set her straight. It mattered to him suddenly that he be precise. Belgian Sarie was not English. Mrs. Turner's husband was. "Gilbert Turner," Majid said. "He's the English one."

A husband! Sugra thought. Dismissing the announcement of the woman's nationality, Sugra paused. Sarie Turner, not a widow? Had she misunderstood the Englishwoman's trembling on the settee? Had she conjured up a love affair where there wasn't one? Or . . . did the husband not matter at all? A husband! Sugra wasn't sure she liked such complicated things. All for love, she was, legitimized or no. But she had standards, too. She frowned a little at her cousin. She'd get details from him later. But, still, she thought. Nevermind for now. There had been a tea. "Tell me who was there." And so Majid told her.

Mrs. Turner and her husband. "Yes, only just the two." In a reconditioned flat on Mchanganyiko Street, in a building that had lots and lots of tenants. Fine, just fine, it was. A home. Not as nice as Kudra House once was, but, still, a piano in the parlor, a picture, he had thought, of the British queen.

While Sarie—*Sarie,* Majid thought—gloomed and loomed

about in shadows, almost like a ghost, a shade, not quite as he remembered (this he did not say), Mr. Turner had, he said, shown off
all his books. Sugra liked the thought of books and she asked Majid
about them. She tucked her legs beneath her on her seat. Leaned
in. Lots of them, he told her. Coastal history, Indian Ocean fish,
agricultural statistics, and even one, a pamphlet, all about Bohoras,
which he had found amusing. And they had talked about . . . He
mumbled, paused, was not sure where to start.

Sugra interrupted. Surely at a tea there would be at least a small
variety of cakes, a splendid table done up on a lawn. "What was
there to eat?" Sugra cared for sweets as much as she did news and
books, as much as she did for Majid and the boys. And she ate them
so rarely. "The food?" Yes, Majid told her, there had been a cake.
But not a very sweet one (something, he'd been told, Sarie had
picked up from a certain nurse). An American treat, Gilbert had
said. "Banana bread," Sarie had explained, voice almost too steady,
looking at her husband. Not a cake, but bread. Sarie had not eaten
any. From her seat at the piano, she had not looked at him at all.
Had treated him, in fact, like an acquaintance of her husband's. And
it had made him, oddly, free to be there, in a way he had not quite
expected. This Majid did not say.

Still thinking of the cake, Sugra cocked her head. "Just one?
Your friend made it herself?" She wanted to know this, had long
been under the impression that British women did not learn how
to cook. Therefore there were Chinese restaurants with linen
cloths and waiters, clubhouses, marinas, men and girls employed to
stew and fry, make tea.

Majid sighed, and told her that the cake was not important. He
had been sensitive enough to see that Sarie or her husband had
gone to the expense of flour and some (too little) sugar and had
hoped that he would find it tasty. He had saved a lump of it for

Tahir, and as Sugra, looking sour, spoke, he felt aware of it, wrapped in ancient news, heavy, dampening his pocket. He rearranged his bony hips so as not to crush it, would keep it in his trousers until Sugra had gone home. No lemon loaf, no cupcakes, no Scottish shortbread from a tin.

They had talked about . . . Majid paused. Sugra watched him like a teacher, as she'd looked at Tahir when explaining how to walk. "Well," said Majid, thinking that if he stated it out loud, a few times, even, perhaps it would not sound to him as peculiar as it felt. "Here is what he said." Mr. Turner had proposed that Majid Ghulam assist him in a business. Keep his eyes peeled, so to speak. An ear down to the ground. Send customers his way. Advise him now and then. On commission. For, eventually, a share. While Majid's too-full stomach turned and rolled inside him—the anxious settling, the undoing, of a sharp excitement he had felt when Gilbert Turner finally let him go—Sugra began, softly first, then fiercely, to twinkle in the dark. He did not know where to look. "A business!"

"Me? Assistant to an Englishman? It's not possible," he said.

But Sugra set him straight. Right before his eyes, Sugra turned the tea, which had made him feel so strange, confused, elated, frightened, shy, into a wonderful event. He was not, after all, she said, repulsing any cisternful of brothers who were eager to help out. Not much coming from that side. Crumbs, the jetsam. As if he needed a reminder, she said to him plainly: "You've lost every fine and fancy thing that anyone has ever placed into your hands."

Majid squirmed beneath his eager cousin's gaze. Massaging his old stomach, he wondered for a moment if Sarie Turner, too, had once been fine, or fancy. If Tahir's leg had been his to lose or find. Sugra's fingers quivered as she spoke. Her voice rose. Majid looked away, thought, *She is brighter than that lamp, and I can neither blow her out nor turn her flickering down.* What was happening to him? In passing, he wondered if the lines might find their way into a poem, something he might title *Brightness.* How dissipated, unpredictable, he felt!

Sugra, once she'd started on a thing, was difficult to stop. "You have scared too many people. There is no one else for you," she said. "Why not a British man for once?" It was true. Sugra knew— in a way that Majid himself didn't, that the boys could not, and much more keenly than even Bibi did, because Sugra had cared for him and also for his wife—Sugra knew exactly how those long nine years had been. Even Sugra's husband, who was very soft on her despite all of his rules, who helped all kinds of people, had drawn the line at Majid. And all those talky aunts, he thought again, had come to visit Tahir and his missing-leg-below-the-knee because they liked tragic news the best. The brothers, who should have minded him the most, those who could say "no matter what," with feeling, had one by one, too long ago, made their way abroad. More quietly, more seriously, Sugra said to him, "There's no one else, Ghuji. You must give this some thought."

Sugra had to go. She gathered up her handbag (vinyl, not unlike Mrs. Turner's) and the paperback she'd brought to read if Tahir fell asleep. She left him with a warning that Majid took to heart, though he would ever be uncertain as to which Turner it applied: "You never know," said Sugra, "just who might be an angel in disguise."

Had it not been for Sugra, he might have let the whole thing go. He might have urged Sarie to come back to him, to what had been before. That evening he missed Sarie with his loins but also with his heart. This, he thought, he could not, could not, do. He would ask her to return, forget her awful plan. The peculiar afternoon at Mchanganyiko Street would become no more than

364 ⬥ *N. S. Köenings*

something awkward to recall. Something they might laugh at or, even better, never talk about again. He'd felt a bit of guilt, of course, at talking with her husband. But what was most awkward for Majid, and he knew it, was principally this: he had experienced pleasure, too—pleasure at her Gilbert, Mr. Turner, treating him so nicely.

At first Majid had been nervous. Gilbert opened the discussion with: "My wife has told me much about you." Majid wondered what, and felt his skin go cold. For a moment he had asked himself if Sarie had not trapped him into something else, a weird uxorial play. Had brought him there to trick and to expose him. But, no, of course she wouldn't. Had he not pressed himself inside that very woman and felt her teeth graze his? Did he not know her ribs and spine and the diameter, the rubbery weight, of Sarie's open thighs? She wouldn't trick him so. She couldn't.

Sarie, for once, had been wearing a long skirt, a gray thing topped by a blue blouse with sleeves that came right down to her wrists. The color made Sarie's eyes very light and clear, like seawater in shallow places where the sand is clean and white. From the doorway of the kitchen, she stole a glance at Majid. Her mouth moved. She looked fragile, glassy. As though she might at any moment throw herself at someone—Gilbert? Majid?—and shatter or collapse. He had looked at her and had attempted by his looking to make Sarie a bit stronger. *It's going to be all right,* he thought. *It must.*

He had turned back to Mr. Turner, squared his torso—and although Sarie hadn't told him very much at all, although wives and husbands had been left out of the thing, been pushed into the corner by the thrashing of their limbs, he had answered, fearless, "She has said good things about you, too." At this, Gilbert had smiled.

After letting Sarie pour for him another cup of tea, Majid had felt better, told himself that there was something reassuring in being made so welcome not only by Sarie Turner but her husband—balding, pink-faced, chatty (*Gentle,* Majid thought) Gilbert Turner. He discovered that he felt no jealousy for Gilbert. He did not begrudge this man any rights to Sarie's body—he didn't wish to take her from him. Watching Gilbert as he now and then looked at his wife, attempting to see Sarie through her husband's eyes, Majid wondered, without any unkindness, without any sense of triumph, whether, had he seen Sarie Turner on the street, without the accident, without her coming up the stairs on her own steam, he would have sought her out. Majid wasn't sure. When he looked up at her again, the woman he had fondled only days before in his own house had disappeared into her kitchen, and bit by bit a strange thing happened. Majid became so comfortable in that front room with the piano and the bookshelves and the droning sound of Sarie pacing in the kitchen that he eventually felt at ease.

Gilbert was both formal, and giddy like a boy. His flattery did Majid good. *She's married a kind man,* thought Majid, and, oddly, he approved. As though he himself had given her away. When Gilbert said, "Sarie lets me understand that you are not presently engaged, am I correct in thinking this?" Majid didn't, out of meanness or for pleasure, say (and he could have, his English was as good as Gilbert's, better even, yes), "No, no! We aren't engaged, dear sir, we are not *that* far along," though this was the kind of sarcasm he might not so long ago have turned against his kin. No, he didn't dare. In fact, he had no wish to.

When Gilbert bravely, clearly, said, "I have been thinking for some time now of going into business," Majid didn't even say, "In these times? A business?" In fact, a lot of people *were* in business; they just didn't let it show. He simply said, "A-laa." And "Oh." In the kitchen, Sarie's pacing sounded now like the tattoo of an army on the march.

Gilbert heard her pacing, too; he was buoyed by Sarie's feet. She was, he thought, keeping time with him, pacing out their future. He recalled how still she'd been all week, and he was glad to hear there was some motion left in her. *She's come to terms with this,* he thought. *She'll buck up any day.* When Gilbert said, a little coy, "I am thinking of spare parts. You know, for the cars," Majid said, "I see." In the kitchen, Sarie's eyes went blank. She listened, leaning in the doorway, where the thick vanilla-colored paint against her arm and cheek was unyielding and cold. She spread her toes along the flat, smooth tile to keep herself in check.

In a voice so sure that Sarie wondered briefly what third man had slipped into the room, Gilbert Turner said, sounding for a moment exactly like his wife, "I have always dreamed of doing something for the motors." And Majid said, "I see," again. Sarie let them talk for as long as she could stand it, then came back into the room and sat at the piano, where she played with her own hands, with the long drape of her skirt, and tried not to look up.

Majid could not remember clearly how the afternoon had ended, what Gilbert had explained, or how he had responded. He did recall that when it was time for him to go, Sarie had stood at a respectful distance from him in the doorway and offered him her hand. "Thank you very much for coming, Mr. Jeevanjee," she said. And softly, "Do consider Gilbert's proposition." He had felt his lover's eyes burning on his cheeks but was not at all disturbed to hear Sarie speak her husband's name. *Gilbert,* he thought. Not an awful sound, though he would have been hard-pressed to place it in a poem.

As Gilbert moved into the hallway to accompany him a bit, Sarie, still holding to the door, called out, "Give Agatha's regards to your youngest boy. To Tahir." He could see how difficult it was for her. He had almost reached out for her shoulder, thought to rest his fingers on her cheek, but didn't. That wouldn't do at all. Gilbert stood, excited, at his side and said he would accompany him part of the way home. On that first walk with Gilbert, down Mchanganyiko and Mahaba, up to Mosque Street, not certain why it should surprise him, Majid sensed, of all unexpected things, a generosity in Gilbert. Sarie's husband: a nice man. He had walked home in a daze.

Spare parts. Majid thought about it in the nighttime, after Sugra had gone home. People needed spare parts then, of course, for all the things that plied the streets and groaned and shuddered and clack-clacked along the dusty roads, for all the things that broke or died and had to be revived. But wasn't that the problem? Everybody needed them. People paid large sums to smuggle needed things into the country. Where did Mr. Turner hope to get them? Did he have a link, a friendship of some kind, with an amenable official? Surely, Majid thought, the man must have a plan. He'd dealt with many people in his time at the High Court, no doubt. Had surely traveled both sides of the law. Gilbert Turner must have made connections. He had, after all, held a respectable *position*.

Clearly Mr. Turner also hoped that Majid would know something, too, about how spare parts could be gotten, handled, moved, dispensed. Whom did Majid know with an interest in cars? Connections? Rahman, if he could be convinced to speak with him again. Or that clever young man Issa, who, so he'd heard from Sugra, seemed to know a lot of men who worked with engineers (and weren't they building *roads?*). Even Sugra's husband, who had a car himself. There were others, too, if only he could let himself think back into the past, if only he could bear it. Hadn't one of his own teachers—a man who had approved of Majid's poems—also driven taxis? Wasn't he alive somewhere? Didn't all those fleet young boys just outside his house fix buses all the time? Did they not know him by sight? Yes, there might be others, too.

Cars. He tried to think of all the cars he'd been in in his life. He himself had never owned one. Before their emigration, his older brothers had—a shiny Benz that had taken him and his once-wife to parties, weddings, birthdays, to the clinic now and then if another boy was on his way. It was in that fine Mercedes, Majid thought, that he had come back from the clinic that sad day without Hayaam. The brothers in Nairobi certainly had cars, and in Mombasa several younger in-laws, too, zipped around with radios blaring, tops rolled down, in Peugeot 504s. *Fiats,* Majid thought. *My sons think those are grand.* Others. The Citroëns that made him think of lemons, low and growling, sleek. The Austins and the Morrises, older, some with cloud-white bonnets, with steering wheels as large as any tire. He thought about the buses and the trucks, their dips and shining curves, the long, enormous bodies of the dog-rib trucks bearing their wood boards. The Leylands, heavy, iron scaffolding on top, fitted with a canvas sheet, some rolling down the roads diagonally, no longer shooting straight. The DAFs, with colored aprons.

Later, Majid dreamed of chrome and squeals and smoke. And of Tahir's metal crutches, crumpling. He got up in the dark and, night-eyes full of diesel fumes, ears sore from hard dream-sounds of metal, he went into the bathroom. As his urine streamed onto the floor, a quiet little spill, he squinted up into the square that had been cut out of the wall, showing him the sky. He thought he saw the stars. His own small boy had been knocked down and split in two by a big bus. A Tata, made in his own India. His grandfather's, more like. A mystery-country far away. Buses. Back in the dim hallway, hands damp against his naked chest, he leaned against the wall. Weren't Hungarians bringing in a bus, these days? *That's right,* he thought. The Icarus, boxy, hopeful, painted red and white. As he fell into his bed, Majid laid an arm down fast across his eyes. He knew all about that story. *Icarus,* he thought. *Sure. Too close to the sun.*

❦ Twenty-five

I n the breeze at the Victorian Palm, Majid was introduced to
Kazansthakis, who, he learned with interest, was Greek.
Gilbert introduced Majid as M.G. and Kazansthakis as the Frosty
King. Majid listened while Gilbert and the Frosty King told him
what they thought. Majid, telling what, if he had not believed it in
the depths of his new heart, would have been a lie, assured the
Frosty King and Mr. Turner that he had in his day managed more
than one successful business. That he had deftly managed them to
death, he wisely did not say. He would do his best. He also said—
and this was true—that he remembered having seen once with a
man he knew (that Mr. Essajee, who could bring dead appliances
to life, who'd been so kind to the boys) a clever youth named Idi
Moto, who could, it was softly said, pull a radio from a pebble, then
make it disappear.

Majid Ghulam Jeevanjee's fine name—for Jeevanjees had managed many places in the world, made them what they are, and also
fought for very honorable things—left a great impression on the
Frosty King. Kazansthakis also wished to be impressive, and while
he had resisted telling Gilbert exactly how much he could help, he
found himself declaring rather recklessly that he could easily procure for them some European brake shoes, screens, and the necessary pumps. The excitement made him jumpy, restless. He left the
Palm before them, saluting as he went. "We'll meet again, my
man," he said, to neither one, to both. "I go to Mrs. Frosty." And
Gilbert raised his glass.

Outside, the sun was low, and the sky over the flat white sea was fluid, turning slowly plum. A kitchen boy, dispatched to the innards of the Palm, turned the generator on. It was time for all of them to go. Gilbert and Majid rose up from their chairs and with a shake of all their legs loosed the wrinkles in their slacks. Majid pushed his chair closer to the table with the care of a new guest at a luncheon who folds a napkin formally before going on his way. He leaned forward on the backrest for a moment. In the leaking twilight, a silver ring on Majid's smallest finger gleamed. Thinking briefly about Sarie, he felt a sharp thing in him tumble down a crevice, leave a tingle, disappear. Majid sighed, and looked for a long moment at the sea. And then he said, "Let us go together, Mr. Turner. We are almost neighbors, after all!"

Gilbert cast a glance towards the bar, where two expatriates were hovering, each over a drink: Jan, the gloomy man from KLM, and a quiet engineer. Gilbert looked above their heads and saw himself reflected in the heavy mirror that rose up behind the bar. He puffed his chest out, just a little, and clapped Majid on the back. He cleared his throat and said, "We *are* neighbors, indeed!" He hoped that the expatriates would hear, and turn their heads to see. *That's right,* he thought. Gilbert Turner might not be flush with funds as yet, and he might not have slapped a bright all-weather road down in any tangled wilds or by himself have conjured spark plugs from the air, but he could, at least, at last, perhaps say that he belonged.

As they reached the steps, Gilbert, made sentimental by one too many drinks, the Frosty King's salute, the promise of success, and the violet of the sky, shook his lowered head as though he had just found a lost thing that had been there all along. Sounding sweet, confused, as though someone were to blame, he said, "Tell me, Mr. Jeevanjee. Why have we not met before?"

Majid gave his partner a gracious little smile. "It was not yet planned for us," he said. "It was not meant until now." And Gilbert, who had often read that certain peoples had a tendency to believe in things like that, that it meant some things were planned by God, felt satisfied at last. Victorious. He patted M.G.'s back. Majid felt light-headed. Tahir would be proud to know that his own dad had sat beside the famous Frosty King—didn't Sugra take the boys for sundaes at the Kreem? They might even go again, together. Kazansthakis, he was sure, would offer little Tahir a vanilla scoop for free.

As Gilbert made his way along the seafront, all aglow, Sarie stepped into the parlor. In the gluey light of the one bulb, she stood before her husband's shelf. Resting horizontally across the other volumes: the dog-eared *Everyman's Car Handbook.* Sarie winced and picked it up. *For the cars,* she thought. *The motors.* Why had she not seen it before? Why had she never paid attention to the things that Gilbert read? She held it for a moment but did not part the covers. Instead, she slipped it vertically between a tattered guide to the attractions of East Africa's long coast and a book on making bricks. What was she looking for on Gilbert's precious shelf? Where had Gilbert put them?

She turned, and looked under the piano, below the rocky table. Not there. She looked under the pillow of Gilbert's favorite chair and wondered, as she did so, if he had ever purchased ointment for his skin. She found a rubber band. She put the pillow back and yawned. On her knees, she paused. Perhaps behind the settee. She crawled towards the wall. There it was: Mr. Frosty's box.

Not a big box, Sarie thought, *but look what it has done!* She'd been amazingly defeated. By the spark plugs, and the tea, her husband.

But she also felt impressed and curious that she had been, at least, thwarted by an interesting, redoubtable, international opponent. Had he said *Japan?*

She plucked a spark plug from the box and lifted it between two fingers to the light. What a clean, smooth middle the thing had, what weight in its small shape. Sarie sighed. With the spark plug in her hand, she went into the bedroom, where she lay down on the bed and thought about the lover she had left. *"Rompu,"* she said out loud. And then she wondered at the word, how "romp," in English, meant something else entirely.

When Gilbert returned home, he found his wife asleep. Exhausted by the nearness and the dazzle of their future, Gilbert took his shoes off, then his trousers and his shirt. He stretched out beside her. Oh, Sarie had done well! He would tell her all about his new good friend M.G. when the two of them woke up. Perhaps she'd make him breakfast. In sleep, Sarie felt the mattress shift. She clutched the spark plug tighter. She was dreaming about Mr. Jeevanjee's high balcony, the bubbling street below. And mountains far beyond. All of Majid's plants. Grown, and shivering with fruit, the little palm, she saw, was bursting through the slats.

Twenty-six

B ibi started out the week thinking happily about Majid
Ghulam Jeevanjee and everybody else she'd spied on
from her balcony. What great moments there had been! She'd seen
them all, she thought, and she was, for once, satisfied entirely with
her rather limited location. *If I were following just one,* she thought, *I
would be missing all the rest.* Indeed, what if she had, like a bird,
followed poor Majid Ghulam—who'd looked so fresh, so nicely
bathed and wasn't that wild mustache now neat!—into the New
Purnima Snack? It's true she would have seen that he had eaten
jalebis and later had bajia mix and not, as she had so firmly
told herself, kachori. But if she had been checking on whether it
was chutney-yes-or-no, she would have missed Salma Hafiz sneaking from her house with her face hidden in a niqab, going who-
knows-where, and also Mama Ndiambongo slipping through
a doorway just three houses down and coming out again
(*Surreptitious!* Bibi thought) holding a big basket. And if she had
been able to sneak into Mrs. Turner's house—a nice one, Bibi was
quite sure—to see what things were like in the long-legged
woman's bedroom, and then, perhaps, unseen, down to the
Kikanga clinic to make certain that Nisreen was not flirting with
the doctors, and to all the other places for which she sometimes felt
a hunger, she would not have seen the most amazing thing of all:
just the other day, Majid Ghulam Jeevanjee accompanied by, of all
things, a British man, who talked and talked and talked while the
new, presentable Majid cocked his head and listened.

She had been amazed to see on the first day that Mad Majid Ghulam walked proudly, decently, in fact. He'd been looking sometimes straight ahead, then to the left or right, without shouting out at anyone or talking to himself. That was already, Bibi thought, a step. *See what an affair can do?* But seeing him a second time, so easy in the company of the almost-bald white man, listening so carefully, was something else indeed. *Perhaps,* thought Bibi, *Jeevanjee's setting out to trick him. Maybe-maybe, there is still a spark in him, a business-flame at last. Is he borrowing money? Will he start the paper up? Make a special deal? Is he offering a service? Something only local men can do for too-soft old white men?* Here Bibi held back a hot chuckle, remembering Mrs. Livery-Jones's red husband and the swaggering alley boys. *Not that, surely. Not a grown man like Majid.* She dismissed that thought with a happy sniff and raised a palm up to her face.

She pondered. This pale man was probably, thought Bibi, not really, really rich.

See how those long trouser cuffs had been stitched up at the hem? See the marred, worn shoes? And what would a rich white man be doing in Kikanga? But one could never tell these days, as Issa and Nisreen so very often said. Perhaps, she thought, having cut his teeth with one light person from the North—the woman with the girl—Mad Majid Ghulam had learned something important and was taking on a second. Things do change, indeed. *What if*—she thought, *what if his fortunes rise!*

She thought about it for a while, turning over in her mind how she might coax Mama Moto into helping her a bit—to make a nice tale for Nisreen. Dear Nisreen, who was (oh, wasn't she?) looking a bit brighter now than she had looked before. Looking almost, Bibi thought—almost but not quite, because the girl *was* really skinny—as well-fed as a bride. And what had gone on in the bedroom not so long ago? And again the other night? Hadn't Mama Moto nodded, silent, yes, but *nodding* and not groaning at the sky when Bibi said again how nice it would be if the girl would only have a child? *Dear Nisreen,* she thought. Bibi wanted to give little Issa's wife a sort of present, a new story about Mad Majid Ghulam that could have a different ending. She needed Mama Moto to help her understand what was happening out there. Then she would sit down with Nisreen and tell her what she knew. And Nisreen might even smile.

But when Bibi called for Mama Moto to come up, Mama Moto didn't come. She called and called: "Hebu, hebu! Hoh! Mama Moto, where are you?" All without an answer. Where was she? Where were people when you needed them? When important things were happening? She would have to go downstairs. Alone!

It was hard. She panted. Scowling, preparing insults as she went, Bibi struggled down the steps, holding to the wall. She found one of Mama Moto's cloths in the far storeroom where she slept and wrapped it round her head and shoulders, tucking in the hairs that had sprung down over her brow. Hobbling, she groaned loudly in case Mama Moto was in fact nearby and playing her a trick. She moved unsteadily from the kitchen and the courtyard, down the hallway to the door, holding her big stomach. For the first time ever, Bibi wished that when Issa and Nisreen had offered her a cane, she had—instead of "Where would I go all alone?"—graciously accepted. A walking stick would help. She hadn't been outside by herself in a long time. But she wasn't planning to go far.

When she opened the front doors just slightly and looked into the street, it struck her that the road looked rather different from ground level than it did from high above. How far up Salma's window was! How chipped and shabby those white doors at Lydia

House were from here! And to the right, how low and wide the ocean looked—how close. Bibi scratched her nose. It was early afternoon, and quiet. Who could she call over? In the alley just across the way, she caught sight of Mama Ndiambongo, old and gray, shelling groundnuts on her stoop. *She would be up and out when other people are indoors, when other people nap.* That was how she did it, Bibi thought. *Mama Ndiambongo steals when everyone's in bed.*

Bibi hissed to get attention. She made a long sound with her teeth. "Over here! Over here!" she said. And Mama Ndiambongo, who could not recall ever seeing Bibi Kulthum on the ground, came over with, because her back was not so good, a little leaping in her knees and her top half bent so far that it was even with her hips. If she had had a broom in hand, thought Bibi, the street would have been swept. "What? What? What?" Mama Ndiambongo said, frowning and excited.

Bibi—who would not have known from so high up—noticed with some pleasure that Mama Ndiambongo was missing her front teeth and that her earlobes were a little more distended than she'd thought. "Mama Moto," Bibi said. "Where is she?" Bibi, though she liked to think so, was not the only one to keep an eye out on the world; Mama Ndiambongo had a ready answer. "I'll tell you," she said. And Bibi, though she herself had asked, was a bit taken aback. "Idi came to take her shopping. I saw her leave just now." Mama Ndiambongo smiled, and tilted her small head to the side. She tsked. "You must have been asleep, or what?"

Bibi was put out. She hadn't been asleep. She'd been upstairs on the balcony, looking at the street. How did she miss Mama Moto when she passed? Did Mama Moto know to walk especially close to Mansour House, just next to the wall and right beneath her Bibi—*Just under my feet in the one place I don't see?* How often did the woman take her leave, like that, without asking permission?

And since when did Idi Moto have any cash to spare? A layabout, a small-time, no-good thief. Since when did he take Mama Moto *shopping?*

"I hear he has a job," Mama Ndiambongo said.

"A job?" Bibi almost snarled. She put her hand out for support and Mama Ndiambongo, who knew how hard age was, held on to her arm. "Since when does Idi Moto have a job he would admit to his own mother?" *And since when does Mama Ndiambongo have news that I don't know?*

"All right, all right," Mama Ndiambongo said, pushing Bibi back towards the wall so she could let go of her arm and hold herself up, too. "Don't go crazy, now. They haven't gone to London." Bibi sniffed. "Let go of me," she said. But she was glad to know that Mama Moto would be back. When Mama Ndiambongo held her hand out for some shillings, Bibi gave her some.

Back inside, she closed the door behind her. Her chest hurt, and her dry scalp itched with sweat. But she'd learned something on her own, in any case. *Mama Ndiambongo doesn't have her teeth!* For a moment she thought she would tell Mama Moto so, but then she sighed. Surely Mama Moto, who spent her time at street level, who did go out, who could walk far on her two legs, knew this much and more.

Bibi shuffled on into the kitchen and removed the cloth she'd worn. Getting back up the stairs would be too difficult, she thought. And so she took a rest on Mama Moto's bed.

Uneasy now, unkeeled, she wondered what else she might be missing. Did Salma Hafiz have crossed eyes? Was Mr. Mehta ugly? Did Kirit Tanna have a mole she hadn't ever seen? Perhaps. She pressed her cheek against the wall and looked at a long crack in the white paint. But she could not stay disappointed in herself for long. She rolled over, righted her sore hips. She closed her eyes and turned again to more interesting questions that could, if she just waited for a while, be answered: Would Majid Jeevanjee become what everyone had hoped he would at first? Would he start a business and give himself some pride? What would Mama Moto bring back from her shopping, and, most of all, would she have witnessed in her travels anything worth mention?

Had Nisreen not returned from work much sooner than expected, complaining of a stomachache and weakness, Bibi would have turned herself full strength on Mama Moto when she finally came home. But here was something else. Nisreen doing something completely out of character. Hadn't Issa married her because the girl worked very hard? Because she was intelligent-and-capable-and-dutiful and wrote things down correctly and filed things right away? What was Nisreen doing, slacking off like this? "What's wrong with you now? Why aren't you at work? Have you lost your job?"

Nisreen was surprised to find Bibi downstairs. "I haven't lost my job," she said. "I'm sick." Sick? This, Bibi was not displeased to hear. In fact, she felt a twitching in the wings. Sick? With what? She called Nisreen over to the bed. "What's wrong with you, exactly?" Bibi asked. "Sick in your stomach? Vomiting? Dizzy? Do you have a headache?" Nisreen didn't answer. She bit her bottom lip and took off her big glasses. She ladled water from the cistern into a metal cup and drank.

"Feeling funny walking?" Bibi kept on asking. "Bleeding from your gums?" And she asked and asked and asked until, at last, Nisreen looked seriously at her. It was not the sort of thing a person shared with anyone so early, not at all, oh, no. But what was she to do, with Bibi so enormous and so close, clawing at her arm? "All right, old woman, yes. All right." Bibi clapped her hands and felt suddenly so well that she sat up directly and put both feet on the floor. "All right, all right," Nisreen went on. "It's true." Bibi all at once could not care less if Mama Moto came back to the house weighed down with electric incense burners, bread machines, and gold. Who cared if Majid Ghulam Jeevanjee was a good-luck man or no? Who gave a blessed corn husk about European men? *That envelope,* she thought, tears springing to her eyes, *was meant for only this. For me. For me and my Nisreen.* How pretty Nisreen looked with that gray tint to her skin, the sweat along her cheeks. How fine a girl, indeed.

Twenty-seven

The week Nisreen admitted she was pregnant, Gilbert got Uncle James's wire. He winced at all the bank fees but was confident that it would be enough. He and Kazansthakis and M.G. had, after all, gone over things together. They also got a customer. And, while Bibi, had she known all there was to know, would have said it was no surprise at all, Gilbert was amazed.

A knock at the one door, which Gilbert, nimble, rose to answer, and there, yes, there he was: Mr. Suleiman, stately in a kanzu gown and blue-embroidered cap, standing in the doorway, leaning on a stick. None other than the owner of the Morris just across the way. Startled but increasingly accustomed to taking on new things, Gilbert asked him to come in. Mr. Suleiman, gaunt and lean, slipped out of his sandals and sat down. He asked after Gilbert's family, calling Agatha by name, which unsettled Gilbert for a moment and made him feel suspicious. Agatha came out from the kitchen and sat down on the floor, laughing at the man as though he were her uncle. Sarie, unsmiling but dutiful, brought a glass of water.

Mr. Suleiman looked evenly around him and admiringly took note of Gilbert's shelf of books. "Sir," he asked, "have you read them all?" He spoke a teacher's English. Sarie saw her husband blush and, despite everything she'd gone through, despite how very tired she was, felt a very faintly mollifying twinge. Their guest coughed discreetly. He crossed his bony ankles, tugged once at the hip of his white gown, and went on to praise *The Mohammedan*

Peoples of East Africa's Coast Lands, adding very comfortably that he would be gratified one day to have a look at *Sons of Sindbad,* too, about which he'd only heard. Gilbert, unnerved, rather, but quite pleased, coughed, too, raised his eyebrows, and said, "Yes. A valuable book, indeed." He was going to suggest that Mr. Suleiman might one day also look over his pamphlets when he realized that the visitor had finished talking about books. His gaze was now on Gilbert's face. He'd come for something else.

Lowering his voice, Mr. Suleiman said, "Mr. Turner. You will forgive me if you find my visit untoward." Gilbert looked at him, eyes wide. Since when was *he* in a position to find a visit *untoward?* It felt awfully nice, and he found himself saying, "Nevermind, my dear sir," quite calmly, and urging his guest on.

Mr. Suleiman shifted in his seat, and Gilbert leaned towards him, hands just slightly shaking. Mr. Suleiman went on. Would Mr. Gilbert Turner please forgive him, but he had heard it from a friend, a man who could be trusted. That he himself would tell the news to no one. Times, as Gilbert knew, were difficult. Dangerous, for some. But they were neighbors, were they not? To whom else should one turn? Was it true there were, perhaps, some *items* that a person could acquire to remedy . . . a certain sort of problem?

Gilbert felt that he was acting in a play, in the perfect role. He felt his eyes go round. He cleared his throat. Could Mr. Suleiman please clarify his point? "What kind of problem might you mean?" Sarie, watching from her place on the piano bench, fought an urge to laugh or maybe cry. She had the feeling she was watching something new and old, an important thing unfolding, right there in her parlor. Gilbert's airs both irked and fascinated her. *Who does he take himself for being?* Sarie thought. She tapped her thighs with outstretched fingers, bit down on her lip.

The smile on Mr. Suleiman's face, small, discreet, made Sarie think of cats. "Vehicular, in fact." Mr. Suleiman leaned in. "Something for the engines?"

Gilbert, smiling a bit slyly, offered their guest coffee, which Sarie, sighing, rose to boil. Gilbert thought how pleasant it was in the parlor, suddenly! How fine! While Sarie moved about, opening a can and searching for a pot, Gilbert, like a schoolmaster himself, brought his hands together in his lap. He'd practiced for this, hadn't he?

He asked Mr. Suleiman: Wasn't it unorthodox, this visit, this coming to him so directly, yes, at home? And *how* exactly had he heard?

Mr. Suleiman did not give a clear answer. The line of whispered things and gestures, little nods and winks, he said, was too complex to follow. Perhaps, in fact, he had been asked by the person who had sent him not to let on to Mr. Turner exactly how he knew. For safety's sake. But he would go this far: "Perhaps, let's say, there are old friends here at work. Or perhaps that cold things are involved. Ice. Cream."

Oh, how Gilbert liked to feel that he could say yes or maybe no. Or, *Come back another day*. Or, *You have been misled. I'm afraid you are mistaken*. Sarie, sucking at her cheeks, watched her husband from the doorway. At last Gilbert said, "It's true."

Mr. Suleiman continued. "My taxi," he explained.

Gilbert breathed out through his nose as high officials do. He tilted his head sideways and watched his guest through half-closed, thinking eyes, then said, "I have admired your blue taxi, Mr. Suleiman, for very many years." Sarie brought the coffee in. Mr. Suleiman thanked her with a raising of his palm and took a little sip. She sat down at the piano.

Gilbert, with his notebook, brought his pen to bear. They talked. Once the business part was done, he showed Mr. Suleiman a book, *On Island Life and History,* which Mr. Suleiman, having come from those green places long ago, was very pleased to see.

When he finally left, Mr. Suleiman passed Gilbert a tight tube of rolled bills, which he had hidden in his sleeve. "A show of faith, you see." Sarie watched it all from the piano, and when Mr. Suleiman rose to go, she gathered up the coffee things and went into the kitchen, where she sat down at the table.

Gilbert, still pink from that first blush, came to find her and said, "Look at that! It's working." And Sarie nodded at him. *My pink husband,* Sarie thought. "Well," she said, a keening in her teeth. "I think you should be proud." Gilbert did feel proud, exactly, yes. And he wanted Sarie to be as glad for him as he was. "Come on, now, Sarie. You're feeling better, aren't you?"

From behind, he placed his palms on her broad shoulders, squeezing here and there. She thought how rubbery his hands were. How hard it was to feel the bones in them, how, really, they were not far off from fat. "When I tell Kazansthakis," Gilbert said, "he will be excited." Sarie made a little sound like humming, thinking, *If it's going to be like this, I will have to look un peu heureuse, I will have to try.* She said, "*C'est vrai.* Your friend will be happy. You've done a good thing here." She couldn't say her husband's name. Since she had first said it to Majid Jeevanjee in Gilbert's presence ("Gilbert's proposition"), it had seemed impossible to say again in private to the man whose name it was. "Very good," she said.

Gilbert rubbed and rubbed. Despite themselves, Sarie's muscles loosened. Gilbert paused a moment, moved her hair away from her long neck to reach her better there. It was nice like this, to have a proper wife. "And that M.G.," he said. "Wait till he hears this." Sarie didn't mean to, but she stiffened. Then took a deep breath.

She looked up at her husband and tried on a new word. "He will feel outdone, I'm sure."

At the new, exciting cafeteria of the Mountain Top Hotel, Hazel Towson paid for Sarie and herself. "I was pleased, you know, to find your little note. It was so unexpected."

Sarie, starting on her second bowl of custard, smiled at Hazel Towson in the white-white noontime light. She was glad the fans were working. "I also took the number of your telephone," she said. "In case you did not fetch the letter soon."

Hazel Towson laughed. She told Sarie that she passed by the British Council office almost every day. As involved as she was, with so many responsibilities, how could she do less? Although, of course, she was very glad that Sarie also had the number now, so that she could call the house in Scallop Bay, oh, any time at all. Sarie stroked the inner circle of her bowl with the long edge of her spoon so as not to miss a single bit of cream. "I'm so glad you want to help," Hazel Towson said.

"Mrs. Hazel," Sarie said, shifting her long legs and trying not to step on Hazel Towson's feet, "I want to know your plan for the syringes. The vaccines." She took a gulp of water and continued. "I was once, you know, almost like a nurse."

Hazel Towson smiled and nodded softly, as if Sarie had just done what she had hoped she would for years. Kindly, she said, "Of course, of course, my dear." And that Sarie ought to dispense with the "Mrs." "Mrs. Hazel!" Hazel said. She laughed and put a hand up to her hair. "It sounds like something from a film, you know, an old one. As if I were an ancient."

Sarie felt embarrassed, but Hazel Towson smiled. "Would you

like another custard, Sarie? It's things like that a woman craves, you know, when she is expecting." She motioned to the waiter, then looked Sarie in the eye. "Are you *sure* you'll have the strength to help us? Though it's true you've done it all before, now, haven't you? You've done well with little Agatha."

Sarie had forgotten. She hadn't thought about the pregnancy since that day in the gift shop, when Hazel Towson had attempted to explain about the precious stones. Hazel thought Sarie's silence meant that Sarie had grown modest and that Hazel had, in her forthright farm girl's way, embarrassed her by laying out the truth. Yet hadn't Hazel overcome her own misgivings and her shyness? Hadn't she forgiven Sarie for being pregnant in the midst of middle age? She reached across the table to stroke Sarie on the forearm, as though she were a child. "It must be difficult, at this time of your life. Oh, it must be a trial. But, still, miracles do happen, don't they? I imagine our dear Gilbert's making plans now, isn't he? To get a little money? You're going to need it, aren't you? Children are expensive. And in these times I have to say that I'm especially grateful, knowing all your worries, that you've agreed to help us. It means very much to me."

Sarie put her spoon down on the table. Around them, men and women talked. Waiters in starched uniforms, bearing dull tin pots of tea and soft drinks on brown trays, appeared to glide, like vultures, circling the room. Outside, Sarie saw a flash of blue. *The swimming pool,* she thought. Had Mr. Majid Ghulam Jeevanjee ever swum in such a basin? She hadn't ever asked. She folded and unfolded her white napkin, set it to the side, and looked Hazel Towson in the eye. "Mrs. Hazel." Sarie said. "There has been a mistake." Sarie looked down at her lap and gestured to her stomach. "I am not expecting anymore."

Hazel Towson, equal as she was to every kind of crisis, only faltered for a moment. She leaned in close to Sarie, so that Sarie smelled her breath, which was very clean, like cinnamon or mint. "Oh, my dear," she said. Her hard, square hand felt soft on Sarie's skin. "I *am* sorry, you know. We did rather think, yes, *I* did . . . well, that it *could* turn out like that."

N. S. KÖENINGS grew up in East Africa, Europe, and the United States. Of Dutch and Belgian descent, she holds a B.A. in African Studies from Bryn Mawr College and a Ph.D. in Socio-cultural Anthropology from Indiana University, where she completed her M.F.A. in Fiction. She is currently teaching in Massachusetts.